Riddle of the Seven Realms

2nd edition

Lyndon Hardy

Volume 3 of Magic by the Numbers

Bartizan Press
Los Angeles

Second edition
Version 1
Print ISBN: 978-0-9971501-8-6
Library of Congress Control Number: 2016907176

Other books by Lyndon Hardy

Master of the Five Magics, 2nd edition
Secret of the Sixth Magic, 2nd edition

Visit Lyndon Hardy's website at: http://www.alodar.com/blog

Cover by Tom Momary http://www.tomomary.com

Map by Ana Maria Velicu http://facebook.com/ancart7

1. Fantasy 2. Magic 3. Wizard 4. Sorcerer 5. Alchemy 6. Adventure

To my daughters, Melinda and Jennifer

Contents

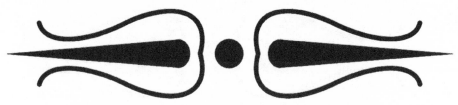

Part One *The Realm of Demons*

Part Two *The Realms of Men and Skyskirr*

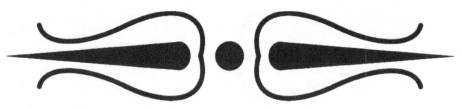

Part Three *The Realm of the Fey*

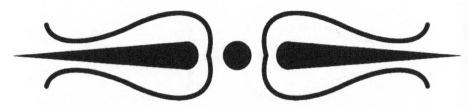

Part Four *The Realms of Order and Chaos*

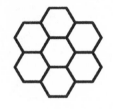

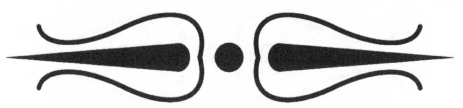

Part Five *The Realm of the Aleators*

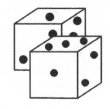

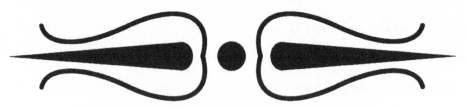

Part Six *The Ultimate Precept*

The Laws of Magic

Thaumaturgy

The Principle of Sympathy — like produces like

The Principle of Contagion — once together, always together

Alchemy

The Doctrine of Signatures — the attributes without mirror the powers within

Magic

The Maxim of Persistence — perfection is eternal

Sorcery

The Rule of Three — thrice spoken, once fulfilled

Wizardry

The Law of Ubiquity — flame permeates all

The Law of Dichotomy — dominance or submission

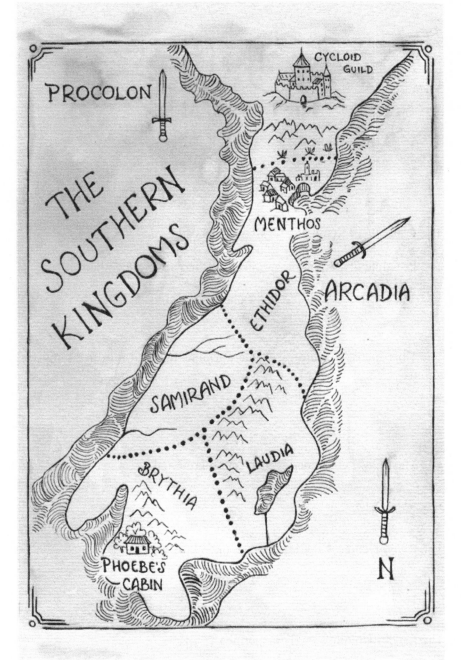

PROCOLON

THE SOUTHERN KINGDOMS

CYCLOID GUILD

MENTHOS

ETHIDOR

ARCADIA

SAMIRAND

LAUDIA

BRYTHIA

PHOEBE'S CABIN

N

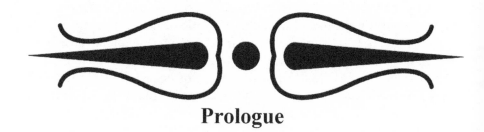

Prologue

KESTREL LOOKED past the flame toward the cabin door and estimated his chance of escape if something were to go awry. Like the lairs of most wizards, there were no windows in any of the walls; the distractions of the outside could well be done without.

He glanced back to the center of the room at the figure standing in the chalk-drawn pentagram that surrounded the firepit. Phoebe was not reputed to be a wizard of prowess and it was no simple devil that she was trying to summon.

If only she had been as greedy as the rest! The price he asked for an entire wagonload just like the branches he waved in front of their faces was usually low enough to hurry all of their thoughts away from testing what they were to receive. Some stored it all in their larders without even bothering to examine any of the leather sacks. Usually he was well into the next kingdom before they learned that a simple woodsman had gotten the better of the bargain rather than they.

But this one chose even to doubt that the sack he brought inside contained only anvilwood and nothing else. She had insisted upon a test to see that more than just the merest of imps was contacted through the realms, once the fire was lit.

Kestrel looked around the cabin. Thick beams bridged stout walls of white plastered mud. On the left, a bed of straw with room for only one stood underneath a shelf sagging with rolls of parchment. Behind Kestrel and extending along the wall on the right were tiers of wood-framed cubbyholes rising to the high ceiling, a scrambled collection of nailed-together boxes and wide mouthed bins.

In most of the openings Kestrel could see the contents stuffed nearly to overflowing and spilling onto the wood planked floor with goat-bladder sacks, vials of deeply colored powders, dried lizard tongue, sunflower seeds, licorice, and aromatic woods; this was as well stocked a wizard's larder as Kestrel had ever seen.

3

Kestrel looked again at the wizard staring intently into the flame. He had sought her out because of the tales of her wealth. All the practitioners in the Brythian hills, though they thought little of her skill, admitted that she was the richest. But if not for that, his interest might have been piqued anyway. Rather than in ratted tangles, her well-groomed hair fell in a cascade of shiny black down the back of her robe. The broad and youthful face was clear and unwrinkled. It carried the open simplicity of an unspoiled peasant girl, rather than the somber broodings of one who dared to thrust her will through the fire. The sash of the robe, adorned with the logo of flame, attempted to pull tight a waist a bit thicker than the current fashion. But at the same time, it accentuated curves that would otherwise be hidden. Despite her caution, her manner had been quite warm. She did not display the disdain that vindicated in part what he did.

Kestrel ran his hand down the back of his head, feeling how well the thinning hair still covered the beginning of a bald spot. He imagined how he must have appeared to the wizard when he had knocked on her door barely an hour ago-brown curls on top, what there was of them, deep-set eyes about a long slash of a nose, and wide lips in a sincere-appearing smile. His clothing was plain but still fairly new. The road dust on tunic, leggings, and boots had just been applied around the bend from the cabin, rather than being the result of a three day journey, as he had said.

How much had his ease in gaining entrance, Kestrel wondered, been because of other thoughts in Phoebe's mind, rather than the possibility of acquiring some of the rare anvilwood that peeked from the rucksack on his back? He savored the mental image which suddenly sprang into his mind. What would it be like to offer a wagonload of true potency instead of the disguised snags and rotten branches and to ask a fair price, rather than display an apparent ignorance of the value of what he possessed, or not to hurry away before his deception .was discovered?

No. He shook his head sadly. He could not take the risk. He had to take advantage of the base impulses of others. It was his only defense. Long ago, he had trusted-and the scars still remained.

Phoebe suddenly stiffened. "I am yours to command, master," she said.

Kestrel immediately sensed that something was wrong. The air above the flame shimmered and danced. A hand emerged from nowhere, and then a head with features more plain than bizarre. The demon was no towering giant with menacing fangs and crackles of lightning, but Phoebe's jaws went slack, and her hands fell to her sides all the same. She had not won the contest of wills; the demon had done so, instead.

Kestrel made a step to the left and then hesitated. The demon might be content with domination of the wizard and pay no attention to him as he slowly glided past. It was still morning. He could be well away before nightfall and anyone else suspected. On the other hand, he would be abandoning what little anvil wood he had remaining with nothing to show for it. In mixed fascination and fear, he watched as the demon continued to tear apart the fabric of reality and emerge into the realm of men.

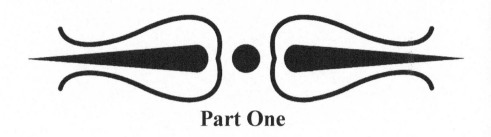

Part One

The Realm of Demons

1

A Summons by the Prince

ASTRON RAN his tongue over the stubs of fangs he had filed away. In the palm of his fist, now clinched with tension, he felt nails ground short in the manner of men. Only two small knobs protruded from his back where one would expect the powerful wings of a splendorous djinn. Unlike his clutch brothers, Astron had no real weapons with which to fight.

The broodmothers' talk was that Elezar's mood was most foul. Only the foolish or those consumed by the great monotony would elect to be near a prince of demons when his disposition was less than ideal. Far more pleasing were the cozy contours of Astron's own den where he could spend eons rearranging the small collection of artifacts he had managed to keep for his own. If hints of boredom did begin to grow, he could catalogue more of the names that the skyskirr gave to their lithons or even start his investigation of what men called love. The summons of his prince could have waited until the next scheduled time.

Astron was standing on a thin plane of matter that hung suspended in the black expanse that constituted the realm of demons. On the flatness, the home of his prince, were massed the splendid domes of his prince — mighty structures that soared into the blackness and blazed with color. In the distance, other pinpoints of light shone against the background of ebony, some steady and pure — beacons of the princes who did not choose to hide. Others flickered at the edge of visibility, lures for the unwary or perhaps evidence of the enormous weavings of warring djinns.

At his feet, the smooth surface of the plane glowed with a soft iridescence, pleasing to the eye. Pathways to the various domes were subtly marked for those who knew the signs. Behind him, the plane ended abruptly not far from where he stood, the edge sculpted in a graceful pattern that encircled the entire periphery. If he peered over the side, he would see a scene very similar to the one above — glimmering lights in a pitch-black sky.

Astron picked out a trail and followed it into the midst of the domes, trying all the while to keep his stembrain silent in his thoughts. The cupolas near the periphery were squat and ornate, no more than simple hemispheres encrusted with arabesques and intricate designs, lairs for broodmothers and little more. Behind them towered the true marvels of Elezar's domain, stiletto spires that soared to heights far beyond what their delicate walls would seem to support. In clusters and splendid isolation, they sat atop broad vaults and fluted ellipsoids. Over a sea of juxtaposed and intersecting bubbles, they pierced the emptiness of the void. Fierce lights of lavender and orange welled from ports cut into the roofs of the domes. Intense beams ricocheted from shiny mirrors on the spires and scattered from curves and planes glittering with twinkling jewels. Elezar, the one who dazzles, did not hide his domain from others who hoarded their meager store of matter in the blackness of the realm.

Astron threaded his way between the outer domes and then entered an archway that opened into one of the larger central vaults. Despite telling himself not to worry, the special summons was troubling. What could the prince possibly want that he was not providing for him now?

He paid no attention to the small devils huddled around the lump of rock in the first chamber, nor to the manner in which the stone jerked and bobbed above their craned necks. Levitating a boulder was beyond his abilities, even if aided by the will of others. He passed sleeping lairs resonating with deep snores, treasure vaults crammed with artifacts from dozens of realms, quiet rooms of dark contemplation, and weaving alcoves shimmering with half-finished constructions. Finally, he entered the grand rotunda itself at the very center of the domain.

The great hall was nearly empty. Except for Elezar, in the pit at the very center, sitting on a pillow of silk and down and with a swarm of imps buzzing about his head, no other demons were present. The prince was clothed in a glittering robe of deep sea green, covering all of his slender body except for his fingertips. Delicate features, an upturned nose, thin lips, and ears that were barely pointed sculpted a narrow face. Straw pale hair ran over a brow flecked with gold, and half-closed eyes glowered under long curving lashes. No great scales or hair-pierced warts marred the smooth skin. Like Astron himself, Elezar could pass unnoticed in the realm of men if he were not too closely regarded.

Discontent smoldered in Elezar's eyes, and Astron's limbs begin to tighten. He started down tile-covered steps toward the prince, not bothering to notice if any weavings had altered the shape of the rotunda since his last visit. As before, the ceiling was a large inverted bowl with a span greater than the outstretched wings of a hundred djinns. Sprays of soft colors caressed its glassy-smooth surface and glowing crystals throbbed with light all around the periphery.

"You are late, cataloguer." Elezar's soft voice floated upward from the hub. "Surely, even one whose only concern is the making of lists must know the folly of displeasing a prince."

Astron's arms and legs tightened further. His stembrain stirred from its slumber. The broodmothers had been right. The prince was troubled and did not care if his irritation showed. With eyes averted, Astron descended the remaining distance to the pit and squatted on a small cushion at Elezar's feet like a prisoner awaiting his sentence.

The prince eyed Astron with a cruel smile. "If I had not watched the hatchings myself, I would not believe that the demon that huddles before me is no less than a splendorous djinn."

Astron kept his head down and said nothing.

"And what of the broodmothers, mighty cataloguer?" Elezar stepped forward and thrust his toe into Astron's ribs. "What of the carriers of our seed? Do they tremble with anticipation in your presence? Does their skin grow moist at your touch?"

The prince kicked forward a second time. Astron felt a stab of pain in his side, but did not grimace, his face a porcelain mask that would shatter with the slightest expression. His hurt was but a mere token of what Elezar could do if he unleashed his great power.

"Or perhaps, instead, they confide their whispers, as if you were one of their own," Elezar continued. "Yes, as if you served no more purpose than they. Why should you not retire to their dens and prove your worth by becoming a warmer of eggs?"

Despite the iron-tight bands of his will, Astron felt his stembrain's awakening presence. Egg-warmer indeed. Only the deformed and slow of wit were charged with such a task. His value to the prince was far greater, as he had demonstrated dozens of times before. Who else had deduced the meaning of the cakes of congealed fats that mortals called soap, the purpose of the forged metal they thrust into the mouths of horses, or, the most perplexing of all, why their warriors grasped right hands in greeting?

He opened his mouth to speak, feeling the words rush upward sharp and cutting, but at the last moment, he slammed his teeth together, biting off the sound. He pushed the hot thoughts away and concentrated instead on visualizing the safe and comfortable contours of his own lair. Let the prince say what he would, he would not be provoked like some minor

11

devil.

For a long while, nothing more happened. Then Astron saw Elezar's shadow retreat and heard the swish of silk as the prince sat back down on his cushion. He raised his head upward and judged that finally he must speak.

"I have been of use to my prince in the past," he said. "Perhaps, there is some additional service that is to be performed as a result of this summons."

Elezar nodded. "Any of your brothers would have replied with bolts of power, even though it would have meant their death. How could one such as you retain clear thoughts after what has been spoken?"

"I am not like my brothers," Astron replied quietly. "I am different in more ways than those that you have chosen to notice."

Elezar grunted. "And it is those very differences upon which I am now forced to depend."

2

The Riddle

ASTRON WRINKLED his nose, puzzled. What should he now say to the prince seated in front of him? Before he could phrase a reply, Elezar looked up into the cloud of imps above his head and gestured. Instantly, the swarm began to twinkle with a kaleidoscope of color, each small devil glowing in a vivid hue. Their lazy hovering changed into a complex tangle of loops and dives, and then a pattern emerged from the random motion, shimmering like a tapestry basking the sun.

Astron's protective membranes slid over his eyes as arcs of fiery red imps, like droplets of molten lava, soared upward in a central column and then cascaded over onto waves of emerald-green that seemed to dance in empty air. Blues and yellows threaded through the rest, knitting complex designs that pulsated and changed in subtle ways that one could not quite follow.

Then, as suddenly as it had begun, the synchronized display winked out. The cloud of imps returned to their aimless hovering above the prince's head. Astron's membranes retracted, and Elezar's eyes refocused, his brow wrinkled with a scowl.

"More than three eons it took to train them all." Elezar waved at the swarm. "Three eons for that one clutch alone." The arc of his arm continued around the expanse of the rotunda. "I will not give them up, cataloguer. Not them or a single dram of hard matter in my domain."

"You are among the mightiest of princes," Astron said. "And the djinns who obey your commands number more than those of any other. What demon could challenge you for possession of —"

"Your skill is reputed to be one of making lists," Elezar interrupted. "Your knowledge of the other realms is the most profound of any in my retinue. Tell me then, what are the seven laws that govern the affairs of men?"

Astron wrinkled his nose. Such knowledge was widespread throughout the realm. Even the prince himself would have at least a casual acquaintance with the seven laws of magic. Why would Elezar choose to exercise him through a memory drill like a broodmother instructing her scion? Astron started to ask the reason for the question, but then the frown deepened in Elezar's face.

"The first two laws are the concern of wizardry," he said in a rush, "the law of ubiquity — 'flame permeates all', and the law of dichotomy — 'dominance or submission'. It is through fire that the barriers between our realm and the others are broken. And when, through it, we contact a dweller on the other side, one must end up the controller of the other; there is no middle ground.

"Of all the realms, ours is unique," he continued. The fires of the other universes connect them only to us and never to each other. If ever men, the skyskirr, the fey and all those who exist elsewhere interact, it is because we have brought them together. And although these others can coexist side by side with no threat from one to another, our own involvements are much more tightly bound. Whenever one of us leaves our realm to sojourn elsewhere, it must be as the master of the one who has summoned or else as his slave."

Astron considered what to say next. "But you know all of this quite well, my prince. No one less than you organized the great plan to conquer the entire realm of men and bend it to your will but a tick in time ago. Had it not been for the one that the mortals call the archimage —"

Elezar's hands clutched spasmodically, and Astron veered back to his original course. The prince did not like to be reminded of his defeat by a mere human. "Shall I continue to the other laws?" he asked. "Or perhaps, the metalaws that lie underneath them?"

He glanced at Elezar's hands, but there was no change. Somehow, the listing of the laws of magic was bound up in whatever was vexing the prince.

"Your eminence," a deep voice suddenly rumbled from one of the rotunda entrances, "the signal lights have been blinking. Gaspar with his retinue is now on his way. There are twenty-two djinns of lightning and lesser devils as well."

On the rim of the rotunda, the entrance was darkened by the massive form of a colossal djinn, his folded wing tips scraping the archway as he entered. Powerful black muscles rippled across his chest as he moved like a wave on a restless sea. Eyes of piercing yellow glowed in a face of darkest black.

14

"What is your command, my prince?" the djinn asked. "Though we are fewer, my clutch brothers and I can make his landing one that will cost."

Elezar turned to answer, "No, no, Delithan. To meet Gaspar on his own terms is a strategy of defeat. Invite him in unchallenged. We will use the time to our advantage."

"A djinn lives to fight, my prince," Delithan rumbled. "He exists to rip matter asunder and drink deeply of its dying shrieks. If that is denied, there is little that restrains surrender to the great monotony."

"There will be many more battles in the epochs to come, Delithan," Elezar said. "Do not deny yourself the opportunity to engage in them by a miscalculation now. Push aside thoughts of the brooding doom. As you have in the past, trust in your prince."

"An epoch ago, none could call himself master of my lord," Delithan growled. "But now there is indeed one who can so claim, and he is only a man. Perhaps Gaspar too is mightier, and the coming struggle is the last."

With a sharp crack, a spark of blue light arched from Elezar's left thumb to his forefinger. His arm swung out from his body in the direction of Delithan, a mask of anger etching the fine lines of his face. The huge djinn brought an arm up over his eyes. The pale outline of a shield began to materialize in front of his chest.

For a moment, the two demons stood frozen, the crackle of ionization masking any words that they might have been spoken. Then, as quickly as it had sprouted, the arc of energy in Elezar's hand winked out of existence. His face softened. He rotated his palms upward in Delithan's direction.

"Gaspar has grown so bold as to attack me in what all the princes acknowledge as my strength," Elezar said, his sudden outburst back under control. "It is a foolish boldness for him to do so, and I will not reply in kind. There may yet be the thrill of battle for you against his djinns of lightning, Delithan, but as long as I am your prince, it will be a time of my own choosing. Now take your clutchbrethren as I have commanded and escort him to me without incident."

Delithan's shield disappeared before it completely formed. He dipped his head in acquiescence. Stooping to clear the archway, he turned back the way he had come. "A djinn lives to fight," he rumbled as he left.

"Gaspar!" Astron blurted as Elezar turned back to face him. "Gaspar of the lightning djinns! Though his numbers are large and mighty, he would not dare to challenge you without due cause. None of the other princes would permit it. They would rally to your aid, and against all he

15

has no chance."

"His attack is not one of djinn against djinn," Elezar said. "Instead, it was something quite unexpected, although, of course, I showed no surprise." Elezar's eyes flared. "He has posed a riddle, cataloguer, a riddle to test the prince most noted for cunning of all those who rule.

"The stakes are familiar, the ones I have accepted from demons with far keener minds. If I answer correctly, then Gaspar and all who follow him are mine to do with what I will. If not, then I and my domain are his."

"A riddle?" Astron asked. "Then there is no threat at all. The likes of Gaspar could not formulate a puzzle that would long give pause to one such as you, my prince. And if you were — were too busy to answer yourself, then many in your domain would have sufficient wit to formulate the solution."

"It is not as simple as that. Gaspar's riddle might be a valid question — one with a definite answer. Ah, for the answer." Elezar looked away. "The answer that would give me dominance over yet another who thinks his power greater than mine."

The prince ran his slender tongue over his lower lip, savoring an imagined victory like a chef testing a simmering stew. He smiled and waved to the hovering imps for another display. But as the complex pattern formed, Elezar shook his head and motioned them to return to stillness. He looked back at Astron. "I have no ready reply, cataloguer," he said. The words were forced and spoken with difficulty. "I stall for more time, and Gaspar guesses at my weakness. He even taunts me with clues, so sure is he that I will fail."

Astron thoughts started to boil and tumble. Elezar, Elezar, the one who was most dazzling of all the princes — he was the one with the keenest mind. The others might wage their games of power by mustering great arrays of djinns into eye-blinding battles, but Elezar, time after time, bested them all with deft strokes of high strategy or bound up the outcome in riddles for which only he could unravel the answer in the end.

And if this time, Elezar could not provide the solution, then there was great peril for all that he commanded as well. The barely controlled rages of Gaspar were well known throughout the realm. None without an equal appetite for ripping things asunder could hope to survive for long under the rule of a prince of lightning. Astron glanced down at his short nails and flexed the wings on his back as if they were there.

But mixed with all of that, the surprise and the fear, there was something else that churned with the rest — a riddle. A riddle that Elezar

16

himself could not solve, a mystery that led perhaps even to the realm of men. What new and wonderful things might then be learned by one sent to observe, or by one tasked to record the labors of those questing to find the answer? What increase in power could come to one who catalogued rather than fought?

Elezar did not notice Astron's momentary inattention. The prince stood up and waved his arms in the air. "As you have stated, cataloguer, for every realm that we can contact, fire is the medium that breaks down the barrier between us. And for each of those connections, we are at the mercy of those who dwell on the other realm to build the flame and send their thoughts through it. We must wait for the call, the tugging at our own being, before we can begin the struggle that matches our wills against theirs.

"How much more powerful we would be if we could initiate the interaction, to go forth into the other realms at our own choosing rather than await events of chance. That is the essence of Gaspar's riddle, cataloguer. He states that the power of the laws pale for the one who has the answer. It is the ultimate precept, he says, the underlying principle upon which all else is built."

Elezar brought his arms back to his chest. "The riddle is quite simply stated, Astron: In the realm of demons, how does one build a fire?"

3

Astron's Task

THE EYES of the prince seated in front of Astron widened. The cataloguer felt a rush of questions but knew better than to speak.

"We have great control over the little matter that has been brought back through the barriers to our realm," Elezar said. "We can weave and transform it into exotic shapes that please the eye for eons. But somehow, in all the epochs that I can remember, no one in our realm, whether mighty prince or lowly sprite, has ever created a flame. None has been able to form the dance of ions that signify the combination of air with other things. The answer indeed must be the ultimate precept, cataloguer, and Gaspar's riddle or no, I, among all the princes who rule, will be the first to find out how it is done."

"But how will you learn?" Astron asked. "Is it perhaps in the realm of men that the answer would lie?"

"None in my personal domain have any hint to the solution," Elezar said. "I have decided that it is elsewhere I must look." The prince intensified his stare. "But there is little time for undirected and random search. First, I must ask the one who might have a greater chance of knowing the answer to the riddle than even I."

Astron's interest vanished. Cataloguing in the relative safety of the realm of men was one thing. Dealing with others of his own kind was quite another. And if it was the one he suspected that the prince had in mind...

"Not old Palodad!" he exclaimed. "The broodmothers say that even mighty djinns cannot return from his domain unscathed."

"Yes, Palodad," Elezar said, "the one who reckons." Astron's stembrain began to struggle harder to free itself from his rational control. Knowledge was power, it was true, but the risk must be commensurate with the reward. Even with a well-disciplined phalanx of splendorous djinns, Astron would not care to enter the domain of the demon reputed to be maddest of all. Besides, his specialty was in the other realms. It would not make sense to send to the domain of another prince one without the ability to weave or fly. It must have been for something else that Elezar had summoned him before the scheduled time.

"Which of your phalanx have you selected to dispatch?" Astron managed to say through jaws drawing tight. "How have you balanced between the need for strength in a far domain as well as here to impress Gaspar when he arrives?"

"*You* are the emissary, Astron. You alone are the one I have selected above all the others that I command."

"But, I am a mere cataloguer." The protest rushed from Astron's lips like water from a dam suddenly giving way. "Far more do I know of the workings of men than the traps in our own realm. I serve best by helping to unravel what information another might bring back from such a trek than braving the perils myself.

"Look at my fangs," Astron spun around. "See the stubs on my back. Look between my fingers. Only the most feeble of sparks can I will to be there. My role is to observe and record. It is the calling of the devils and djinns who can weave to perform actions for their prince."

Elezar shook his head. "The broodmothers are likely correct. Palodad's lair will be dissimilar to any other in the realm. But it is because you cannot fight that I have chosen you, cataloguer. The unfamiliar will not provoke you to rage. You above all else will keep your stembrain under control — because you must."

Astron looked beyond the prince to the cool, serene walls of the rotunda; familiar sights that he had viewed many times before. He thought of the comforts of his own lair with the artifacts whose purposes were yet to be discovered. Even the realm of men with the strange customs and exotic structures was to be preferred to the dangers that lurked for the unwary in his own realm. He felt the tug and pull of his stembrain straining to be free, to run amok and control his limbs in a frenzy of chaos and self-destruction.

"There is more at stake than the rule of my domain," Elezar said. "Gaspar will treat my own djinns with dignity. Grant them a final battle that would satisfy even their lusts for destruction." He bored his sight into Astron. "But as for you, my wingless one, a nimble wit and knowledge of arcane lists will have little value for him. At best, your torture would serve as a moment's distraction. You might hope that the process would not be a lingering one."

19

Astron's stembrain stirred. He had heard the tales of Gaspar's cruelty. How painful would it be if flayed alive? Would he remain conscious as his limbs were torn from his body, one by one? It was a fate beyond comprehension.

He studied Elezar's eyes, searching for even a hint of indecision, but saw only the resolve of a prince. His shoulders slumped like a deflating balloon. The last thoughts of his den faded away. Finally, he willed his tongue to move. "Arrange for the djinn who will transport me," he almost whispered. "I will perform my duty as the prince commands."

4

The One Who Reckons

AS THE flickering light grew brighter, the overwhelming emptiness of the realm began to fade. Astron craned his head upward at the djinn who carried him, each shoulder tight in an unflinching grip. Like a manikin in the realm of men, the larger demon showed no change in expression as they closed on their destination, the boredom of flight just another indication of the encroachment of the great monotony into its mind.

Looking over his shoulder, Astron could no longer distinguish the shine of Elezar's domain. It was lost in the sparse scatter of glowing dots that gave a feeble hint of pattern in an otherwise featureless expanse. Despite countless eons of wresting matter through the flame from the other universes, the great vastness was still the true character of the realm. Only in the small confines of one's own lair or in the ever-changing patterns of the domain of a prince could one temporarily forget the meagerness that enshrouded imp and djinn alike.

Endowed with the power to cover great distances almost without effort and the ability to transform whatever was seen into unlimited other shapes, the cruel jest of it all was that there was so very little on which those powers could be exercised. It did not take long before the farthest corners of the realm had been explored, all the interesting weavings formed and destroyed, and the bizarre mysteries of men and those of the other realms sampled and discarded. Ultimately, all that was left was to sit and wait, contemplating the curse of an immortal lifetime — sit and wait until the great monotony drove one to surrender to the stembrain and self-destruction in a new and interesting way.

Astron shook his head free of the brooding thoughts as the features of Palodad's lair became clear in the darkness. Just like the other domains, the province of the one who reckoned hung in space like a ripe fruit dangling from an invisible tree. Unlike Elezar's, however, it cast forth no shafts of brilliant light. Only the glow of a single imp marked the entrance to a long, sloping tunnel that led to Astron knew not what.

After he was deposited at the entrance, Astron bade the djinn to wait and cautiously entered. He felt the smooth surface of timeworn stone beneath his feet, true stone of condensed matter, rather than a web of fleeting energy that merely hinted at substance. Around his head and shoulders, the gnarled tunnel walls squeezed downward in the emptiness. The solidity of the steps was a surprise, and the darkness proved too much a reminder of the cold and depressing emptiness of the realm. But there was no other choice. Astron clasped his fingers into fists and began descending as rapidly as he could, each step taking less than a heartbeat.

Images of what could happen if he did not succeed flitted through his mind — Gaspar's rasping laugh. The small mites that crawled in the greasy stubble on the prince's chin. His minions ripping asunder the delicate columns and domes that Elezar had taken eons to weave, demigorgons crushing the skulls of the imps in their massive hands and degutting the larger devils with searing bolts of flame.

Astron tightened the coils of his fists. He, for one, was not ready for such a fate. His hatching had been less than an era ago. The great monotony did not yet dampen his will to live as it did for some of the others, those who had sampled a dozen times over all that Elezar had to offer, others who would have to be goaded out of a jaded lethargy even to die. No, if they came for him now, surrounding his slight body with stares and gloats, it would be far too soon.

He grimaced. If they came, he hoped that, for once, he would have the strength of his clutch brothers, strength to deny Gaspar of any satisfaction, strength to be able to look back with unblinking eyes and stand silent, even while they pulled away his fingers and toes one by one.

It was all because of arrogance, he thought. His prince had been too proud not to accept Gaspar's challenge on the terms with which it was given. Elezar should have denied the fairness of the riddle. But he was too concerned about what the other princes would think if he refused a test in which, after all, he was supposed to be the strongest of all.

The tunnel turned sharply to the left without warning, and Astron banged his head against a jutting overhang. His thoughts jangled back to his immediate concern. More than a million steps in total darkness. This Palodad constructs an approach of more than a million when a few hundred would do. Even a sublime devil guards his lair with only fifty. Fifty steps, though he might be able to weave the essence of a rose.

Astron rubbed the throb in his temple with one hand while he extended his other forward. 'There must be some truth to the accounts," he said to himself. "What sane demon would dare to be so wasteful? To squander his wealth on stride after stride of featureless rock when he could occupy himself for epochs building intricate sculptures instead."

His question echoed unanswered down the dark tunnel, and Astron paused a moment, willing himself into placid composure. To approach in a state of visible apprehension would place him at an immediate disadvantage. He was, after all, the emissary of a prince. He squeezed his fists all the tighter and set a grim mask on his face. In silence, he trod the last ten thousand steps, not even bothering to count.

Finally, he reached the entrance barrier and pulled it aside. The tunnel blazed with light. Translucent membranes flicked over his eyes as he stared into the brilliance. The drone of tiny wings mixed with the slur of countless curses, creating a din that assaulted even the most insensitive ears. The walls expanded outward from where he stood to form a giant sphere, dotted with smaller globes of incandescence that banished all shadows from its interior. He stood on a ledge that circumnavigated this globe — a small pathway that curved and disappeared out of sight on both sides behind the massive constructions that filled the enclosed volume.

Directly in front, a causeway arched from the ledge to link with the nearest of the structures. The edifice resembled a gigantic game board, a collection of tightly packed cubical cells built of rusty iron spars with row upon row of repeated patterns forming an immense vertical plane. Thousands of cells were stacked into a single column, and thousands of columns ranked together from left to right.

Each cell was occupied by an imp, mostly rock gremlins with pale green skin, warted eyelids, and thick leathery wings. But here and there were other types: water wisps, smoldering succubae, and pigmy afreets almost as tall as the span of his forearm.

Every imp, regardless of type, was collared with iron and linked with short pieces of chain to the lattice. The inhabitants of each row were joined together by lengths of rope that draped from cell to cell and looped around right wrists outstretched above slumbering heads. The end of each rope terminated on a separate shaft of steel at the edge of the lattice that ran to other constructions farther back in the sphere. More cords dangled from shafts above each column, connecting the left wrists of the demons positioned in the same vertical line. Although all seemingly were asleep, about half had their mouths open and long dangling tongues oozed a drool onto those confined below.

Astron's nose wrinkled as he tried to make sense of what he was seeing. A shaft on the side of the lattice twitched, joggling the arms of the

23

row of gremlins to which it was connected. They all sprang alert. An instant later, one of the rods on the top also lurched from its resting place, waking a column as well. Another moment passed with the aroused demons tensed and eyes open wide. Then, almost as quickly as they had awakened, they returned to their rest, facial expressions the same as they had been before. They all returned, that is, except for one, the one who had been common to both row and column, the one who had had both arms tugged. The selected imp waited restlessly until another gremlin, free flying and unfettered, buzzed into view to position itself in front of the lattice.

"Bad news, mint breath. It's a togueout," the newcomer squeaked. "And from the way things are cycling, I doubt another change will come for an eon or so."

"Gimme a break," the awakened imp answered. "I'm way ahead on tongueouts. I had to drool for over an eon just a few cycles ago. My jaw still aches from the effort. And I can remember my state in my head just as well as you. Wake me in an era and I will still recall whether I had been set to be in or out."

"Tongueout," the hovering gremlin insisted. "Or do you want me to report you stuck? If the upkeep crew replaces you, then you will be sent to the register pit. At least here you get to sleep most of the time."

The imp in the lattice grimaced and then finally spat out its tongue at the messenger. With a growl, he pitched his head forward on his chest, letting his body dangle from its fetters. The fluttering gremlin then flew away just before another tug on the rods aroused a succubus and the cycle started again.

Astron shifted his attention to other lattices nea the first. Some were identical in construction — giant arrays of sleeping imps. In others, tall columns of sprites were bound spread-eagled with a limb stretched tight toward each corner of its cell and the fetters running from the leg of one to the arm of another. In spasmodic waves, the demons twitched and shuddered, jiggling the left leg if only one arm were tugged and the right if both were stretched instead.

Astron's mind whirled. He had been prepared for strangeness. If nothing else, his many trips into the worlds of men had accustomed him to the unusual, but the expanse was too great. Never before in his own realm had he seen so much matter concentrated in one place. Countless numbers of fetters and chains, cell placed upon cell, lattice after lattice, receding into the distance. Elezar was reputed to be among the richest of the princes, but all his fanciful domes would be lost among the massive constructs in the sphere.

24

"With no matter for payment? One dares to come with no matter?" A raspy voice sounded over the noise.

Astron turned his attention upward. A platform jutted from the wall of the sphere some hundred spans above where he stood. Descending from it in a rope-hung bucket was a demon of about his size, although certainly not his shape and form. The posture stooped; a long curved neck cantilevered from the deep valley between bony shoulders. The scales of the face were cracked and peeling. Near the gnarled ears, some scales were missing altogether, revealing a pulsing underlayer that quivered like freshly flayed flesh. Eyes squinted out from grimy hollows, one rheumy with phlegm and the other jerking in erratic directions, independent of its mate. Emaciated arms terminated in three-clawed hands, one wrapped permanently about a crystal of some polished metal, the webbing between the fingers spread like a threadbare cape over the gleaming surface.

"And no wings as well, I see," the voice continued as the basket descended to eye level. "Quite presumptuous to come without wings to get you from here to there."

Astron stared at the demon as it swung a spar from the basket over to the ledge and hobbled across. "I am unfamiliar with the tradition of this domain," he said to the advancing figure. "This is the first time I have come. I act upon the request and demand of my —"

"What did you say?" The demon cupped his free hand behind his ear. "This is the first what?"

'The first time," Astron repeated. "The first time that —"

The rest of his words were drowned in sudden laughter. The approaching demon tilted back his head and boomed with a repetitious grate, each rasp more dissonant than the last. Astron opened his mouth to speak again but then thought better of it, waiting instead for the other to lapse back into silence.

"Time," the demon repeated with his last rasp. "Not only time but the first time. Here, hatchling, look at this."

The good hand reached into a small pouch hung over a pointy hip and produced a curiously shaped glass, two bulbs, one above the other with a small constricted passage between and grains of sand draining from top to bottom.

"This is time, hatchling. See it flow incessantly. In a continuous stream. Eons, eras, epochs, one after the other without seam, without division, apparently without start and finish. There is no first time, there is no last. There is only time and it is one."

25

Astron retracted his membranes and stared at the figure before him. The awe for the surroundings gnawed at his resolve. "Palodad?" he asked. "Are you the devil, Palodad, the one who reckons?"

"I am indeed he." The demon straightened his back slightly, his demeanor suddenly sober. "And you no doubt are the messenger of some prince who cannot see his way out of a problem. This may be your first visit, but across the eons, it is but one of countless others."

"I come by the command of Prince Elezar," Astron said. "He strives against Gaspar of the lightning djinns for the right of supremacy."

Palodad's good eye brightened. He put away the sandglass and looked over Astron far more carefully than he had before. "Ah, Elezar, Elezar, the one who dazzles," he replied.

"Yes, and as you say, I come with a riddle that is in need of its key."

"If Elezar cannot answer, then it must be an enigma indeed," Palodad said. "I have advised him before on matters of weight. If this is of like proportion, then a mere fistful of iron will not suffice for payment."

"Nevertheless, the answers the prince must know."

Palodad grunted. He stared unblinkingly at Astron, then put away his glass and turned to hobble back onto the spar. "Come," he called over his shoulder. "Come and tell me what perplexes the great Elezar so. I will elect to be flattered by his attention, even though it has been slow in coming. It is about time he has decided to ask for my aid again."

Palodad jerked to a halt and smiled. "Yes, it is about time," he repeated with a rasp. "About time. It could be for nothing less." He tilted his head back and opened his mouth into a great circle. His laugh filled the air and echoed from the wall. For a dozen cycles of the nearest lattice, the demon clutched his arms to his sides, rocking back and forth, oblivious to everything around him.

Then, as abruptly as he had begun, Palodad stopped and resumed his shuffle toward the bucket. "I had instructed you to follow," he called back as he entered the basket. "Or did your prince send just an imp still afraid of its broodmother?"

Astron stared into the interior of the sphere, at the bound and jerking sprites. Around him on all sides were the howls of pain and maledictions. The scene troubled him greatly, far more than any mystery in the realm of men. A reluctance coursed through his stembrain, putting stiffness into his limbs when he commanded them to move.

"I will remain untouched," he muttered to himself. "I need only stay until I have information for the prince." With a pace no swifter than Palodad's, he moved toward the waiting bucket.

5

Lore of the List Maker

ASTRON LOST track of the number of pulley baskets he rode before he reached Palodad's destination, deep in the interior of the sphere. As the last bucket whisked from view, he found himself in an open-top box of stone as solid as the steps that had led to the entrance of the old demon's lair.

To his immediate left, in front of one of the four confining walls, a continuous belt moved on rollers and creaked off through a dark recess into the sphere beyond.

Directly in front stood a collection of glass jars, packed with swarms of swirling mites. Behind them were stacks that resembled shallow baking sheets, some piled in precarious columns and others only two or three deep littering the floor. Through an archway in the distance was a small devil brushing a sticky glue onto the surface of one of the sheets and adding it to another stack. A cloying sweet odor drifted from the glue and hung heavy in the air.

More strange structures, Astron thought, each one a riddle in its own right. How much more of this could his stembrain take? On the right, the wall was covered with tiny glow sprites, each one crammed between the limbs of his neighbors, but somehow arrayed in precise lines. The small demons winked on and off with random bursts of light across the spectrum. All the colors of the rainbow stirred in motley patterns, each imp no larger than a thumbnail, but with thousands of neighbors producing a pulsating and almost hypnotic glitter.

"It is here that questions are composed," Palodad said behind Astron. "Here I affix the mites to the matrix and send the instructions to my minions who await beyond."

"But to what purpose?" Astron turned and shook his head, unable to contain himself any longer. "Why the million steps? How can so many submit to such an existence?"

"These are the questions of your prince?" Palodad asked.

"No, no, not these. His is much more profound."

Astron regretted the words as soon as they had left his lips. They revealed that Elezar's messenger was not unimpressed by what he saw and hinted therefore that Palodad's power might be the greater. The prince would not be pleased.

"But nevertheless, I am a cataloguer," Astron added. "It is my nature to ask so that I can observe and record."

"A cataloguer. Indeed." Palodad squinted. "No doubt the lack of wings and protruding fangs gives you greater satisfaction with your amusement."

Astron turned away his eyes. Things were not starting well at all. "I am, in fact, a splendorous djinn," he said. "At least my clutch brethren are. But I was hatched without wings and grew in stature no greater than you see me now."

He stared back at Palodad. "But no matter that I cannot weave great cataclysms or burst asunder condensed rock with the wave of my hand. I am a cataloguer and a good one. I filed my fangs myself so that the effect would be complete. With hood and cape, I have passed among men, raising not a modicum of suspicion. And yes, I even managed the domination of a strong-willed one or two."

"No doubt," Palodad replied. "Even the smallest imp declares he has a few wizards under his spell."

"What I say is true. I have no need to speak otherwise."

"It does not matter." Palodad waved the words aside. "I have little use for the boasts of others in any case. The workings of my domain tell me far more of what has happened and what yet will come to pass."

He stared at Astron. "Perhaps, as a cataloguer, you might appreciate that more than the others. Tell me your name. We will see what I know of the followers of Elezar the one who dazzles."

"It is Astron — Astron, the one who walks."

"Ah, Astron. Yes, of course." Palodad turned to pick up one of the metal sheets from the floor. "Not thousands of syllables that record all of your exploits like some who have come."

He placed the sheet on the belt and pulled a lever to stop it moving. Then he turned the lid on one of the jars at his feet, releasing a cloud of mites. Moving with a quickness that surprised Astron, the old demon began plucking the tiny imps from the air one by one and affixing them to the sticky surface of the sheet like a baker positioning cookie dough. With the metal ball in his other hand, he smashed them flat so that they would stay. In a few heartbeats, he had immobilized several precise rows of mites, some with their heads aligned along the lines and others perpendicular to it.

Palodad surveyed his handiwork and then kicked the empty jar aside, waving the unused mites away. He hobbled back into the stacks behind them and returned with several more sheets, these already filled with imprisoned imps. He formed a chain of the trays on the belt. With one final grunt, he pulled the lever to start them moving toward the slit in the wall.

"Pay attention to the glowsprites," Palodad instructed. "It will take a while for the framing instructions to be obeyed. After that, the images will unfold quickly enough."

For a short while, nothing happened. Then, the pattern of dancing lights changed. The glowsprites began pulsing in unison, creating bands of color that seemed to move across the wall. Kaleidoscopic shapes formed and dissolved. Scenes of other parts of Palodad's lair exploded into sharp focus and then faded away. Faces of great djinns snapped into view, one after another, faster than Astron could follow. Then the flickering stopped. A single image remained for him to view.

Astron stared at what he saw. A slight demon somehow familiar seemed to frown back from the plane of the sprites. About the figure was a clutter of trays and jars. In the apparent distance stood a gnarled old devil that looked exactly like Palodad. The second demon scratched absently at a pockmarked cheek with a hand clutching a metal sphere. Astron whirled to see Palodad do the same.

Astron spun back to look at the vision, took a step forward and extended his arm. The image on the wall copied his motions. He touched his forehead and bared his filed-down fangs in a grotesque grin, watching in fascination as the face staring at him responded in kind.

"How is this possible?" Astron asked. "For all of demonkind, none of us cast a reflection."

"Truly not." Palodad smiled. "Light is altered when it is scattered from our bodies. It subsequently can be adsorbed but not reflected again." He waved his arm at the wall. "What you observe here is merely what I have instructed my sprites to do. They watch how you move and then each glows in the required hue and intensity to form an image that mimics exactly. They form a precise copy so that you see yourself as you appear to others."

Astron examined the wall. He straightened to full height and squared his shoulders, staring at what he had never seen before. His head was oval and symmetric like a perfect melon, with the small knobs where the horns of his brothers would be. No tufts of hair grew from the delicate swirl of his ears, and on the supple pale flesh, only a hint of scaling was visible in the glow of the sprite light. The eyes were deeply set and the nose and lips a trifle large. But as had been said about him, without close scrutiny he could pass for a native in the realm of men. It was for these features that he had found favor with Elezar, he knew. The prince himself was unlike most demonkind and, rather than minimize the difference, he flaunted it.

"Evidently in the grand scheme of things," Palodad said, "there was need to collect more than just superficials about you, cataloguer. That is why the image is so sharp and clear. Look to your left. There is more that can be displayed than physical form."

A second pulsing of color appeared next to his reflection. It distilled into the image of a brood lair, with pieces of broken shell littered among the coarse grasses like the refuse from a wild celebration in the realm of men. Four tiny djinns, tufts of down still clinging to rapidly flapping wings, danced above the lair while one smaller demon cowered in the straw. With a shock, Astron realized what he was witnessing. No sound accompanied the animation, but he remembered the shrieks an era ago as his brothers had swooped down upon him, claws gleaming sharp. Even worse, he recalled, was the laughter as they turned aside at the last instant, barely avoiding contact. The two more precocious of his brothers already had felt the first intuitive grasp of weaving and formed bolts of crackling pain that they sprayed upon Astron's back as they sped by.

Astron clinched his long, slender fingers as the memory of impotency flooded through him. Four brothers, all splendorous djinns, and he with no more power than a lowly sprite, able to convert the air he breathed into food and water and nothing more.

But before Astron could dwell further on the memory, the image formed by the glowsprites shimmered and shifted. He saw himself half grown, eyes wide with membranes pulled back as he examined the object he cradled in his hands. The devil who stood next to him in the image had his arms folded across his chest and a face showing uncompromising pride.

Astron remembered that he had not cared. Acknowledging the magnitude of the feat that brought condensed matter of such quality through the flame had not been in his thoughts at all. He had leafed through the delicate sheets that were stitched along one side, studying the rows and rows of markings and occasional drawings of other objects equally strange. Some he had recognized: coins, belt buckles, forks; a random sampling of things retrieved by other demons on their journeys through the flame. And for some of these, he had understood their use and meaning from the context in which they were drawn.

Astron nodded his head as he watched. He remembered the electric thrill that had arched down his spine. Who among all of demonkind would have guessed that the cylindrical cap guarded a human's fingertip against pricks from the tiny sword and trailing thread that bound together two pieces of cloth?

There was more merit than mere mass in an object fetched from beyond the flame, he had realized. There was knowledge as well, knowledge that might be of use to a prince who wished to astound his peers. And with knowledge came stature and regard, even for a djinn without wings or the ability to weave.

"All the artifacts that I possess," he remembered he had said, looking up at the devil at his side. "The web of the spider, the pollen of a flower, everything in exchange for this."

As the trade was made, the image dissolved. When it refocused, Astron recognized a scene of only months ago as measured in the realm of men. He stood in his hood and cloak beside a cottage hearth. Only the last embers remained of the evening fire. At a table across the room, a human serving girl stared in Astron's direction, her eyes wide and unblinking, completely under his command.

"What are your instructions, Master, while I wait for you to return," she had mumbled.

Astron remembered his hesitation. He knew what would happen to her when she was found after his departure. Men professed to feel compassion, but they dealt with demon possession with a zeal that was hard to understand. And she was not a wizard, boldly reaching into the flame to test her will against Astron or his kin. Only by accident, had she looked too long into the hypnotic dance of the fire and allowed Astron to pass through the barrier between the realms.

Elezar would be satisfied enough with what has been learned, Astron had decided. The purpose of the little orb attached to the side of the door had been explained. None of the other princes would guess that it was to be rotated before being pulled.

"Return to the way you were," Astron had said. "I release you from my control. The prince cannot care about one mind more or less. Besides us, who in the two realms would know?"

The scene began to fade. Astron turned away to face Palodad. "How did you find out?" he asked. "I have told no one of what I did. Indeed, why even bother to record my affairs, rather than the lives of the princes that rule?"

"I have the relevant information on them as well," Palodad replied. "Do not prejudge your role in the scheme of things. I am, after all, the one who reckons."

The old demon squinted his good eye at Astron. "The more interesting question is not how, but why. Why did you release the human female when you had no need? Even without wings, one would not expect such behavior from the clutch brother of a splendorous djinn."

"I, I do not know," Astron replied. The vividness of the memories was unsettling. The impact of all he had seen began to numb his mind. His thoughts started to go off balance like a scale with weights on only one side. His limbs tightened. Was this the madness that came with a visit to the one who reckons? Was his lair so overwhelming and knowledge so great that one could not hope to keep his head clear in the old devil's presence?

Astron flicked down the membranes over his eyes and concentrated on the comforts of his own den. He had not one book by now but three. Some of the strange symbology that accompanied the pictures he was beginning to understand. Of all of Elezar's cataloguers, he was held in the highest regard. He had pledged to his prince and had a mission to perform, regardless of the great powers exhibited by the old demon at his side. And the results were needed soon, before Gaspar lost his patience and it was all too late.

Astron firmed his resolve. He would not waver. Digging his shortened nails into his palms, he retracted his membranes and regarded Palodad.

"Questions concerning Astron, the cataloguer, will be for another time," he said. "I am here now by demand of Elezar, the prince."

Palodad did not immediately answer. He pointed at the imaging screen indicating that he could show more, his lips curved in the hint of a mocking smile. But Astron held his determination. The urgency of his visit locked firmly in place. He willed his thoughts to calmness and waited for the devil to speak.

"Questions concerning the one who walks will be for when?" Palodad asked at last.

"For another time."

"Yes, for another time, another time," Palodad echoed. He kicked one of the metal trays aside and dissolved in a fit of laughter. "There is no getting away from it," he gasped. "It is always a matter of time."

The devil clutched his sides and crumpled into a ball at Astron's feet. Rolling about on the hard stone slab, he flailed his spindly legs like an overturned spider and bellowed incoherently, giving no signs of ever stopping.

Astron scowled in annoyance. Now with his focus away from his own personal history, the pressure to obtain results felt all the greater. He scanned about for the presence of a broodmother who might give aid to the stricken devil but saw none. With a shrug copied from the humans, he turned and began to walk toward the doorway behind the stacks of trays.

Palodad stopped laughing before Astron had gone two paces. "You have not yet told me the question of your prince," the devil said.

6

A Matter of Payment

ASTRON WRINKLED his nose. Now there was no hint of madness in the tone in the one coiled at his feet. It was as if the devil was as unaware as a hatchling of his actions just moments before. Astron shook his head, trying to toss off the behavior as he had all the rest. He turned back to face the devil and waited until the old one was erect.

"Gaspar's riddle is most unusual," Astron said after Palodad had finished smoothing his pouches and straps. "It is most unusual that the likes of a lightning djinn would even conceive of one of such difficulty."

"But nevertheless, he did," Palodad replied. "No matter how unlikely the conundrum, the agreement is no less binding."

A faraway look came to the old devil's eye. The corners of his mouth rounded in the beginnings of a grin. "So, quickly now, state what it is that your prince wishes to know. You already have wasted enough of my precious ..."

Palodad's cheeks lifted further like curtains about to open on a stage. The hint of a giggle started in his throat.

"How does one start a fire?" Astron said quickly. "On the worlds of men, in the 'hedron of the skyskirr, and in all the realms that we know, there is fire and flame."

"It is the means by which the barriers between our realms are overcome and mind is linked with mind," Palodad said. "Elezar does not need the one who reckons to tell him that."

"In every realm there is flame except for one," Astron shook his head in the manner of men. "Except in the realm of demons itself. We have pulled through the barriers artifacts that are solid and ones of liquid and gas. But never, in all the epochs, can any remember has there been fire in the domain of any of the princes."

Astron stopped. He peered at Palodad to judge the old devil's

34

response. The only sounds were the background cries echoing in the confines of the sphere. Palodad shuffled to the jars on the stone floor and released another swarm of mites. For many cycles of the lattices, he grabbed them from the air as if his arm was the tongue of a frog and affixed them to one metal sheet after another, feeding the completed trays through the slot in the wall. When he was done, he turned his attention to the glowsprites, watching the random blink of colors and form. This time, they did not shape coherent images, but Palodad nodded and smiled, mumbling to himself when he seemed to distinguish one particular pattern from another. For how long he remained waiting, Astron could not tell, but one by one, the sprite lights winked out, leaving a surface of muted gray like an old cloth bleached by centuries in the sun.

"There is the matter of the payment," Palodad said at last. He rubbed the metal ball he carried in his hand against his leg and then looked at the shiny surface. "Did your prince delegate to you the bargaining as well?"

"Then you do know the answer!" Astron exclaimed. "You have calculated it with your strange devices even as we waited."

Palodad held up his hand before Astron could say more. "As you have stated, the riddle is most profound. It is no wonder that even the likes of Elezar could not fathom the direction in which to proceed."

The devil fingered the pouch containing the hourglass at his side. "In fact, even I do not bargain with the solution to the conundrum," he continued. "I can only indicate where it is the most — the most profitable for Elezar to look. As for the details of the answer, he will have to find it on his own."

The sudden buoyancy of Astron's hopes drained away. Despite all the tales of the broodmothers, the old devil knew little more his prince did. Elezar already suspected that the answer lay outside of the realm of demons. Merely being told where to seek would be worth far less than the answer itself.

"You speak of payments," Astron said. "A mere hint carries little value at all."

"Many others have found my prices reasonable enough." Palodad waved his arm out across his lair. "With each enigma I solved, I obtained a few more spars, stone for another trio of steps, cages for one or two more imps. Each exchange in itself has not amounted to much, but over the eons, I have managed to build all that you have seen. And, rather than waste my wealth on trivial amusements for the senses, I have focused it on increasing my ability to compute, to collect and store even more of what happens in the realm, and to predict with greater and greater accuracy what the future will bring."

Palodad smiled and tapped Astron's chest with the ball he clutched in his fist. "Elezar chose his emissary well," he said. "I get no great amusement spending eons maneuvering through complex negotiations for the last dram of mass. Your prince will have to fetch for me something from the realm to which I will direct him. That will be payment enough."

"If what you desire is more than base iron, then it will not be so easy for any of Elezar's retinue to wrest it back through the flame," Astron disagreed. "The prince will not care for an agreement that carries such a complication."

"I am aware that the living residents of the other realms can transport objects through the flame far more easily than can any of our kind," Palodad said. "Elezar will have to enlist help from men, skyskirr, or some other beings, it is true. But I have faith in his ability to figure out a way."

"It is a complication," Astron repeated. "As Gaspar presses for an answer, my master will have less ability to comply."

Palodad scowled. He pressed the heavy orb of metal to his chest. "Tell him that I will validate his answer," he suggested. "Whatever he discovers, he can bring to me before he risks exposing it to Gaspar. I will weigh the plausibility of correctness with the computations that are at my disposal and no one else's in the realm. In exchange for a modicum of matter, he will know not only where to look, but be certain that what he finds is correct.

"Tell him, cataloguer. Tell him what I offer. He will ponder, and then finally acquiesce. It is only a question of time."

Astron grimaced, but Palodad took no heed. He slapped his arms about his waist and staggered back into the conveyer belt, howling in apparent glee. "Time, time, time," he gasped. "The focus always returns to time. When will it ever end?"

Astron slumped to the stone slab in frustration. He felt the beginnings of doubt that his journey had accomplished anything at all. Perhaps all the talk of computations and hints were no more than the ravings of madness, a perverted defense against a growing presence of the great monotony.

He shrugged. But if there were anything else to try, his prince would have so directed him. Palodad represented the last hope, as slim as it was. In resignation, he watched the old devil flail on the hard stone, waiting for the seizure to end.

Eventually, Palodad stopped and righted himself, wiping away a mucus-filled tear as he stood. "You should now go," he said, waving to a bucket descending from a level above. "Repeat to your prince the offer I have made. Come again and tell me when he has agreed. Then I will instruct in detail where it is you are to search and what you will bring back for me in exchange."

Astron nodded and rose to meet the descending basket. The outcome of the meeting was far from satisfactory. He doubted that the duty to his prince was yet quite completed.

7

Princes of Power

THE DOMES of Elezar were just as Astron had left them. The talons of the transporting djinn released their grip on his shoulders, and he dropped the last few spans to the decorated plane on which the structures stood.

"Until the prince gives me cause to return to Palodad's lair, I will have no further need," he said to the djinn still hovering above him. "Return to your own den and await command."

The mighty demon gave no acknowledgment, and with one beat of his wings, he soared upward. Soon he was but a speck vanishing from sight. Astron watched him go and for a moment followed the flights of others as they transported objects and smaller devils to and from Elezar's domain.

He was a cataloguer, Astron thought, the best in all the retinue of his prince. He understood the value of knowledge and traded it for power far beyond what one would expect for one of his size and lack of ability to weave. He was a cataloguer and yet ...

He flexed his arms, trying to imagine for perhaps the millionth time the sensation of darting between the uppermost spires of his prince's towers, of swooping down into the dark abysses, or even of visiting distant lairs without the assistance of a djinn dangling him from great talons and protecting him from danger.

Astron closed his eyes, wiggling his fingers in exaggerated slowness, straining for the feel of the matter about him, trying to caress its form and texture, molding it into the shapes that he commanded, and transforming even its innermost structure and bonding so that it became as he desired.

But as always, the feelings did not come. His weight pressed all too firmly on the soles of his feet. His palms and the tips of his fingers felt no more than the tenuousness of air. He was only Astron, the one who walked. Besides, there was no time for such reverie, he decided. He must report to the prince.

Astron navigated through the maze of peripheral domes to the main rotunda. The slight give of the thinly stretched web of matter to each stride as if walking on just congealed lava reminded him of the firmness of Palodad's crude steps of true stone. The outer passageways were empty. The flitter of imps and bustle of messenger devils had stopped. When he arrived the central rotunda, Astron found that every demon in the domain had gathered. In concentric circles, they hovered and squatted like a flock of vultures around prey with only a few more moments of life. . All eyes were focused on the hub in which were conversing no less than two princes of the realm.

Astron's limbs stiffened. He might already be too late. Gaspar and his minions had already arrived. Elezar was sitting on the same pillow of silk and down. Ignoring the other cushions, Gaspar stood with arms folded across his chest, his massive torso rippling with muscle that seemed just barely under control. Cruel eyes brooded under a brow like an outcrop of rock overhanging the face of a mountain and shadowing a face that never smiled. With a wave of irritation, he brushed aside the mites that swarmed about his chin. Small bursts of unwoven energy crackled from his fingertips, arching from joint to joint. In the dreams of men, it was demons such as Gaspar that they feared the most.

Astron hesitated. One part of his mind willed his legs forward to tell the prince what little he had learned. Another bade him to remain still. It would not be prudent for Gaspar to hear the extent of Elezar s ignorance. In nervous anticipation, Astron waited for some indication of what he should do.

"I have come to settle our wager," the lightning djinn's voice rumbled throughout the dome like distant thunder. "Either you know the answer to my riddle or you do not. There is nothing to be gained by delay. Submit to your doom as you have agreed."

The guard of colossal djinns behind Elezar, six in all and each identical to the tiniest scale to his brethren, tensed and bared their fangs like leopards preparing to strike, but the prince motioned them to remain calm.

"Your haste hints of weakness," Elezar replied. "How bored has your following become?"

'There is no trace of the great monotony in a single one." Gaspar waved at the brace of lieutenants he had brought with him, now standing off to the side. He glanced about the dome and eyed the web of vaults and spars that held the expanse of the great roof aloft. "Every one of them looks forward with anticipation to when they can reduce all of this to base iron."

"And even if your challenge should prevail," Elezar said, "after a brief instant of destructive fury, what then? What new amusements will you promise? How can you hope to keep alive their will and allegiance for even an epoch more? In the end, you will lose, Gaspar. The eons and eras stretch before you farther than you dare imagine."

Elezar lowered his voice to a whisper, although all present could still hear. "Are you not already weary, Gaspar? Does not the futility of it all begin to gnaw? Will one more orgy of destruction be that much different from the last? Submit, submit to me, and at least the ending will be amusing for all."

"No," Gaspar boomed. He unfurled his wings and rose a span above the floor cushions. The air around his shoulders began to crackle and hiss. Sparkles of color pulsed into existence above his head. The guard djinns interposed themselves between Elezar and the other prince. Gaspar's lieutenants vaulted over the smaller demons between and formed a rank alongside their leader, their synchronized wing strokes creating a wind that whistled through the rotunda archways.

"Are these the actions of a prince secure in his command?" Elezar continued his questioning as the djinns maneuvered. "Why do the images I propose prick at your stembrain so?"

"I will have your existence to do with what I will," Gaspar roared back. "It has been promised. Agree to the conditions of the challenge and surrender. If you do not, it will not only be the lightning djinns that you must face. All of the realm will aid my just cause."

"And if you hurl one bolt at what is mine before that surrender is made, what then of the agreement?" Elezar said. "If a single atom of my domain is disturbed before I accede you the right, on whose side will the realm render succor and aid?"

Pops of thunder exploded from Gaspar's hands, intense bolts of power arching between his fingers. Then the demon curled one hand into a fist and smashed it into the other, smothering the pulsating energy. He roared an incoherent bellow of frustration and waved his lieutenants back to their positions. With a sullen face, he drifted to the rotunda floor, folding his arms across his chest. Elezar's guard djinns resumed their positions behind the prince. For a long while, there was silence throughout the vast dome.

"I will illustrate my point in a less destabilizing manner," Elezar said at last.

He motioned to an archway and four devils responded by carrying in a sculpture on a stand of marble. It was molded in heavy bronze, a cluster of bubbles popping from a viscous broth, a copy of an art form prevalent in the realm of the fey. As the devils positioned it between Elezar and Gaspar, six more demons waddled forward, each one squat and broad, with eyes that squinted from between deep folds of flesh. They positioned themselves behind Elezar and gazed at the sculpture from expressionless faces.

"Now pick one of your lieutenants," Elezar instructed. "I give him leave. He may do with this matter as he wishes."

Almost in unison, Gaspar's djinns expanded their chests. Crackles of energy began to dance from their fingertips and eyes. Their alertness for possible battle before was a mere shadow of the excitement that gripped them now. Gaspar grunted and motioned one near the middle forward. The selected lieutenant arched across the intervening distance and landed with a heavy thud near the sculpture. His eyes widened. He wiggled his fingers, letting short arcs of piercing blue jump from one hand to the other.

"Wait until the shield demons are ready and then you may begin," Elezar said. "I wish to minimize the effect of your craft upon the dome and the others who watch."

Gaspar's lieutenants nodded. The shield demons begin to hum in a six-voice harmony. Simultaneously, the lightning djinn started to fade. On the top, bottom, and each side of the demon, a plane of haziness began to form, six sheets of growing opaqueness that intersected and confined him and the adjacent sculpture into a box. As if they were filling with fog, the surfaces grew less and less transparent, hiding the djinn from view. The glow of imp light around the rotunda walls reflected from the cube. The shield demons had constructed a confining barrier. Little energy could penetrate it from either direction, coming inside or going out.

But then the interior of the cube pulsed with light. In a heartbeat, a searing bolt of yellow ripped from the djinn's hand and struck the sculpture with a devastating force. The power released was so immense that even the small fraction of energy that trickled through the barrier was sufficient for all to see what was happening. The sculpture ripped asunder where the bolt struck it at mid-height. Globules of molten metal sputtered from the point of contact. Two jagged halves ricocheted from the walls of the confining box. Before the image faded, the djinn struck a second time with two quick bolts that hit each of the tumbling pieces. Again, the metal shrieked and tore. Four fragments bounced about the cube.

41

With increasing speed, the djinn aimed strike after strike at the fragments, ripping them into finer shards and filling the confining volume with light. Astron flicked his membranes over his eyes. The outwelling residue of the destruction was too painful to watch, even with the shield demons' barrier in place.

The confined djinn begin to froth and gesticulate wildly, barely in control of himself as he sought to rip the cloud of scrap into even smaller rubble. The onslaught continued unabated until only a hazy dust filled the cube. No recognizable part of the original sculpture remained intact or any of the metal of which it was composed.

With no more targets on which to focus his power, the djinn slumped exhausted in one corner of the box. Elezar motioned to the shield demons. The side of the confinement nearest to Astron dissolved away as quickly as it had formed. Amidst pulses of escaping light and heat, the djinn tumbled out to lie at Gaspar's feet, limbs scattered haphazardly and with a smile on his face beneath glazed eyes.

"Such is the amusement that you offer to those who would follow you," Elezar said, "and to any who has not tasted the pleasure of total destruction, the allure might be strong indeed."

The prince looked down at the djinn regaining his composure. "But I wonder, Gaspar, now that the experience has been savored, what more can you promise that will not be repetition of the same. And after the second, the dozenth, perhaps the hundredth time, what then will be your hold over these mighty djinns?"

"You speak of events that are in epochs yet to run," Gaspar replied. "None of my lieutenants, nor any of the legions that they command, have tastes so jaded that they do not look forward to repeat for your entire lair the small sample we have witnessed here."

"My point is not yet complete." Elezar raised one robed arm to cut off the other prince. "Let us see first the principle upon which the allegiance to my domain is founded."

As Elezar finished, a small devil came forward, barely larger than Astron himself. He entered the box from the open side and sank into a deep contemplation of the still swirling dust as the missing side reformed after him. For a long while, nothing happened. Then a tiny spark of light blinked into existence before the devil's eyes and, following that in rapid succession, a series of others. Gaspar rumbled with impatience, but Elezar and the concentrating devil paid him no heed. For a long while more, there was no visible change in the haze, but then, a sparkling precipitate began to fall to the bottom of the box.

"A significant fraction of the matter has been lost to light and other rays," Elezar said. "But it is of no concern. The weaver will work with what is at hand. He will first reassemble the basic particular components back into copper and tin, reversing the transmutations of your lieutenant. Then he will reconstitute the sculpture, coalescing the particles together one by one, if need be."

The prince smiled at Gaspar. "It took this one an era to make the first sculpture — staring from a hoard of bronze another of my minions had obtained from the realm of the skyskirr. It will take him eras more to reconstitute and restore what he had before, or, perhaps, create something of greater beauty still. Eras, Gaspar, eras, not mere heartbeats before it is done. He will be constructing, weaving, paying attention to painstaking detail to ensure that each little mote is in its proper place. It is a matter of rational control of the stembrain, not surrender to its lust.

"Eras and not heartbeats, Gaspar. That is why princes such as I will endure long after djinns of lightning have long since surrendered to the great monotony."

"The stronger shall endure the longer," Gaspar said. He motioned his lieutenant to resume his position in line. "And there is little doubt between the two of us as to which it will be."

Gaspar unfolded his arms and stuck a bulbous thumb toward his chest. "My will has forever been my own," he continued, "but in cold reality, Elezar, you can make no such claim."

The djinn looked around the assembled demons in the rotunda. "It is no less than another conundrum. How can any here choose to ally themselves with one who has been enslaved by a mortal?"

"It was no common man," Elezar shot back. "No less than the archimage did I contest in wills. And I am not ashamed of the result. No prince of the realm would have fared any better than I. Certainly, not a coarse djinn who has not even dared to answer a single call when it has come through the flame."

"So you assert," Gaspar said. "Such is your interpretation of the events. But if this mortal is so great that even princes bend to his will, why are there no others who also call him master somewhere in the realm?"

"I have spoken with accuracy," Elezar replied. "The archimage knows quite well the folly of too much interaction with our domains. It is a mark of confidence in his power that he has no compulsion to exercise it wastefully."

"Spoken like a true slave of a dominating master." Gaspar laughed.

"A lowly imp could not have put it better. Come, Elezar, Prince Elezar, Elezar, the one who dazzles, submit to me now before my followers discover that the victory does not represent that great an accomplishment."

"I will not be distracted by your words." Elezar beat his right arm against his chest as the agitation billowed in his face like a stormcloud. He stirred uncomfortably. Against Gaspar, Elezar's strength lay in his wits, not the plasma that glowed about his fingertips.

"If dominance by a man is of such little consequence," Gaspar continued, "then why does it upset you so much that I discuss it in front of those who blindly follow? Perhaps, there is more to the story that you have not told."

"Be gone!" Elezar stood and shouted. "Flutter back to your rough stone lairs and await the answer to your riddle. I will reveal it to you when the time is proper."

"I have come for it now," Gaspar growled, unfurling his wings.

"I said, 'be gone'," Elezar clapped his hands together. The air above his head hissed. Traces of blue sparked about his ears.

Gaspar flexed his fingers, letting small tendrils of light race up from the webbing near the palms to the fingertips. "You warned of the consequences that would accrue from the rest of the realm if I struck outside the bounds of our agreement," he said. "Do you not think that the other domains would judge with equal disfavor one who professes to know what in fact he does not? Admit the truth, Elezar. You might once have been a prince, but now you are nothing more than the dimwitted doll of a man."

Elezar snarled, baring fangs that he seldom showed to others. With a flick of his wrist, a bolt of ionizing blue arced between the two princes, striking Gaspar on the shoulder and spinning the djinn to the ground. Gaspar swooped into the air, a small rivulet of smoke wisping from where he had been touched. A glaze of pain clouded his eyes. Sparks showered off his knees and elbows into the air.

"The prince of lightning djinns does not submit to such insult," he yelled. "If you are so foolish as to test the strength of my lieutenants and me, then so shall you meet your doom and meet it now."

8

Demon Battle

WITH AN ear-shattering roar, Gaspar unleashed a huge bolt in Elezar's direction that slammed past the weaving devil and into the midst of the shield demons. One was hit in the chest and exploded in a spray of bone, sinew, and gore. Those on either side were hurled from their feet like duckpins, colliding with Elezar's guards, who scrambled airborne to get out of the way.

Gaspar's lieutenants rose in reply. Almost instantly the upper expanses of the rotunda filled with brilliant bursts of light painful to see. All of Elezar's followers who had surrounded the hub stood in a mass confusion, some scrambling for exit tunnels and others surging forward to aid their prince. Astron shouldered aside the imps and sprites lesser than him who raced past. His stembrain said to run, but he knew that his duty was to help Elezar as best he could. The air imploded in a great clap of thunder and then rang with the crash of falling matter from somewhere across the rotunda. Shrieks of pain blended with the crackle of ionization. One of Elezar's guards plummeted to the floor a wingspan away, the odor of charred flesh bubbling from a smoking hole in his side.

Near the apex of the dome, two more djinns converged on one of Elezar's lesser devils who had soared forward into the fray. One methodically countered strokes of crimson with larger bolts of his own, meeting the thrusts of energy head-on and dissipating them harmlessly into the air like windblown shards of parchment. The other unleashed his power unimpeded, each stroke blasting asunder a limb or wing.

The prince must withdraw, Astron decided. Elezar's guard demons were too few. Despite their battle lust, they would not prevail against massed lightning djinns in the confines of the rotunda. The prince must retreat to a position where he could direct all the demons at his command — draw Gaspar's minions into separate battles where superior numbers could harry each one separately.

But how to withdraw safely? Astron's thoughts raced. He wrinkled his nose. Even though his membranes were down, he had to squint his eyes against the fierce glare as he looked in the direction of the hub. There were arcs of energy, his prince, the master weaver, the scattered shield demons, and Elezar's guards trying to form into some sort of protective array.

Then, with a sudden flash, Astron realized what must be done. He whirled about, looking for a devil to carry a message to the prince but saw only chaos. There was no one to listen. He squeezed shut his eyes for an instant, picturing the smooth walls of his den in which he stored his artifacts and the comfort of leafing through his books and deciphering their meanings.

"Duty," he muttered at last. "Without duty, there is no purpose — only a surrender to the impulse of the stembrain and the great monotony."

Wondering if he would ever see his treasures again, he waved aside a cloud of imps winging past and headed for the hub. A blob of plasma from a fallen djinn roared by his left, hitting a small devil in the back as he ran, incinerating the tiny wings and burning its way through to the chest. Astron ducked away from the searing rays, scrambled over the body of another fallen demon, and reached Elezar's cushion that had been kicked aside like a rotten pumpkin shell. The prince, outlined against the fierce glow, blocked bolts of energy with his own and yelled commands to his guards above the din. Astron scrambled around the periphery of the hub to where the shield demons sprawled in disarray. Their opaque screens had dissolved, but the squat demons were too slow-witted to do more than move a few feet from where they had originally stood.

"Form your barriers," Astron shouted to the one closest. "The prince commands and needs your aid."

The nearest shield demon grunted. The space between him and Astron began to fog as it had before.

"Faster," Astron commanded, looking over his shoulder to verify that Elezar and his retinue still stood their ground. "And make it horizontal, on top of your head."

The forming barrier began to tip toward the ceiling and Astron scrambled aside to instruct the next in line. As he did, one of Gaspar's lieutenants saw the activity, broke off his engagement with four lesser demons, and turned to attack. The djinn folded his wings and dove. As pulses of energy leaped from outstretched fingers, Astron sprawled flat on the rotunda floor, feeling waves of heat roar past his head. High above, the djinn swooped on by and then turned to dive a second time. Astron rose to his knees and scrambled beside the shield demon constructing his screen. The next volley spattered harmlessly from the thickening barrier as the djinn roared overhead.

Astron instructed the other three shield demons that remained alive. Before the djinn could attack again, he was safely inside a box with an open bottom resting on the rotunda floor. The attacking demon released three bolts in frustrated fury, then turned his attention back to Elezar and the few remaining guards that still stood hovering over their prince.

With the attention diverted, Astron rearranged the positions of the shield demons, rotating their opaque planes until they too were inside the protective enclosure they had created.

"Now, in unison, toward the hub," he commanded. "First the left foot and then the right." The strange mechanical way that men used to move in synchronization was proving to be a most useful piece of information. The shield demons lumbered forward, their barriers bouncing and banging against one another as they moved. The seals between the edges did not remain perfect, and backwashes of energy spilled inside to carom about the interior. Astron danced about to avoid the stray ricochets while he directed the demons forward, concentrating on how many steps to take before he reached the vicinity of Elezar and his guards.

After a dozen steps, he ordered a halt and then directed the demons controlling the shield nearest the hub to rotate his barrier floorward. Astron threw his arm in front of his eyes and stared out of the enclosure. Elezar was down on one knee, his right arm grasping the other near the elbow. The prince's face was frozen in a mask of pain as he steadied himself among the dead and dying at his feet. Two remaining guards stood on unsteady limbs between Elezar and three towering lightning djinns. Behind them all, Gaspar's laugh boomed as he urged his minions on against the other devils who flitted about the huge hall.

"Hasten, my prince. You need shelter to compose your thoughts," Astron shouted as he darted out from the protecting shields. He sidestepped a spent pulse of energy and stumbled over smoking cushions to Elezar's side. The prince turned as he approached, released his injured arm and prepared to defend against the new attack as best he could.

"No, it is the one who walks," Astron said. "Command those that you can into the shelter."

Three more bolts of plasma screamed overhead. One of the remaining guards reeled backward, clutching his shoulder and trying to stop the flow of green ichor from a gaping wound. Astron shoved away the reluctance coursing up from his stembrain and did what he had never dared before. He touched Elezar's extended hand, wincing as much from the thought of contact as from the prickles of pain created by the sparks that ran along the prince's palm.

Elezar's eyes flared at the familiarity, but then in resignation stumbled backward with the tug. With his injured arm, he somehow waved others to follow. In a rush, all of the nearby imps, sprites, devils, and demons abandoned their defenses and scrambled after the prince.

Gaspar roared when he realized what was happening. "After Elezar," the lightning djinn shouted. "Ignore the lesser devils. We will make game with them at our leisure. Focus your energies. Stop the one who dares to call himself a prince."

Bolts of plasma lanced into the protective enclosure as Astron and the others tumbled under the upraised barrier. Shouts of agony echoed through the air. Sprays of wet stickiness like warm fat globules from a slaughterhouse fell on his back as he directed the shield demon to drop the open side back into place.

When the panel sealed with the others, the scene plunged into near darkness. Except for a rumble transmitted through the floor, the sounds of battle faded away. Then, just as suddenly, the top of the enclosure blazed with light, a diffuse glow that spread outward from a focus and slopped over the edges of the plane. The pulse decayed, but it was followed by a pair and then a half dozen or more as Gaspar's djinns converged to attack.

The shield demons inside of the protection were undisturbed by the onslaught, however. The plane pulsed and glowed, but except for the visual light, they deflected the energies away. The bursts moved methodically from the top panel to the one nearest the hub and then around to the others. Gaspar was testing each one in the hopes of finding a weakness in the defense. But all the shields held, each as well as the next.

Astron's stembrain retreated backward from his conscious thoughts. Elezar could not hold out forever within the confines of the box. Eventually, Gaspar would think to attack from underneath the thin flooring upon which there was no shield. But at least it bought some time for the prince to think and plan a counterthrust in conditions that were more favorable. In the diffuse darkness, he groped to find Elezar and tell him of what he had learned in Palodad's lair.

9

Through the Flame

"SO, EVEN Palodad did not know the answer," Elezar whispered through pain-clenched teeth when Astron had finished reporting on his trip to the old one's domain. "All that he can offer is the direction in which to look and verification of what is found in exchange for some exotic form of matter. It makes how the likes of Gaspar came upon the conundrum a riddle of its own."

Astron shifted uncomfortably. He had little room, sandwiched between the legs of a stone sprite and with his back pressed against the barbed wings of a messenger djinn like a new clutch of hatchlings huddling for warmth. Elezar's ability to force aside the distractions of pain, the bursts of light, and what was happening outside of their enclosure might indeed be the necessary talent of a prince, but it was disconcerting, nevertheless.

The assault of energy against the barriers of the shield demons had continued unabated while Astron had informed the prince. In dim outlines, he caught glimpses of the destruction of the rotunda and several of the other domes beyond. Muted cries filtered through even the thickness of the woven walls as more and more of Elezar's followers were routed out of their hiding places and made the sport of the lightning djinn's lust for battle and destruction. Soon, all the rest would be gone, and the attention of every demon that Gaspar commanded would be turned to the box that sat on the rotunda floor.

"How Gaspar possessed the riddle is of little enough consequence," Astron said. "And since you struck the first blow, the lightning djinn will feel justified in his destructions whether you can solve his puzzle or not."

"The key is the disposition of the other princes who rule." Elezar disagreed. "If I can get word to enough of them undetected, then sufficient might can be marshalled to drive Gaspar from my domain. And once he is removed, the others will judge what he has already done to be sufficient compensation for my momentary indiscretion. He will be able to unleash his will only if I indeed fail to present to him a satisfactory solution to the riddle."

All four sides of the enclosure flashed in unison as if bathed in a sea of sudden light. Images of falling spires filled Astron's mind.

"All that you suggest will take time," Astron protested. "The aid I have rendered is at best temporary." Already his feeling of accomplishment was fading. The baser emotions of his stembrain had begun to reassert themselves. "Would it not be better now to focus on Gaspar's immediate threat to your well-being?"

"I must go by stealth to another node in the realm." Elezar ignored Astron's words. "One that is dark and not the lair of any demon of power. From there, I can dispatch my messengers while Gaspar dissipates his energy with fruitless destruction here."

"But how will you journey there?" Astron asked. "Not — not all of your present retinue are winged. The few djinns here cannot carry us all."

"Do not despair, walking one," Elezar whispered. "You still possess value. I would rather you not be wasted like some lowly imp. Look at those crowded about you. You are the only one with more than a bulb of pulp riding atop his stembrain."

The prince reached out and squeezed Astron's wrist. "Your mission is a different one, cataloguer, and I bid you to begin it now. It is with you that I must entrust the quest for the answer to Gaspar's riddle. You are the one to bring true flame into the realm of demons."

Astron's feelings bubbled like gases escaping from a pool of molten rock. It had been quite enough to visit Palodad's lair once. He had returned with what he could and had saved, at least for the moment, the prince as well. What more could be asked of one such as him? His stembrain forced him to look through the translucence of the barriers, to estimate his chances to skitter away while Gaspar and the others concentrated on targets that were more important. But even if he escaped, what if Prince Elezar then fell? What then would be the demands of duty? What reason would there be for the existence of a cataloguer? Would there be any other prince who would appreciate the value of one who studied the puzzling details of other realms?

The shriek and tear of matter from outside the barriers pushed its way into his thoughts. Astron shook his head. The speculation was not the substance of a true enigma. There could be no other choice.

"When Gaspar breaks through, be sure to command a djinn to return me to Palodad's lair," he said at last. "I will tell him that you agree and find out in which realm the search is to be conducted."

"No, no, not Palodad," Elezar whispered hoarsely. "You will be unable to transport into our realm whatever it is that Palodad wants. You will need the aid of a being from outside of our realm. A strong one with great will and equal to the task. You must find him first so that you will be ready."

"But where?"

"From the realm of men. You must go through the flame first to the realm of men. Dominate whomever you contact and instruct that one to carry you to Alodar the Archimage. Only he will have the wisdom to decide and choose among his minions the one best for the quest. Have the archimage contact me back through the flame so that we can agree on his succor and aid."

"The archimage!" Astron exclaimed. "He is the one among men who has mastered all five of the mortal magics — the only one to bring a demon such as yourself ..."

"That is why you must link minds with another mortal," Elezar said when Astron did not continue, "someone with lesser strength or will whose mind you can control. Use the one you dominate to guide you to Alodar. Then you can converse with him with your own faculties intact, rather than wrestle to speak freely while under his power."

Astron started to say more and then thought better of it. The groan of twisting matter and flashes of crackling plasma had intensified rather than abated. It would not be long before Gaspar, even in his rage, deduced how to renew his attack on Elezar. No time must be wasted to ponder it more. If Elezar commanded him elsewhere, then he would go. He must make contact with a mind that at that very instant was probing into the realm. Make contact and hope that his will would be the stronger.

Astron twisted into a comfortable position as best he could and fought to push the light and sound out of his thoughts. He breathed deeply — a curious practice he had noticed in the realm of men — but it helped no more than it ever had before. With his membranes down, he tried to imagine the emptiness of his own surroundings, vast expanses of black desert sprinkled with rare oases of matter.

His thoughts soared as his body could not; past glittering lairs swarming with imps, feebly glowing fortresses of devils who no longer cared, and dark nodes unclaimed by any prince. Astron imagined himself in total darkness, undistracted by anything in his realm, his mind as blank as a child's slate in the realm of men and open to the tendrils of thought that pierced through the barrier from beings on the other side.

He willed his mind to stillness, but even his stembrain knew that he must be careful, avoiding the lures that were the most tempting. As Elezar had warned him, he could ill afford a struggle with a wizard of great strength. The law of dichotomy admitted no middle outcome. When contact was made, one of the beings would dominate and the other must submit.

Yet it would serve no purpose for the battle to be an easy one. Control of the likes of a mere serving girl did not provide the means to gain audience with the archimage of men. No, the linking of minds must be chosen to be correct, a grapple with a being of some will and hence possessor of power, a being of consequence, but not so great that Astron would find himself the one dominated as the final connection was made.

Astron tested one probe and then flitted to another. For a mere instant, there was a vision of dancing flame and behind it some gnarled wizard pushing with his thoughts and daring mighty djinns to accept his challenge. Astron felt his way past a dozen more, retreating from most with haste and discarding the rest as not worthy of even such a demon as he.

Finally, he touched upon one different from the rest, a being of inner strength, but also, with a softness that perhaps could be molded to his desire. Astron let his own mind engage the tendrils of beckoning thought. The essence of his being coiled like smoke and intertwined with the wisps reaching out for him. First at a single point, then with many others, the two minds meshed and flowed into one another, preparing for the struggle that was soon to come.

It was a female, he realized with a shock as the intimacy increased — a female and yet a wizard, nonetheless. Her flow of will began to stiffen and push back against his own thoughts as he tried to maneuver them so that they surrounded and confined hers. Astron increased his concentration, imagining strong, sinewy vines looping through a flimsy trellis and pulling it to ground. His hands tightened into fists. The muscles in his back bunched in bulging contractions on his slight frame.

He perceived more of the universe that was joined through the flame, a pentagram of chalk, the wizard in dark robes staring into a firepit cut through a planked floor, and the strong odors of aromatic woods. Behind her was another, a dark-headed man with eyes of gray, his furrowed brow beaded with sweat as he watched the struggle unfold.

The interlocking thoughts lose all their pliancy, congealing first into stiff ropes, and then bands of steel. At every juncture where they crossed his own, there was a sudden tugging, an urging to push through the barrier and travel from one realm to another. He set his teeth and pushed out with his arms against the protecting walls of the shield demons. He wanted to vault through the flame and into the other world, it was true, but only as he willed it, a master of the one who beckoned, rather than her slave.

The floor buckled and then spattered up ward sprays of molten metal. Two of the lesser imps a few feet away from where Astron struggled screamed in pain as a ball of pulsing plasma tore through from underneath and bathed them in its destruction. The edge of a gaping hole fizzed and steamed where before had been a plane of matter.

"Demons, surround your prince," Elezar called out. "Guard the portal so that the lightning djinns do not pass."

"Let none escape," Gaspar answered. "We will catch and then fry them all. Pursue them no matter where they flee. I will boil Elezar and his minions, even if they vanish to another realm."

Astron was only dimly aware of the scramble among the devils and sprites who had sought the refuge with his prince. He struggled to concentrate on his own battle and strained to buckle the resistance to his thoughts.

Another loud crash shook Elezar's entire domain with a shudder. The flooring split asunder, disintegrating into disconnected platelets of twisted matter. The support of the shield demons tumble away and then a sense of falling into the emptiness of the realm swept over him.

"Yield," he shouted across the barrier as he fell, "yield to him who is the stronger." In desperation, he pounded his clenched fists to his chest and strained with a final gasp to end the struggle with the wizard.

The inky blackness exploded with painful light. A stab of singeing heat rolled across his back. He heard death cries barely a span away. The panic building in his stembrain pushed against its restraints. If Elezar lost now, what could his quest matter? It would only be a question of time before Gaspar's lieutenants hunted him down for a far more ignoble death.

But just as he prepared to relax his straining will and submit to his fate, there was a reduction of the tension and then a collapse of resistance.

"I am yours to command, Master," a voice said in his head. Astron did not bother for one final look to see how those around him fared. Determined, he thrust himself through the barrier into the realm of men.

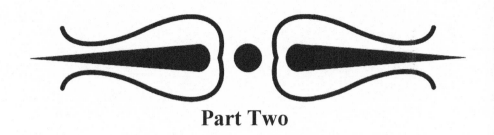

Part Two

The Realms of Men and Skyskirr

An Agreement of Honor

KESTREL SHIFTED uneasily as the demon materialized above the flame in Phoebe's cabin. In barely a dozen heartbeats, the creature stepped from the flame, as solid from head to toe as the wizard he had just subjugated. If he dared reach out, he probably could touch the apparition.

"I am Astron, the one who walks," the demon said. "I command you to take me to Alodar the Archimage of all men, so that the message from my prince to him can be made known."

"I am a wizard of Brythia, the hindermost of the Southern Kingdoms," Phoebe answered like a sleepwalker being questioned. "The great Alodar resides in Procolon far to the north, beyond Samirand, Laudia, and even Ethidor." She turned her hands palms upward and shrugged. "The petty squabbles of the princes have closed the border between us. Unless you are willing to wait for several months more, you will need the service of men-at-arms to cross it, not the skills of a master of the arts. Give me some other task, one for which there is some hope of success. "

Astron scanned the room. "The rate of time is never quite the same among the realms," he said, "but several of your months will be far too long." The demon's eyes fell on Kestrel as he finished stepping clear of the fire that was fading into glowing embers and curls of smoke. "If not you, then perhaps your lackey. Why cannot he lead me to the archimage by your command, just as you must obey my wishes as your own?"

"Ah, pause here for a moment," Kestrel said. "There is a slight error in your logic." More anvilwood he could obtain somehow. Getting entrapped by a devil was another matter altogether. "I am a simple woodchopper, not a hero from the sagas. I was just stopping by to show my wares. If the lady is not interested, then there is no obligation I have to her."

Kestrel stepped to the side, aiming to place Phoebe between him and the demon. He glanced at the door and calculated how many more glides it would take to be away.

"The task is as I have stated it," Astron persisted. "My control of your mind, wizard, is not so great to smother all thought. Perform what I command and I shall set you free. Let your creativity be the key to your release."

Kestrel slid two more steps to his left. He kept his head down and avoided looking at the devil. Catching a demon in the eye was to be avoided at all costs, he remembered.

"Acting together, the wizards of my local council might petition for a writ of safe passage," Phoebe said. "But it is difficult to get them to agree on anything so concrete, especially if there is no gain in it for them."

"What then is the motivation that would prod them to act in haste?"

"All the wizards of Brythia are enamored of the tangible rewards from their craft," Phoebe replied. "It is to the golden brandels of Procolon or the magic tokens of Pluton across the great ocean to which they listen the most."

"What of these things do you have?" Astron asked.

"My wealth is the greatest of any on the council, it is true," Phoebe said. "But divided and spread among them, the enticement would not be all that strong. There are ten of them and each has at least three-quarters of what you see here."

Kestrel stopped in midstride. Ten times three-quarters, he thought. More than seven times the potential gain of what he had hoped for from Phoebe alone. If there were only a plausible story with which to approach the entire council, something that would appeal to their individual greed but force them to act collectively, some dealing with the realm of demons that no wizard could afford to let pass by. The allure would have to be quite spectacular, something that would withstand the scrutiny of not one but half a score.

He jerked up his head and peered at Astron. The demon did not appear very ferocious, more like an alchemist's factory drudge than a devil. Perhaps, with Phoebe under his command, he had no lust for another. Perhaps, in fact, the sagas were distorted and the risks far less than the babblings that had been recorded. It would be just what he expected of wizards — concocting a great peril to enhance their own importance and the magnitude of their fees.

Kestrel had hoped for ten brandels from Phoebe's purse. If he could get the devil to agree, he might leave these hills with over a hundred. And besting not one but ten so-called masters in one stroke would be even more satisfying as well. The more he pondered it, the more the risks dissolved away and the rewards grew increasingly tempting.

"Your first instincts were correct," Kestrel called to Astron as he returned to Phoebe's side. "I am the key to getting the necessary petition from the wizards' council. Just do as I say, and we both shall be compensated as we desire from our efforts."

Astron wrinkled his nose. "As *you* say? It is I who has asserted the more powerful will in coming through the flame. I control the wizard who called me and, through her, any of those bound to her own command. "

"This is not like that," Kestrel replied in a rush. "Your command of the wizard is part of the plan I have in mind, but between you and me, it is more of a mutual agreement."

He stretched his face into a smile. "A contract between partners that we both swear to uphold — like the formal exchanges between alchemists and apothecaries for rare ingredients and tested formulas."

"If not the wizard, then who is your prince?" Astron asked. "And what do you mean when you speak of contracts and swearing to uphold?"

"I am a free man and have obligations to no one, neither king nor master," Kestrel said. "My will is my own." Astron's face distorted further and he rushed on. "The important thing is that we agree to act in each other's behalf — on our honor, not by threat of penalty but by being true to our innermost values of being."

Astron did not speak for a long while. He looked back and forth from the placid face of the one he controlled to Kestrel's sudden enthusiasm. "In my realm, one serves a single prince and no other," the demon said at last. "Breaking allegiance is such a personal shame that the will to resist the great monotony is shattered as well. Is that what you mean by contracts and honor?"

"Why, exactly so," Kestrel said. "I could not have explained it better myself."

"And if I follow your instructions, you will arrange my audience with Alodar the Archimage?"

"Yes, that will be our agreement — on our honor."

Astron's face relaxed. The demon stuck out his right hand toward Kestrel. "I do know some of the customs of the realm of men. I agree, human, to what you call a contract, working to mutual benefit upon our honor. Here, clasp my hand to seal the agreement and then let us begin."

Kestrel grasped the offered hand and shook, hardly noticing the coarse texture next to his palm, like the new skin from a snake that had just molted. "Here is my plan ..."

But his thoughts were elsewhere. Something about the demon was disturbing. He had agreed all too quickly — too soon for Kestrel to figure out what his real motives were. An agreement on their honor. It sounded as if the devil actually meant it.

The Council of Wizards

KESTREL CLAPPED his hands for attention. Several hours had passed since he outlined his plan to Astron. Now it was almost noon, and nine wizards had gathered in the small garden outside of Phoebe's cabin. The eldest three sat on a long wooden bench next to a small pond lined with smooth stones. Behind them stood the rest, all robed in black and wearing faces heavy with the seriousness of their craft. Kestrel stood next to Phoebe on the other side of the pond, next to a tier of dove cages and neatly trimmed bushes that flashed waxy leaves in the high sun. He glanced once at the small scroll of parchment he had tossed into the pond before the wizards' arrival and smiled. As yet, none of them had called attention to it. It would serve its purpose well.

To the left, Kestrel's wagon stood hitched and ready, his mare nibbling contentedly on a bed of flowering hornweed as if it were permanently allowed to do so. The birch-framed canopy over his pinewood-filled sacks fluttered in a quickening breeze. The last of the doves dispatched with a summons circled overhead, building up the courage to return to its roost just beyond Kestrel's reach.

Kestrel ignored the hovering bird. The message tied to its leg probably stated only that the last wizard in Phoebe's council would not come, he thought. Enough were already present to make the production worthwhile. Judging from the pleasant jingle of their purses, the effort would be worthwhile indeed.

He took a moment to study the masters seated in the front. Undoubtedly, they were the ones to convince. Then the others would follow. The one in the middle, Maspanar, appeared the most bloated with self-importance. Any revelation of facts would have to be his. Monetary aspects were of less concern.

On Maspanar's right sat Geldion, a shriveled hulk that stared back with piercing blue eyes. He seemed to dare Kestrel to speak, to commit some error that could be pounced upon and exposed to the others.

The last of the three, Kestrel decided, was his primary target. Benthon's black robe was a trifle newer than all the rest. Golden rings adorned slender fingers not smudged by charred embers or sooty ash. The eyes danced about the confines of Phoebe's garden, searching for an opening, an opportunity for gain that would continue to feed his expensive habits.

"Masters, if I may have your attention," Kestrel said after he had satisfied himself that he could predict how the assembled wizards would react. "Your colleague in craft apologizes for the lack of words of greeting and sweet wine."

He waved his hand in Phoebe's direction. "But her startling discovery is of such great importance that she dare not break her concentration for trivial amenities. When you have witnessed what she has to demonstrate you will understand why."

"Who is this that speaks for the wizard Phoebe?" Geldion demanded. He looked over his shoulder and spoke to the masters standing behind the bench. "He wears no robe with a logo, nor have I heard her talk of any bondsmen in her service."

"I have interrupted my studies as a courtesy," Maspanar said. "I doubt that the youngest of our council — and a woman at that — has found anything not yet well known to most of us." He shrugged massive shoulders beneath a robe that had been patched more than once. "If the dabbler has found a means of amplifying our powers as her note indicated, then let her explain her alleged discovery and be done. There is no time for the smooth tongues and empty thoughts of others."

Kestrel forced his smile wider. Years ago when the opinions of other mattered, such rude manners would have hurt and given him pause. But now, like tempered steel, he was as hardened as the rest. He would give them what they deserved, matching their insensitivities with a disdain of his own. Kestrel watched out for himself and no one else. Let the masters beware.

"A simple flame." Kestrel pointed back through the open doorway into Phoebe's cabin, ignoring the challenges. It would serve no purpose to spar with Maspanar or Geldion until after Benthon was hooked. "You can all see it burning within the pentagram on the floor. Perhaps the keenest among you, even from the distance, can guess what fuels the blaze."

"Simple pine logs," Maspanar shot back. "The height of the yellows, smoke with little soot, and the lack of intense blues mark it as nothing else."

"Yes, dried pine it is," Kestrel said. "The tunnel between the realms for small imps and sprites and little else. For demons of true power, more exotic woods and powders must be consumed to bore through the barrier that keeps them from us."

Kestrel replaced his smile with a serious mask. "More exotic woods are needed for demons of true power," he repeated, "or so one would expect."

With a sudden thrust of his arm, he reached into the cabin and grabbed the door by the knob. In a blur of motion, he repeatedly opened the door a crack and then slammed it shut, a staccato burst of sound like the beat of a marshal's drum calling to arms filling the small garden. After perhaps a dozen slams, he flung the door all the way open, again permitting the wizards to view the interior.

Kestrel's smile returned as Astron strode forward from the flame, exactly as he had planned. The decorum of the wizards dissolved into a babble of excited voices.

"Impossible," Geldion said. "No demon of that size could come through such a simple flame."

"Some trace element, perhaps," Maspanar replied. "A substance of great power so that a small amount was necessary."

"But what of the control?" Benthon spoke for the first time. "That is indeed no small imp of little will. Our voices distract too much and place Phoebe in great peril. "

"I am yours to command, Master." Astron bowed to Phoebe as he exited from the cabin. "Give me your instructions so that I may serve."

Phoebe frowned as she heard the words and mouthed them silently. She shook off her lethargy. "Do not concern yourselves with the risk, my colleagues. Observe. I need to devote only a fraction of my attention for control."

She turned and looked at Astron as he emerged. "Go among them, devil," she said. "Let them examine you at will. Perhaps the experience will be of interest." Then, with a flourish, she turned her back and began picking a bouquet of flowers from a bed near her feet, her features hidden from the others. Her face relaxed to a lifeless stare as her hands groped for the nearby stalks like a blind woman.

Kestrel glanced back at the wizards, but their attentions were all focused on Astron as he came forward. Things were going well. He would be far away before anyone deduced that Phoebe's words were the ones the demon beforehand had commanded her to say.

"Not an imp but neither a mighty djinn," the talk of the wizards continued.

"But if from simple flame and with no great struggle of will, the phenomenon does deserve some investigation."

"This is indeed most surprising, I admit. My respect for the woman must climb a notch. She may become a credit to us yet. Tell us, Phoebe, what is the name of the one you have so effortlessly summoned? How was his domination achieved?"

"I am called Astron, the one who walks," Astron said. "But that is of little matter. I have done my part. Now I wish you to perform yours with haste. Surrender to the man whatever it is that provides my audience with the archimage. It is the agreement that we have sworn on our —"

"Masters, your attention, please," Kestrel cut in. "Your interest should be more on how Phoebe was able to perform her feat rather than its result."

He frowned in the direction of Astron. He had been so busy beforehand explaining how Phoebe should be controlled that he had neglected to tell the demon to keep his own mouth shut as well. "I have been instructed by your colleague to explain her discovery while she keeps the devil under control. But be advised it might take several hours, and any attempt to rush could destroy what is being demonstrated."

"Several hours," Astron said. "How curious. It must be a ritual I have not witnessed before. Under any other circumstances, I would be most eager to add the details of its performance to my catalogues."

"Masters, if you please," Kestrel persisted. He flexed his shoulders trying to dislodge the tiny burr of apprehension that had made its presence felt under the smooth blanket of confidence in his scheme. "The key insight that Phoebe exploited in her experiment was the willingness of the demon to come. It is true that mighty djinns, virtual kings in their own realm, are ill disposed for the journey through the fires. Only with exotic woods to reduce the barriers and great struggles of will have you been able to woo them.

"But consider instead another approach — an approach in which you provide a bait, an enticement for the devil to journey on his own accord. Phoebe has shown it to be true. Simpler flames are all that is needed, and the demons' spirits are more docile when they appear in our realm. One must provide in addition only the cadence of sounds that sends notice of the lure to the realm where they live."

Kestrel looked at the assemblage, one by one. "Think of it. Mighty djinns for you to command. No more costly expenditure for rare powders and woods."

"Another example," one of the wizards behind the first row called out. "Although this one before us is no simple imp, he seems to have little more value beyond his increased size."

"Little value?" Astron said. "I am a cataloguer. I know perhaps more of your realm than any other of my kind. My prince values me highly. Because of that I am here rather than any other —"

"Exactly so, a cataloguer." Kestrel scowled at Astron again. "He was enticed here by the scroll that Phoebe laid out before the flame. See it there in the pond. It was the lure that made possible a transition even in the fire of pine."

"That is the second time you have looked at me that way," Astron wrinkled his nose. "What message are you trying to convey?"

"What is the demon asking?" Geldion said. "Phoebe, have you given him leave to speak of his own free will?"

Master and Slave

"NO, NO, pay him no heed," Kestrel took another step towards the wizards. "Focus instead on the second experiment. The key is to assemble a lure from your possessions that will entice another demon here. I will manipulate the door as before and you will see."

"What kind of lure; what do you mean?" Benthon asked.

"Anything," Kestrel said. His apprehension lessened. Benthon speaking now could not have been better timed. "Anything at all. It seems the greater the quantity, the mightier is the demon that responds."

He paused a moment and rubbed his chin. "I guess there is one thing, however, that you, of course, will not attempt to employ. I heard the jingle of your purses and could not help thinking of it. A brandel from Procolon will fetch a gold imp, a sack full of them, a bigger devil of the same bent. Their only interest is in hoarding. About the only useful command you could give them is to go and find it in the ground where it is not yet discovered by men."

Kestrel shrugged. "Of course I realize that you are all men of ethics and would not use your powers for such base gain of a few nuggets of metal."

"You stated that the bigger the lure, then the more powerful the demon which would respond and the more able he would be to perform his special talents?" Benthon asked.

"Yes, that is the fact of it," Kestrel replied. "Why, I would imagine that a gold djinn would not even have to look. He would transform the metal out of base rock, as much as was commanded."

Benthon's eyes widened. He opened his purse and thrust it at Maspanar like a gambler with a sudden hunch. "Then such an experiment it will be. Empty what you have into mine and we will share in whatever is gained in return."

"I think that we proceed without sufficient caution," Geldion said. "I am not yet satisfied with the explanation of what little we have seen transpire."

"Then do not participate," Benthon said. "Only those who take the risk shall benefit from the returns as well." He turned back to Kestrel. "What would it take to fetch the likes of this gold djinn to do our bidding?"

"From what Phoebe has instructed me, I would say about eight or nine times the amount in your purse alone. And with such a demon in your power, he should be able to produce tenfold that amount in less than a day."

"What do you say, Maspanar?" Benthon persisted. "If you decide to join, then the others will follow."

Maspanar grunted, looked at Astron and then back at the dying fire in Phoebe's cabin. He shrugged and reached for his belt. "What is the harm?" he asked. "The worst that can happen is that the claim is not true. And with woman's work, I suspect, that somehow, that is the case."

"But if she is correct?" one of the masters in the second row asked.

"With nine of us here, we can dominate whatever comes through the flames." Maspanar shrugged a second time. "If it proves to be small, we can command it into a bottle for study at our leisure. If something of greater size appears, we can call forth clouds of imps on our own that will harry it until it too is subdued."

For a moment, no one moved. Then, in a flurry of jingles and flailing straps of leather, the six wizards who stood behind crowded around Benthon like children buying candy from a traveling peddler and added their contribution to a growing store. Finally, Benthon himself held his bulging purse in front of Geldion, waving it to back and forth. Geldion scowled and reached for his own pouch. Showing no pleasure, he emptied his coins in with the rest and then folded his arms across his chest.

Kestrel tried not to let his excitement show. The wizards had all come better prepared than he had dared hope. Now, for a little more maneuvering and it would all be done.

"But, but your ethics," he said. "If you get too much gold, then even the economy can be altered — just as it was on Pluton across the sea some two decades ago."

"A wizard indeed is entrusted with a most solemn trust." Benthon stepped forward, thumping his chest with his free hand while his sack hung heavy in the other. "Therefore, we judge the risks and take only those that are prudent." He turned and waved back at the others. "And here our judgment is unanimous. What Phoebe has discovered must be verified with all expediency. Any reward that is possible for our efforts will be administered with discretion."

He caught Kestrel's eye. "There might even be a brandel or two for the lackey who made the process all the quicker rather than throw up objections that are of no real concern to one of his station."

For a moment, Kestrel stared at the sack and then ran his tongue over his lips. "I guess there is only one more thing to be aware of, and then my conscience is clear," he said. "Whichever one of you controls the demon will have some advantage over the others. And, as Phoebe has explained it, the closer you are to the flame, the greater your chances of being the most likely to grab the demon's will. But then, of course, the closer you are, also the greater the danger. In good faith, I recommend that you all stay outside as did the woman, rather than try to crowd around the flame inside the cabin."

"Clear a path for me," Benthon said. "My will is the strongest and I am not afraid."

"Wait, drop the gold here in the pond," Kestrel stepped aside. "By the scroll that lured the first demon to Phoebe. You must be between the lure and the flame for the connection to work."

"Watch this for us, Phoebe," Benthon gathered up speed. He tossed the sack into the water. It fell with a plunk satisfying to Kestrel's ears. "We will be back for it in a few moments, and, if you indeed are correct, for a good deal more. "

Maspanar and two more wizards followed Benthon. Then, in a mass of elbows and shoves, came the others.

"The cadence of sound for calling a gold djinn is fifteen immediate slams and then a wait of some thousand heartbeats," Kestrel said. "If the door is opened before then, the connection is broken and the entire effort wasted." He nodded with satisfaction as Geldion started to join the rest. Mentally, he measured the strides from the pond to his waiting wagon.

"I have pondered the existence since you first mentioned it," Astron interjected suddenly, "and I cannot think of a single example. No, I am sure of it. None in Elezar's domain nor any of the princes who hang in the void near him has ever known of such. It is an extraordinary occurrence. I devote my life to cataloguing the mysteries and surprises of other realms and find that there is still much I do not know of my own surroundings. Gold imps and even djinns of gold. Yes, it is extraordinary. There is no other word for it."

Geldion paused in the doorway and turned around. "What did he say?" It sounded as if he is questioning the existence of what we are about to seek. Phoebe, make him explain what he meant."

Kestrel scowled. He ran forward and grabbed for the doorknob, blocking the wizard's exit with his body. "There is time for that later," he said. "Wouldn't you rather I get the cadence started right away? You know I won't be able to begin until you are inside and the door able to hit the jamb."

"Phoebe, answer me," Geldion persisted. "Stop denuding that flowerbed and answer me."

"Go ahead and speak, Phoebe," Astron said. "I am anxious to get things concluded as much as anyone."

Phoebe rose and turned toward Astron. "What shall I reply, Master?" she asked. "You have not instructed me this time as to what you wish me to say."

"Wait a moment," Geldion said. "Who is the master and who the slave? Maspanar, step back here for a moment. Now that I think of it, Phoebe has been acting most strangely. She should be examined at once to verify the freedom of her thought."

"The gold djinn! Look, he comes now through the flames." Kestrel pointed back into the cabin. It was an act of desperation, but things were unraveling fast. He pressed against Geldion's side but the master did not yield.

"But if not Phoebe, then who is manipulating the devil?" Geldion continued as his eyes danced about the garden from Phoebe to Astron and then to Kestrel at his side. He glanced at the wet sack of gold resting on the bottom of the pond, his eyes suddenly wide. With a strength surprising for his size, he pushed through Kestrel's restraint and staggered back into the garden. "Guardsmen," he shouted, "guardsmen, attend at once."

A squeak of leather and rattle of steel sounded from a clump of trees near a bend in the road a small distance from the cabin. Kestrel scowled at his bumbling, first with the demon and then not checking the environs to ensure a path of escape. At least one of the wizards was suspicious enough not to come by himself. The size of the treasure had been too great, and he had dreamed too much about how it would be spent, rather than ensuring its capture.

Half a dozen men-at-arms emerged from their hiding place and begin jogging toward the cabin, their swords drawn and shields in place as if they were assaulting the gate of a fortress. With a sudden surge, Kestrel pushed Geldion to the ground and bolted over his sprawling body. He leaped to the edge of the pond and scooped out the bulging sack of gold. He glanced a second time at the approaching warriors and back at the wizards now spilling out of the cabin. It was going to be close, but, considering his mistakes, no less than he deserved.

Kestrel ran to his wagon and started to fling the sack into its interior; but as he did, a well-aimed rock cracked into his shoulders, forcing him to release his grip. Like a ripe melon spewing its seeds, the wet leather pouch hit the ground and burst apart. Circles of gold flung in every direction, some rolling under the wagon and others arcing all the way back to the pond.

He bent to the ground and then hesitated. The first of the wizards was almost upon him. He would be an easy target once he crouched over. He watched the last of the coins stop their spinning and settle to the rough ground, sparkling in the sunlight. It was more than he had ever seen at one time. With an almost painful regret, he pulled himself up into the wagon, empty handed, and grabbed for the reins.

"Block his escape! Don't let him get away!" the wizards shouted to one another.

"We have the woman. They should be punished together."

"A barrier across the road. Quickly, before he bolts!"

Kestrel slapped the reins against the hindquarters of the horse. The wagon jumped into motion. He grabbed his whip and increased its pace, all the while looking down the road and trying to judge on which side to try to run past the converging men-at-arms. Upraised hands grabbing at the side of the wagon were wrenched away as he gathered speed.

The cart surged forward, and Kestrel leaned to his left, looking back over his shoulder past the covered awning toward Phoebe's cabin. Only one wizard ran after him in labored slowness. Three more were sprawled on the ground where they had fallen away. Most of the rest fluttered around the spilled sack like feasting black birds fighting over the coins in the sand. The last two held Phoebe in tight grips on each arm, pulling her forward towards the rest. Perhaps the demon mingled among them, but in the confusion of black robes, he could not be sure.

Kestrel's eyes lingered on the woman. With him safely away, the wrath of the other wizards would all fall on her, even though she bore no responsibility for what had happened. He recalled his feelings when they stood together inside her cabin and then shook his head at the sudden impulse that welled up within him.

Madness, he thought. The only course was to be gone before the men-at-arms could organize to block him. But the impulse remained. Her blank face made him remember the sweet smiles it once bore, even when it carried her own caution.

"It may as well be three errors," he muttered as he pulled the reins to the left, circling the wagon just before the road narrowed to a single lane. Without reducing speed, he raced back toward the cabin, aiming directly toward the wizards who held Phoebe in their grasp.

The Truth of Things That Are Not

KESTREL TURNED the wagon around well before the men-at-arms could reach him. He slapped the reins across the mare's hindquarters, urging her back toward the cabin. The master who had chased him down the road scrambled to the side and let him pass. The others, intent on scooping coins from the ground, took no heed until he was almost on top of them. Then, they too scattered in a flurry of flapping robes and tinkling coins.

Kestrel aimed his wagon at the wizard on Phoebe's left. As he expected, the master dropped his grip and jumped out of the way. The horse slowed, and Kestrel leaned over to the side as he passed. He extended his arm around Phoebe's waist, and she flopped against the rough planking of the wagon like a rag doll as it careened by. Even though the mare was slowing, the momentum was too great for the remaining wizard. He let go of Phoebe's arm with a protesting cry.

With his free hand, Kestrel pulled the horse to a stop.Dropping the reins, he lifted Phoebe up beside him. Her eyes were glazed, oblivious to what was happening. He let her sag into a heap like a sack of tubers, then leaped from his seat onto the mare's back and jerked the beast's head to the left. There was too little time to back up and turn.

Hoping that the front wheels had sufficient free play, Kestrel started the horse forward, pulling it to the side as much as he dared. The mare whinnied in protest and started to rear, but Kestrel kept his grip firm and kicked her onward. Stepping into the flowerbed, the horse bumped the wagon wheels over the low boundary stones that separated the garden from the walk. Stomping the small bushes and spring blooms, they edged by the cabin on the right, the hub of the rear wheel scraping as it passed.

Just as the wagon bumped out of the garden and back onto the path that led to the road, the men-at-arms ran forward, shield and sword arms blocking the way. Kestrel did not falter. Focusing on the shield of the man on the far left, he dug his knees into the mare's sides. As the troops converged, without thinking, he circled the horse's neck with both arms and swung from its back in a giant arc. Feet extended, he hit the upraised shield with a jarring blow like a battering ram, sending the man-at-arms sprawling before he could strike.

Perhaps he would be able to pull this off.

The impact sent Kestrel swinging backward. He raised his feet as high as he could to avoid the stomping hooves of the mare, now thoroughly frightened and running as fast as it could. A sword's-length distance opened between him and the men-at-arms who were nearest, and then two lengths more. The warriors rallied to run after, but weighted down by shield and mail, they realized that they could not keep up. In a few heartbeats, the clatter of pursuit and shouts of anger started to fade.

Kestrel clung to his precarious hold while the mare raced onward. The occasional clump of trees at the roadside grew into groves and then merged into the beginnings of true forest. Stately elms crowded the pathway like encroaching multi-armed giants, enfolding a canopy over his head. From above, the sunlight alternately burst through unabated or completely hid from view. A gentle breeze swirled away the dust thrown up by the wagon's rapid passage. Finally, the mare spent her wind and slowed to a gentle walk. Listening between the hoof clops, Kestrel could hear no sound of the wizards or men-at-arms. He dropped to the ground and grabbed at the reins, pulling the horse to a stop.

Kestrel gave himself the luxury of a long deep breath. He was getting too old for such theatrics, he thought. And now he probably would have to move on to the next kingdom to practice his skills. He could not count on the shame of the masters in being outsmarted to keep his presence secret. Soon every wizard within the flight of doves would know to watch for a woodcutter and his wagon. He would have to change his tale altogether and target another of the five arts as well.

And what of Phoebe? She might not think that snatching her from the other wizards was much of a rescue. Of course, in her present state, she might not think much of anything. What was he going to do now?

Suddenly, there was a movement from within the awning. A figure stirred. Like a child cranking his first jack-in-the-box, Kestrel dropped his jaw in surprise.

"Why did you turn back?" Astron called down from where Phoebe still slumped. "Even more than the location of the lair of the gold djinns, that is the part I most want to understand. Why did you return to fetch the woman?"

Kestrel recovered his senses and shot back. "What are you doing here? How did you follow where no one else could?"

"I climbed in the back of this — this conveyance while you were pulling the female wizard in through the front," Astron said.

"But why?" Kestrel inched back from the wagon. Astron looked no more menacing than he had when he had first appeared in Phoebe's cabin with his almost human face and muted scales, but the apprehension Kestrel had felt then returned to his thoughts. And now, there was no lure of gain to distract him from the risks of dealing with demonkind.

"I doubt control of my will would be that interesting." He brushed off some of the road dust from his arms and straightened his tunic and rucksack, trying to look as imposing as he possibly could. "It would be better for you now to find some convenient fire and vanish back whence you came,"

"The law of dominance or submission applies only when one of my kind transits between the realms," Astron said as he vaulted from the wagonbed to the ground. "Once I am across, there is no need to wrestle any further. I will do you no harm. Besides, there is the matter of the contract. I have yet to meet with the archimage. You have sworn on your honor to provide the means."

"That was only half of it," Kestrel snapped back. "I was to have received something to line my purse in exchange for my efforts. Thanks to you, I have nothing to show. The contract is balanced on both sides. We each entered the agreement with nothing and now neither is any the better because of it."

"That is not quite so." Astron stepped forward and opened his fist. "In the confusion that followed the bursting sack, none of the wizards seemed to mind that a demon was scurrying over the ground with them. This is perhaps not what you anticipated, but it is far from the nothing of which you speak."

Kestrel studied the offered palm. There, in a neat stack were more than a dozen brandels, glinting with the light that filtered through the canopy of trees shading the road. Several dozen brandels — less than he had hoped but as much as he had expected from convincing Phoebe to buy his wagonload of wood in the first place.

He reached out to grab the coins as Astron tipped his hand. "This is compensation for the errors you made by speaking out, is it not?" he asked. "A settlement and then we can be on our separate ways?"

"This is payment in full," Astron said. "I have honored my part of the bargain. Now you must honor yours."

Kestrel shook his head in disbelief. The devil was indeed serious! Or so he professed to be. Doubt immediately followed in Kestrel's thoughts. Honor, contracts, and trust — such things were mere abstractions. They did not actually exist — not for him anyway, not since he had trusted too much and paid the price. Could it be any different for the demon?

Kestrel stared at Astron's unblinking expression, trying to fathom the true motives that lay behind it, but Astron did not speak. Kestrel glanced away, noticing almost absently the foam standing on his mare's withers. He reached into the wagon for a coarse rag and began to wipe the moisture away, his mind churning with what he should say next.

He finished rubbing down one side of his mare and then started on the other. "Do you not understand?" The words burst forth at last with more bitterness than he would have liked. "Understand what it means to bargain with one such as me. I am no hero from the sagas, performing great deeds for kings and masters of the five arts.

"No, my satisfaction comes from motives much less lofty. I prey upon these so-called heroes. The masters most regarded give me the greatest thrill. I tempt them where they are the weakest and appeal to the baseness in their characters that is as great as mine.

"Was Phoebe interested in the properties of anvilwood or the fact that the price I seemed to offer in innocence was a tenth of what it would fetch from Procolon to the north? Did the wizards care about the effect of gold nuggets common as pebble stones on all those about them or wonder which one would end with the greater share?

"Honor, heroes, the masters," Kestrel continued. Each time that I succeed, each time that they reveal the rotten core beneath their masks of righteousness, it piles proof upon proof. There are no such things as heroes, only men, and not one any better than I."

Kestrel slumped his shoulders. Why had he said so much? His values and how he acted were his business alone, not the concern of a being from somewhere beyond the flame. It was best to end things so he could be on his way. He stared at Astron, waiting to see how the devil would react to what he had said.

"You speak with great passion," Astron replied after a moment. "A passion that I never before have observed." He reached into the wagon and grabbed a second cloth. Eyeing Kestrel's work critically, he dabbed at an apparent wetness on the mare's hindquarters that had been missed. The horse whinnied and backed away, but Kestrel patted her neck and calmed her back down.

"I wish that I had the time to pause and understand it more fully,"

Astron continued, "but for now we must continue. Tell me, what is your plan for gaining the attention of the archimage?"

"Didn't you just hear what I said?" Kestrel flung his rag to the ground. "The merging of our paths was an accident, an alignment of the random factors, as the alchemists would say. Now that the business at Phoebe's cabin is done, there is nothing more to bind us together. Here, keep the brandels. But look elsewhere for a hero with honor, if one you must have."

"I do not know as much as I must of the realm of men," Astron said. "For that, I must rely on you. But of sprites and wizards, my knowledge is perhaps the deeper. For the foreseeable future, that will be your greatest need."

"What do you mean?"

"Wizards are most proud. Their wills are not easily diverted, once they have set upon a goal." Astron stepped around the mare, thrusting his face into Kestrel's, his eyes glowing with intensity. "Do you actually think that every master who visited the woman's cabin will forget what has happened and let you continue unimpeded on your way?

"Or will they call forth from my realm the most powerful devils that they dare and send them searching — searching until you have been found and cast in some dim dungeon as punishment for your deed?"

A chill like ice water raced down Kestrel's spine. Maybe Astron was right. Simply disappearing and starting over might not be so easy. And years in a cage, he could well do without.

"We are cleanly away," Kestrel said. "Once we reach the juncture, the road will be one well-traveled. Demon-aided or not, I will be able to fade successfully from sight."

"It will take time." Astron shook his head. "But eventually, you will be found. At first, they will dispatch hundreds of small imps or perhaps even thousands if their ire is truly great. Tirelessly, these will dart throughout every corner of your world, examining the features and actions of you humans as closely as they dare. Those who match the descriptions given to them will become the subject of a more intense investigation by devils with greater capacity above the stembrain. Even though, to ones of our realm, you all look very much the same, in the end all the possibilities will be eliminated except one."

Astron halted. He flicked transparent membranes down over his eyes. The demon's face seemed to take on a distant and preoccupied look.

"Now that I think of it," Astron continued, "our urgencies are intertwined. The same imps and devils called forth by the wizards could have a second mission as well. If Gaspar has already triumphed, then the visitors to your realm will be instructed in addition to search for Elezar's missing cataloguer so that he can be returned to his fate.

"Yes, woodcutter, I need your help to navigate through the realm of men just as you need one such as me, one who knows the signs of the presences of my kind."

Astron held up the rag in his hand and tossed it to Kestrel. "My eyes see reds that men cannot, especially when my membranes are in place to filter out the distractions of the blues. That is how I can detect the areas of moisture that you missed on this creature's back. In like manner I will notice the imp glows far sooner than could the finest wizard in your realm. I can alert you of the danger while we pursue our common goal."

"What common goal?"

"Why to find the archimage, of course," Astron said. "If he stands to these wizards as a prince does to the djinns of my realm, then only he will be able to turn aside their anger and tell them to desist."

The hint of a human smile crept onto Astron's face. "So you see, what we seek is the same, as well as what we want to avoid."

Kestrel felt the dampness of the cloth that Astron had thrown him and dropped it to the ground with the other. He patted his mare and frowned. "You can detect the presence of these imps before they can get too close?" he asked.

"Far before what you might dismiss as a fleeting spark of light or a distant buzz of an insect, I can recognize for what it truly is."

"And once detected, you can confine them as well?"

"They would bite my fingers just as surely as yours," Astron said. "It is the bottles made by your magicians that are best to keep them in."

"Such jars cost a great deal," Kestrel replied. "Far more than a dozen brandels. I have — have dealt with a guild of Procolon to the north and know what one might bring."

"Then too there is the matter of the gold imp and others of its kind. For those, I do not know for sure that I can even detect."

"If you have not heard of such, then they most probably do not exist," Kestrel said.

"But you spoke of them to the wizards."

"It was a lie." Kestrel shrugged, dismissing the thought. Astron's unblinking eyes were disconcerting. Not being able to snatch even a glimmer of what he really was up to made him very uncomfortable. But what the demon had said made sense. The pride of not a single wizard had been bruised, but that of almost a dozen. The archimage probably was the only one who could get him out of his fix. Only Alodar would have enough power to turn aside the masters' wrath once he somehow was convinced it was all a simple mistake. And surely, he could come up with a plausible explanation before he got to the capital of Procolon. Crossing the border would be the only problem.

Kestrel smiled. Now that he thought of it, being in the presence of the archimage might lead to other opportunities as well. The master of five magics was a man just like the rest. What satisfaction there would be in giving him the chance to outsmart a simple woodchopper. The archimage! Yes, it would be the greatest triumph of all!

"Very well," he said. If the demon had any ulterior motives, he would deal with them when they became more apparent. For now, he would continue as he had been asked. "Our paths are still joined. I will get us to the archimage — as we, of course, have agreed."

"A lie," Astron ignored Kestrel's words. "You spoke something which was not a reflection of the truth, or at least your interpretation of it."

"Of course. I explained to you already what I am about, what all men are about. Concern yourself about it no longer. The only difference is that some of us are more skilled in seeing through the words to what stands behind."

"You have this skill of observation?" Astron asked.

Kestrel sighed. The events of the past hour had already been too draining. He did not want to experience any more intense feelings. He shook his head and turned away.

Astron waved at the mare and wagon. "I understand," he said, "that you do not have the means of transporting us as swiftly as a mighty djinn. One is bound by his honor for no more than he is capable of giving."

He reached out and tugged on Kestrel's sleeve. "There will be time, therefore, that can be most profitably spent with no hint of disgrace — time to tell me how you learned to discern the truth of things that are not."

The Sorceress' Tyro

KESTREL STUDIED the expression of the demon standing before him. There was no trace of mocking judgment. Astron's words of honor and trust unlocked memories that had been suppressed for too many years. Unbidden, they bubbled up to be examined again. They would not go away until they had been acknowledged. And if only a being from another realm heard them, who would care?

"I did not have such skills at first," Kestrel said. "Not at first, when perhaps they counted the most." He waved his arm up toward the wagon where Phoebe sat entranced. "In many ways, the wizard reminds me of her - at least in the way she speaks and smiles."

Kestrel focused on the brandels he clutched in his hand and ran his fingers over the bust of the old queen. "Evelyn was a wandering sorceress, so she said, unaffiliated with those on Morgana across the great ocean. The logo of the eye on her robe was plainly stitched and unadorned. Of great beauty, she was as well, as fair as Vendora, the ruler of Procolon, in her prime.

"Her love for me knew no bounds, she told me. Anything that I asked that was in her power would be mine. And who was I to believe otherwise, a lad barely out of his teens?

"The request was simple enough — to go with her among the townspeople I knew, add credence to her tale, and hold the pledges for safekeeping that each of them subscribed. When the total was sufficient, she would add a matching amount of her own. Then, while I waited outside the gates, negotiate with the Cycloid Guild for the sale of some properties — properties that would aid in the enchantments. With them, she would form great illusions of healing and relieve the deep-set pains that even sweet balm could not touch. Our village would become famous for the soothing comforts the charms provided. Everyone would share in the fees that such wonders would bring. And I would learn the words of the spells and be second only to her in the eyes of the grateful.

'Three days I paced in front of the forbidding doors of the guild before some of the more suspicious townspeople came and asked to count again the contents of the sacks I so carefully guarded. When they were opened and iron disks instead of soft gold spilled out, I was as much shocked as they. Even when told how the switch must have taken place in a moment of intimacy, I would not believe. At any moment, I knew, the gates would open and Evelyn would emerge with a satisfactory explanation.

"But she did not come; she left by another exit from the guild almost as soon as she had entered. No, she reappeared not then nor during any of the four years I wasted away in a dungeon in punishment for my part in the crime.

"So when I finally was set free, I started learning to look intently at the faces, to read behind the words and to serve to magicians and other masters some of the same formulas that they would brew for me."

Kestrel shrugged. "It is not so difficult if you set your mind to it. Every man betrays his innermost thoughts with slight gestures and the tugs of muscles in his face, master as well as slave. You merely have to put yourself in his place and feel as your own what must be his driving desires. Each time you observe, the readings become clearer, the hidden motives behind them easier to read.

"And with that understanding comes the power to manipulate, to guide and channel according to your own desire. One can twist a master of the arts like a magic ring on his finger and show to the world, as did Evelyn, how undeserving he is.

"So, in the end, I have become a sorcerer as much as any other. No, I know nothing of the incantations that are so hard to say but if spoken thrice bind the spells. I do not bend others to my will by force of magical art. The illusions that I spin are fabrics of the other's own thoughts, rather than my own. I encourage the impulses that are already there and enable them to flower for a brief moment for my own gain before they are smothered by shame."

The sadness in Kestrel's face tugged like a great weight. "I do have the skill of observation," he said. "I can see through men to their true worth. And unfortunately, I am among the best."

He stopped his rambling and looked at Astron with questioning eyes. "Now do you understand any better?" he asked.

"No," Astron said. "It is all very interesting, but in fact, I guess I do not. Why would this Evelyn say she would return and then change her

80

mind without letting you know?"

Kestrel sighed again. At least for a while, the bitterness was expunged. And it was far better for a demon to hear his confession than for someone who could manipulate the information against him.

He waved back to the wagon. "Climb inside and let us be going, I have some clothing that you should don so that you will not attract notice as we travel northward."

Astron nodded. "But you have not yet told me of the wizard. Why did you return for her at such great risk?"

"I do not know." Kestrel shrugged. "But it does not matter. Into the wagon, I say. Let us be gone."

"You had no real need," Astron persisted as he climbed aboard. "As I understand it, it could only be the act of a hero."

Talk of the Thaumaturges

THE RACE across the Southern Kingdoms was swift. Kestrel pushed the mare as much as he dared, barely stopping for food and sleep. Astron had no requirement for nourishment and Phoebe in her entranced state needed little. In three days' time, they crossed Samirand and Laudia and entered Ethidor, which bordered Procolon on the north. During their trek, Astron saw no sign of the searching imps, but the compelling sense of urgency did not abate. At any moment, the wizards could discover where they were and subject them to their wrath. The tale of what awaited Astron back in his own realm, if he did not succeed in time, Kestrel could scarcely believe, but the demon remained steadfast in urging the wagon onward.

Toward dusk of the third day, they arrived at the port of Menthos as the onshore breeze blew thick plumes of dark smoke from foundries across the isthmus. Kestrel pulled his horse to a stop at the head of the main street of the town. He glanced back at Phoebe, who appeared to be sleeping on a rough bed under the wagon's canopy. The branches and snags meant to be foisted off as anvilwood had long since been discarded. Astron sat at Kestrel's side, wearing a long cape and hooded like a master, although no logo was displayed. A worn tunic, leggings, boots and gloves covered most of his faintly scaled skin.

On the left side of the main street, behind a sidewalk of rough planking, stood a long row of apothecaries, wooden-faced structures mainly of one story. Some were brightly painted and prosperous looking, others were dull with isinglass windows scratched and hazy. 'Galena and cinnabar', some of the placards over doorways proclaimed; 'Fresh vacuum of all quantities, created daily', was written on others.

"An alchemist's town, no doubt about it," Kestrel said as he pointed to the storefronts. He had decided it best to explain things to Astron as soon as something new was seen by the demon. It would reduce the chance of questions at inappropriate times, like those that had been asked at Phoebe's cabin.

They had stopped at the end of the street, just before the first apothecary. There in a jumble were a dozen small cages, each slightly taller than the height of a man. A small crowd had gathered in front, and with laughs and jeers were throwing eggs and rotten fruit to spatter on the bars or sometimes sail within. Each cage held one prisoner who, rather than trying to avoid the onslaught reached to catch the hurled garbage before it hit the ground. It was the first meal they had received in three days.

The punishment of the wizards and masters of the other crafts was swift and cruel in Ethidor. No trial, no jury, and confinement for months or perhaps even years for even the pettiest transgression. Four years in a dungeon was one thing, Kestrel thought, but on open display in baking sun or howling rain, grasping for food to forestall starvation was quite another.

Kestrel knew about the cages. It was a known risk for what he did, but something not to dwell upon. Seeing at first-hand what it meant if he were captured made him shudder. Until now, he had always been clever or perhaps just lucky enough to avoid the wrath of a wizard when he worked his swindles, but now, the stakes were higher.

He turned away to shield the image of the captives from his thoughts. On the right, steep stairways led down a short cliff to docks and quays. Riding at anchor were broad-beamed galleons, all lying high in the water, though some had their decks filled with closely packed bottles, their sails unfurled. Like straining stallions, they were ready to weigh anchor. At the other end of the street, behind high fences, large smokestacks towered into the sky, belching dense black clouds and blemishing the blue. Even from the distance, one could hear the roar of huge bellows feeding air into furnaces like the labored breath of fettered dragons and smell the hint of metallic fumes.

Except for the crowd in front of the cages, the traffic on the street was the usual mixture of scurrying messengers, maids hawking vegetables and material from simple carts, merchants in animated conversation, and an occasional litter bearing someone of importance. Mixed with the rest were men-at-arms in groups of twos and threes, wandering aimlessly, looking for something to spark their jaded interests.

By this time, Kestrel had become quite used to the physical presence of the demon. The oddity of his bizarre origin had long since faded away. A wrinkled nose, Kestrel now understood, indicated puzzlement, the flicking of the eye membranes a retreat into the deep logical thought. But beyond these simple signs, he still could not fathom any motives behind those that the devil professed. Hopefully, they would become more apparent as they drew closer to the archimage.

Despite his statements about his experience as a cataloguer of the realm of men, Astron was completely ignorant about some of the simplest things. Abstract concepts beyond what one could see and touch took a good deal of explaining. But the demon was an eager and attentive pupil, asking questions until he was sure that he fully understood.

"If this is the lair of alchemists, then what formulas do they work?" Astron asked. "The chance for success must be quite high, judging from the number who are congregated all in one place."

"Vacuums," Kestrel said. "By melting metals, the alchemists of Menthos can produce the hardest vacuums on the great ocean. They are in demand by magicians and thaumaturges for their own rituals and simulations."

"But a vacuum is the total absence of matter. How can that have any value at all?"

"I do not understand the details," Kestrel answered, "but by connecting one of the bottles produced here to another vessel, the air can be removed far better than by any pump. Lids can be sealed with greater force than that provided by the finest waxes. Huge pistons can be made to move along long cylinders, raising bridges over navigable rivers."

"The absence of matter," Astron mumbled, "and in the realm of men great effort is put into its creation." He wrinkled his nose. "Another fascination. If only there were more time."

Kestrel started to say more, but he spotted what he was looking for on the crowded street. Half a block down from where they had stopped, three brown robed young men were performing their services for a queue of men-at-arms standing on the sidewalk, waiting their turn. Kestrel pointed out his destination and started the mare forward.

"Thaumaturges," he said, "a journeyman and two apprentices. See, one wears but a single wavy line on his sleeve; the other two are unadorned. But no matter that a master is not present. They will know what is happening by the nature of their trade better than most."

Astron leaned forward to watch the activity as the wagon approached. One of the apprentices clicked short shears through the long hair of a sergeant who sat in a portable chair set up on the sidewalk in front of the line. The second scooted about on his knees sweeping up the locks as they fell and passing them on to the journeyman seated at a table a little distance away.

The last of the three extracted a single strand of hair from the rest of each tress and dipped it into a pot of glue at his side. With a smooth motion, he aligned the sticky hair along the length of a piece of twine in front of where he sat. The men-at-arms chatted among themselves, oblivious of the apprentice and the other activities about them.

"I recognize the craft," Astron said as they approached. "The one with the doubled blades is called a barber. In exchange for a coin he removes hair from the head and face."

"In the Southern Kingdoms, there is no fee." Kestrel pulled the wagon to a halt in front of the line of waiting men. "The hair itself is payment enough."

"Something new for sale?" one of the men-at-arms called out, jingling the purse at his waist as Kestrel vaulted to the ground. "It has been a fortnight of staring at the fires across the marsh. This is our first day of leave. "

"How much for an evening with the wench?" A second poked his head into the interior of the wagon and spied Phoebe's reclining form.

"Although she is mine to command, such base use is not —" Astron began before Kestrel reached up and laid a hand of warning on his arm.

"A fortnight without rotation." Kestrel smiled. "A long time without distraction. Tell me, how have things fared on the border for those who might wish to pass?"

The two men-at-arms turned silent and resumed their place in line. Kestrel noticed the glower of the sergeant who sat in the apprentice's chair. "My business is with the journeyman," he said. "What he has learned from all who have sat here is not the fault of your own fine squad of men."

The sergeant relaxed back into the chair as if settling in for a nap while Kestrel walked down to where the journeyman worked his craft. As he approached, he noticed the hatchet-sharp nose that split the thaumaturge's elongated and melancholy face and how, with eyes furrowed with concentration, he arranged more than two dozen pieces of twine in front of him, each with a hair glued down its length from the head of a different man. The journeyman mumbled something that Kestrel could not quite catch and then began to weave the strings into a stout rope the thickness of a man's thumb.

Simultaneously a second hair from each of the clippings before him disentangled from the rest. Like worms on a hot griddle, they danced toward one another and then began to intertwine. In a perfect mimicry of the weaving of the journeyman, the hairs wove into a tiny replica of the rope but with a diameter smaller than the shaft of a pin.

"What is your greatest length?" Kestrel asked as he approached.

"Over ten times the height of a man but with a carrying strength for its size greater than anything but the strands of a spider's web. You have no need for bulky ropes of hemp or cotton when you can possess such compact beauties as these braids."

"Only ten times the height of a man? Oh, then it is a pity." Kestrel backed away. "I was hoping for something more like the distance from here to the quay."

The journeyman looked up from his work. His eyes ran over Kestrel's rumpled tunic and he frowned. "Even with the aid of thaumaturgy that weaves the tiny strands as quickly as if they were bulky twines," he said, "what you request would take much effort to produce. Each short length must be knotted together. You speak of something measured in golden brandels rather than the mere coppers of Ethidor. Are you sure you do not waste my time?"

Kestrel shrugged and smiled. "Perhaps you are right. There are probably others who have what I want on hand." He turned to go and tossed a brandel onto the table amid the braids of hair. "For your trouble," he said.

The journeyman eyed the coin as it spun to rest on the rough surface. He looked at Kestrel a second time and then made up his mind. "Luthor, to the master's den," he commanded. "Fetch the other braidings with length of ten. I will knot them all together for a price that would be most fair."

As the apprentice scampered off, the journeyman called out to Kestrel, who was halfway back to the wagon. "Here, I will show you how it is done while we wait. Watch as I join together the short length I have just made with another of similar size."

Kestrel hesitated, but then continued toward the wagon.

"You ask of the border," the journeyman continued. "Perhaps there is something of interest I can tell you to pass the time." He waved his arm at the remaining apprentice, now working on the next who stood in line. "There is much that we learn from those with whom we trade."

Kestrel turned and shrugged. "I have heard that there are many who mill about in the bogs."

"And for no real purpose," the journeyman answered. "Our own Prince Rupert's troops are there only because his alchemists could not abide by each other's agreements with the miners of Procolon — ambushing and waylaying each other's shipments of galena and other lead ores as they came south to the foundries. When Celibor rips his mind from lusting after some wench, he is the worst, and his rivals little better. It is no wonder old Queen Vendora dispatched a garrison to guard the way.

"Then Rupert's pride could not stand the presence of Procolon's banners on his soil," the journeyman continued. "So his own legions were dispatched to ensure that none remained on this side of the border. And now they sit staring at each other, with no traffic at all going either way. "

"None at all?" Kestrel asked.

"A month ago, a small wagon about the size of yours attempted to run past Procolon's lines, after bribing some squad on this side of the marsh." The journeyman shrugged. "Their archers gave him no chance to speak before everything was consumed in flame."

"And writs of safe passage?"

"A profitable business." The journeyman laughed. "I can point you to a dozen scribes who would write the most impressive documents for a suitable fee. The trouble is that the men who walk the Procolon line are as testy as ours. They swing their swords first and then ask their sergeants if it was the proper thing to do. But never mind all of that. Let me show you how I will make the length of braid that you request."

The journeyman positioned two lengths of woven rope in front of him, the strands in each one cemented to individual hairs. He grasped a single twine from the end of each and with nimble fingers knotted them together. Then he selected a second pair, interwove them with the first and joined them as well. Proceeding methodically, a pair at a time, he spliced the ends in a strong bond.

Kestrel did not follow the motions of the two corresponding braids of hair but he knew what was happening. They too were becoming knotted and bound in exactly the same way as the easier to manipulate ropes in the hands of the journeyman. The laws of "like produces like" and "once together, always together" were being used to perform a perfect simulation.

Instead, Kestrel was looking in the direction in which the apprentice had sped away. When he recognized a blur in the distance that indicated the young man's return, he reached out and tapped the journeyman on the shoulder.

"The sergeant seemed a little perturbed that his men might talk of the border," he said. "What do you suppose he thinks when he hears the same words come from you?"

"What I have related will cause no harm," the journeyman answered.

"He is concerned only about the regulations laid down by his captain."

"Still." Kestrel pointed at the brandel lying where it had fallen. "How would you explain that a stranger was willing to pay gold for what he has heard?"

"But you said that is for —"

"I see his frown deepen." Kestrel smiled back to the sergeant waiting for his men. "Perhaps the two of us should go over together and explain."

"No, the braided —"

Kestrel reached down and scooped up the coin.

"On the other hand, perhaps it is best for everybody if this transaction never took place."

Before the journeyman could say more, Kestrel glided back to the wagon and climbed aboard. Just as the apprentice came panting up with coils of the tiny rope about both his arms, Kestrel motioned the mare to start away. The only problem was getting across the border, he remembered thinking. It looked as if it was not going to be quite so easy.

A Minority of One

THE AFTERNOON faded into darkness while Kestrel pondered how to proceed. He had navigated the wagon up and down the streets of Menthos a dozen times, looking at all the shops and factories, but no inspiration had come. With a growing fatigue, he studied in the encroaching dimness the last of the foundry fires as they winked out for the night like fireflies starting to slumber. Somehow, the solution to getting past two lines of armed men and into Procolon had to involve the large works of alchemists, but he could not quite put all the elements of a solution together.

Kestrel glanced at Astron, sitting patiently at his side. The demon had halted all his questions when he had been told that interruptions would not be appreciated for a while. Kestrel glanced back into the interior of the wagon at Phoebe's still slumbering form. He sighed. He was bothered about that little detail as well.

What good had it done to rescue her from the other wizards, if she remained in a semi-inanimate state under the control of a demon? Someone was bound to get suspicious about a woman in a trance, wearing the robe and logo of a wizard. Word would surely get back to her peers. Crossing the border would be difficult at best, and Phoebe in her condition was an added complication.

On the other hand, if Astron were to release her from his domination, Kestrel was not sure what would happen. She might try to contact her council and aid in Kestrel's apprehension as well. How easy would it be to convince her to keep quiet about her traveling companions?

"What about the wizard?" Kestrel asked aloud after some more thought. "Is it harmful to keep her in such an unnatural state?"

"Eventually, yes," Astron said. "The muscles atrophy and the thoughts turn sluggish, even after one is released. In time, she would become no more than a vacant doll with drool on her chin."

Kestrel jerked the horse to a sudden halt. "I still do not know quite why I brought her along," he replied, "but certainly not for a fate such as that." He wavered in uncertainty but then thought of the warmth of her smile. "Perhaps it is better to release her now."

"By eventually, I meant a long passage of time," Astron said. "As for the present, do you think it wise? I have held her to avoid more struggle of the wills, but if I were to set her free, she might not be similarly inclined. Most likely, she would try to dominate me instead. The first contest was hard enough. I do not wish to undergo it again."

"No, somehow, I will take care of that," Kestrel's thoughts raced as he spoke. Now that he had decided, it was important that the deed be done. "She can be the key element of the exchange. A role that she is to play. A — a countess. Yes, a countess is what we need. A countess to impress one of the alchemists with the possibility of a very large reward."

"A reward? In exchange for what?" Astron asked.

"Transport across the border in exchange for — for a mine," Kestrel said. As he spoke, everything fell into place. Phoebe was the missing element that he had been searching for! By posing as a countess, she would give them the credibility that was lacking in his half-formed plans. Never mind about the risk of letting her decide for herself. He would work out something when everything could be explained. Kestrel turned the wagon into an alleyway and halted.

"Quickly," he commanded. "Release her now so that we can purchase some clothing appropriate for her station. At dawn tomorrow, we must be ready to start."

"Your motives regarding the female I still do not understand," Astron replied. He wrinkled his nose, and for a long while, nothing happened. Then abruptly his face cleared and he turned his attention to studying the tackle of Kestrel's mare.

"Awake," he said. "I release you, wizard, to command your own will."

Phoebe's eyes fluttered like newly hatched butterflies and then sprang open. She looked up at the wagon's canopy in the darkness and then at the two figures hovering over her. Her eyes widened further, and she clutched her fist to her mouth, preparing to scream. Kestrel reached down and stroked her arm. Gently, he placed an extended finger on her cheek as if it were a mother's caress.

Phoebe's eyes flashed in the gathering darkness. She drew a deep breath and returned her hand to her side.

"Where am I?" she asked in a controlled tone. "What is it that you want?"

"Remember the anvilwood?" Kestrel tried to make his voice soothing. "I am the woodcutter who brought it to your cabin. You summoned a demon more powerful than you could control."

Phoebe's eyes shifted from Kestrel to Astron. "Yes," she said in sudden recognition. "The demon. His will was too strong. I could not resist. I am his to do with what he will." She shuddered and snapped shut her eyes. "The council was right after all. Their barbs and jeers are true." She tugged at the folds of the robe about her hips. "I wear the logo of a master because of my father's wealth, not because of skill. Go ahead, devil, do with me what you will."

"No, you do not understand," Kestrel continued. "Test your thoughts. They are free. The contest is finished and you are dominated no more."

Phoebe cowered in silence for a dozen heartbeats but then the tension faded away. The wrinkles vanished from her brow like the departure of the wind from a suddenly calm sea. She sat up and shook her head as if trying to toss away thoughts that did not belong.

"Free-willed I am, woodsman," she said. "Thank you for your aid." She reached down in confusion to her waist and patted for a purse that was not there. "Your product is as good as you bragged it to be. You need not show me the contents of each leather sack as I originally intended. Let us go back into the cabin and I will pay you your price though I must say that I am getting the better part of the bargain."

"Ah, things are not quite that simple," Kestrel responded. "You see, we are not outside your cabin, but in Menthos, near the border to Procolon."

The tension in Phoebe's face returned. "Menthos? I do not understand."

"Your council of wizards has become enraged," Astron said. "As we speak, they no doubt have many imps scouring the countryside looking for —"

"You," Kestrel cut in. "Yes, you are the one they seek, a wizard in flight from what they construe as the justice that is your due."

"Yes, the council and their hidebound ways," Phoebe shook her head. "But Menthos? I still do not understand."

"Well, this is the way of it," Kestrel looked into Phoebe's questioning eyes. He should have thought things through a little more thoroughly before having Astron release her from his control.

"Yes," Phoebe asked. "What indeed is the way of it?"

"The council of wizards think that —" Kestrel began, but this time,

Astron interrupted.

"We need your help," the demon said, "to cross the border and see the archimage. Kestrel sees you as the key element of the plan. Despite what he has done to your reputation back in Brythia, we need your help here and now."

Kestrel grimaced, expecting Phoebe's face to knot into one of displeasure. Next time, he just had to get the demon to understand and follow his lead, rather than cut in on his own. Not that there would be a next time if Phoebe decided to rectify what had happened to her good name. He shook his head, awaiting the outburst. Why had freeing the wizard been such a good idea?

But the hard words did not come. "You need my help," Phoebe repeated, "the service of a wizard, and you have come to me."

Kestrel blinked at the unexpected tone. "Wizardry, why no," he rushed to say. "It was something rather different from that."

The words of deception were becoming harder and harder to get out of his throat. "We must get to the archimage," he continued while he could, "and for that, we must first cross the border. I think that I have a means of accomplishing it. We need an impersonation of a countess, one who is the seeker of thrills, one who can convince an alchemist to grant favors in exchange for profit to be received later."

He hesitated and then added in a mumble, "The archimage will be able to set things straight between you and your council as well."

"Then it is true!" Phoebe exclaimed. "I was indeed dominated by the demon. If it is skill in wizardry that you desire, elsewhere is where you should look."

"No, no, if wizardry is called for along the way, you are the one to whom we will turn," Kestrel said. "It is just that there are other requirements as well. "

"You need me?" Phoebe questioned again.

Kestrel just nodded, trying to fathom the motivations behind the pretty smile. He was having difficulty reading the wizard, just as he did with the demon, but for a different reason. The emotions were on her face clearly enough, but when he looked at her, distracting images warped the logical cadence of his thought.

"And it will help you with the council," he repeated weakly.

"The council." Phoebe shook her head. "I have little doubt that they have found some way to give me censure." She smoothed the folds of her robe and shrugged. "It has not been such an easy struggle. Without the largess of my father, I would never have been able to pay the triple fees the masters charged to initiate me into their art. The stocking of my larder comes less from the few payments I receive for my craft than the continued openness of his purse.

"'Far better for all concerned',"" he would say despite the largess, "'It has been made quite clear more than once, if Phoebe behaved more like her cousins and sisters, lounging in the dresses of brocade and attending the balls of the prince.'"

"What do you mean?" Astron said. "I cannot yet follow when men speak in such abstraction."

"Men, indeed," Phoebe scowled. "I suspect the realm of demons is much like what you see about you here." She narrowed her eyes and looked at Astron. "Tell me how it is that only the males answer the summons through the flame and grapple with the wizard's will. Why no females? What have you done with them?"

"Why, that is not the purpose of the broodmothers," Astron answered. "They serve one function and no more. It is unthinkable for it to be any other way."

"And you, Kestrel, how many wizards of my sex have you encountered in your peddling of woods?"

"Ah, you are the only one."

"Yes, the only female wizard in Brythia, perhaps in all the kingdoms that border the great ocean. Despite all the regulations that were thrown in the way, the unapproving stares, the whispers behind my back, I became a master — an equally accredited master in a local council, whether they liked it or not."

"Then, if your council does not look with favor on you at the moment —" Kestrel began.

"It can only be an intensification of what already was there. I am an embarrassment to them because I am so different and do not assume their airs. But no matter, I have won the robe and they cannot take it away."

"What is important to me now is not their thoughts, woodcutter, but yours, she continued. "What do you think of a master who happens not to be a male? Would you use me when you could elect to choose a man instead?" She glanced over at Astron and her voice softened to a whisper. "Use one who has already proven that a demon such as that is her better in a battle of wills?"

Kestrel blinked. "I have considered you a master, no different from the rest," he protested. The question went deeper than that, but his answer was a truthful one. She had been chosen for the anvilwood because of her greater wealth, not anything else. As for the rest, he felt the old barriers sliding into place. No good could come from raising the innermost feelings and trying to strip away the scarred layers of pain.

"Well said." Phoebe smiled faintly. "Perhaps my instincts in the matter were correct from the first. Stand in the light so I can see you better. No, not you, demon, only the man."

Kestrel climbed back down from the wagon and into the brightness of the street.

"Yes, it is all coming back now." Phoebe's smile broadened. "I remember why I invited you in. And as for now, wizardry or something else of equal value, it does not matter. Just so I am a full partner and not a tool to be manipulated like a sorcerer's slave."

"You will not try to continue our struggle for dominance?" Astron asked.

"No, why should I?" The smile vanished from Phoebe's face. "If you still desired to control my will, I do not see how I could resist a second time, knowing I had lost the first." She turned her eyes away from Astron and lowered her head. "I have already proven myself worthy to wear the logo of the master. Perhaps, in the end, that will be sufficient."

"There is no more to it!" Astron exclaimed. "Kestrel, you are most remarkable. I apologize for my doubt. When there is more time, you must explain how you achieved such an agreement of wills."

Kestrel lightly touched Phoebe's arm again. Despite the inner warnings, it felt good to do so. "Things are not always what they seem, demon," he snapped. "I have already told you that."

Astron did not answer. He wrinkled his nose and stared off into the distance. Images of peeling skin and ripping limbs surged from his stembrain.

"Let us get on with your plan," he said. The flickers of light that I now see at the end of this alley — I do not believe that they are the simple fireflies of your realm."

The Alchemy of Air

KESTREL HIT the tapper against the brass door with authority. The gong reverberated all along the high metal-plated fencing that ran around the foundry. Even though it was barely dawn, smoke was already spilling out of the stack on the other side of the enclosing barrier and the wheeze of the bellows was quite loud.

Astron had not been sure how much longer it would be before the wizards became certain of their location, but they had little time for additional delay. They had to get over the border and to the archimage soon, or it would all be too late.

Kestrel cupped his hands to his mouth and spoke directly at the demon, the noises within the foundry masking his words more than a few feet away. "Now remember, Astron," he said. "You are the consulting alchemist for the countess. You will observe the process and say nothing. Occasionally shake your head slightly in disapproval after an explanation. Under no circumstances, ask any of your questions. Just be on the lookout for more of your kind."

"But an alchemist I am not," Astron said. "I cannot speak that which does not reflect reality."

"That is just the point," Kestrel replied. "Do not say a thing. Let those inside draw whatever conclusions they will. For what they think, you are not responsible."

"To stand and shake my head is not very interesting, Kestrel. At least, I should be able to find out something to add to my catalogues."

"I will see to it that you are suitably amused. Just keep quiet while you are about it."

Kestrel turned his attention to Phoebe. The gown they had purchased the previous evening with eight of the dozen brandels suited her well. She carried herself as one would expect of the nobility, erect and straight like a ramrod. She returned his approving look with a smile, but he pulled his eyes away. She had enthusiastically taken on the role he had outlined to her and did not even bother to ask any more about what had happened at her cabin or even the reason he was originally there.

So long as she did not ask, Kestrel decided, there was no reason for him to explain more. He darted one more furtive glance in her direction. And yet, his logic did not quite ring true. For the first time in a long while, he was somehow uncomfortable about what he was hiding from someone else.

The door opened and Kestrel turned to meet the gateman. "The grand countess of Brythia, second cousin to the king, is here to discuss terms for the shipment. Show us to the head alchemist without delay."

The gateman puckered his prune-like face into a mass of wrinkles. With studied disapproval, he examined Kestrel's plain clothing up and down. He frowned at Astron, hooded by the woodcutter's side. "I have received no instructions about a visitor. You will have to wait until I check with Master Celibor."

"Surely we can wait inside, rather than here on the street," Kestrel said. "Perhaps even a chair so that my lady can sit. The purse she carries is most heavy. And from what I hear of Master Celibor, he will be most anxious to meet her."

The gate man glanced at Phoebe, hesitated, and then snatched at the brandel that Kestrel waved in front of him. "You may use my stool." He waved as he headed off across the interior of the foundry yard.

Kestrel and the others stepped inside. He surveyed the enclosure from one end to the other. The fencing formed a huge square, each side the length of a sprinter's race. In the rear corner of the left stood dumps of ore, huge boulders ripped from deep running mines, glinting with crystals of gray in the morning sun. A dozen laborers swung hammers at the larger ones, reducing them to smaller chunks and dust that were shoveled onto a belt squeaking over a long row of wooden rollers. Spinning flywheels and convoluted belts moved the rock into massive grinders and then through acrid chemicals dripping from glazed retorts. At the terminus of the conveyor, a fine powder fell into a chute leading to a huge brick-lined athanor in the center of the square. On the backside of the furnace, barely visible from where Kestrel stood, two three-man bellows alternately expanded and shot air into the burning firepit.

A tall shed spanned the opposite side of the square, covering loads of sand that fell from hoppers into a red-hot cauldron. There a dozen glassblowers dipped long hollow tubings into a transparent slag. With bursting cheeks, they blew huge flat-bottomed bottles with tiny necks.

These too were conveyed to the furnace and entered on the side opposite from the processed ore.

Astron's face curved in the manner of a human smile. He had never seen such things in any of his previous journeys to the realm of men. The only thing he recognized were the two men robed bearing the logos of alchemy.

Near the front of the athanor stood the two alchemists, each furiously writing on parchment, giving life to the formulas that formed the basis of their craft. They stood on either side of a third conveyor, this one discharging a sequence of lead-capped bottles that were collected and arrayed in designated squares throughout the yard. Behind the back of the second master, in a cast-iron trough, a river of molten metal ran into an array of molds, presses, and rollers.

A bright lead foil extruded from the last of the rotating cylinders. Intricate objects that even Kestrel did not recognize dropped from the presses into a hopper. Some of the molds were simple ingots, shaped for resale elsewhere. The rest formed struts and geometric figures, destined for a vast array of dull gray structures beyond the cooling area.

Among the distant sprawl were skeletons of dodecahedrons in three different sizes nestled with solid-sided cubes and small spheres clustered like grapes on long cylindrical stems. Beyond them, giant pylons soared twice the height of a man. Hollow balls of lead, ten arm-lengths in diameter, shone dully in the morning sun. To the left of the completed spheres stood one in mid-construction, the bottom of a mesh-covered skeleton sheathed in a foil of lead, while laborers heated and fused additional sheets above its bulging equator.

"Somehow, in the final step of the formula that the alchemists guard in their grimoires, the smelting of the metal produces the vacuum," Kestrel explained to the others. "The lead is used as a seal only because it is conveniently here. As you can see, the bulk of it goes into the molds and presses for resale elsewhere as a byproduct. I think the geometric shapes are used in magician's rituals, although some of the foundries make small statuary to sell to the nobility as works of art as well.

"But beyond that is where our interest lies, where the vacuum is tested to verify its quality. As you may know, not a single formula of alchemy can be guaranteed to succeed every time. Indeed, the more powerful have the least chance of all. Each product must be verified to ensure that the process has resulted in what was desired."

Astron and Phoebe turned to look where Kestrel pointed. Two workers dragged one of the larger bottles from a square and placed it adjacent to a stitchery of cured hides lying on the ground. One connected bellows to the collection and began pumping. In a few hundred heartbeats, it grew into a perfect sphere. Then the second worker thrust the neck of the vacuum bottle into the bellows opening and broke the seal.

With a powerful hiss that the three could hear even from where they stood, the sphere buckled and warped, although not back to the flattened shape it had before. Like a lumpy pillow, it sagged on the ground at the workers' feet. The first bound off the opening at the bottom and the other set it apart from the rest of the gear so that it received the full glare of the rising sun.

"Yes, what is it?" A master wearing the logo of the inverted triangle had emerged from a hut near the glass works and followed the gatekeeper back across the foundry yard. He was short and swarthy with small quick eyes that squinted in distrust. His jaws hung heavy like those of a bulldog. Kestrel wondered whether, if he got his grip on something, he would ever let go.

"If it is a large order, you had better place it quickly." The alchemist waved toward the pile of rock waiting to be crushed. "When that is gone, there will be no more for vacuum for a good while, at least until the border to the north is once again open."

"Master Celibor, I presume," Kestrel said. "This is Countess Phoebe and she indeed is most anxious to buy." Kestrel forced a smile. "Her mind as yet is not made up, however, between dealing with you or the establishment across the street."

"What! Iliac!" Celibor exploded. "He is no less than responsible for the blockade in the first place. You should be blaming him for the rise in prices, not giving him aid by favoring him with trade. If he had not persisted in trying to divert ore wagons rightly meant for me, then none of this confrontation at the border would have happened. Even the archimage would be visiting our fair kingdoms rather than wasting his good time entertaining the ones who call themselves skyskirr from some forsaken place or another that is far away."

"Nevertheless, he has the reputation for a splendid product," Kestrel smiled.

"Lies of the market-place," Celibor spat. "He turns out great volumes of glassware and at less cost, it is true. But how many prove to be nothing more than jars of clear air rather than vacuum of prime hardness, answer me that? Why, look you at the pains we take to ensure that each batch has indeed run its course, rather than randomly fail as is sometimes the case."

Celibor paused to catch his breath. The ruddiness of his cheeks began to fade. He waved in the direction of the hidden sphere. The crushing indentations had vanished. The sun had warmed the air that remained until the skin was again tight and firm. As everyone watched it began to rise from the ground and tug at the single fetter that held it in place.

"Elsewhere along the street," Celibor said, "they let the balloons rise to their maximum heights and do no more. Those batches that produce the highest they label as premium grade vacuum, no matter that they might be half as good as the ones produced the day before.

"Here we do more than that. We calculate the degree to which the jars are empty from measuring the balloon's ascent. Nowhere else are such quantitative tests made, not in a single foundry along the street. We know the volume of our balloons; the hides have been cured so that they no longer stretch. From the height to which they rise and equilibrate with the lesser density of air outside, we can compute the mass that rides within. From these numbers, we then determine precisely how well the test bottle extracted some of the original contents and thence from that how good was the vacuum it originally contained."

"That is most interesting," Astron said. "A quantitative calculation aimed at showing nothing as the result."

Celibor frowned. "Not every batch produces a balloon which rises so well," he explained. "Some bottles extract only half the air because only half was removed from them by the random perturbations of the creation process. Some draw no air at all, total failures the likes of which you are much more likely to find across the way."

"How high do these balloons rise?" Phoebe asked.

With a deliberate coolness, Celibor ran his eyes over her body. "A most interesting question, my lady. We usually test only a single bottle in a batch. So, like the one you see there, they rise only perhaps as far as the top of the athanor's stack or a little higher."

Kestrel noticed Celibor's reaction to Phoebe, but surprisingly, the satisfaction of a plan going well did not come. Rather than being pleased that she had excited the alchemist's interest, he felt irritated by the degrading way in which he showed it. It would indeed be soon enough when they were well away.

"And no gondola attached for one to observe?" Phoebe asked as Kestrel tried to draw back Celibor's attention.

"Why no, not every time, my countess, it would be a great waste." Celibor did not take his eyes from Phoebe. "Although we have baskets and the necessary riggings obtained from the thaumaturges up the street, the purpose is to test, not to lift a considerable weight. And with the onshore breeze, there is risk as well. A parted tether would mean the occupants would sail right over the encamped armies and deep into Procolon itself."

"But then think also of the thrill of it," Phoebe said in a bored tone. "If only for a part of an hour, floating like a cloud and looking down on the coastline as far as one could see. So much more exciting that all those dreary teas and receptions. Yes, Kestrel, see to it. Do business with the one who will offer a balloon ride as part of the bargain."

"You are talking a considerable expense," Celibor replied. He turned his attention from Phoebe back to Kestrel and Astron. "And although I have been most free to point out details of my trade, I know nothing about you other than what you profess."

He motioned back the way he had come. "Visit me in my chambers, my lady; I will ask more of you there." Celibor again looked up and down the length of Phoebe's gown. "Never mind the clutter along the way. It is quite safe since we keep it well away from the flames. Just lift your hems a trifle and they will not be soiled as we walk."

"The countess and *I* will gladly follow," Kestrel said. "But consultant Astron's time is perhaps better spent in evaluating more of what takes place here. Pair him with someone who talks well and fast. He is the best of listeners."

Astron opened his mouth to speak, but Kestrel grabbed him by the arm. "There, the man with the pen and quill — perhaps you will be amused by learning more of these calculations. Or even the sculpturing — see, look at that scaffolding going up on which they are hanging those foils of lead. Surely, those will be of more interest than standing around listening to the countess and the master exchanging pleasantries."

"The calculations and the structures, why yes," Astron agreed. "The sculpturing is akin to what I call weaving and, for one who cannot do that, it would be interesting indeed. I need to feel no guilt. While I wait I can no better serve my —"

Kestrel squeezed Astron's arm tighter and the demon stopped. He nodded and started to move in the direction Kestrel had indicated. Kestrel whirled to catch up with Celibor and Phoebe as they walked to the hut. The alchemist had his arm around her waist while he pointed out other aspects of his foundry. Curse it, Kestrel thought. She permitted it just as he had instructed her to.

Phoebe tried to shield from her eyes the afternoon sun streaking into the hut through a low window like from a beacon standing just outside. Kestrel shifted uncomfortably on his stool, kicked at the cracked and discarded parchments that cluttered the floor. In the foundry yard, Astron with some sort of sextant sighted the top of the huge lead spheres and then the pylons at their side. The bellows whooshed. A blistering heat radiated from the openings of the athanor. Throughout the yard, the bustle of the activity continued as if the border blockade did not exist.

Kestrel frowned at the lengthening shadows. Despite Celibor's other interests, his first concern turned out to be for his profits. For most of the day, they had argued, and no agreement was yet in sight. Soon the sun would be setting, and they would have to come back the next day, something that Kestrel did not want to do. He would have to play through the last part of his plan, whether the alchemist gave him an opening or not.

"But do you not see?" Celibor waved his hands around the confines of his hut. "This is no palace with rich furnishings paid for by the profits of my trade. Iliac across the way has seen to that with his low prices and inferior products. I need the coin to pay the workers as the effort is done. I cannot afford to wait until the order is complete no matter how alluring is the bounty I would receive."

The alchemist appraised Phoebe slyly. "Besides, I cannot believe that a few hours aloft is the primary reason you are so anxious to do business with me. Why the concern, my lady, about pretending you are a bird?"

Kestrel became alert. Celibor's statement was what he had been waiting for. "You drive a hard bargain," he laughed. "And this day grows long." He smiled at Phoebe. "With your permission, my lady," he said.

Phoebe nodded. Celibor leaned forward from where he sat.

"There is the matter of the new mine," Kestrel continued. "One not in the mountains of Procolon to the north, but in the very hills of Ethidor itself."

"There are no such mines," Celibor scoffed. "Our own hills have been scoured many times over."

"But not from a height, not from a vantage point that no other has taken." Kestrel lowered his voice to a whisper. "And not with a sketch of what to look for drawn by a sorcerer while under a far-seeking trance." Kestrel pulled a tightly rolled parchment from his belt and waved it in front of Celibor's face.

The alchemist reached for it but Kestrel pulled it away with a nod. "You understand how critical it is that word of this reach no one else. Your craft can ill-afford a repetition of what has caused the impulse to the north to occur."

Kestrel waited for Celibor to withdraw his hand and then continued. "Of course, our original plan was to find the location and then keep it from all, offering our ores to the highest bidder." His smile broadened. "But you deal with such skill that a direct share might be more in order. Enough perhaps so that you see the raising of the balloon is as much in your interest as in ours."

Celibor glanced at Phoebe and then back to Kestrel. "How do I know that these are not more words, perhaps as empty as the rest?"

"You do not." Kestrel shrugged and rose. "There is a risk here that must be taken — a single balloon ride for half share in what may be the only source of ore while the blockade continues. Perhaps those across the street would indeed be more receptive."

"No, wait," Celibor said. "In good faith, I have made investments as well. Come outside and see what I have instructed the workers to do while we talked. If we can agree on a fair price, then even today the deed can be done."

Phoebe tilted her head slightly a second time. Kestrel shrugged and turned his palms upward to Celibor. "Evidently, she likes you. A few hours more she has graciously granted."

Celibor grunted and scurried past where they sat into the afternoon sun. He squinted his eyes against the harshness and motioned for them to follow over into the testing area. Kestrel and Phoebe left the hut with regal slowness and stepped out into the daylight. They walked past the cooling lead ingots, lattices, and polyhedra and through the shadows cast by the great spheres and pylons. Astron glanced up from what he was studying and motioned, but Kestrel waved him away. The hook was nearly set and he could not afford to be distracted.

Kestrel noted the contents of other huts as he passed. One on the left was piled high with cured animal hides and beyond it were seamstresses lashing them together into a growing pile of balloons not yet used. On the right, knot makers tied lengths of braided hair into canopies that would fit over the balloons when they were inflated and tether them to the ground.

When they caught up with Celibor, he was pointing at a long row of bottles all connected to a hose of some rubbery fiber. Like a giant centipede, the construction wandered through the open area where the tests were performed.

"More than one bottle will be needed to remove enough air so that the three of you can be borne aloft," Celibor said. "My craftsmen have labored long and hard to connect all of these bottles in parallel so that the evacuation quickly can be done."

'Then we are almost ready," Kestrel contemplated the snaking line. "Why haggle over details when we can be at the task right away?"

"It is not quite as you make it seem," Celibor answered. "Two more bottles must be connected to the chain. That is no easy matter if one wishes not to lose the entire vacuum in the process. Then we have to bind a valve to the balloon itself, one that will not leak once it has been removed of its air."

Celibor waved to one of the leather spheres resting on the ground. It was partially inflated and tugging slightly against the beginning of a breeze like a child tentatively trying to get free of his nursemaid. "And the heating arrangement I have not yet contemplated. Much air will be extracted for this ride, not just a little amount. Heating what remains to regain the original volume is an intriguing challenge all in itself."

Kestrel studied Celibor's expression, trying to judge the truthfulness of his words. He resisted the impulse to grab the end of the hose nearest him and hurry the process along. Then, as he wrestled with what to say next, there was a loud pounding on the metal doors that led to the street.

"Open the gates," a voice sounded over the fence. "In the name of the wizards of the Brythian hills. You house the ones we seek."

Foundry Fight

CELIBOR GLANCED at his gateman in annoyance and then back in the direction of his hut toward a pile of shields and swords. Next to him, Kestrel spun around to look at Astron pointing into the air. Though it was not yet dusk, a swarm of lights could be seen dancing along the fence line in a confusing buzz. The demon had been right. The wizards had caught up with them and far sooner than Kestrel would have thought. Now there was no time left for subtle maneuvers. Every instant would count.

"Defend your property rights," Kestrel shouted at the puzzled alchemist. "A direct attack from your rivals across the way. They strike in desperation to prevent the ascent of the countess into the air."

Celibor continued to hesitate, and Kestrel turned his attention away. He had to get the foundry workers to act. "You, and you with the sextant," he directed. "Back to the weapons store and arm yourself against the entry. Delay them as long as you can." He waved at the apparatus in front of where he and Phoebe stood. "Never mind the last two bottles. Quickly, affix the valve." He grimaced at the blank stares of the workers and tried not to think how much more must be done.

With a sudden crash, the doors shattered like the collapse of a dam, and a squad of men-at-arms burst into the foundry yard. Behind perhaps twelve warriors, each clad in mail, came a quartet of wizards, shaking their fists and urging those in front forward.

"Benthon and Maspanar!" Phoebe exclaimed, "And two others of my council. What you said was true. They pursue me with great vigor."

"To the weapons." Celibor shook off his indecision when he saw the men-at-arms. He picked up the hems of his master's robe and ran for his hut. "The visitors speak truly. Iliac seeks to get my share of the mine for himself."

Kestrel looked from the gates and back to the master's hut. Perhaps eight of Celibor's workers would arm and provide some resistance. He glanced at the two struggling with the valve. They were now working as fast as they could.

"What of the devils?" he asked Phoebe. "Where are the ones bigger than the imps on the wall?"

"Benthon is quite conservative," Phoebe said. "He will use demons of as little power as he can. Perhaps the imps are all that they have under their spell."

"Then help with the balloon," Kestrel decided. "I will aid in the defense to give us as much time as I can." He bolted to Celibor's hut and pushed two of the slower workers aside. Then he reached for one of the shields and grabbed the sword that was closest of the lot. The blade felt heavy and not balanced to his liking, but there was no time to choose.

Swinging his arm back and forth like over-energized pendulums in what he hoped were menacing arcs, he advanced with Celibor and four others to meet the first of the attacking men-at-arms. Six of the wizards' men raised their shields to meet them. With a ringing clang, steel crashed on steel. Kestrel lunged forward, trying to get around his opponent's guard, but the man who faced him was skillful and dodged nimbly to the side. The rest of the wizards' men moved behind the first and spread to outflank him and Celibor on both sides.

Kestrel retreated a step backward and darted a look towards the gate, sucking in his breath. Another dozen men poured through the opening, lance men and archers who fanned out across the yard. The limp balloon that was to be a passage over the border made an ideal target and in a heartbeat, three arrows pierced the hide as if it were paper. The sphere crumpled and sagged to the ground. The lancers ran to the ore heaps and glassworks, pushing all resistance in front of them into a disorganized retreat.

"Another balloon from the storage hut," Kestrel shouted in desperation. "Start the bellows while there is still a chance." He tore his gaze away from the scrambling and barely ducked a swipe at his unprotected neck.

Kestrel retreated another two steps and stumbled backward over a fallen worker, trying to block out the growing sense of futility that hammered at his thoughts. There was a crash behind him, and then a clatter of metal. A hot blast of air roared from the athanor and almost blistered the back of his head. Flames shot up from the glassworks. Globs of molten slag arced over the yard, starting small fires in the debris wherever they landed. One hit the stack of uninflated balloons, and Kestrel groaned. Their remaining means of escape burned along with the rest.

He rubbernecked around for Phoebe or Astron, but acrid smoke was beginning to obstruct his view. One of the pylons fell and then a second. The huge lead sphere seemed to lumber from its pedestal and lurch his way. Kestrel staggered backward and felt the wall of Celibor's hut. The alchemist had dropped his sword and was on one knee, begging for mercy. A trickle of crimson ran from his forehead.

The smoke thickened. Kestrel took a deep breath and plunged into where it was densest, just missing another swipe at his side. The fumes hurt his eyes. He squinted into the dirty grayness, just barely able to make out the indistinct objects towards which he ran and the menacing forms pursuing him like ghosts from the grave.

Kestrel staggered a dozen steps forward and burst back into clear air. Tears clouded his vision. He shook his head in surprise, trying to understand what he saw. Almost directly in front were Phoebe and Astron, standing in the gondola Celibor had planned to couple to the balloon. Frantically, the two were waving their arms and beckoning him forward.

He took one step, puzzled. The gondola was made of straw. Soon it, too, would be in flame. It was better to run as best one could. But while he pondered, the box lurched in his direction, scraping along the ground. A shadow passed over Kestrel, and he looked up, astonished. The gondola lifted from the ground and started to climb over his head. Astron reached out over the edge of the box while Phoebe held the demon by the waist.

"Grab my hand, mortal," Astron shouted. "This is no time for your stembrain to assume command."

Kestrel nodded. He raised his arm and felt a surprisingly strong grip on his wrist. Then, with a stab of pain in his shoulder, he was lifted clear of the ground, just as a man-at-arms made one last stab at his dangling feet. Kestrel gazed down at the foundry. With gathering speed, it seemed to move more and more rapidly away. He glanced skyward for the second time. There was no mistake about it. The gondola was tethered to a sphere of lead.

Escape Aloft

"WHAT WIZARDRY is this?" Kestrel said as he climbed into the basket. "Balloons of lead cannot fly."

"There was no other choice," Astron replied. "The ones of animal hide were all rendered useless by the minions of the wizards."

"It is not a matter of choice." Kestrel shook his head, still dazed by what had happened. Over the edge of the gondola, the foundry yard shrank into toy-like smallness. To the north, the camps of the two armies began to take shape into recognizable forms. The green wetness of the border marsh faded into the dark shadows of the setting sun. Low hills that led to the mines of Procolon grew closer with each passing heartbeat. The onshore breeze was pushing them in the direction Kestrel wished them to go.

"It is not a matter of choice," he repeated. "The metal is too heavy to be borne aloft."

"The calculations shown to me by the alchemist were most interesting," Astron said. "It seems that the force carrying a balloon aloft is proportional to its volume. The greater the size of the sphere, the more it can lift."

"One need not study one of the five arts to understand such a fact. The key point is that the weight of the balloon itself must be included in the total."

"And so it is," Astron said. 'The mass of a balloon increases as the square of its radius while its volume and lifting power increase with the cube. Regardless of the density of the material, there is a size large enough that it can be buoyed aloft."

A smile of pleasure crossed the demon's face like that of a squire being asked by a comely damsel for a dance. "I was fascinated by the concept of the vacuum," he continued. "And once I understood the principles, it was easy to perform the calculation for the lead sphere to which you directed my attention. Not only was it large enough to carry the skeletal structure inside which gave it shape but, as you can see, the three of us as well. I connected the gondola harness and the bottles of emptiness as soon as I saw that it was the last balloon remaining."

"It never was intended to be a balloon." Kestrel started to protest again, but then he stopped. Of course, for him, or any other man for that matter, connecting the vacuum bottles to the lead sphere would never have occurred as a possibility. But Astron was not blinded by the obvious. The demon merely thought it fortunate that the great ball was large enough to carry the three of them. There was nothing of the five arts involved at all. Kestrel let out a deep breath. They were safely away and soon would be visiting the archimage.

But as he scanned groundwards, a twinkle of light near the foundry wall caught Kestrel's eye. The feeling of relief vanished. He studied the dancing pattern until he was sure, a scowl deepening on his face all the while. He pointed the light out to the others, and Astron nodded in confirmation. The cloud of imps that had tracked them to Menthos still pursued their flight. The small buzzing demons would have to be dealt with immediately, or they would have gained only a little respite from the wizards' wrath.

"Perhaps a magic bottle." Phoebe pointed at the trailing swarm. "Compared to other objects of magic, they are inexpensive. Others of my council have spoken of them often. They use them to confine the imps that they summon through the flame. If we can capture them all before any returns to report where we are, then we will be cleanly away."

Kestrel stared out at the imps and pondered what Phoebe had said. His thoughts raced, pulling together the elements of another plan. "I think the wizard is right. We have nothing to aid us in this empty gondola. And there are so many that we must find a way to deal with all of them at once. Let us land while there is still a bit of light and continue on the ground."

He gazed to the north, trying to judge their rate of motion. "If we are lucky, we will travel far enough that we can reach a guild that I know of— one which specializes in the making of those magic jars. Perhaps, if we can intercept a single magician on the road, the odds against us might not be all that great."

Kestrel began constructing the details of what to do next but stopped in midthought. The urgency of the moment was as great as ever, but somehow he still felt puzzled. Despite the explanation about the balloon, something else was bothering him just under the surface of his thoughts. He glanced over at Phoebe and took in her smile. He put his arm around her waist to steady their stance as the basket began to rock in the quickening breeze. Phoebe did not protest. Instead, she brought her pleasing softness to press against his side.

The full realization of what had happened thundered into focus. First the demon, and now the wizard. By his own cunning, Astron had managed to secure a means of transport over the border. Phoebe had joined him in the gondola. She alone would have been sufficient to see him the rest of the way to the archimage. There was no reason for them to pull him into the basket as it ascended. No reason at all — and yet they did.

Honey and Vinegar

KESTREL BARGAINED with the baron whose crops had been damaged by the descent of the balloon and the metal sphere was traded for another horse and wagon. Soon the trio were on the main road leading to Ambrosia, the capital of Procolon.

While Kestrel guided the steed, Phoebe and Astron held torches aloft on the moonless night. The swarm of imps that tracked their progress would not be deterred by lack of light, and the increased speed was worth the illumination.

They were on the road but for a fraction of an hour when, as Kestrel had hoped, he caught the reflecting glint from a huge bottle on the shoulder of a cloaked traveler on the crest of the hill ahead. As the wagon grew closer to the solitary figure, bent far to the side by the weight of his load, Kestrel smiled with satisfaction. The cloak was turned inside out, but his trained eye could make out the stitching for the ring logos sewn to the other side. The man was a magician on the way back to the Cycloid Guild.

"Do you care for a ride, stranger?" Kestrel called out as the wagon drew abreast. "Your load looks heavy and you in the need of a rest."

The magician looked up with eyes dancing with suspicion. He was short and broad like a plowman, rather than shallow-shouldered like so many practitioners of the arts. "I can manage my own way," he said. "There is no assistance that I need."

"Not even if you carry an imp bottle?" Kestrel replied. "I recognize the shape, straight sides of wide diameter and the narrow neck."

"What do you want?" the magician growled. He stopped and set the bottle on the ground. With his free hand, he reached for a small dagger strapped to his belt.

"Why, to buy, of course." Kestrel pulled the wagon to a halt. He reached back under the covering and pulled out the wizard's robe Phoebe had abandoned for the dress of the countess. He pointed at the logos of flame. "We travel to avoid notice, just as you do. What is the price that you would set in your guild? We will pay double — double if it can be proven impregnable to the weaving of simple imps.

The magician examined Kestrel and then Astron at his side. His eyes widened as Kestrel pulled away Astron's hood, and he saw the fine network of scales. Kestrel reached into his pocket and pulled out the remaining brandels of the Brythian wizards. With a flourish, he flung them at the magician's feet. "Double the price, and three pieces of gold more for the trouble of the demonstration."

Kestrel smiled. "Just think how satisfied the other masters of the guild will be when you report to them that you have sold the bottle, not for the going price, but one and a half times that amount. Twice for you but only one and a half passed on to the coffers of your guild. It would serve them right. You are the one who has had to toil in the blackness while they wined and dined in anticipation of the fruits of your labor."

The magician looked down to his feet at the gold coins sparkling in the torchlight and grunted agreement. He stooped to his knees, retrieved the brandels, and thrust them into a purse next to his knife.

'That the bottle is a true prison of imps there can be no doubt," he said. "Magic rituals lead either to perfect results or else to nothing. And I have performed the last step myself — alone in a flat field when the moon was at nadir. I completed the square of numbers precisely in the order prescribed. The cymbals were struck thrice and then buried.

"And then the glass hummed of its own volition," the magician continued, "sucking strength from the cosmic spheres and forming an unbreakable crystal. It would not have rung unless my actions were the perfect last steps to a perfect ritual, producing a jar like the imps it will surround, one that will last forever."

The magician drew the dagger from his side and flipped it over in his hand. Pommel first he crashed it down onto the side of the bottle, causing it to ring like the seductive harmony of the finest bell. A second time he banged on the glass and then a third but the bottle wall held firm and did not shatter.

"See," the magician said. "That is no ordinary container but one that has been transformed by the skills of my craft. You cannot break it or its stopper. More proof than that you do not need."

"Nevertheless, this purchase is not one of little consequence," Kestrel replied. "You cannot deny us the assurance of putting imps in the bottle and seeing that they cannot escape."

"Well, if I were the buyer, then perhaps I would want to know for sure that —" the magician began.

"Wait a moment," Astron interrupted. "There is the matter of volition. Only the wizards that command the cloud that pursues can will them into what they know to be a trap."

"I have thought about that," Kestrel said. "We will just have to hope that the motives that drive your kind are not so different than those that push upon men."

"What do you mean?"

"Are not imps noted for their curiosity?"

"Except for their vanity, it is the strongest of traits," Astron agreed. "They are always chattering that their abilities are the equal of the mightiest of djinns. But their inclinations have nothing to do with control of their will. There is no —"

"Such is what I have heard from the writings in the sagas," Kestrel said, "and such I will use. The only other thing I need is a lure. What is it that would attract them the most?"

"In the realm of men? Why, vinegar, I suppose. At least, it is told that you can catch more imps with it than with honey."

"Then vinegar it is," Kestrel said. He motioned the magician into the wagon and grabbed the large bottle as it was pushed upward. "We will hasten to the next village and buy a few coppers worth."

He eyed Astron's wrinkled nose, and his smile broadened. "Observe carefully, cataloguer. We will see if there might be another power that operates among the realm of demonkind, another power than what you call 'weaving'."

Imps in a Bottle

KESTREL SHIFTED uncomfortably in the tree and pushed Astron to the side. It would have been better if the demon had not come, but his curiosity could not be thwarted.

Astron glanced down at the bottle below them in the nearly empty field and whispered in Kestrel's ear. "In the first place," he said, "this is no hiding place at all. They will spot you to be here as if you were on the ground. In the second, even if one were in the bottle, you could not spring downward and insert the stopper quickly enough before he flew to safety."

"I know," Kestrel whispered back. "Those are exactly the things I am counting on. Now be quiet and watch. The sooner we settle down, the quicker they will come."

He gazed back to the road in the distance where the wagon was parked. The magician leaned against one of the wheels talking to Phoebe and was distracted. Kestrel glanced out over the field. In a perimeter perhaps the span of a dozen men, small fires burned at each of the corners of a pentagram under bubbling pots of lilac water that scented the air with a sweet fragrance like that of a lady's newly drawn bath. Imps hated it, Phoebe had said, and oftentimes wizards used bouquets of flowers to keep them away when they probed for more powerful demons through the flame.

Kestrel sighted the distance between the fires for the last time and judged that they were properly placed, enough of a nuisance to make approaching the bottle under the tree a challenge but not so close together that the imps could not do so if they wished.

For a longer time than Kestrel could judge, nothing happened. Then a single twinkle of light swept in from the distance and hovered over the open mouth of the bottle. The imp circled the glass jar twice and then darted up to within a few feet of where Kestrel and Astron hid in the branches of the tree.

The small demon hovered with his wings buzzing like a scouting bee who had found a fresh blossom. Kestrel could see the tiny eyes staring into the foliage. Then abruptly, it abandoned its scrutiny and plunged in a straight line to the ground. With tiny hops, each about the span of a man's stride, it measured the distance to the bottle.

The imp looked back up into the tree and then along the path it had traversed on the ground. It rubbed a bony hand along a pockmarked jaw and squinted its eyes in thought.

A second imp appeared near the top of the tree, buzzing within inches of Kestrel's back. With a shrill cry, it dropped to the ground and hopped toward the bottle as had the other. The first sprite soared skyward as soon as he heard the shriek, shouting what sounded like insults as the second jumped along the ground.

The second stuck out his tongue at the first. He turned his attention to the bottle at his side. Cautiously, he paced around the perimeter, extending each foot lightly and testing the firmness of the ground as if it were filled with hidden mines. He reached forward, placed a palm on the smoothness of the glass, and then jumped backward as the first imp dove within a wingspan of his head, laughing raucously.

The second imp waved some gesture that Kestrel did not recognize and glared at the first until it stopped and hovered at the height of the tree. Satisfied, the second vaulted up to the open mouth of the bottle and peered inside. He hesitated, extended first a finger, then an arm, and finally his entire head into the smooth walls of the mouth. All he would see was the large cup of vinegar that had been placed inside.

The sprite lowered himself to the bottom of the bottle and repeated the same slow approach to the small bowl. He stuck a finger into the cup and then touched it to his lips. A moment passed and then the imp abandoned his caution altogether. He plunged his head into the liquid and began slurping.

The first imp saw what was happening as well. He dove into the bottle, knocking the other one aside. Like two children fighting over a single toy, they began pushing each other away from the tasty prize. Instantly, a half dozen more sprites appeared from the distance. In a rush, they raced into the bottle one by one, bowling those that preceded into the hard glass walls and lunging for the cup for themselves.

"Do you see any more?" Kestrel tensed.

"None at the moment," Astron said. "But —"

Kestrel did not wait to hear more. He dropped from the tree to the ground with the stopper in his hand just as the imps had decided he would. One that had been knocked the farthest from the cup of vinegar spotted his motion and shrieked a warning. In unison, the imps stopped their fighting and took to flight. Like bees discharging from a shaken hive, they buzzed up the height of the bottle into the neck.

Kestrel sprinted to the jar as fast as he could, but, as he had guessed, he did not have to hurry. The buzz of the imps died in the grunt of crashing bodies. In a tangled mass, they wedged into the neck and could ascend no further. The ones underneath the first cursed and pushed against those above but to no avail. Kestrel dropped in the glass stopper before a single one could escape.

"Why, that is most remarkable. " Astron jumped to the ground after Kestrel. "They are trapped just as surely as if you were a wizard who could command their will."

"As I told you earlier," Kestrel said, brushing his hands in satisfaction, "knowledge of the push and tugs that compel one to action can indeed be a great power. Evidently, beings are the same everywhere, whether they are men or demon."

Astron started to say more but instead pointed at the jar. Kestrel's satisfaction evaporated. A single glow of light flittered in from the south, made two circles of the bottle, and then with a burst of speed raced away in the direction from which it had come.

"A straggler," Astron said. "One that was distracted and did not fly in formation with the rest. Imps are well known for their lack of discipline. Perhaps that is a fact that you should have utilized as well."

"Never mind that," Kestrel snapped. "He has seen what has happened. You can bet that he will streak back and tell the wizards where we are without fail."

Kestrel began running back to the wagon. "Come! At least, I know the thinking of my own kind better. I suspect there is very little time before some of your more powerful cousins will be visiting us on this very spot."

Kestrel waved to the magician as he passed the master running into the field. "We do not want it after all," he called out, "but you can keep the imps to demonstrate to the next buyer in exchange for your trouble."

He pushed past the open-mouthed magician without bothering to offer any more explanations. He clambered onto the wagon and lent an arm to help up Phoebe. Then he whipped the back of the horse. In a sudden cloud of dust, the three again were on the road.

Kestrel pushed the horse recklessly, not bothering to make sure of holes and ruts before he chose his path. The more distance they put between themselves and the field, the longer they would have before rediscovery by demons who would not so easily be fooled.

"I do not deny it, mortal," Astron said after they had bounced along for more than an hour in silence. "You have shown me that there is more to learn in the realm of men than the things that are described in my catalogues. "

He looked Kestrel in the eye. "But also I wonder," he continued. "I wonder if any amount of your tugging and pulling would have gotten the lead balloon off the ground."

Temptation

THE RACE up the coast was a blur. There was no time for the luxury of sleep or even food for the horse. How long it had taken, Kestrel could not recall. Through half-open eyes, he spotted the simple sign that marked the turnoff from the main road to the ward of the archimage. With aching arms, he steered the wagon onto the narrow gravel lane that wound into the low hills on his left.

After they had climbed to the pass between the nearest peaks, he could see down into the valley that lay between him and higher buttes farther away. Birch and aspen climbed partway up the hillsides. Tall green grasses filled the valley floor, waving in the breeze like ripples on a stagnant pond. One area was cleared of vegetation near the center. In it stood a dozen wooden cabins arranged in a circle around a two-story house of stone. Pulsing bellows like those at the foundry spat blasts of cold air near the closest cabins. Curls of wizard's smoke rose from the chimneys of the next two in line. Three spinning energy wheels of the thaumaturges whirled on the far side of the compound. Next to them, magicians added spars to a complex latticework in step to the intricate jingling of hundreds of tiny bells. A few of the cottages were dark, sorcerers' lairs with even the windows painted black to block out the sun. On the grounds between the structures, knots of robed masters argued and gestured as they walked from one experiment to another.

"I see no high walls or metal gates," Kestrel said. "Anyone could approach the archimage with no resistance at all."

"There is a little hut at the foot of the road." Phoebe pointed. "I believe one states his reason for calling to a page therein, and, if he is worthy, he arranges an interview. As for security, the power and reputation of the archimage is such that he has no need for walls and gates. If not for honorable means, it would be folly to approach."

Kestrel grunted and urged the horse onward. There was yet no sign of imps or more powerful devils, but, even with having to reestablish the trail, they could not be far behind.

Phoebe reached out and grabbed Kestrel's arm as the wagon gathered speed down the last incline. "Before we meet the archimage and I am questioned about my craft, Kestrel, I must understand all that has happened at my cabin." She lowered her eyes. "Perhaps it was something that would embarrass me," she said. "Yes, that is it. The demon made me do something quite unladylike in front of the other wizards. You are too much the gentleman to tell me about it."

Kestrel pulled his lips together in a grim line. He gazed at Phoebe's attractiveness in the fancy dress. Despite the fatigue, he felt a great longing. Without the immediate rush, it would be easy to say the words that would result in another conquest of a master of the arts.

But the well-spun phrases would not come, not even ones that set the foundation for later. Phoebe's apparent trust was too overwhelming. How could he deceive her as he had done to all the others when what she wanted had so little value?

"The past cannot be changed," Kestrel said, "no matter how much one might wish it. If you were embarrassed, would you want to know?"

"No, I would not," Phoebe answered. "Not if it caused me to lock all that I am behind a barrier through which no one else can see."

"What do you mean?" Kestrel asked.

"You know full well," Phoebe replied. "For the length of this headlong flight, I have been chattering away, telling you everything about myself that came to mind. Perhaps it took my thoughts from what would happen if we are caught, but I have said much nonetheless."

"I did not wish it otherwise," Kestrel said. "If you suspect that I was bored but just being polite, put your mind at ease. I enjoy your company."

"And so about the wizard you can now recite volumes," Phoebe continued. "About the woodcutter, what can be said other than that he indeed did at one time chop some trees?"

Kestrel slumped over the reins, wishing the entry hut all the closer. Mixed with everything else, he felt an onrush of discomfort. It was not enough that he refrain from further deception. Phoebe wanted more. She was asking no less than that he reveal things that, except for the demon, which did not really count, he had vowed never to share again.

"I can be only one of many possibilities," he said while continuing to look straight ahead. "Why me and not some other? One more suited to your station."

Phoebe tightened her grip on Kestrel's arm and pulled herself closer to him. "It gets to be lonely in the cabin of a wizard," she said. "Lonelier than you might otherwise believe. And at first, I admit my thoughts were for a brief interlude. You appeared far better than most that I had seen in the past year.

"But there was something else," she continued. "Something I saw behind the eyes of one who professed to be a simple woodcutter."

"Do not probe too deeply," Kestrel warned. "You might not like what you will find."

"No, my first impression has been confirmed."

Phoebe reached up and turned Kestrel's face to hers. "I saw the excitement when you explained to me how we would cross the border. I witnessed the swordsman rushing to defend when he was outnumbered two to one. There is perhaps more to Kestrel the woodcutter than he dares to admit even to himself."

"Does not the ritual prescribe that the male pursues and the female demurs?" Astron poked his head out from under the wagon's canopy. "Or does the fact that the woman is the one that wears the logo of a wizard alter that? It is no wonder there is so much anguish and confusion in the matter. The variations are too many for one to keep track of them all."

Phoebe pulled back her arms, like a child caught in the fruit larder. She frowned at Astron as she dropped her hands to her lap. Kestrel felt a wave of relief and then a twinge of annoyance. He could work out his feelings without any help from the demon.

He darted a glance at Phoebe. No, perhaps it was best that Astron had come forward. What he would have said if he were forced to answer at this moment he did not know. A silence descended on the three. For the rest of the distance to the entry hut, no one spoke.

Archimage and Skyskirr

WHEN THEY arrived at the page's hut, Kestrel glanced over his shoulder and then back to Astron. The demon shook his head, indicating that he detected nothing. Kestrel vaulted from the wagon and into the shack. Soon all three stood facing an ancient page, bald-pated with splotchy skin, sitting behind a high desk. His folded hands rested on a huge appointment book bound in gilded leather. Kestrel returned the page's stare and glanced about the small room, trying to seize on the story that would get them immediately to the archimage.

"Elezar," Astron said before anyone else could speak. "I have a message from Prince Elezar for the archimage that should be heard at once."

The page looked at Astron through half-closed eyes. He leafed through the pages to the very front of the book and scanned a list of names. "Elezar," the page repeated, "Elezar". He stopped, and his eyes opened wide. "Ah, exactly what is the — the nature of this prince?"

"He is a demon," Astron replied. "A mighty ruler of over a hundred djinns."

Like a sprung rattrap, the attitude of the page shifted from bored indifference to obsequious concern. He climbed from his high stool and motioned the trio to follow.

"It is the foremost of the archimage's instructions," he explained. "Certain visitors are to receive priority over the others who come asking no more than a boon. But above all else, Archimage Alodar has written that he is to be interrupted on any news of Elezar the demon appearing in the realm of men. Quickly, follow me."

In almost no time, they were across the courtyard to the house of stone and ushered into a large library, brimming with scrolls and books of crackling vellum. A ladder was propped on each of the four walls to reach shelves that stood beyond the grasp of the tallest man. Three round tables were covered with piles of parchment rolls. On a fourth stood a bubbling retort and convoluted runs of glass tubing like the intestines of a disemboweled sprite. A model of a crane and small blocks occupied the fifth, next to a clump of bar magnets and needles of steel. On the far left, the light of a single candle worked its way through tiny slits and a series of lenses that alternately expanded and contracted its radiance.

Astron's membranes flicked down when he saw all of the books. After the page left to find the archimage, the demon stood motionless for a long while. Then with a delicate reverence, he approached the closest table, reached out and touched the gilt letters that spelled *Practical Thaumaturgy* on the volume on top. Oblivious to the reason they had come, the demon gently opened the cover and stared at the pen strokes on the first page.

A doorway deeper into the interior of the cottage clicked softly. Kestrel turned to see who entered. As if shocked by a death in the family, his face stiffened in surprise.

"We are manipulants of the skyskirr"," said the first of four thin beings who filed into the library. "We understand the astonishment that shows on your face. Many of the strange happenings of your realm affect us in a similar way. Be at peace. All that comes to pass is guided by the great right hand."

Kestrel shook his head. Astron looked almost human. The imps that had been captured in the bottle were no more than gross copies of a normally shaped child. But these four were distinctly alien, unlike anyone else he had ever seen. They were tall and slender, impossibly thin for a man. Large, puffy lips protruded from faces of bony gray planes. Primitive jewelry hung from ears and noses. Each wore a simple loincloth coiled about his hips.

"You too are djinns from Astron's realm?" Kestrel asked. He backed into one of the ladders and pulled Phoebe protectively to his side.

"No, we are skyskirr," the first repeated. "On our lithons, we sail through the 'hedron's sky. The wind whistles with our passage. With graceful arabesques, we circle the larger stones and from them scavenge what the great right hand provides.

"Our realm is self-contained, as distinct from that of the demons as you judge yours to be. We must use the might of a djinn and the intermediary of the flame to travel from our universe to here."

Kestrel ran his hand over his mouth. Not from the realm of demons but elsewhere beyond the flame, he puzzled. He glanced at Astron. Yes, there are other realms, he thought. Just as the demon had said.

"Besides those of men and demons there is a third?" Phoebe asked. "I have heard whispers of such a thing and of metalaws behind those that we know so well."

"Indeed, it is true," the first skyskirr replied. "For us, the laws of magic are different. We, in fact, change them all the time. Our visit here and now is to see if your thaumaturgy is a craft that will be useful besides the ones we already know."

"Of course, there are consequences in any such venture," the third interrupted. "Perhaps it was the intent of the great right hand that such knowledge we were not meant to possess." The skyskirr pounded a shovel he was carrying against the floor and then touched the blade to the chest of the fourth, who slumped almost hidden behind the other three.

Kestrel eyed the last skyskirr for the first time. The deep-set eyes seemed not to focus but dart almost independently about the room. A thick drool ran from one corner of his mouth. With his hands, he picked at his loincloth, removing small pieces of lint that were not actually there.

"Mortonzel has seen too much of gently curving horizons," the third skyskirr continued. "He has felt for too long the oppressive pull of the great lithon that binds all of you humans. Only occasionally are there winds to caress the full length of his hair." He turned and poked with the blade of his shovel at the chest of the first. "Now even the archimage dismisses us for something he says is of greater importance. It is a sign of the great right hand, I say. Let us be gone. I feel the sickness of mind beginning to bubble within me as well. Build the flame, Purdanel, and summon the djinn that will return us whence we came."

Purdanel looked at the second skyskirr and then around the room. For a moment, his eyes rested on Astron, who was turning the pages of the book. "You may have the volume," he said. "It was to be a gift from the archimage, but I think it will provide no value in the realm where the lithons fly."

Without waiting for an answer, he grunted and pounded his own shovel twice against the floor. Purposefully, he marched out of the room. The other three skyskirr followed, the last being gently led.

Kestrel shook his head again. Lithons, the great right hand, soaring through the sky — it sounded most bizarre indeed. His intuition had been confirmed. If the skyskirr reacted so poorly to the realm of men, then surely he would fare as badly if transported to where they were from. But before he could ponder more, a second door opened as quietly as the first. Someone else entered the room.

"I am Alodar the Archimage," the newcomer said. "Tell me. What is the news of the sighting of Elezar the one who dazzles? What is it that you have seen?"

Kestrel jerked his thoughts back to why they had come. He studied the archimage as he approached. Streaks of white ran through fine yellow-brown hair like slender fish swimming in a shallow sea. Furrows of concentration had become permanently etched at the bridge of the nose. The purple robe hung simply over a slight frame. On one sleeve were the logos of all five of the crafts.

Kestrel stared at the eyes. They were alive with intelligence and a driving will shone through like from a fire that could never be quenched. He felt a surge of doubt about what he hoped to accomplish. The archimage was not one to be either easily fooled or tempted.

"It has been almost thirty years," Alodar continued. "Thirty years since our one and only encounter. " The furrow above his nose deepened. "And the truth of it is that one is sufficient for any man. For all this time, I have hoped there would not be the need for another."

"There is also the matter of the wizards of Brythia," Kestrel said. He pointed at Phoebe and her robe that she carried over her arm. "They are ill disposed toward this master who has traveled a great distance to seek your aid in clearing her name. Ah, hers and the ones who accompany her as well."

Alodar looked about. "Forgive my lack of hospitality. Find a chair to your liking. It is just that dealing with the likes of Elezar is so urgent that —"

Alodar's eyes narrowed. "What demon is this?" he pointed at Astron. "Which of you have him under control, and why is he dressed as a man?"

Astron glanced up from the book he was perusing. His stembrain rumbled. The urgency of why he was here rushed back to him. He threw back his hood and tilted his head in Alodar's direction. "My will is bound only to the service of my prince," Astron said. "I am Elezar's messenger, bidding that you contact him at once through the flame."

Alodar frowned. "Elezar can pass through the barrier only after many lesser demons have preceded him. Since our first battle, all wizards everywhere interact with great caution so that never do too many come through to our realm at any one time."

"Contact only, not passage, is what my prince desires. " Astron stepped forward. "He is in great peril from his own kind and seeks out aid from the only one he acknowledges as greater."

"Few enough know even the name of the prince," Alodar said. "But perhaps you have somehow learned. If you are truly from the dazzling one, then you will have knowledge that others would not."

"His eyes are green, and his brow flecked with gold," Astron answered. "His stature is but finger-widths greater than mine. Hooded, he, too, could pass unnoticed in the realm of men. His —"

Alodar waved Astron to stop. He slumped into a chair at one of the crowded tables and then eyed Kestrel with a weary smile. "I would much rather handle a squabble among a dozen councils of wizards," he said, "or spend more time trying to squeeze one more secret from the lore recorded in this room."

He arched his back and stretched. "But three decades of running from one crisis to another take their toll. The glamour of being world-saver wears thin after perhaps the dozenth time."

Kestrel did not respond. He looked out of one of the high windows, but still saw no sign of any imps or djinns. There might be time enough after all. Soon he would learn which of Astron's words were no truer than the fancies that he himself wove. Hopefully, from what he discovered, he would be able to spin his own scheme to turn aside the Brythian wizards. He glanced at Alodar's intense expression, deciding how much his tale should dare.

"If you would assist," Alodar said to Phoebe, his reluctance shoved aside. "I will light the fire in the hearth and attempt to see if what this demon says is true. " He pointed to a well just outside one of the windows. "But if he has warped his words, be ready with a full bucket. I will want the flames doused before any great harm can be done."

"I — I am not sure that I am worthy, Archimage," Phoebe stepped forward cautiously. "Although I won the logo of flame fairly, even the small devil who is with us I could not command."

"I am the one who will challenge Elezar. " Alodar shook his head. "Such a task I would wish upon no other. I do not need your skills as a master, just a quickness of eye and arm."

Phoebe let out her breath. She scowled, annoyed at herself for the image that she had presented. With a quick nod, she scurried to do the archimage's bidding.

Alodar brought a simple flame to life in the stone-lined fireplace along the north wall. He left for a few moments and then returned with some powder that he flicked into the blaze. The fire billowed and flashed into a rainbow of color.

As Phoebe returned with the water, Alodar pulled his chair in front of the growing blaze. Making himself comfortable, he stared into their hypnotic dance. For three dozen heartbeats, nothing more happened.

Kestrel shifted his weight from one leg to another in discomfort. His eyes darted around the room, wondering about the propriety of taking a second chair for himself. Then, just as he had about made up his mind to move, the flames flashed green and an eerie voice whispered from out of the hearth into the room.

"Ah, Master, you have come." There was a gentle sighing. "Astron has done well for his prince."

"He is so weak! " Alodar exclaimed. "This is hardly the one with whom I wrestled so long ago."

The archimage paused, and then shook off his astonishment. "What is it you wish?" he asked. "We have decided long ago, Elezar, that the affairs of the realm of men were no longer to be your concern."

"So they are not," Elezar replied. "But I am one prince among many. I maneuver to keep the interests of the others away by your command and have succeeded because of my own great power."

The fire spit and sputtered as if it were gasping for air.

"My prince has not recovered from his wound." Astron took a step toward the hearth. "And by the weakness of his voice, I would deduce that he has received another."

"But consider this, Archimage," Elezar continued, not paying any attention to the voice of his cataloguer. "If my own power were to wane, who then would keep the other princes from coveting the realm of men as I did myself? And unlike creatures of my kind, you age, Master. Are you ready again to undergo the test of wills that you undertook in your prime?"

"What other prince?" Alodar leaned forward in his chair. "Who else in the realm of demons focuses his thoughts in a way that should not be his concern?"

"There is Gaspar," Elezar said. "He has proven far more potent an adversary than I did first suspect. My own domain he has ripped from the void. And before his attack a full dozen other princes he had allied to his cause. My hiding places in the blackness he has found, one by one. The dark node I now occupy is the last. There is little time left before I am overwhelmed. Do as my messenger directs. You can fight to save the realm of men now or wait till later when the outcome will be more in your disfavor."

Kestrel shook his head. He could not believe what he was hearing. Imps and sprites or minor devils summoned with anvilwood were one thing, but warring demon princes and archimages were quite another. Astron's story was correct, just as he had stated from the first. What had he got himself into?

"These events are all very sudden," Alodar said. "I find it hard to believe that one as crafty as you, Elezar, would be reduced to such straits. I will need time to verify if what you say is true."

"Time is the luxury that you do not have, Master," the flame whispered with Elezar's voice. "Gaspar hunts not only me but all who serve as well. In the last few ticks of the eon, many imps have crossed the barrier between our realms. Some have been instructed, I know, to track down my cataloguer — track him down so that mightier djinns can pluck off his limbs one by one, just as surely as Gaspar wishes the same fate for me. Each moment you hesitate brings closer the time when you must confront not one demon passing through the flame but more than a score. Discover what must be done before it is too late."

The One Who Carries

THE FLAME sputtered. Elezar's voice faded into the glow of the hot coals like spent echoes. Kestrel strained to hear more but the whispers of the demon dissolved into indistinctness. For a moment, he and the others gathered around the fireplace were silent.

"What then is the message of your prince?" Alodar asked Astron at last. "What would he have me do that would restore him to power and protect the realm of men as well?"

"The prince needs a transporter," Astron replied. "One to carry matter between the realms. One whom he trusted you to choose."

"We have little traffic with the realm of the skyskirr," Alodar shook his head. "Ever since the metamagician Jason restored our laws to their natural state, the path between the two universes has been opened but rarely. It is by chance that you have arrived while some manipulants are also here."

"I do not think it is to the skyskirr that we must go," Astron said. "Their realm has little more diverse matter than my own. It would be somewhere else instead."

Alodar's eyes narrowed. "There are others, are there not?" he asked with sudden excitement. "It was, of course, obvious after I learned of the existence of the 'hedron, but I dared not seek the definite proof. Contact with one other realm was disruptive enough. It would have been folly to explore too far."

Astron nodded in the manner of men. "Yet, just as the number of laws number more than seven, so does the counting of the diverse universes that populate the void, each with its own essence and rituals, distinct from the rest."

Kestrel stirred uncomfortably. The conversation was about things he could well avoid. He would have to divert its course to matters of more direct concern.

"The wizards of Brythia are responsible for the imps of which this — this Prince Elezar speaks," he said. "Restricting the masters from such reckless action might help with your other problem as well."

Alodar nodded but kept his attention on Astron. "What else then, demon? Of what other wonders should I know besides the multitude of realms?"

"There is the ultimate precept," Astron replied. "That is what my prince seeks — the ultimate precept, a concept superior to the laws of magic, one transcendent to the metalaws behind them, the answer to the riddle that provides the greatest power of all."

"In which realm does one search for this ultimate of precepts?" Alodar asked.

"Only Palodad knows that," Astron said. "In exchange for bringing him some exotic matter from whence he directs us, he will tell us where to look."

"Palodad, additional realms, ultimate precepts." Alodar's frown deepened. "It is all too much to swallow in one sitting. Perhaps Elezar has constructed what we men call a fancy and expects somehow to convince us that it is real."

"It is a chance for redemption," Phoebe interrupted. She had placed the bucket of water on the stone floor. Her cheeks were flushed with excitement.

"It came to me while the two of you conversed," she said. "I cannot continue through the rest of my life always blushing in apology for a single failure in my craft. I must strike out again and somehow prove a woman's worth. It is by accomplishment that I will yet show the wizards of my council the meaning of respect. By proven deed will I gain comfort, even in the presence of the archimage of all the crafts."

She took a deep breath. "And even though the archimage hesitates, then I will not. Tell me, Astron, is this Palodad strong willed, like your prince?"

Kestrel bolted across the room. He put his hand on Phoebe's arm and looked over his shoulder at Alodar. "She has not quite recovered from the haste of our journey," he said. "Dismiss her words as some nervous prattle."

He spun his head back around and stared at Phoebe. "This is no game with imps and sprites. Did you not hear the words from the flames and see the strange beasts the skyskirr were? Be careful or you will get us into a pit deeper than we presently are."

Kestrel stopped abruptly. He studied Phoebe's expression and did not like what he saw.

"Imps and sprites," she shot back. "Is that indeed all you think me capable of? If the need arose, despite your words, would you trust me with more?"

She disengaged herself from Kestrel's grip. "I know I stated when we began the journey that the adventure was all that mattered. But how can I be other than the demon's slave, if deep inside you cannot judge me to be your equal."

Kestrel opened his mouth to speak, but he did not know what to say. For Astron to talk of other realms was his own business. No doubt at the root of his desires was the wish to return safely home, regardless of where that actually was. And the affairs of demon princes were the concerns of one such as the archimage. But Phoebe was another matter altogether. He glanced at her sudden determination and shook his head. He must have been right when he first explained her words. It was the fatigue of the journey. In a calmer moment, she would see the folly of dealing with such immensities just as clearly as he.

Phoebe ignored his outstretched arm. She grabbed the sack of powder still at Alodar's feet and, like a miller fulfilling an order, threw another handful into the dying flame. Thrusting the pouch into her cape, she took a deep breath as the fire roared back to life. "Palodad," she said. "Palodad, come forth. I command you to submit to my will."

"Who tugs and pulls at the one who reckons?" a deep voice boomed from the hearth in response. "He is no mighty djinn who can be commanded to burst asunder great rocks or wield bolts of awesome lightning. Be gone! Let him be! Wrestle with someone else, someone more worthy of your mettle."

"If you are named Palodad, then you are the one I seek," Phoebe said. "Submit now to your master so that you might answer the questions that I have about realms other than my own."

"It is not the one who reckons whose tendrils of thought intertwine with yours. He is my prince. I speak on his behalf for all who come asking at the doors of his domain."

Kestrel hesitated, not knowing whether to rush forward and pull Phoebe away or let her be, so her concentration would not be disturbed.

Astron released one hand from the book he still clutched to his chest and tugged on Alodar's purple sleeve. "If the one that has been touched serves old Palodad, then it is just as well," he said. "He can learn from the old one and tell us in turn in which realm we are to seek — tell us what is to be brought back in fulfillment of the bargain to the one who has him duty-bound."

Astron shuddered. "In fact, the intimacy of mind is all the better with a minion than with the old one himself," he said.

Alodar's expression did not change for a moment, but then he nodded. He indicated for Phoebe to continue.

"Whose mind then do I touch?" Phoebe asked. "Speak your name as token of submission to my will. Tell me how it will be that you will convey Palodad's thoughts. Be swift about it. There are many assembled here and the waste of time is great."

The flame flashed hotter. Kestrel felt a blast of warmth like that from a kiln on his cheeks.

"I am Camonel, the one who carries," the voice rumbled. "Prince Palodad has instructed that I submit to what you ask. We need not exercise the ritual of struggle. Feel my thoughts. I do not resist. He can speak through me as if my mouth were his own."

There was a brief pause while the fire danced wildly, and then the demon behind the flames spoke again. "Time, did you say time?"

The words rolled out from the hearth. "Time, there is no way either to save or waste it," Camonel said. The flame spat and crackled. "It flows regardless, marching past to be lost forever. Do not speak to me of what even the most powerful of wizards cannot bend to his will." The laughter boomed again, this time more forcefully, echoing from the stone walls and filling the room with sound.

"The riddle of the ultimate precept. " Alodar forced his voice through the din. "Ask him if it is no more than a cleverly worded ruse on the part of Elezar the prince to seek again control of the realm of men."

"Elezar, the one who dazzles, is but a few time-ticks away from being but a memory," the voice answered through the flame. "His domain is gone, dissipated into a fine dust that slowly drifts in the realm. Only one dark node remains his to command, and soon it too will be found. I will record in my domain his many exploits, but, except for that, he will be forgotten like the rest. His only hope lies in looking elsewhere — elsewhere in a realm for which I alone have calculated the identity."

"Then where is this place?" Alodar persisted.

"From there you will have to bring back to me the pollen of the giant harebell flower. In exchange, I will tell you in more detail how to seek the riddle's solution. Will you agree to that — the pollen for what I will then reveal?"

"I make no —" Alodar began.

"Yes," Phoebe interrupted. "Yes, tell us and we will go."

"No, you have no authority," Alodar cut back in. "Wait, Tell Palodad. Only I am —"

This time, the words of the archimage were cut off by a second blast of radiation from the hearth. A billowing ball of orange flame rolled into the room, pushing Kestrel backward and to the side. A heavy black smoke coursed along the stone floor like a runaway playball, and an acrid smell, more intense that the ones from the Ethidorian foundry stung Kestrel's nose.

A large brown djinn stooped to enter the room from the fireplace, thick scales covering limbs that pulsed with tight muscles. The tips of leathery wings scraped against the slope of the ceiling, the fire behind shining through a network of blackened veins. A single row of coarse hair sat atop eyes set in rugged and angular bone. Tiny nostrils flared with each breath above a mouth distorted to the side in a permanent sneer.

"I am Camonel." The demon's deep voice rumbled much louder than it had on the other side of the flame. "Palodad instructs me to transport whomever you have selected into the realm of the fey."

"The fey," Alodar asked. "What manner of place is that?"

Camonel's deep laugh again filled the room with sound. "You men know of it in your fancies. Underhill kingdoms, trilling pipes with melancholy airs, creatures you think no larger than the smallest imps."

"Not the realm of the fey!" Astron interrupted. "They are all wizards, everyone. It is no place for a cataloguer who is merely striving to serve his prince. Why can it not be someplace gentle, as is the realm of men?"

"I am ready," Phoebe said. With her chin thrust high like the commander of a legion, she stepped forward to where the djinn stood in front of the hearth.

"Wait," Kestrel shouted." Wait, Phoebe, this is madness. Think of what you are doing. You cannot follow that monster, aided by no more than the likes of Astron."

"Why, I did not intend to." Phoebe looked back. "It is to be the three of us, just as from the beginning."

Kestrel lunged to a halt and stared. This indeed was madness. The affairs of archimage and demon prince might be of great importance to some, but they were no concern of his. Let some other so-called hero step forth for the honor and the glory. In the end, like always, the rewards would turn to bitter ashes. The one who jumped through the hoops would find that he had been manipulated for the benefit of others who would not take the risks themselves. This was no role for Kestrel the woodcutter. There was nothing whatever in the bargain for him.

He watched Phoebe as she drew closer to the waiting djinn, her nose clamped shut to hold out the pungent odor. His thoughts tumbled in confusion. He was here only to clear his name and perhaps win a few pieces of gold from the archimage so he could boast of it in the tavern.

But there was Phoebe as well. Her life probably was forfeit as soon as the leathery wings closed around her willing frame. He thought of his rescue from the foundry of the alchemist, the pleasure when she had pressed against his side, and her insistence on seeing the good in him when there was none to be found.

While Kestrel hesitated, there was a sudden commotion at the door. Four wizards in sweat-dampened robes burst into the room." There they are," the first one shouted. "The very ones who conspired to cheat the august council of Brythia. Come forward, Maspanar, and the rest. We have caught them at last."

Alodar peered sharply at the intrusion, but before he could speak, the high windows along the wall above the doorway shattered in a spray of tiny shards. Two demons almost as large as the one in the hearth plunged into the room, circling overhead like prowling eagles and with crackles of blue flame pulsing from their fingertips.

One of the wizards who rushed in added his voice to the commotion." Please forgive the interruption, master archimage. Forgive the interruption, but we come to rectify a great wrong to our craft."

"Yes, since I have had time to ponder it," another one said" I recognize the one bearing the rucksack from before, some five years ago in Laudia to the south. "He pointed at Kestrel, his face beet-red with anger." A swindle then of my hard-won gold, just as it was at her cabin. Do not be deceived, Archimage. Their words are smooth but carry not a word of truth, not even the ones of the demons that they command. Give him over to us. His fate is to spend time in a cage."

One of the wizards raced up to Phoebe and tugged at her robe from behind. Kestrel slapped his arm away. He eyed her critically as her bold composure began to falter in the confusion. Stepping to the side, he barely missed a searing bolt of blue that crackled from above and sputtered the hard stone at his feet into a bubbly slag.

Astron moved toward Phoebe as well and that made up Kestrel's mind. "It is because of her and no one else," he yelled above the noise of the others. "For her alone, do you understand? Not for the sake of great princes or the well-being of mankind. Only for Phoebe am I doing this.

The rest of you matter no more than you did before."

He grabbed Phoebe about the waist. Desperately, he put the thoughts of what might be even worse than smacking lips and soaring lithons out of his mind. Closing his eyes, he pushed her forward toward Camonel's chest. He felt a smothering heaviness on his back as the wings closed around them and Astron's elbow pressed into his side. Almost absently, he grasped the book the demon thrust at him and shoved it over his shoulder into his rucksack. He reeled from the dizziness. Reality seemed to spin. The last thing he remembered was the words of one of the wizards.

"If they escape, Archimage, I want the word broadcast even across the sea. Apprehend them at all costs and bring them back. There is to be no place in the realm of men where safety will be theirs. And for each day that they are gone, the slippery-tongued one will serve one hundred more in a cage."

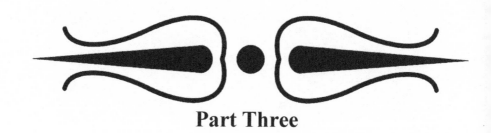

Part Three

The Realm of the Fey

Legends of the Sagas

THE DJINN vanished back into the flame. Astron glanced at Kestrel and Phoebe and saw what he more or less expected. Both stood transfixed in wide-eyed wonder. He remembered how his own stembrain had seized control on his first visit and how he had barely hidden in time.

The trio stood next to one of three small fires, beside a stream that flowed between the rising slopes of a sylvan glade. The hillsides were covered with a carpet of thick grass, each blade the size of Astron's legs. Scattered here and there were huge flowers of red and gold, towering into the sky on giant stems from clumps of thick foliage. The proportions were all wrong, but in the realm of men, they would be called foxglove, white thorn, primrose, and thyme. A ring of mushrooms, each as big as a small hut, circled the hillsides in a single precise line halfway up the slopes. On the crests, the flowering bushes merged into a thick forest of glistening leaves.

No one else appeared to be present, but behind them on the bank stood a large granite-gray boulder with a wooden door incongruously on the side. The trilling of distant pipes blended with the sigh of a gentle breeze. Astron pointed to the hillcrest. He guided the other two upward and into the shadowy cover. They moved perhaps fifty steps and then ducked beneath a low-lying leaf that was the size of the largest djinn. The soft sky glow that was everywhere the same winked in and out of the inky blackness. The click of large insects in the distance blended with the crunch of lichen underfoot. Astron sniffed the fungal pungency of his surroundings and waited for his eyes to adjust to the darkness.

"Where are we?" Kestrel found his voice. "And look at the size of this — this ragwort! What kind of giants are we among?"

The canopy of leaves was not complete. The diffuse light from the pale blue sky trickled between jagged edges and painted the thin spots between the huge, webby veins with an iridescent glow. Behind them, perhaps some ten paces, was a coarse and woody trunk that soared as high into the sky as the tallest structure in the realm of men. Thick emerald branches cantilevered out into a shower of leaves that hung nearly to the ground. Between the stem and the circling umbrella of foliage was the shelter in which they hid. One had to proceed cautiously in the realm of the fey, Astron knew, much more so than in the worlds of men.

"We were lucky we arrived when we did," Astron retrieved the book of thaumaturgy from Kestrel's rucksack. "From the looks of things, the ring has not yet begun to form."

He wrinkled his nose, wondering what to do next. Somewhere in this realm, according to Palodad, was the answer to the riddle. But beyond that, there was no clue. And from the tone of his prince's voice, what little time had been left was almost gone.

Astron felt the tug of his stembrain, but wrestled it into submission. The imps that had tracked him in the realm of men did not help matters. With all the traffic between the realms, Gaspar could not help but be close behind. It would be a race to see if he or Elezar would be the first to fall. And what of the humans? At least one would be needed to wrest the harebell pollen through the barrier when the time came, but what would happen after that? His own realm had grown increasingly inhospitable and was no place for any other kind.

Phoebe drew near Kestrel, and the woodcutter put his arm around her. She smiled at him in the dimness. A bond was growing between the two — perhaps even the one that men wrote so much about in their sagas. What could be so different from the duty to couple with a broodmother whenever a prince commanded? The crease in Astron's nose deepened. He had been with these two far longer than with any other mortals and he had learned many things. But if he were asked to explain their behavior to his prince, he would not be able to do so.

The one called Kestrel could speak of things that had no existence whatsoever in the reality of any of the realms. After the flight from the cabin of the wizard, he had seemed reluctant to continue the journey to the archimage. Then, after the terms of their agreement had been satisfied, he had continued the quest through the flame, not in response to the command of any prince, but of his own volition. Despite these contradictions, Kestrel had the skill to manipulate half a dozen imps as if he were a practiced wizard. There was much more to be learned from this mortal and new experiences to be felt and tasted before their journey together was over.

"I knew you would come," Phoebe said to Kestrel.

"Yes, and now we must see it to the end," he answered. "Instead of weaving a story for the archimage, all we have to do is solve a demon's riddle, discover the most powerful natural law of them all, transport harebell pollen, whatever that is, across a flaming barrier, and restore a prince to power, thereby saving the entire realm of men. Then we might have a chance somehow to return to the archimage and convince him that we were right all along."

"You left out the part about a female wizard proving her worth," Phoebe laughed.

"At least, it does not appear quite as bad as I had imagined," Kestrel sighed with relief. Some of the tension ebbed away. "Except for the size of things, this could well be a sheltered valley in any of the kingdoms that border the great ocean," the woodcutter continued. Once we understand better what goes on here, we just might survive after all."

Astron was not so sure. He surveyed the glade a second time. The trill of the pipes was louder, and soon there was motion on the crest across the way. A row of flute players bobbed into view. Behind them, several rows of dancers were leaping in unison to the sad melody that wafted through the air. The leaves rustled at Astron's side and he smelled a sweet fragrance as Phoebe drew near.

"We must be dreaming," she squinted up at the procession. "Look, Kestrel, creatures of a childhood tale, what else could they be?"

The pipers and dancers were drawing close enough that rough features could be seen. The tallest would tower two heads above Astron, but a weighing scale would tip in the demon's favor. Slender limbs protruded from tunics of deep green, and long delicate fingers almost like small tendrils arched over the shafts of the flutes. Tumbling curls of gold bounced above delicate features that gave no hint of gender. They were lithe and thin, like the skyskirr, but somehow shrouded in a delicate beauty, rather than a repulsiveness that made men want to turn away.

The step of the pipers was light, and those of the dancers lighter still. In impossibly long glides, they darted from one point of the slope to another, hovering in mid-leap until they barely touched the ground.

"Do men know of the fey?" Astron asked. "The words of the archimage lead me to believe that this realm is as new to your kind as was that of the skyskirr some few time-ticks ago."

"Only in legend," Kestrel whispered back. "Tales for wee ones to send them to sleep. Strange beckoning music that one must at all costs avoid. Outwelling light from deep forest mounds. Tiny enough to hide in the bowl of a flower or under a curling leaf — not the size of a man. The scale is all wrong."

Kestrel stopped and darted a quick look around at his surroundings. He reached upward and stroked the fine hairs like the bristles on a brush that lined the underside of the leaf overhead. "Legend," he muttered, "a coincidence. It can be no more than that."

Wizards in Abundance

MORE RANKS came over the crestline of the hill, most showing the dull sheen of copper on their chests. Two more lines of pipers marched in precise step behind the dancers, their faces all grim and unsmiling like men-at-arms on review, and each with unsheathed blades attached to their belts. While those before them descended to the stream that transected the glade, the sentrymen fanned out to circle the shallow bowl. In a matter of a few heartbeats, they were standing at attention, a sentry next to each of the toadstools that ringed the glade. One was barely a stone's throw from where Astron and the others hid.

The trilling of the pipes intensified. A litter came over the crest of the hill. Surrounded by fluttering attendants, what could only be the equivalent of a prince's carriage jostled down the slope. The one inside was dressed in a tunic like the rest, but fancy embroideries of brilliant reds decorated a green deeper than that worn by the others. A garland of tiny blossoms crowned the brow where the yellow curls had faded to the color of pale straw.

Behind the first ruler came a second and a third, and then a disarray of others, some in clumps of twenty and others in twos and threes. The chatter of many voices began to mingle the melody of the pipes. Occasionally, what might be tinkling laughter sounded with the rest. Finally, the litters came to a halt in front of the door into the rock. All the music faded as if swept aside by the breeze. The richly dressed occupant of the first rose to his feet and spread his arms to the sky. His face showed the first signs of age, and there was a cruel hardness in his eye. His melodic voice, barely deeper than that of a human woman, filled the air.

"What is happening?" Kestrel whispered. "Can you understand the tongue?"

"Yes," Astron said. "On my previous visit, I learned it well from one kinder than the rest."

He concentrated on the words coming from the streamside and began translating for his companions.

"Come forward, high king Finvarwin, venerated judge. It is the season," Astron repeated. "Come forward, Finvarwin, and decide which creations have sufficient beauty, which will be granted the privilege of continued life. Tell us all who will receive the rewards for their efforts and who must render service as penalty for failure. I, Hillsovereign Prydwin, speaking for all the others, request your presence."

The wooden door swung outward. A frail and stooped figure shuffled out into the light. The top of his head was bald except for a few long stringlets of bleached gold hanging to his shoulders. His face looked caved in, as if struck by a mighty blow. Squinting eyes sat atop a flattened nose. The chin jutted out from under a mouth long since vacant of teeth. Rather than a tunic of green, the newcomer wore a long robe of white, cinched at the waist with a rope made of vines.

"I am ready," Finvarwin said. "I will judge as I have so many times before."

Finvarwin waved his hand out over the assemblage and then shielded his eyes. "Which one is Nimbia?" he asked. "Which one attempts to create without the aid of a mate?"

One of the fey standing somewhat apart from the rest came forward and dipped her head. "It is my creation that you have asked to inspect, venerated one. May your judgment be keen and fair."

"Look at that one!" Kestrel gasped in a voice almost loud enough for the nearest sentryman to hear. "I do not know how these creatures judge, but if she were in Procolon, men would fight for just one of her smiles."

Nimbia was a bit shorter than the rest, about Astron's own height, and wore a plain tunic, with no added embroidery. Her face was slender, with soft angles, high cheeks, and a tiny upturned nose. Large eyes danced beneath a halo of gold. The way she moved was in some subtle way different from the rest, a dancelike flow of smoothness like a well-oiled alchemist's machine.

She indeed would be judged a great beauty, Astron thought, and from what little he did know of the fey, in their underhills as well. He puzzled for a second time about the lust that went beyond the duty to couple and wondered if it affected those before him in the same way as it did Kestrel and his kin.

"You will be the last," Finvarwin said to Nimbia. "I will judge first those more likely to prove worthy. Vastowen, prepare the ring for the use of all."

The occupant of the second litter, more heavy-set than the rest, bowed and then addressed the assemblage. "A dozen djinns," he said. "At least a dozen for I am confident that what I have started has begun to grow of its own volition."

The pipes again started trilling. Everyone present focused his or her attention to the three fires burning on the stream bank. Vastowen motioned to one of the females standing nearby. Shyly, she came forward and clasped his extended hand. Together they waded across the stream to the side on which Astron and the others hid.

Vastowen grabbed a handful of powder from a pouch at his waist. With a fluid motion, he distributed the dust into the three fires. The flames roared skyward, each a brilliant purple of glistening heat.

"Come forward, djinns of the circle, I command you," Vastowen called out. "Come forward and make the bridge so that we can see into elsewhere."

"He is a wizard!" Phoebe exclaimed. "A wizard, but a foolish one at that. One djinn is sufficient a contest of wills for anyone. Against a dozen no one can withstand."

"They are all wizards," Astron replied. His stembrain stirred at the thought. "The high king, the hillsovereigns, the litter bearers, even the sentrymen formed into the ring. It is what makes a journey here so risky for one of my kind. The struggle of dominance or submission could occur with each and every one that I meet."

Astron waved at the figures before him, now all concentrating on the three fires at Vastowen's feet. "And if a single one of them has insufficient strength, he can enlist the aid of another. In twos and threes or even scores, they can meld their wills as one. A solitary devil or even a prince is no match for the scores you see before you here. They can summon and control a dozen djinns with ease. It is no wonder that none of the princes who rule cast covetous thoughts toward a realm such as this."

As Astron spoke, a transcendent djinn materialized in the first of the three purple flames. In an instant after, the other two populated as well. Vastowen waved his arm in a great vertical circle. The great demons grunted acquiescence, bowing their massive heads to their chests.

The djinn from the second flame beat his wings. With one great stroke, he vaulted onto the shoulders of the first. Wisps of purple plasma trailed along with his jump. When the third took position on top of the second, the slender column of flame rose to an unbelievable height. The air roared with bubbling energy. Astron felt the heat penetrate even the shelter in which he hid.

More djinns appeared in the two abandoned fires. After his display of submission, each placed himself on top of those who had preceded him. In a matter of moments, a column of twelve djinns encased in a sheath of dancing flame ascended high into the pale sky.

"And now the circle, I command you," Vastowen said when the last had taken his position. "A great ring of demonic flame from the realm of the fey to the one that I direct."

A terrible groan like that from prisoners before their execution escaped from twelve mouths in unison. For a few heartbeats, nothing seemed to happen. But imperceptibly at first and then moving faster, the column bowed from the vertical and arced toward Astron's right. The djinns each gripped their hands upon the legs of the one above and the topmost of all extended his arms over his head, reaching out into the empty air.

Like a supple blade of steel, the column of djinns bent more and more to the right, the one at the base leaning farther and farther in the opposite direction in response to the lateral forces that pushed on his shoulders.

The tower bent into a great hook and tightened. What had been the topmost djinn touched ground a span away from the fire into which stood the very first. He walked his hands across the ground and thrust the other demon's feet onto his shoulders. The dozen djinns had formed themselves into a fiery ring that was four times the height of a tall man.

Phoebe trembled. The power of twelve mighty djinns bent to a single purpose was something that she could not easily imagine. But in the realm of the fey, such feats evidently were commonplace, she thought, a single element in their rituals. As she watched, the pale sky that was surrounded by the ring clouded and darkened. The groans of the djinns intensified into shrieks of pain. The air heaved and buckled, distorting the view of the hillside beyond the ring. Bolts of lightning materialized out of nothing. Rolling thunder echoed throughout the glen.

The scene within the ring dissolved into a blur of dull colors. The hillside appeared to melt into a formless slag that oozed outward to the edges. Eventually, the entire area of the enclosed circle was nothing but an indistinct gray that occasionally pulsed and twitched.

"Is this sorcery?" Kestrel whispered. "An illusion like the ones constructed on Morgana across the great ocean in my own realm?"

"Of the five arts used by men, only wizardry is employed by the fey," Astron answered. "They are using that single art now to command those of my kind to open a passage into yet another realm."

Astron squinted at the amorphous blandness contained by the ring. "But look how they accomplish it! Not a small path that flits an imp from one universe to another. Yes, I understand now that I witness the event firsthand. Within the ring we can all see from one realm to another."

Judgments of the High King

AS ASTRON spoke from the hiding place, the grayness within the djinn-enclosed ring began to take on shape. Colors deepened. Bright lights started to shine through the gloom. Muted tones appeared first, and then saturated reds and yellows. In sunbursts of color, tiny, bright, pinpoints, closely packed and forming a square array came into sharp focus.

Simultaneously, all of the colors changed to deep-lake blue. After an expectant pause, the first column on the left shifted to a mustard yellow, immediately followed by the next adjacent. Like a painter's brush repainting a wall, the change of color marched across the ring. More patterns followed, each more complex than the one before: concentric rings expanding from a central point, an array of spinning batons, small circles of color pursuing one another in a spiral chase. Finally, the field of blue returned, and then after another moment faded to the original gray.

"Savor the vibrancy of the dance," Vastowen said, "I — "

The female next to Vastowen pulled on his hand. He stooped forward to listen to what she had to say. For a moment, they exchanged animated whispers like star-struck lovers. Then he nodded and reached into a second pouch at his belt.

"And there is yet more, Finvarwin," he called to the high king. "My soulmate's inspiration soars beyond the richness of what has already been revealed. Look, we cast in more pollen and with our combined effort cause there to be more."

A cluster of small nodules sped from Vastowen's grasp and through the ring of djinns. The female fell to one knee with a gasp, although she did not release her grip on the hand of her mate. Beads of sweat popped into being on Vastowen's smooth brow. Wiping away the salty drops that streamed into his eyes, he stared at the opening, straining until his arms and legs began to tremble.

In silence like that at a king's funeral, everyone around the glen watched the murky grayness of the disk. Then, as quickly as it had formed, the hazy fog retreated to reveal once again the array of the brightly colored points of light. Only this time, the circular patterns they formed would collide with a burst of brilliant light. In the wake of the collision, dozens of even smaller circles, each as bright as its parent, popped into being and exploded outward in wild arcs of their own.

"It is not rich enough." Finvarwin waved his arm at the display. "I need not waste time by seeing more. A multitude of such dim fuzziness soon becomes tiring. I suspect that eventually all of those tiny blobs will dissipate far from one another, devoid of interest. No one will want to watch. Everything that you have shown will all fade away."

"No!" Vastowen shouted. "The creation has volition. I know it does. I can feel the energy of its life forces pulsing inside. Suspend judgment for now. Let the patterns intermingle and produce new variations. We can all wait and thrill in its blossoming richness when we gather the next time."

"You know the rules as well as any hillsovereign." Prydwin stepped forward to stand next to Vastowen. "Once shown to the high king, a creation cannot be withdrawn and substituted with another."

"But we added to the basic premise even as you watched. Surely that —"

"Enough," Finvarwin said. "You have presented fairly, and fairly have I judged."

Vastowen opened his mouth as if to say more, but then he scanned the glade and stopped. Even the retainers that had come with him had backed away from his litter as if retreating from a leper. Vastowen dropped his mate's hand to his side. The scene within the ring of djinns returned to a muted gray. With hushed expectancy, all of the fey awaited Finvarwin's next words.

"To Prydwin," he said. "Yes, to Prydwin. The *entire* underhill in its entirety. To dissipate Vastowen's holdings among the rest might encourage similar exhibitions of little skill."

"Thank you, venerated one." Prydwin sank to one knee and tilted his head. "I will make great use of the resources that you have so generously —"

"Enough," Finvarwin commanded. "Who is next? What does he present?"

"But the disposition of your largesse." Prydwin rose to standing. "It is only right that everyone knows."

Finvarwin grunted. Prydwin's face broke into a smile. He turned to face Vastowen and his mate. "For you, Hillsovereign, my mercy will be swift. You may choose which of my sentrymen will guide his dagger to your heart."

The expression on Vastowen's face did not flicker. "My sovereign," he mumbled. Glancing for a final time at his mate, he squeezed her hand and then pointed out randomly at the circle of mushrooms. "That one," he said. "That one will be as good as any."

"Not yet." Prydwin put up his hand to stop the sentry from leaving his post. "First, there is the matter of the rest. You will probably want to hear."

Prydwin turned his attention to the litter bearers and the others of Vastowen's retinue. "For those who remained underhill and did not come, their penalty is to travel to my own domain and there begin service as I direct. You there, carry back the empty chair so that they will know that their hill sovereign is no more.

"As for the rest who were so bold as to accompany their liege." Prydwin's smile broadened. "Your yells and screams shall serve to inspire me to greater creations still. The pain may not be brief, but at least you will have the consolation of adding to the greatness of the art."

Several of the fey around Vastowen's litter suddenly started to run like mice fleeing from a cat jumping into their midst, but before they had traveled a dozen steps, the sentrymen cut off their escape and herded them back toward the stream.

The first two began whimpering softly as their hands and feet were bound with a vine bristling with thorns. Like slaughtered pigs, they were fastened to a beam that was placed between two pairs of crossed stakes. The oily contents of a plant bladder were spilled over their tunics. Then, without further ceremony, they were set ablaze.

The fires burned slowly, billowing up dense clouds of pungent black smoke. Through a growing haze, the march of the smoldering flames burning outward from where they were first lit, down each leg and arm and toward the head.

The death cries of the fey were high and piercing, so much so that even Kestrel had to release Phoebe so he could cover his ears. The complexion of the two humans washed chalky white as they stared at what they saw.

"Let us be away," Phoebe whispered urgently. "They are so many. This is no place for us."

"We do not know where." Astron shook his head. "A moment more

148

and perhaps something of value might be learned. See, the sounds have stopped and the Hillsovereign Prydwin speaks again."

Astron translated Prydwin's words. "Those are enough for now. The rest I will save for later when there will be more time to enjoy."

The hillsovereign looked at Vastowen's wooden face and chuckled. "I have saved the best for last," he said. "Your mate, Thuvia, is a comely one. I think that my creations too will benefit from the experience of her pleasures."

Vastowen looked toward Thuvia, tears streaming from his eyes. "Do not be afraid," he said so softly that he could barely be heard. "Perhaps he will be gentle."

"Gentle?" Prydwin suddenly barked with laughter. "To my underhill and remove her of her garments," he roared. "We will see if you judge me gentle."

"Enough of the unimportant," Finvarwin's reedy voice cut in. "Who is to be next in the judging?"

"I am, venerated one," Prydwin said,

He turned his attention away from Vastowen's followers, their fates dismissed from his mind. The hillsovereign gestured to the females who stood by his litter, and one came forward to stand with him in front of the ring of demons.

"Join the two of us, my king," Prydwin said. "Come closer to the ring so that all of the detail can be seen. There is not one but two realms that I wish to show you."

As the Finvarwin drew nearer, Prydwin dissipated the muted gray in an instant with a casual wave.

Within the ring, in looping trajectories, what appeared to be frozen warriors clothed in blood red leather armor, copper swords raised and ready to strike, soared through a black void. Occasionally two would collide, and exchange a blow before they bounced back apart. Some careened swiftly; some moved hardly at all. From center to rim, the activity was the same, featureless and unending chaos with no beginning or end.

"I sense the power of your creation," Finvarwin said after several hundred heartbeats of watching movement within the ring. "It does not repeat. It does not dissipate. It continues on. Yes, the creation is worthy — not as complex as those that have been seen before, but vibrant and long lasting nonetheless. I have no need to see the second. This one is enough. There is no penalty, Prydwin. Instead you fairly may receive a boon."

"You have blessed me many times already, venerated one," Prydwin said. "Of material things I have little want. I ask instead that you give me knowledge, arcane knowledge of our own realm that only you remember — knowledge so that my own worth might grow."

"Very well then, the answer to three questions shall be your prize. Think of them carefully, Prydwin. When all ceremonies have been completed, then you may ask."

Prydwin tipped his head to the high king and retreated to his litter, satisfaction wreathing his face.

"Who's next?" Finvarwin repeated. "Who's next to be judged by the high king?"

A soft murmur like that of a spring breeze ran through the assemblage on the other bank, but neither the owner of the third litter nor any other came forth. Finvarwin waited a moment more and then motioned toward Nimbia.

"Then the time has come," he said, "the time for the reckless one who dares to create without a mate."

Hillsovereign Defiance

NIMBIA WADED across the stream and addressed herself to the ring of djinns. She performed no bold display, but the gray began to dissolve away. But rather than into a riot of color, it transformed into a field of deepest black.

From the hiding place, Astron squinted to shield his eyes from the glare of the sparks that danced around the circle of djinns. He drew his membranes into place, and that helped even more. In the smoothness of the deep ebony, there was the beginning of subtle movements and then a texturing that rippled across the field of view from left to right. An occasional glint of light, reflecting from an unseen source, gave a sheen to the surface like light reflected from a pond at sunset, highlighting at first regularly arranged depressions and then ribs and furrows that oscillated in sinuous patterns.

With each passing moment, the texture of the surface changed from one form to another. Astron watched fascinated, not able to predict what would happen next, but delighting in each new variation as it emerged. The effect was totally unlike the presentations of either of the other two hillsovereigns. The slow melodic pace soothed, rather than agitated with jerks and starts. Astron glanced at the high king, wondering what his judgment would be.

"Enough," Finvarwin said. "I let us view longer to give you the benefit of the doubt. But there is little there to distract one from a boredom greater even than the attempt of Vastowen. The punishment can be no less. To Prydwin with your underhill, Nimbia. It is for hillsovereigns who are proficient in their art to hold sway over the fey."

"Sentrymen, to your duty." Prydwin motioned from his litter. "Arrange an escort and bring her with Thuvia. It will be a pleasure deciding which will be first."

"Never," Nimbia suddenly shouted in a voice almost as deep as that of a male. "I will not meekly submit like Vastowen, just because a few wish it so. Our traditions are ancient ones, but there are times when even they must be disobeyed."

She kicked at the dagger of the first sentryman who approached, sending the blade twirling to the ground. Then scrambling in front of him, she retrieved the knife before the surprised guard could react. With a wide swipe, she spun about, waving off the others who had begun to approach.

She looked at those who stood near the high king and then at the sentrymen converging from across the stream. "You all saw the images," she shouted. "You do not need the age of Finvarwin to search for small subtle differences. Be true to what your eyes have shown you. Mine was a true creation, a difficult balance of predator and prey. Prydwin's was no more than the bubbling flow of plasma, thick pastes swirling with convection in a heated pot."

Except for the closing sentrymen, no one moved. Finvarwin squinted at Nimbia, and then shook his head. "Your underhill is no better protected than all the rest, Nimbia," the high king said. "Against all the rest, eventually, it will fall. You are dealing with the inevitable. Prydwin has offered to accept you as his mate. Go with him in peace. Perhaps together the two of you will combine to produce an imagination greater than either of its parts — just as the fourth dictum states."

"Prydwin!" Nimbia spat. "Never." She waved the dagger in the air. "Who among you has the courage to act as his heart tells him?" she called out. "The courage to aid a lady of the realm when she calls in distress?"

"The hill sovereign speaks with too much boldness for one defending herself alone," Prydwin said. "Fan out and cover all of the trails. She may have aid just beyond our view."

"That is the signal that we start to move." Kestrel tugged at Astron's arm. "I doubt it will do us any good to be mistaken for part of the losing party."

Astron shrugged off Kestrel's hand. "The one named Finvarwin is one that we need to interrogate further. Perhaps more than any other he would know of harebell pollen and even the ultimate precept."

"Yes, the old one certainly," Kestrel whispered back. "But at a time when not so many are about. Now we must be going — before it is too late. Being hunted in two realms should be enough, even for a demon."

The ring started closing in on Nimbia. Astron glanced over his shoulder in the dimness. Kestrel was right. There was a path leading through the dense underbrush, and he should lead, because he was more familiar with what they would encounter.

Kestrel also had been right about how to get the imps into a bottle the demon thought. The way the human had planned to manipulate the wizards at Phoebe's cabin was something no demon would have conceived on his own. For the dozenth time, he realized there was much about the mortal that he wished to learn.

But the words Kestrel spoke were sometimes so unexpected and peculiar that Astron could not fully comprehend the intent: duty to oneself rather than a prince, lures for gold djinns when none such existed, or traveling through the flame for Phoebe and no other.

Perhaps mere words would not be enough to unravel the mysteries of men. Perhaps their experiences would have to be sampled before understanding could come. Astron glanced one final time at Phoebe and Kestrel, standing close together with their arms about each other, and made up his mind.

He stripped away the hood and cape from his back. Gripping the book of thaumaturgy firmly in both hands, he suddenly sprang out from the cover of the heavy leaves. The sentryman standing nearest turned in the direction of the rustling sound, but grappled for his dagger too slowly to defend himself as Astron rushed forward. The demon swung the book high overhead and then crashed it down on the skull of the startled guard.

The fey crumpled to the ground. Astron staggered to retain his balance and somehow managed to tuck the bulky volume under his arm. He bounded down the hillock toward where Nimbia still waved a dagger of her own. A shout of alarm went up from the onlookers. Everyone seemed to freeze in his or her tracks like ice sculptures on a winter day. Astron felt the beginning of a compelling pressure in the depths of his thoughts.

He grimaced in resistance, pulling his face into a tight little ball, forcing the mental probes away. Through eyes half closed, he ran to Nimbia and extended his free hand. As he did, she cautiously lowered her dagger.

"To safety, through the underbrush," Astron shouted as he closed. "If no one else will defend you, then I am the one." Nimbia hesitated a moment, but then firmly clasped Astron's outstretched wrist. He felt a surprising tingling when the smoothness of her skin touched his, but pushed the sensation away. Almost jerking Nimbia from her feet like pulling a weed from a garden, he reversed direction and began racing back up the hill.

The pressure against his thoughts increased. The fey dealt with a demon by force of will, not slashing blades. He felt the probes of many minds mold into one. "Stop, desist," a voice inside his head seemed to say. "We are many and you are one. You cannot resist the combined might of us all."

Astron stumbled over a small rock, but continued his climb. His limbs began to stiffen. The panic in his stembrain stirred from its slumber. As they reached the sentryman Astron had felled, Nimbia drew even with the demon. In half a dozen more steps, she was tugging on the grip between them, pulling Astron forward into the cover of the bush.

"Why did you do that?" Kestrel shouted as the pair ducked under the leaf. "Have you gone mad? Has some wizard put you under his control?"

"I do not know for certain," Astron said thickly. He waved at Phoebe and then dropped his arm heavily to his side. "But then I would not have had to, if you had explained — explained why you rescued your wizard when you could have been safely away from her cabin."

Merging Minds

A DAGGER soared into the underbrush over Astron's head, entangling in the drooping leaves. Retreat deeper into the foliage was an immediate necessity or else Nimbia would not be the only one captured by hillsovereign Prydwin.

But Astron's thoughts became much more sluggish. His limbs would barely move. It was difficult enough understanding the words of both Kestrel and Nimbia as they spoke in their respective tongues.

"There are only three of you!" Nimbia exclaimed. "And none from my own underhill as I had supposed."

Another dagger crashed into the canopy. Kestrel pushed Phoebe to the ground out of its path. "Well, what is the rest of the plan, demon?" he asked. "You know this place as we do not. In what direction do we proceed?"

"Only three," Nimbia repeated, "but then effective, nonetheless. Prydwin's kind are so used to his will being obeyed without resistance that his sentrymen have little chance to do more than serve as a frame for the presentation of his creations. As I think of it now, none of my kind would have succeeded. The daggers were too many. A bold action, demon, was precisely what was needed."

Her grip tightened in his hand. "Come," she said. "If we escape back to my own underhill, even though you are not one of the fey, you will be rewarded."

Nimbia turned into the darkness toward the huge trunk and pulled Astron after. He clutched the book of thaumaturgy to his chest and struggled as best he could not to stumble. Dimly, he was aware of Kestrel and Phoebe following behind.

The little light that filtered through the overhanging leaves vanished altogether. Nimbia pulled a gnarled root from her belt and, with her free hand, extended it overhead. The tuber glowed with a feeble yellow light like a dying candle that just managed to illuminate the obstacles that lay in their way.

The thick trunks that supported the overhang grew closer together. Aboveground, suckers caused more than one stumble as they ran. Grub-like insects with bodies as big as the arm of a djinn scurried out of their way. Rasps and loud clicks blended with the stomp of their feet against the ground.

For how long they raced, Astron could not tell. Except for Nimbia's glowroot, the darkness was as deep as the void in his own realm. His chest began to hurt from the exertion. Sharp pains crackled through his knees. He was a demon of contemplation and not used to such stressing of his body. What little weaving he was capable of to supply his basic needs was being severely overburdened.

Nimbia stopped at the base of a particularly large trunk. She gestured upward and released her grip on Astron's hand. Like an acrobatic gibbon in the realm of men, she grabbed hold of a low branch and swung herself upward. Kestrel grunted in understanding. He cupped his hands to give Phoebe a boost. With Nimbia astride the limb and pulling, Kestrel pushed from below. Phoebe clawed her way onto the limb in a tumble of cape and long skirt, and Kestrel followed. Only Astron remained on the ground.

The pressure to submit grew in intensity. Astron found he could barely move. With agonizing slowness, he raised the book for Phoebe to grasp and then cupped the branch in his hand.

"Hurry," Kestrel whispered. "They cannot be far behind. "

"It is the contest of wills," Nimbia said. "The followers of Prydwin command him to be still." The thought that Kestrel and Nimbia had no way of understanding each other floated across Astron's mind. He should serve as translator, but somehow he no longer cared. Perhaps it was hopeless to run further. Eventually, they would be found anyway. Why not at least take a rest at the base of this bush, rather than exert himself anymore?

Astron felt his grip on the branch loosen. He slid to the ground. Slumped in a heap at the base, perhaps he would not be seen. Or even if they did see him, what did it matter? Curled up in a tight ball like an armadillo, a crooked smile formed on his face.

But just as consciousness began to fade, a thought of piercing sharpness ricocheted through his head. Resist, it commanded. I am the closest and have the greater influence. Resist their wills because I wish it so.

Nimbia! Astron stirred from his dimness. She was a wizard like the rest. Her thoughts churned with the others. And somehow they were different — strong because of her nearness. But the crushing drive to dominate was held in restraint. Her will was adding to his, repelling the others, giving his own consciousness room in which to function, time to construct barriers against the pressure to quit.

Astron vaguely became aware of many hands tugging on his body and of being lifted into the air. He felt the rough fiber of the stringy bark against his skin. He flailed past the first horizontal level of branches and then several tiers more. Finally, he felt an embrace that held him firm. Nimbia's arms coiled around him. He smelled the exotic aroma of her closeness and heard the rustle of her tunic against his own.

"Do not fight me, demon," she whispered. "Blend your will with mine. Cling to me and do not let go. When they pass below and do not find us, their command will be for you to come forth, and you must not."

The glowroots danced in the distance, and a line of sentrymen fanning out along the crude path on which they had fled. Phoebe sucked in her breath. The four stiffened into nervous silence.

As Nimbia had predicted, the voices inside his head changed. No longer was he implored to stop and freeze. Instead, he felt a growing urge to take action, to bolt forth and run into the open, to flee the dismal dark cover into the gentle light of the glen.

Astron's limbs began to tremble. With all the concentration left to his command, he clutched Nimbia harder, willing his arms to stiffen. He must hold on.

Nimbia seemed to sense his struggle. Her grip tightened, and her thoughts blended with his. He felt the strength of her inner being, like a vault of steel. He poured his own essence into it, molding to the contours of the container, pressing against her like an annealing of the alchemists that could not be torn away.

The followers of Prydwin drew closer, peering into the inky darkness and listening for some sound of their flight. Some passed in the distance to either side, but three came close to the enormous bush in which they hid.

Come forward, the voices commanded. Come forward. It is the will of the fey. Astron slammed shut his eyes and crushed Nimbia to him. She gasped for breath from the force of his embrace. He felt her nails dig into his back, even though the thickness of his tunic. The trembling of his limbs shook his entire body in spasms. He ached from the effort to

157

remain silent and still.

He tried to keep the image of Nimbia's in focus, pushing against the surface of her being everywhere he could. He felt her accepting his struggle, welcoming the intertwining of what he was with her. Beyond the quiet strength that she projected, there were recesses of her existence that went beyond the immediate struggle — hints of great pride in her creations, the agony of defeat in competition with Prydwin, the frustration of the petty jealousies of her courtiers, and a profound melancholy that perhaps even she did not understand.

The images fluttered in Astron's mind, then faded away. If he were struggling to dominate her across the barrier of the flame, he would have pursued them further, exposed them to view, analytically picked the one most painful, and then exploited it until her will was his own to do with as he chose.

But Nimbia was sharing his struggle. To meld the fullness of her strength to his, she had to expose the foundations from which it sprang. She bared the innermost essence of her being in trust. He could do no more than accept the gift that was given.

The urge to howl in pain rose in Astron's chest. He clamped his jaws shut, feeling that his teeth would explode into fragmented shards from the pressure to remain silent. Every muscle in his body ached from the conflicting commands to stay immobile on one hand and to dance into fevered action on the other.

He felt the strong walls of Nimbia's mental vault buckle on the bottom and the band about the mouth wrench apart in a silent scream of ripping metal. Although he strained to resist, the top stretched wide and, as if pushed by giant thumbs, the bottom bulged upward toward the opening. Helplessly, he felt the container wrenched inside out, exposing his own being to the relentless will of the others.

But then, just when he could stand remaining silent no longer, the pressure lessened. Almost in disbelief, Astron darted a glance out of one eye to the ground below. Whistled commands sang through the leaves. The sentrymen were moving on through the brush.

As the searchers departed, so did the pressure in Astron's head. The trembling of his limbs slowed to random twitches and then stopped altogether. His own consciousness expanded to fill all of his being. Almost with a sense of reluctance, he felt Nimbia's presence within him withdraw as well.

No one moved, however. All four remained frozen, lest the smallest sound draw the attention of Prydwin's sentrymen back to where they hid in silence. The whistles and calls grew fainter until only the buzz and click of the insects remained. After an immeasurable time, Nimbia shifted slightly and uncoiled her arms from around Astron's back. With muscles stiff from fatigue, he released her as well. Nimbia pulled the glowroot from her pouch and brought it up to eye level. She looked him in the eye and then darted her glance aside. A hint of redness blossomed in her cheeks.

"Forgive me," she said. "When we struggled to resist the will of the others, I could not help but learn things that you probably do not want to share."

"And I of you," Astron responded. "I sensed I should not but —"

"If those are thank-yous you are exchanging, they can come later," Kestrel cut in. "No doubt the others will return this way when they have convinced themselves they have lost our trail. Ask the nabob if she knows of a more permanent shelter we can reach before nightfall."

Astron shrugged and told Nimbia what Kestrel had said. Serving as the intermediary came easily now. The conversation flowed almost as swiftly as if they all spoke the same tongue.

"There is no nightfall," Nimbia explained. "The soft blue that you saw in the glen remains eternally the same. Finvarwin and the old ones before him say that our realm is a globe centered inside a hollow sphere that radiates light and heat uniformly. There are no days, no seasons. It is the reason that we find such delight in our creations.

"And as to safety, we will journey to the hill under which I am the absolute ruler. Perhaps, before the other sovereigns decide on how they will combine their forces and attack, there will be enough time to create again, create before the next judging with something that even Finvarwin cannot deny is the best."

"Would not moving and staying hidden be better?" Kestrel asked. "To face again the pronouncements of your high king seems fraught with risk."

"I must," Nimbia said. "It is my duty, my duty to my people."

"Duty," Astron repeated. "I know of duty or at least I thought I did. I come to your realm in search for the answer to a riddle because my prince demands."

"Come." Nimbia touched her finger to Astron's lips. "The human is right. We must get underhill before Prydwin's sentrymen return."

Under the Hill

FOR WHAT would be hours in the realm of men, Nimbia led Astron and the others through the darkness of the brush. They encountered no sign of Prydwin's followers and eventually emerged on the edge of a clearing similar to the glen in which they had first arrived. Rather than slope down to a stream, however, the grass-covered ground rose from where they stood. From all sides of the open space, at first gently and then with increasing slope, the soft greenness under foot tilted upward to form a high hillock in the very center. Like a great upside-down bowl thrust against the ground, the bulge dominated the landscape. Its broad, flat apex stood higher even than the crest of the bushes that edged the clearing.

As Nimbia moved out into the open, the ground underfoot began to vibrate with a great rumbling. The music of pipes and lyres filled the air. The hillock shuddered slightly and then began to move. The ground parted with a clean horizontal slit. On dozens of stout pillars, the central portion of the hillock rose majestically into the air like a cake rising in a warm oven.

Brilliant lights, laughter, and music sweet and pure poured out of the opening. Long banquet tables groaned under piles of glistening fruit and heavy flagons sparkled with a patina of dew. Scores of lithe dancers pirouetted in complex patterns. Laughing jugglers kept dozens of small objects whirling above their heads.

"Nimbia, Nimbia," dozens of joyful voices called out.

"Our hillsovereign returns."

"She has triumphed at last."

"Finvarwin has been pleased. Look, he gives her three changelings as a prize for her great worth."

"Alert the scribes and the tellers. There will be work for all."

A throne of polished stone was pushed into a position of prominence on a dais bathed with colored lights. Two long lines of young pages formed on either side. Small girls began strewing delicate flower petals from the base outward onto the grass of the clearing. Stout-cheeked musicians stuck long-stemmed pipes into bowls filled with nearly solid gels. With straining lungs, they forced upward bubbles of air that burst and sprayed all those about to their laughing delight. Fragrant odors tickled Astron's nostrils and beckoned him forward.

Nimbia said nothing. With a grim smile, she walked on the path laid for her and beckoned Astron and the others to follow. Accepting a cape embroidered and encrusted with jewels, she mounted the steps and sat on her throne. Nimbia looked about the gaily-decorated surroundings, and her face saddened.

"I do not return in triumph," she sighed. "And these that accompany me are the reason that I return at all."

Like a festival cut short by a sudden storm, the music stopped as did the clank of flagon and flatware from those who prepared the feast. Smiles fell from the faces of those nearest. Eyes lowered. Many looked away. For a dozen heartbeats, the silence filled the hilltop. Even the creak of boots and rustle of tunics against one another stilled.

Then, from the periphery of the hillock, a single piper began playing a slow, sad melody. Others caught the tone and added to it. One of the females close to Nimbia choked on a small sob. Tears began to glisten on the faces of a dozen more. In an instant, the infectious joy transformed into a chilling sadness as if there had been no other emotion before.

Nimbia nodded in acceptance of the changing mood. She motioned over the heads of those nearest and the ground began to vibrate as it had when they had approached. The narrow band of pale blue sky started to shrink into nothingness. Like a great piston sinking into a cylinder, the surface on which everyone stood descended into the earth. In an instant, the hilltop again rested firmly on the ground.

The bright lights reflected by the jeweled panels and mirrors shone with undiminished intensity. Even though Nimbia had retreated underground, the area around her throne remained far brighter than the daylight outside. As the descent halted, Astron saw lit passageways radiating in all directions. Great bins lined the hallways, like the walls of Phoebe's cabin. From some spilled the powders and woods that the demon recognized as essential for the summoning of great djinns. Others bulged with strange prickly spheroids, covered with sharp barbs or intricate lattices of thorns. In the distance were rows of doors and dark cross-corridors radiating farther into the earth. The extent of the queen's underhill could not easily be judged.

Two of the pages, taller than the rest, pushed each other timidly from the crowd that had gathered about the throne. Each wore a tunic embroidered with the same designs as those on Nimbia's cape. Their copper daggers were sheathed on belts inlaid with gold.

"Perhaps what you created survived despite Finvarwin's judgment?" the first one asked.

"My creation will live on unaided for a lifetime or more." Nimbia nodded. "Such strength am I sure that it possesses. But without the thoughts of others, it will not expand to be more than what it is now. Eventually, it will grow sluggish and decay."

Nimbia looked over the heads of the assembly. She closed her eyes to absorb the mood of the piping that now swelled to a persistent resonance that could not be ignored. Tears appeared from fluttering eyelids. She slumped into the folds of her cape like a bat retreating to sleep in the blaze of a sun at noon.

"The penalty is a severe one." She opened her eyes again at last. "Servitude to Prydwin for us all. This underhill to become one of his, rather than our own. We will be toiling to carry his baskets of pollens, blowing on the pipes as long as he commands, plucking the blossoms that he decrees, whether they are part of our harmonies or not."

"You should not have attempted it without a mate," the second page said. "All of us regard your craft to be of the greatest quality, as strong as your own great beauty. But forgive me, my queen, even so, the challenge was far too great."

Nimbia studied the second page a long time before speaking. "You knew of the risk as well as any other," she said. "You and every other page underhill. Almost any would have sufficed, provided that he had the strength of heart."

"But it could not be me," the page stepped back. He waved his arm about those who clustered around the queen. "Perhaps someone else," he muttered, "someone more worthy. Your beauty is too great. One such as I would never have a chance."

"A single page," Nimbia repeated, "And yet not one came forward. Not one chose to accompany his queen, despite what decorum demanded. I do not understand. Can the prize be of so little value?"

"A prize has greater value the less it is shared." A third voice, deeper than the first two, sounded from the rear. A male slightly more heavyset than the rest push his way forward, the lines of a frown etched into his forehead as if drawn by a plow. Dark black ringlets of hair curled above clear lake-blue eyes. He was older than the other pages, and several of the females followed him with keen interest.

"This is not the time and place to air old accusations, Lothal." Nimbia stirred on her throne. "They are no less true now than they were when the two of us —"

"The rages have cooled, my sovereign," Lothal interrupted, bowing deeply with an almost jeering smile on his face. "I do not come forth pressing a suit that you have more than adequately demonstrated I can never win. I speak merely as another loyal and concerned subject for the benefit of us all."

Nimbia stiffened but said nothing. She motioned for Lothal to continue.

The courtier bowed a second time and then stood to face Nimbia with his hands on his hips as if he were the sovereign and the queen his subject. "Your wit is a sharp one. Despite everything else, I will always have admiration for that. Perhaps, from what you see happening again and again, you can finally deduce a basic truth for your conduct."

He turned to face the others, extending his arms in great arcs, hands opened outward. "The queen can have anyone here she chooses." He looked at several of the females who wore bands about their waists with the same markings as those of a nearby male. "Even ones already bound can hardly resist the great persuasion of her beauty we all know that in our hearts."

Lothal whirled abruptly and again faced Nimbia. "Anyone she chooses, that is, so long as her choice is for one only." His cheeks flushed. Veins stood out on his neck. "I did not submit to share with another, and by all that lives of its own volition, neither will any other here. Amend your ways, Nimbia. Change the greed for more than one. That is all you deserve, despite the loveliness you possess. Amend your ways, and then a champion will come forward to share the tasks of creation with his queen."

"I was faithful to you from the first day to the last," Nimbia said. "It was your jealousies and no more, Lothal, that churned in your heart. You saw evil where there was none. Nothing I could have done would have convinced you otherwise." Nimbia threw up her hands. "And we could not create, so long as your own inner being was so troubled."

"If you were not queen, I would not let such assertions go unchallenged," Lothal shot back. "You try to use the power of your station to gain what even your beauty cannot grasp."

"Challenge whatever you will." Nimbia shook her head and pulled the edges of her cape in tightened fists, with knuckles showing white. "I give you leave as I have given you leave each time before. Try to find any proof that I was ever other than loving. You cannot, because none was ever there. Come, Lothal, I would forget the pain and accept you even now, if it would spark the creation that would save our underhill."

Nimbia looked at Lothal expectantly, but his jaw was set. He would speak no more.

"We waste the time of all those that have assembled here," she sighed. "And there is little time that is left." She waved her arm at the banquet rooms beyond. "Feast, my people. Make merry while you can. Prydwin's sentrymen will come for us all soon enough."

The mournful melody of the pipers stopped. There was a moment's pause and then they began again, this time with the lively air that Astron had first heard when he arrived. Tentatively, two of the younger females began to dance. With a sudden enthusiasm, three of the pages mimicked their steps. Nimbia started clapping her hands. A smile reappeared on her face. In what seemed like an instant, the mood transformed into the gaiety it had been before.

"I do not understand." Phoebe raised her voice above the music. "What has happened to her? The moods of the woman on the throne change faster than the purest quicksilver."

"My previous sojourns were brief," Astron said. "I witnessed the ring of djinns for the first time just as you did."

"The mysteries of the realm can wait for later," Kestrel said. "More important is the reason why we came. If this Nimbia thinks we are her savior, then ask her for a boon before she forgets. What does she know of the things we seek?"

Astron hesitated. Nimbia had saved him from the sentrymen of Prydwin — far more than what he had done for her. And the passions shown by the fey evidently were quite similar to those of men. He would like to have listened for much longer.

"Excuse me, Queen Nimbia," he said, "but I have a request — knowledge in exchange for the small service we have performed on your behalf. If perhaps you know the location of harebell pollen or how to gain audience with a sage among you who knows the riddle of the ultimate precept ..."

Nimbia stopped in mid-clap. She turned and regarded Astron with an amused smile. Then she broke into a gale of laughter, clasping her sides and poking her elbows at whoever was the closest.

"Yes, harebell pollen," she said. "That is all it would take. Who needs the logical precision of the male to temper the leaps of intuition if harebell pollen could be tossed through the ring? Even Prydwin's greatest triumphs: the realms of order and chaos — both could be challenged in a single judging. Yes, harebell pollen indeed."

Nimbia tried to say more but she clasped her sides again, unable to speak. Astron looked from side to side for an explanation, but saw only other mirthful faces. His nose wrinkled. He turned back to face Kestrel with a shrug.

Nimbia suddenly stopped laughing. She tapped Astron on the shoulder. Her face was sober. "It is the way of the fey," she explained. "We cannot sip life in only half measures, but must drink deeply from the cup of emotions. It is no less than the first dictum, 'reality mirrors passion'. How else can we create with a vividness that will live of its own volition?"

Astron started to reply but Nimbia shook her head.

"For now, no more words," she said. "Do not disturb the joyousness of the feast. I owe my people no less." She reached out and touched his arm. "Even though you are no more than a demon, I wish that you would abide with me for a while. Abide with me, since your saving of a queen might not yet be complete."

Power of the Fey

ASTRON BLEW out all the candles except for the one on the far end of the oaken table. The remaining light was feeble, but he had had more than enough time to get familiar with even the tiniest details in the small circular room.

His door was snugly shut. A row of small gouges lined the frame. Upon each rising from sleep, Kestrel would add another mark to those already there. Now there were fifteen.

The apprehension about surviving the transition into the realm of the fey had long since faded, but with each passing day, Astron sensed Kestrel's growing restlessness. Time flowed at different rates in every realm, but with each new mark, the demon reasoned, the human would multiply the total by one hundred. The woodcutter would become less sure of what would happen even if they were able to accomplish the task before them and return to the realm of men.

Astron too felt the tension. There was no sign of Gaspar's minions yet, but it could only be a matter of time before they appeared. And despite the urgency, he had achieved no new progress toward his goal. The growing frustration made his stembrain active. A feeling of constant uneasiness ached just below his consciousness. He could not still the rumbling, no matter how hard he tried. With each passing tick of time, the chances of the survival of his prince and hence his own shrunk even more. Something had to be done soon, no matter how interesting the other distractions.

They were not prisoners, but Nimbia's sentrymen made clear with the force of their thoughts that wandering around underhill was highly discouraged. After the queen had dismissed them, they had not seen her again. Astron and his companions were left to their own devices until she saw fit to call them back to her presence.

The idle time had not been a total waste, since there was much he had learned. The oaken table with the candle was straight on three sides, while the fourth was curved to meet the contour of the stone wall to which it was pressed, even though square cells would have been a much more efficient use of space. Using stone instead of wood must stress the mechanism that raised and lowered the hilltop, but evidently, such practicalities were not the concern of the fey.

Next to the candle, hung from a cantilevered scaffolding made of twigs and branches like a tiny crane, was a water sack from one of the large vines that grew aboveground. Astron had pierced and drained the bladder and then refilled it with lamp oil obtained from another resinous herb. With bits of copper wire hooked into the surrounding leaves, the spherical globe was elongated and flattened, distorting it into a thin vertical disk.

At the other end of the table, the book of thaumaturgy that Astron had obtained from the skyskirr stood upright in a scaffolding similar to the first. The candle flame flickered through the orb of oil and cast a diffuse glow of light on the upright parchment, illustrating an image quite similar to the one Astron had constructed on the bench.

Astron studied the illustration for a moment more and then the arcane symbols written beneath it. The abstractions had been difficult to grasp at first, but the examples had helped a great deal. He turned to the bag of oil and moved it to a mark he had calculated before, roughly midway between the candle and book.

The diffuse halo of light on the parchment coalesced into a much sharper dot. Astron grunted in satisfaction. He cupped his hand in front of his lens so that only its very center received the candle glow and watched the focus on the book decrease to a single point of whiteness.

The demon moved the position of the book toward the candle and then adjusted the lens to regain the proper focus. He measured the distances from page to oil bag and oil bag to candle and checked the results with the predictions of the formula. After a half-dozen trials, he blew out the remaining light and sat in the darkness, contemplating what he had learned.

The ones who call themselves masters in the realm of men treated knowledge in strange ways, he thought. The basic principles of bending rays of light had no intrinsic connection to thaumaturgy or any other of the crafts known to mortals. But because these laws were used by practitioners of the magical arts, they were shrouded in secret like the rest. One went to a thaumaturge for telescopes or heating lenses, even though a glassblower could construct what was needed just as well without any recourse to the art if he knew a few simple formulas. Unlike Prince Elezar's riddles, which extracted a price but once, knowledge in the realm of men was hoarded and reused, demanding a fee each time.

Astron's reverie was broken by a pounding on the door. "The hillsovereign commands your presence," a voice on the other side said.

The demon scrambled out of his repose, opened the door, and burst into the hall. Perhaps at last he could continue the search for the answer to Gaspar's riddle.

He was joined shortly in the narrow curving hallway by Kestrel and Phoebe. While Astron had pondered the mysteries of thaumaturgy, they had spent much time together learning the fundamentals of the language of the fey. And the demon could not help noticing how much stronger the attraction between the two of them had become.

He had no chance to comment on the fact, however. In a few heartbeats, they were ushered into the presence of Nimbia in the central throne room. The queen wore a gown of iridescent pink that billowed like a parachute and filled the high chair on which she sat. On either side, two pages stood at solemn attention, their copper spear points straight and aimed at the sculptured ceiling overhead. The openness that was present when Astron had first arrived had been replaced by substantial-looking panels that blocked everything behind from view. Footfalls echoed from the unadorned walls. Somewhere in the background, pipers still trilled melancholy airs.

"I apologize for my lack of attention," Nimbia said as they entered, "but the emotion had to run its course. Nothing has changed, but at least now I can be a more proper hostess."

"How do you seek?" Astron ignored the courtesy. He reviewed the questions that he had decided to ask at the first opportunity. "I deduce from what I have seen that you command the ring of djinns to bridge between realms that you have never seen before. How do you know they are there? Would not the action be one of discovery, rather than creation?"

A weak smile appeared on Nimbia's face. "I see our control of your kind is not something you ponder lightly," she said.

"I appreciate the extent of your power," Astron answered. "The youngest hatchlings are taught to avoid the lure of the fey." He wrinkled his nose. "But even the mightiest djinn cannot respond to an order that is ill-formed. He cannot pass through the barrier to another realm unless he is directed there. If he does not know it and neither do you, there is no way an opening can be formed."

"But we do know the realms where the ring is commanded," Nimbia replied. "We know them because they are formed by our thought. We do not discover other realms, demon. They are created by the fey exactly as you have heard us say."

Astron opened his mouth to speak again, and then slammed it shut as the significance of what Nimbia had said began to sink into his stembrain. She spoke casually, as if what she said was of no great matter, but the words brought forth images as staggering as those in Palodad's lair.

"You *create* realms," he said, trying to fight off the stunned numbness that began to tingle through his limbs. "You are the ones responsible for the realm of demons, the realm of men, and all the others."

"No, no, not the demons," Nimbia corrected. "As you well know, your realm spans the space between all the others. It must have existed far before the oldest memories of our own. Somehow, it is different from the rest.

"And as for the realm of men, none of my brethren would admit to such an act — conceiving something so malformed. Perhaps ages ago, before our art reached its present level of perfection, it was accomplished — or maybe it was the other way around, we are all the product of the fancies of men. Otherwise still, both could be the discarded first attempts to achieve perfection by yet some other beings. If that is so, it explains why so many of the realms are similar."

"What do you mean?" Astron persisted. "What realms?"

"Of the ones you saw on the slopes of the glen," Nimbia answered, "I was the author of the last. I conceived the waves of black and the forces that gave them motive power. It was my thoughts that strained against the compressive forces that push against all the realms, trying to crush them to nothingness."

"I am sorry," Astron said. "You speak too quickly. I do not understand."

Bubbles of Reality

NIMBIA'S SMILE broadened slightly beneath her sad eyes. She gestured to one of the sentrymen standing in a doorway at the rear of the throne room. "Pipes and cooling gels," she commanded. "I must explain what to the fey is common knowledge and second nature."

Three pages appeared, each one carrying a bowl of a steaming and viscous liquid. Behind them came three more, these bearing tripods and long metal pipes under their arms. The bowls were set erect in the stands and each of the trio handed a horn.

"You saw the pipers display this art when we returned from the judging," Nimbia said to Astron and the others standing before her. "It is a festive symbolism of what we accomplish with our thought." She pointed in Phoebe's direction. "Let the female start. The brew before her is the most fluid."

Phoebe handled the horn tentatively, but Nimbia waved her on. "Insert the pipe and blow. Show the power of creativity."

Phoebe thrust the flared end of the horn into the clear broth and took a deep breath. She exhaled forcefully and a riot of tiny bubbles cascade to the surface like the foam churned by a river's rapid and then burst.

"Secondly, the man," Nimbia said.

Kestrel frowned but positioned the long pipe into the liquid. He tentatively puffed into the horn and then strengthened his efforts. There was agitation in the broth but little else. Kestrel's brow tightened. He inhaled deeply and pressed his lips about the mouthpiece of the horn. With bulging cheeks and eyes, he forced his breath through the long passageway into the brew.

The surface rippled and then a single tiny bubble floated upward. Kestrel lowered the pipe from his mouth, breathing deeply from the effort.

"And now the demon," Nimbia said. "Show who is the mightiest of breath."

Astron stepped forward and placed his hands on the pipe. He had no great need for moving large quantities of air in and out of his body and doubted that his strength matched that of a man. Nevertheless, he blew as hard as he could into the resistance.

For several heartbeats, he strained and nothing happened. He concentrated on constricting his chest as far as he could. He clamped his elbows to his sides and strained with the muscles in his back. Then, just as he was preparing to abandon the effort, he felt a sudden lessening of resistance. In the broth, the beginning of a bubble began to emerge from the bell of the horn. With a hatchling-like delight, he pointed at what he had done but halted in mid-gesture as the fluid collapsed the emerging bulge back into the pipe.

Nimbia nodded. "Imagine each realm as a bubble in a great sea, resisting the surrounding pressure by outward forces of its own. If the powers of expansion are insufficient, the bubble collapses into nothingness; but so long as they are strong enough, the realm survives.

"And what is the nature of this outward-directed power? Nothing less than the belief that the realm does indeed exist. If I can formulate a consistent system that has enough clarity in my mind, a rift occurs in the great universal sea. A tiny bubble forms that pushes back the oppressive forces and exists where there was nothing before.

"The effort required is a staggering one, far, far greater than what you experienced with the gels. It is not everyone who can do it. But to the extent that I give my creation a compelling richness, others will also become enamored of its beauty. They, too, will think of it often, adding to the forces that keep it alive. So long as we ponder its being, the crush of destruction can be withstood."

Astron wrinkled his nose. He pondered what he had heard. "It sounds like the balloons in the realm of men," he said. He propped the mouthpiece end of the horn onto the floor and the bell end rose from the clinging viscosity in the bowl. "Are you the only ones with such a power?"

"Beings in other realms can perform these creations as well," Nimbia said. "Why, even humans with their fancies and tales for the sagas have created universes, even though they know not what they have done. Their passions can sometimes be as great as our own. The recording of these ideas on parchment is an analogue to what we do with our song tellers — spreading knowledge of the creation, so that others can experience the wonder and aid in its existence."

Nimbia's eyes took on a faraway look. "As for the ability of the fey, it is the nature of our very own realm — the dictums of magic that are part of it, the storm of our emotion; these are the things that make us perhaps the most proficient."

"When the tales are put away and men read them no longer?" Phoebe looked up from where she was stirring the thinnest of the three fluids with the end of her horn. She spoke in a halting voice, the unfamiliar words of a new language setting heavy on her lips.

"If the creation has by that time not achieved a sufficient vitality of its own," Nimbia answered. "If it has flaws and inconsistencies like a poorly constructed watch, it will eventually run down and be compressed back into the nothingness of the sea — just as you saw with the attempt of the demon."

Nimbia's eyes widened. "But if the construction has been a skilled one, with sentient beings of its own that believe in themselves, in their own existence, then the realm remains. Those inside provide the outward pressure that keeps the crushing forces of the all-enveloping sea at bay — a true creation of great art.

"That is what we strive for. It is the ultimate goal to which any fey can aspire — to create a new realm equal to our own, one that exists in and of itself, with all the thought being provided from inside, rather than the continued attention of those who first brought it into life.

"You saw the vitality of my creation when viewed through the circle of djinns. It lived, lived of its own volition! There should have been no way for Finvarwin to judge it inferior to empty motions of Prydwin's — despite the fact that what I did was accomplished without a mate."

"If you think the outcome of your efforts not to be fairly determined," Astron said, "then why do you try? With all that you command, I would think that there are other amusements that would serve as well."

Nimbia shook her head. "There is nothing to compare to the joy of creation. The sense of accomplishment of bringing into being an existence out of the void. To be denied that pleasure is the greatest penalty that the high king can exact."

She waved her arm about the throne room. "The melancholy is not only my own. Even though only a king or queen is able to force a realm to spring from the void, everyone who serves contributes his or her thoughts to make it grow. They all savor the feeling of accomplishment, the thrill and wonder when the realm takes on a sense of being of its own, the pride when other underhills view what they have wrought."

Fresh tears glistened in the corners of Nimbia's eyes. "It is the duty of a hillsovereign to provide the basis so that all can share. Her own sadness is all the greater because she must bear the responsibility of so many in addition to her own."

"Duty," Astron said. "Is not that due from the subject to the prince? You seem to state that it is the other way around."

"The other realms have witnessed this melancholy, although they do not understand." Nimbia ran on, not hearing the interruption. "In times past, other underhills unable or forbidden to create on their own have been reduced to watching. But just to observe realms who owe none of their existence to your craft makes the restrictions all the more heart-piercing. Usually, we remain underground, so as to block out even the hint of pipes from others who are more fortunate."

"Then you do look into the realm of men?" Kestrel asked. "It could be that our tales are the same not by mere luck after all."

"My own underhill has not viewed the affairs of humans," Nimbia replied, "but that does not preclude the actions of many others. And as you probably have surmised, the ring of djinns can be seen through from either side. No doubt if you have legends of strange beings, piping music, and forced gaiety appearing out of the mists and then vanishing again, it is because of the fey."

Nimbia stopped speaking. She dabbed at one tear on her cheek and stared off into the distance, consumed by her own innermost thoughts.

"We asked before about the ultimate precept," Astron said. "Could it be that it too plays a part in the construction of these creations?"

Nimbia looked back down at Astron. She shook her head. "Of such I have not heard. Our realm is governed by seven dictums of magic, like all the rest. The last two are those of dichotomy and ubiquity, as you well know. They are the basis for the communication with the mighty djinns of your kind."

"Then perhaps one of the others," Astron said.

Nimbia rubbed her cheek dry and flicked back a golden curl over her shoulder. She shrugged again and began reciting as if she were a broodmother instructing her latest clutch. "Of the first I have already spoken — 'reality follows from passion'. Our temperaments are not placid, like those of the skyskirr. Instead, they are the fuel that fires our imaginations when we attempt to wrest a new universe from the void.

"The second, as simply stated — 'strength comes from the lattice' — guides our thoughts as we try to create. It is easier to conceive of a realm with dictums of magic close to our own, rather than more exotic ones about whose existence we can only guess.

"The third is a warning — 'weakness comes from contradiction'," she continued. "As I have already explained, a realm will eventually wind down and stop, because the postulates that we use in its beginning do not mesh into a harmonious whole.

"Of the fourth, even you have probably already heard enough— 'two is greater than one and one'. Somehow, when we are paired as loving mates, the creations are more fertile, more exotic, more likely to live.

"The fifth is stated— 'reap what you sow'. It is the pollens we toss into the rings that somehow unlock the thoughts deepest within us that give rise to our most exciting creations. Each type has its own —"

"Wait. Pollen did you say?" Astron interrupted.

"Yes," Nimbia said. "We do not know for certain how they play a role in the process, but none of the fey attempts to create or embellish without a large supply on hand." She motioned to one of the sentrymen standing in the entryway. He retrieved a small chest that he brought forward and placed at the hillsovereign's feet.

Nimbia opened the arched lid. She reached in to withdraw a prickly sphere similar to the one Astron had seen Vastowen toss into the ring. It was far larger than the others, however, as big as a small melon. Nimbia held it with extended thumbs and forefingers.

Astron studied the globe and, after a moment, understood Nimbia's cautious touch. The entire surface of the orb bristled with clusters of tiny barbs. Smaller hair like shafts radiated in all directions from each of the prickly pylons and, in a blurry haze, these were anchorage for tinier projections still. Beyond the craft of the finest weaver in his own realm, the structure of sharp piercing points iterated into infinitesimals, far smaller than the eye could see.

"We toss pollens through the ring of djinns to seed our thoughts in the void," Nimbia said. "Our success seems greater the more massive they are. To create something of value before Prydwin comes, I would need to use the largest of all, but in my entire underhill I have only this one."

"Are they hard to find?" Phoebe asked. "Could a human wizard help in their retrieval?"

"The flowers that produce them abound in a glen not too far away. The problem is not in harvesting them but harvesting them now. At present, the glen is alive with the hum of its guardians, and no one dares enter until they have gone on their way. After so many did not return,

174

wisely did Finvarwin issue the prohibition."

"We seek a pollen as part of our quest," Astron said.

"This one that you desire, what is its name?"

"This would be called harebell in the realm of men."

Nimbia nodded at the sphere in front of her. "That is why your question on our arrival struck such a melodious chord. Of all that I could wish, they are the only things I have not been able to obtain."

"Harebell pollen, and then you can create," Kestrel said, excited. "Create for Finvarwin so that you can get answers as a boon — answers that Astron seeks." His face broke into a broad grin. "Wipe the tears, Nimbia," he said. "I have a deal for you."

The Paradox of Beauty

ASTRON ADJUSTED the straps that ran across his chest. He had gotten quite used to the tunic and leggings of men, but now the rucksack was a new sensation with the rough fabric rubbing against the stubs of his wings like a poorly fitting shoe over callus on the feet.

Between the columns of the raised hilltop, Kestrel urged him to hurry. Beside the human stood six of Nimbia's sentrymen, each carrying a long copper tipped spear in addition to the dagger at his side. Their faces were rigid with tension. None showed Kestrel's enthusiasm to be under way.

Astron took a step forward and then hesitated. The opening in the wall to the left led to the throne room. He poked his head through the doorway. Nimbia was alone, still sitting on her ceremonial symbol of power where they had left her when the planning was complete.

Despite the short length of his training, Kestrel had been most glib. Whatever dangers lurked in the harebell glen, he had said, they well might not affect human or demon at all. With a modest escort to protect against a chance encounter with Prydwin's forces, he and Astron would fetch the pollen and share with Nimbia what they obtained.

Then, with boosted confidence from the pollen's potency, Nimbia could create something that Finvarwin would approve. They would not wait for the next judging or to see if they could fend off Prydwin's attack, but go directly to the high king for a special presentation. Phoebe could even help in the control of the ring of djinns. At the very least, Finvarwin's previous judgment would be reversed and Nimbia's underhill regain its independent status. With Finvarwin's answer to the riddle and the harebell pollen as payment for Palodad, the old demon would get Elezar restored to power and he, in turn, would explain to Alodar the innocence of Phoebe and Kestrel. With a little luck, everyone would achieve what he or she desired.

When Kestrel had finished, Nimbia's spirits begin to lift. Now, a few hours later, as he prepared to leave, the sadness had vanished from her eyes. She stared off into space, thinking of a possible new creation.

Astron scraped his pack along the doorjamb and Nimbia turned at the distraction. She smiled and beckoned him to enter, "Any more questions, inquisitive one?" she asked as he drew closer.

Astron studied the perfectly sculpted face and graceful limbs. Another unanswered puzzle leaped into his mind. "You spoke of the great melancholy that comes when those of your kind cannot create," he said. "I have seen your tears and I believe. But before we came, before Finvarwin's judgment, what then was the corresponding joy?"

Astron folded his fingertips to his chest. "We shared thoughts in the forest," he continued. "There I glimpsed a sadness even deeper than that which is lifting now."

For a moment, Nimbia did not reply. She sighed and beckoned Astron to sit on the steps leading to her chair. She gathered her jeweled cape about her as he squirmed to get comfortable with the pack pulling on his back.

"Yes, indeed it is a conundrum." Her voice took on a hardened tone. "As you say, I am no less than a sovereign of an underhill. My life should be like the foolish tales that men record in their sagas, with scores of smitten pages vying with one another to do my bidding and any hinted wish their fondest desire. Eventually, from all the rest I would pick the bravest, the kindest, the one most fair. Together we would spend our lives in a blissful happiness, about which others can only dream.

"It is not so, demon." Nimbia shook her head. "No hovering suitors are trying to outdo one another to gain my favor. Most of the males in this underhill seem dumbfounded in my presence. Their self-esteem seems to melt with my smile. Hardly any dare believe that they would succeed against what must be many others and so they do not try.

"And the few that do hold their own value in high regard, the ones that, in desperation, I have run to, offering to subject my will to theirs — without exception, they have proven to love themselves far more than me. To one of them, I have been no more than an object, a trophy to prove yet again his own great worth."

Nimbia sighed. "Even if I were able to accept that part of it, despite how much I might try, the liaisons have never been pleasant. Underneath the bragging of conquest, my mates have been consumed with insane jealousies, irrational fears that they cannot forever hold me as their own, and that I will tire and shame them in front of another.

"It is a fantasy, demon. I do not fully understand why, but for one such as me, there is no such thing as living happily ever after."

Nimbia looked at Astron with eyes once again filling with sorrow. He felt a strange stirring. The queen had shared with him some of her innermost feelings and done so unbidden. There was no question of the domination and submission of wizardry of which he was familiar. She had trusted and given of herself freely. He knew something of another thinking being in a way that he had never experienced before.

A sense of compassion for Nimbia's plight bubbled up within him, and more importantly, an urge to show that he was worthy, that he understood, and that her trust was well placed, with a friend rather than a stranger.

"I — I was born without wings," he blurted without thinking. "Unlike my clutch brethren, neither could I soar through the realm nor weave more than the simplest of matter. I have become a cataloguer, an observer of the bizarre in other universes, and a value to my prince."

Astron lowered his voice to a whisper and continued. "But I know of what you speak, of pains deep in the stembrain that no higher logic can ever completely cover. I am only a shadow of a demon, Nimbia, only a small part of what it is my birthright to be. I look at the mighty wings of the splendorous djinns as they send the air into pulsing eddies with their strokes and a rage at the unfairness of it all burns deep inside. I lower my membranes and cover my ears from the power of the great explosions that my brethren can ignite at will, and a melancholy perhaps as deep as yours stirs from its deep burial."

Astron opened his mouth to say more but the words escaped him. What was he doing? His mind recoiled in numbness. The thoughts that he struggled so hard to keep buried were whirling unabated. And he had done no less than articulate them to one who was not even in the domain of his prince. He rose on one knee to withdraw but his limbs began to stiffen.

"Forgive me," he mumbled. "Those words, they were not meant for another. I, I have —"

Nimbia reached out and placed her hand on Astron's shoulder. "Thank you," she ignored his sudden discomfort. "That is exactly what I needed. You serve your hillsovereign better than many of my own kind."

Astron managed to shake his head, straining against the tightening tendons. Then he caught Kestrel entering the throne room and felt a sudden relief at the human's presence.

"Yes, I am coming," Astron said. Awkwardly, he rose to his feet and adjusted the pack on his back. "A final word with the queen to learn more of the dangers."

Kestrel shrugged and motioned over his shoulder. "Walk with the rest of us now or catch up later," he said.

Kestrel left the throne room as rapidly as he had come. Astron scrambled to follow. Another confusion had piled on top of the rest. He had not spoken to Nimbia of dangers. For the first time in his life, just like a human, he had told an untruth.

Harebell Pollen

THE TREK to the glen of harebells proceeded uneventfully. The constant twilight did not waver. No one else was seen on the grassy trails. Shortly after Kestrel and the fey arose from their second sleep, the party began climbing a final hillock crested with giant ragwort and broad-leaved thyme. Astron inhaled the aromatics that hung heavy in the air.

Behind them, the lush green carpet spread as far as the eye could see, eventually vanishing into the softness of fog and mist. Like blemishes on smooth skin, clumps of mushroom, golden cowslips, and foxglove scattered across the grasses indicated the presence of springy marshes with ground far wetter than the rest.

"What is it?" Kestrel growled ahead of him. "We have come too far to begin slacking the pace now."

He peered up the trail. The fey had stopped, and Kestrel had almost closed the distance between them. The woodcutter scowled and flexed his back, pulling at the straps of the rucksack he bore. The adjustment did not help. Irritated, he slipped out of the burden and let it fall to the ground.

"The shrill vibrations are worse than I have ever known them before," the first of the fey said as Astron caught up with the rest.

"What vibrations?" Kestrel shook his head. "I do not hear a thing." He flexed his back again. "All I know is that we have been pushing hard for two cycles of sleep and the end is in sight. Now is not the time to have second thoughts."

"The irritation is part of the effect," another of the fey replied. "Perhaps the sounds are too high for your ears, but they are there, nonetheless. You feel them, even if you cannot hear."

Astron strained to catch some sense of what the others were talking about, but he heard nothing. Although demon sight was keen, their hearing was inferior to that of many other beings. Nor did he feel any of Kestrel's irritation or the growing agitation of the fey.

"The risk is too great." One of the sentryman shook his head. "Better to bear the burdens of Prydwin's pollen sacks than not to exist at all." He glowered at Kestrel. "Your words may have been smooth enough for the queen, but she does not risk the dangers of the glen herself."

He flung off his pack and grabbed at the arm of another of the guard. For a moment, the two hesitated and then, after wide-eyed glances back up the hill, they bolted in the other direction like stallions racing out of an open barn door, gathering speed as they ran. The panic was contagious. The remaining four did not even bother to lighten their loads. Fighting each other for the center of the trail, they sprinted off after the others.

As the fey departed, Kestrel kicked at his own rucksack. Astron shrugged but said nothing. He stepped past and continued up the slope. For a long while, Kestrel stood with hands on hips, scowling. Then he gathered up his equipment and scrambled to catch up with the demon. In a moment, they were peering out from under the cover of a ragwort leaf into the glen of the harebells.

The hill sloped downward from the ridge under a cover of thick-leaved grasses, just as it had on the other side. But midway down the slope, a wall of skyward pointing leaves poked out of a heavy mist and blocked the view. From a dense forest of upraised green swords, fragile stalks rose even higher, almost to the crests of the surrounding hills. Impossibly slender, the ropelike shoots wavered in gentle rhythms, as if trying by an act of delicate balance to keep from crashing to the ground. And on the end of each, looping over and hanging as a massive weight, was a deep-bowled blossom that swung back and forth. All the flora of the realm possessed prodigious proportions, but the harebells seemed among the largest of all. A man or demon could hide within a single flower, if he climbed that high.

After a moment's observation, Kestrel stirred and started down the hillside, but Astron grabbed his arm and held him back. The demon pointed at a hint of blurry motion above the mist and then at a second and a third. One of the harebells rattled with energy. Brilliant orange-and-black stripes emerged from the petals and then hovered still.

"Bees!" Kestrel exclaimed as the recognition came to him. "Giant bees, the size of the flowers." He put his hands over his ears. "And the noise — it is their wings. They buzz so fast that one barely can hear."

The large insect darted away. Knowing what to look for, Astron spotted several more flitting through the flowers. Large, multifaceted eyes, like blackened shields, rode above a mouth siphon bristling with golden hairs. The wings were a blur about the bright abdomen, to which were attached. Legs folded in an intricate maze. From the rear protruded the sharp tip of the stinger, glistening with venom.

Astron shook his head. Judging from the size, the poison would be unnecessary. The thrust of the lance would bore right through the chest as surely as a shaft of steel.

"If it were not for the tales of no one returning, we could risk it," Kestrel said. "Just walk out and pick a stalk that none of the bees seems interested in. Perhaps we could even shake some of the pollen to the ground."

Astron did not immediately respond. He ran over in his mind what he had learned of bees in the realm of men. "Smoke," he said after a moment. "Perhaps the ones that venture close can be subdued, if we surround ourselves with sufficient soot and ash."

"There is little here that will burn." Kestrel shook the leaf overhead to release a shower of water. "Nothing about is sufficiently dry."

"There is one thing," Astron reached into his pack and pulled out the single grain of harebell pollen he had brought with him to ensure positive identification. He placed it on the ground just beyond the cover of the ragwort, frowning in distaste at the many prickly barbs that pierced his fingertips. He withdrew one of the oil bladders he had used when studying thaumaturgy and stretched it into a crude lens with his thumbs and forefingers. "I had wanted to try the experiment when we got above ground, anyway," he explained as he adjusted the focus. "Even with diffuse light, the energy might be converged enough if the material is sufficiently combus —"

The harebell pollen grain began to smolder like an oily rag. A ringlet of dense black smoke bubbled from the surface and rose into the air. Kestrel coughed. Astron put down the lens. The surface of the pollen grew into incandescence around the origin of the fire, and the circle began to spread outward in a growing ring. The smoke thickened and cascaded from the pollen in billowing waves, far more than what one would expect from such a small amount of flame. Like a sooty fog, it began rolling down the hillside toward the harebells.

"Smoke subdues bees in the realm of men." Astron motioned Kestrel to follow him as he stepped forward from under cover. He stopped and picked up the pollen grain. "Let us move quickly before it burns itself out."

Astron proceeded halfway down the slope, and then Kestrel raced to catch up. Together they reached the slender stalks of the harebell without alarming any of the bees that buzzed overhead.

"You stay here and keep the fire going," Kestrel said when they reached the base of the nearest flower. "I will climb up and shake loose what I can."

Kestrel wrapped himself around the rope-like stem that soared into the air. The demon placed the pollen grain at the base of the plant. With both hands, he fanned the dense smoke upward, enveloping Kestrel as he rose.

Kestrel reached the bowed apex of the harebell without incident. Then, letting his feet hang free, he descended hand over hand onto the bowl of the flower itself. He tested the strength of an individual petal and then paused, apparently trying to figure out the best way to get inside. Two of the bees swooped in Astron's direction, but at the last moment, they both turned aside and buzzed off toward different flowers. The smoke was not something that they wanted to encounter. Astron kept fanning the heavy billows outward and upward, watching for any signs of agitation among the darting insects.

Kestrel dangled in midair, one hand holding the tip of a bluish petal and the other reaching for the knobby stamen that protruded from the center of the bowl. In an instant, he vanished inside the bloom. A few moments later, a shower of pollen grains just like the one that was burning began to cascade downward to where Astron stood.

Astron stopped his fanning and removed his pack from his back. Scampering about like a small child, he harvested the grains and stuffed them into the empty pouch. He gathered a dozen and then three or four more until the pack was filled. He brushed his hands with satisfaction. Nimbia would be well pleased with what they had done.

When the flap was secured and the pack returned to his back, he glanced at the burning pollen grain. The color of the smoke lightened into soft grays. The burning ring of fire started to sputter. Only a tiny disk remained of what once had been a substantial volume. He looked upward to call Kestrel down, and his stembrain jolted in spasm by what he saw.

The bright abdomen of one of the bees protruded from the flower into which Kestrel had vanished. A second was buzzing around the stem, awaiting his turn. Astron reached back to untie the pack, but then the wings of the first bee fluttered to life in agitation. Its stinger began to extend, and the entire body contorted inward toward the blossom.

Astron shook his head to rid himself of his stiffness. He bent forward and blew on the smoldering pollen grain, bringing the flames back to life.

A wave of smoke billowed out over the ground and covered his feet in inky blackness. The demon started to fan the coiling tendrils skyward, then thought better of it. They would be too diffuse at the height of the flower. He grabbed the grain in one hand and cupped its prickly surface carefully against his tunic. Pushing aside yet another wish for wings, he grabbed the stalk and began to climb.

As he struggled upwards, a high-pitched whine caused by the confines of the harebell petals against the insect's wings echoed from all sides. In agonizing slowness, he proceeded, occasionally catching glimpses of Kestrel's dark silhouette through the translucent blues of the petals. The human's body was pushed into a tight ball at the very base of the flower, trying to avoid the larger blob maneuvering itself deeper into the bowl.

Astron reached the height of the drooping calyx of the harebell. All he could see of the flower's interior was blotted by the carpet of coarse orange-and-black hairs on the back of the bee. He wrapped his legs as securely as he could about the swinging stem and stretched out his hand containing the burning pollen grain.

Only a small curved disk remained of what once was a sizable sphere. He blew down the length of his arm but the flame responded hardly at all. A few wisps of black rose into the bowl of the flower. Astron exhaled vigorously, pushing as much life as he could into the remains of the smoke. The twitching of the bee as it twisted itself deeper into the harebell slowed but did not stop altogether.

Something more desperate would be needed if Kestrel were to be rescued. Almost without thinking, he discarded the last dying embers and coiled himself up into a ball on the wavering stem. Then kicking as best he could, he hurled himself across the distance to the dangling flower, grabbing the hairs on the bee's back with both his hands. With a noise like ripping paper, the bee's claws tore through the petals as the added weight pulled it downward. In an instant, the insect was dragged free. With Astron clinging to its back, it hurled toward the ground.

Once free of the confines of the blossom, the huge wings exploded into a blur of action. Stinging blasts of cold air raced across Astron's body as the insect tried to right itself. The bee lurched to the right and Astron felt a stab of pain in his shoulder as he struggled to maintain a grip. With a flip that hurled the demon up over the insect's back, the bee wobbled into a horizontal position. But the ground came rushing up too fast. With a jarring thud, they crashed into it.

The air rushed from Astron's lungs as he slammed into the bristly back. Stunned, he rolled to the side and fell to the ground. The bee tried to rise on its legs, but only uncoordinated spasms shook its body. Its wings fluttered out of synchronization, blowing up a scatter of dewdrops among the broad blades of grass that covered the slope.

There was motion near the base of the stem, and the demon guessed that Kestrel was scrambling to safety. A pungent odor began to fill his nostrils. The stinger of the bee at his side was fully extended and glistening with a foul-smelling oil. In awkward steps on three legs, the insect was turning its abdomen about to where Astron swayed as he tried to regain his composure. His head still rang from the contact and, against his will, he fell to one knee.

"Come on," Kestrel shouted behind him. "Somehow they can communicate. Look, the others are corning to the aid of the one you brought down."

Astron felt a firm grip on his arm and rose to his feet. He followed Kestrel's tug and began to place one foot in front of another. Mindlessly, he picked up speed and started running up the slope. The ringing in his head grew more intense and almost painful. He placed his hands over his ears, trying to concentrate on keeping up with the human as he ran.

Almost without knowing that he had done so, Astron reached the ragwort and burst over the hillcrest. His vision began to clear. The high buzz in his ears started to fade away. In a few moments, they had raced down onto the wet flatlands and were heading back to Nimbia's underhill.

"You did it, Astron," Kestrel said after they had caught their breaths. "You saved me when you had no real cause. First Phoebe and then you. I'm starting to expect it. It's almost enough to restore my faith in hum ..."

For a moment, Kestrel studied Astron's demonic features and then laughed. "Well, maybe that would be going just a bit too far," he said. "A single ring of mail does not make a full suit of armor."

Abandoned

ASTRON AND Kestrel retraced their journey across the hills and glens as rapidly as they could. Without the fey to guide them and no directional aids in the sky, their progress was slow. More than once, they wandered away from the faint trails and were set right only by Astron's keen eye and memory for detail. After Kestrel had risen from his fifth sleep, Nimbia's underhill was drawing near.

The last lush green hill beckoned them forward. Sparse groupings of blooming foxglove and withered cowslip past its prime dotted the hillocks. A carpet of ferns crowded close onto the muddy trail that squished in wetness with each step.

"So you knew nothing of thaumaturgy before possessing the archimage's book," Kestrel said as he paused for breath where the slope steepened. "Burning lenses and alchemical balloons. You are well on the way to becoming a master of many arts yourself."

Astron shook his head. "No, as I have tried to explain, nothing I have done involves any magical skill. I have learned only of adjuncts that can be used independent of the crafts — by you as well as any other."

"This journey has given me no more knowledge of the magical arts." Kestrel shook his head. "Indeed, if it were not for Phoebe's safety, I would not even be here." He shielded his eyes from the diffuse glare, trying to catch sight of something familiar. "Come," he said, "we have wasted too much time already."

"It is because I am a cataloguer," Astron continued as they resumed their march. "Unlike my brethren, I look beyond the facts as they are presented to the deductions that logically follow."

Despite his rush, Kestrel laughed. "If I were to judge, looking beyond what is apparent is perhaps where your faculties most need to be sharpened."

"What do you mean?" Astron wrinkled his nose. "As you have said, I was the one who calculated that balloons of lead could fly, that —"

"And the one who did not understand how a group of wizards would react when presented the opportunity for monetary gain." Kestrel held up his hand to stop the protest. "Nor even how to entrap the imps which you say you have known for eras. There is more to thought than a logical progression from one truth to another, Astron. Sometimes there is value as well in postulating alternatives, in letting ideas flow free."

"I do not understand. How can such lack of discipline help me in my quest?" Astron's puzzlement deepened. "Our course is clear. We have to follow the path to its end."

Kestrel rubbed the back of his neck and frowned. For a while, they trudged in silence. "Well, for example, consider the matter of this Gaspar of yours," he resumed after they had climbed thrice the height of a man.

"He is not my prince," Astron said. "He would find my existence not pleasing. In a tick of time, I would be given to the lowest of his djinns for sport. I serve Elezar, who find pleasure in conundrums and delicate weavings, rather than explosion and chaos."

"Exactly so." Kestrel panted. "From what little you have told me, Gaspar is a demon most unlikely to compose a riddle that would baffle your prince. Even if he could, it would not be his style. Think of it, Astron. Why has Gaspar acted as he has? From where has he obtained the plan to act as he did? There are inconsistencies here that cry for an explanation."

Kestrel shrugged, and then put on a fresh burst of speed. "That is what you should be thinking of," he said, "the deeper meaning of the riddle, not the relative weight of air and lead."

Astron adjusted his pack and hurried to keep pace. "Then what is the answer?" he asked. "Tell me what secrets this other way of thinking reveals. Do you mean to say that Gaspar is under the control of a wizard, just as Elezar has succumbed to the archimage — that there is a being in some realm with a will great enough to subdue a prince of the lightning djinns?"

Kestrel stopped a second time at the crest of the last hill while Astron struggled to catch up. "I do not know enough of your realm," the human said. "Perhaps there is no substance to my conjecture, and everything is proceeding as it has been presented. But, as I have suggested, let your thoughts roam free. Perhaps, when you least expect it, an insight will come."

"It is hard to see the utility of such speculation," Astron wrinkled his nose. "Although if that is the process by which you found a way to put imps in a bottle ..."

The scene that stretched before them reached Astron's consciousness. He glanced once at Kestrel and pointed. They both began to race down the slope. At the nadir of the glen, Nimbia's hillock stood elevated on the slender pillars as it had on their first arrival. But this time the underhill was quiet and empty.

They ran onto the heavy stone flooring that had been raised from below the ground. No one was about. Many of the interior walls and partitions had been removed and carted away. The dais of the throne room was bare. Where before had hung a delicate tapestry of vines, empty sky shone through. . Two empty vats tipped on their sides were all that remained of the store of pollens and seeds. Several flutes and horns were scattered in a litter of leaves and copper swords on the stone floor. Here and there, spatters of blood, like carmen tears flicked from an artist's brush, mingled with the remains of other debris.

Kestrel and Astron raced about the empty corridors and then descended into the passageways below ground. They found almost everything ransacked there as well. In Astron's cubicle, only the book of thaumaturgy remained, tossed into a corner, pages down, its strange script of no interest to whoever had come. Astron turned to leave, but Kestrel ran to the tomb. He flipped it over and pointed excitedly to the inside of the front cover. There in a precise hand, like an author's signature for a buyer, Phoebe had left a final message.

"Pipers of Prydwin have been seen in the glen," Astron read aloud. "Nimbia fears that he plans to come just before the next judging and claim the bondage that is his due. Even without the pollen, she must create for Finvarwin. It is one last desperate chance, even though Prydwin will be there. I will accompany her and aid with my wizardry as best I can."

Kestrel counted on his fingertips and eyed the notches carved in the doorjamb. "It is already the time of the next judging," he growled. "To the glen by the stream! If Phoebe and Nimbia escaped before the arrival of Prydwin's sentrymen, that is where they will be."

Astron tapped the bulging pack on his back. "But without the pollen, there is little chance they will succeed."

"Exactly!" Kestrel shouted as he sprinted back up the stairs. "Somehow we must break through the ring that guards the glen and get them the help they need."

Astron's stembrain stirred. Pulling Nimbia out of the ring with total surprise was one thing, but breaking through to Finvarwin's rock long enough to use the harebell pollen properly was quite another. A shuddering spasm squeezed the breath from Astron's chest like a cruel vice. He remembered all too well the crushing power of the combined wizardry of the pipers. He had expected one of Kestrel's clever deceptions as the means to allow Nimbia to compete again, not an insane dash that the humans seemed to enjoy so much.

Kestrel bounded up the steps three at a time. The thought of Phoebe in peril had been too much for him, Astron thought. The woodcutter had surrendered to the panic of his stembrain, rather than think through what must be done. Grimly, the demon forced calm onto his own churnings. He would have to use the best of his reason to convince Kestrel to formulate a plan.

Demon Deception

ASTRON LAID a hand on Kestrel's shoulder to restrain him as they peered out from the cover of the ragwort. The temptation to wrestle with the human's will flitted through his mind, but he put the thought aside. There was no time for that. He would have to hope that the logic on which they had agreed would work instead.

"Look at them down there," Kestrel whispered. "They are all alone, with not a single piper to guard them. At worst, Nimbia will become a slave to Prydwin, but who knows what will happen to Phoebe."

"Yes, look at them," Astron answered. "Phoebe is cloaked. No one questions that she might not be one of their own kind." He touched the reassurance of the hood he had scavenged from the debris of Nimbia's underhill. "I can pass through the ring with the same pretense. Your presence will sound an alarm."

"You are a demon and know nothing of this sort of thing," Kestrel growled. "If it were not for the fact that your command of the language is better, I would be the one wearing the cape."

"It is what we have agreed," Astron protested. "Propose another plan if you have one better."

The muscles in Kestrel's face contort with indecision. He sighed and slumped to the ground. "Go ahead," he whispered. "Just remember to answer any challenges the way I have indicated, quickly and with confidence — as if it is bizarre that there should be any suspicion."

Astron nodded and began to rise, but Kestrel caught him by the arm. "And none of those fool questions. There is much at stake here, not a petty exercise in collecting data for one of your catalogues."

Astron pushed away a sudden rush of irritation. "Cataloguing is by no means petty," he muttered. "No other djinn under Elezar's command —"

He slammed his mouth shut like the door to a vault. Kestrel was right.

There were more important things to attend to now. He looked down toward the bottom of the glen, from under the cover of the ragworts. Finvarwin stood adjacent to his rock. Next to him, a circle of djinns arched into the sky as they had upon Astron's arrival. Prydwin stood in front of the flaming ring, partially blocking a view into another realm.

Within the fiery window, two armies engaged in hand-to-hand combat, breaking limbs and spattering blood with intense dedication. The warriors on each side were thin-framed and delicate, like the fey. Their blows struck and parried in an almost stylistic dance, creating complex visual patterns that grew and decayed as the battle progressed. From the very center of the conflict, paths of ebony-black radiated out in many directions on a plane of eye-blinding white and continued into the vanishing distance. Astron shook his head. He had never seen or heard the likes of such a place before.

A little farther to the right, he recognized Phoebe, despite the cloak, and next to her, similarly disguised, must be Nimbia, nervously pacing like an expectant mother waiting for the first contraction. As before, copper-daggered sentrymen ringed the slopes of the glen, adding the force of their wills to the control of the djinns who strained to bridge the gap between the realm of the fey and those that lay beyond.

Astron grimaced and concentrated for the last time to push the tuggings of his stembrain far beneath his conscious thoughts. He adjusted his hood to cover as much of his face as possible and stepped out onto the grassy slopes.

He walked down the hillside toward one of the sentrymen, looking past him toward the bottom of the glen.

"Halt," the guard said when Astron was close enough for him to hear the swish of his cape. "Prydwin defends his creations against a challenger from a far underhill. He displays no less than his realm of order. There is to be no interference until the judging is done."

"I bring pollen that is plentiful in that far underhill for my queen," Astron replied. "She is expecting my presence and I must pass."

A strange thrill ran through Astron as he said the words. They were filled with untruth and tasted strange on his tongue. Yet he noticed that the sentryman did not immediately reach for his arms. Instead, he rubbed his chin in indecision and looked closer at what had interrupted his concentration.

"Lower your hood so that I see that you indeed are not from a local glen," the sentryman said. "King Prydwin did not capture Queen Nimbia and all of her followers when he seized what had been granted to him in the last judging."

Astron's sternbrain rumbled. He felt sharp impulses rip through his legs, compelling him to step backward. He clenched his fists and willed his thoughts into control. "I am disfigured," he whispered. "A dagger such as yours severed an ear from my head and left an enormous scar. I wear this hood to cover my shame. Surely you can let me pass so that no one will see."

The sentryman hesitated. Astron stepped boldly forward. "In any event, I am within your ring," he said as he glided past. "You will have the opportunity to challenge me again after the judging is done. For now, I must obey my queen, who bids me come forth."

The sentryman frowned, but had not attempted to follow. Through squinting eyes, he watched Astron march down the slope. The strange thrill blossomed into delicious triumph in the demon's mind. He ran his tongue over his teeth, trying to savor every aspect of the feeling.

He had succeeded in getting past the guard, but not with a display of strength, as would one of his clutch brothers, or even with the knowledge of the cataloguer. He had woven an appearance of reality, and it had been accepted. It was as if Elezar had thanked his service before an assembly of all others in the prince's domain.

Prydwin stood near the circle of djinns as he approached. Nimbia and Phoebe paced nearby. He reached over his shoulder and grabbed the topmost of the prickly pollen grains from his rucksack. "The seeds for your planting, my queen," he said. "May your thoughts grow and prosper."

Nimbia's eyes widened in surprise, and then she smiled. She did not reply but pointed to the ground at her feet where Astron was to dump his burden. He removed the pack from his back and glanced again at the opening into Prydwin's realm. The dancelike battle continued with an almost glacial slowness. A few spans away, the hunched figure of Finvarwin squinted at the motions with unwavering concentration.

"You see the vitality of the combat, my high king," Prydwin said. "It intensifies rather than diminishes."

"Enough," Finvarwin rumbled. "Let us see the offering of the cloaked ones who come from far away."

"Yes." Prydwin waved the demon ring to opaqueness. He smiled at Nimbia's cloaked form. "I too have curiosity about this new creation — indeed, the creation and creator both."

Nimbia tugged at the corner of her hood and turned away. While everyone watched, she took a position in front of the ring. After a moment, she gestured that she was ready and dropped to the ground, coiling into a tight ball and pulling her arms around her knees. Without speaking, she began rocking herself back and forth like an old grandmother in the realm of men. For more than a hundred heartbeats, nothing happened. Then a tiny spark of brilliant red burst into being in the precise middle of the ring.

Nimbia screamed as if in pain and then forced a hearty laugh from deep within her chest. The amplitude of her rocking increased as more peals rang from her lips. She tossed back her head and the hood fell away to reveal her golden curls.

Astron felt a twinge in his stembrain. There could be no doubt about who she was. Two of Prydwin's sentrymen snapped to alertness and step forward with daggers drawn. But their hillsovereign waved them to be still. With the broad smile still on his face, he struck an exaggerated pose of complete ease.

Nimbia's agitation increased. With a violent tug, she flung aside the cape and rose to her feet. Her laughter turned to tears. With violent sobs that racked her body, she raised her arms toward the ring, imploring the grayness to dissolve away.

Corrected Vision

NIMBIA HAD known that the disguise would not long be effective, Astron realized in a flash as he watched her, not more than a dozen paces from him. Her identity could not be hidden when so much passion was required for what she must do. There had not been time to create before the judging. It had to be done while all the others watched. And yet, she had come, rather than slink away to safety in the brush when her underhill was attacked. It was her duty, she had said, her obligation to those over whom she was the queen. Astron shook his head. Such a thought would be foreign to the prince to whom he owed his fealty.

The pinpoint of light expanded into a small disk, pushing against the gray void and slowly growing in diameter. The circumference seemed to tremble in a series of spasmodic expansions and contractions, oscillating in a complex rhythm like a coin spinning on a vibrating drum. When the disk had become the size of a small melon, Nimbia nodded to Astron, pointing at the pollen at his feet and then the disk.

Astron grabbed one of the harebell grains and lofted it at the vibrating circle. The aim was good, and it struck near the center but bounced back at his feet. Of course, he thought, transporting solid matter between the realms was a hard task for even the strongest of djinns. It was the reason why Elezar had sent him to the realm of men in the first place.

He motioned to Phoebe to pick up the pollen and try where he had failed. The wizard frowned in confusion at first but then understood what must be done. Her lob struck the disk near the edge, but close enough to what Nimbia desired. The circle exploded into a blaze of deepest-red, expanding to banish all of the gray.

"An empty palette," Prydwin called to Finvarwin. "There is nothing there. As soon as Nimbia releases the pressure of her thoughts, the creation will collapse back into the void."

"Nimbia, here?" Finvarwin turned his attention for an instant away from the ring.

Nimbia ignored the taunt and directed Phoebe to continue tossing the pollen. The wizard hurled another grain and then, with increasing speed, began throwing more. The orbs sailed through the ring like balls tossed at a carnival and struck the disk near the center. Each seemed to transform as it flew. The prickly spines grew and bent at right angles, forming transparent squares of yellow. The bulbous central body wasted away so that only the boxes remained. Like checkerboards with some of the cells cut away, each pollen grain deposited a haphazard pattern of connected squares in the new realm, some with only two or three components, and others with dozens or more.

Then, after the last grain thrown had been transformed, there was a sudden pulse of light. The plane of red shifted to a brilliant blue. But more importantly, the patterns of squares had all simultaneously transformed as well. Some had vanished. New ones had appeared. The background pulsed a second time, shifting back to red and then again oscillating to blue. With each change, the patterns of boxes transformed, some dying, others growing in grotesque and complex ways, seemingly spawning children that evolved on their own. Astron watched fascinated as the patterns unfolded.

He concentrated on the simple ones that cycled through a series of repeating shapes and then deduced the law that governed their behavior. He smiled at Nimbia in admiration, struck by the clean simplicity of what she had done. Each square lived or died in the next cycle, depending on the number of its neighbors. With two, it remained from one oscillation to the next. Otherwise, it vanished. New squares were born according to a similar rule.

The elegance of the creation swept through him. He felt a great longing to plant a seed grouping of cells himself and see what would happen and to watch the pattern live and die. It was exactly the type of thing that would satisfy the cravings of the fey. Nimbia had created a most unique realm with a vital life force all its own. Surely, Finvarwin would see the merit of what she had done.

"I call this the realm of the conways," Nimbia panted in almost total exhaustion. "It is a universe based upon —"

"I apologize for the wasting of your time with meaningless competition," Prydwin interrupted. "This is no better, Nimbia, than your offering the last time you were called forth."

"It is worse." Finvarwin squinted into the ring of djinns. "I see

195

nothing but the dull repetition of red and blue. A well-defined realm, it is true, but one that bores after the briefest of inspections."

"But it is my best!" Nimbia tried to regain her feet, but could not find the strength. "Look at what is there, Finvarwin. How can you so lightly dismiss what I have done?"

"Nimbia," Prydwin smiled. "Even with the cloak, you must have known I would suspect an unknown hillsovereign who mumbles to the high king the minimum necessary to be granted a turn to present. An unknown hillsovereign indeed!"

Prydwin turned to Finvarwin. "You have already granted me the boon of Nimbia's underhill, venerated one," he said. "What additional might I expect now that I have won the wager doubled?" He turned and called back up the hill. "Sentryrnen, seize them. This time she will not escape."

Finvarwin was unmoved. He swayed on unsteady limbs but otherwise did nothing to explain his decision.

"No!" Nimbia cried out. "A second punishment will only add injustice to the first. It is not the fault of those who have dwelt in my underhill that these creations have failed to find your favor, Finvarwin." She extended her arms trembling from exhaustion, offering her wrists for bondage. "If any payment is to be made, it is the duty of their queen and no other."

"What, this is Nimbia?" Finvarwin said. "The hooded queen and she are one and the same?"

Finvarwin's squint deepened as Nimbia struggled to stand. The hunched figure reminded Astron somewhat of Palodad, infirm yet continuing as he had for perhaps eons before. Age should have brought increased wisdom and the ability to judge better what his senses presented to …

Astron stopped in midthought. The explanation burst upon him like a star suddenly exploding. "He cannot see!" he shouted to Nimbia. "He can no longer discern detail — only large movements and general shapes. Finvarwin has judged your creations inferior because he never noticed the structures of what was actually there."

Astron's thoughts raced. Just as in his experiments, the sharpness of vision in a living being was a matter of lenses and bending light. He remembered the book of thaumaturgy and the many interesting diagrams it contained. Dropping to the ground, he began pawing through the contents of his pack, looking for what might give Nimbia one last chance.

With a surprising nimbleness, he fashioned some bits of copper wire into two small circles, connected them with an arc of metal and then attached longer straight segments on either side. He grabbed at one of the large flat leaves near the stream bank and tore it into two disks that fit over the rings of copper, hoping the oozing sap would hold them firm. With a last segment of wire, he punched a tiny hole in the center of each of the green orbs.

"Here, try these." He raced up to Nimbia's side, extending his construction forward for Finvarwin. "Place them astride your nose and over your ears. The scene will be dim but a pinhole works as well as a fine correcting lens. I have tested the effect in Nimbia's underhill and seen how sharp the focus can be."

Astron's hood flew backward as he ran, but he was too excited to care. Finvarwin must see Nimbia's creation as it was meant to be viewed.

"The demon," Prydwin shouted in recognition. "The one who kept Nimbia from me, as was my due at the last competition. Challenge him, pipers! Make him submit to our collective will!"

Astron grimaced. The memory of his last ordeal sprang into his mind. And within their circle, there would be no way he could resist.

"Like this." Astron demonstrated with the glasses without changing his direction and then thrust them into Finvarwin's hand. He started to say more but felt a sudden compelling jolt. Staggering under crushing pressure, he sagged to his knees.

Through glazed eyes, he watched Finvarwin with agonizing slowness bring the strange object to his face. Astron pushed forward a resistance against the mental onslaught, but deep in his stembrain, he knew he would fail. His thoughts became sluggish, compressing in ways that were distasteful and bizarre. The sentrymen strode closer, and among them, Kestrel pounded down the hill with the rest.

"This is most amazing!" Finvarwin exclaimed. "There is more to your creation, Nimbia, than I first suspected. Yes, look as it — most clever, far more elegant that what Prydwin has offered to be compared."

"What is the ultimate precept?" Astron shrieked. "What law is supreme over all the rest? How does one start a fire in the realm of demons? The prize for winning — the answers I must know."

"No, I am the winner." Prydwin swiped at Finvarwin's glasses, knocking them to the ground. "Do not be misled. It is some sort of demon trickery."

The hillsovereign looked about the glen. "Yes, there are four altogether. Get them all, the one still hooded and the other sprinting down the hill. Get them all while I reestablish contact with my second creation. Look again as you have before, my high king, and you will see even more of what I can accomplish."

Astron struggled to think what he should do, but he felt his very being compressed into nothingness, all the sharp corners of his essence being smoothed away like the result of a using an unrelenting rasp. With a dull thud, his head sagged to the wet earth. In a strange detachment, he noticed Kestrel being shoved to earth near his rucksack and Phoebe thrown beside it.

"Be careful, Prydwin," Finvarwin said. "Even a hillsovereign must abide by the decisions of the high king."

"I will accept no punishment for the likes of this," Prydwin growled.

"First, a competition that has been fairly won deserves its just reward," Finvarwin continued, "and then we will see what additional judgments are appropriate besides."

The high king cleared his throat. "Realities are no more than bubbles," he said. "That is the most profound truth that I know. If there is an ultimate precept, then somehow that knowledge must be a component part."

Astron tried to pull meaning from Finvarwin's statement but he could not. All he could do was focus on Prydwin's strident voice.

"There shall be no reversals of opinion, I say. If I cannot have Nimbia, then neither shall she have control of me. Sentrymen, I command you — all of them through the flame."

Phoebe's scream blotted out what was said next. The last thing that Astron remembered was a sensation of being lifted and then being hurled through the air.

Part Four

The Realms of Order and Chaos

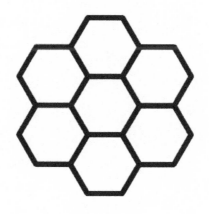

The Oasis

KESTREL SHOOK his head, trying to force his thoughts to order. The disorientation was not as great as the first time he had traveled between realms, but it was there, nonetheless. Astron's pollen sack slid from his grip. Vaguely, he remembered grabbing at it as he was hoisted from the ground by Prydwin's sentrymen and bodily tossed at the ring of djinns. When he hit the plane of the circle, he had felt a tremendous deceleration, like a ball of cotton hurled into a vat of thick molasses. The sack almost wrenched away, but somehow he had held on and burst through to the scene that lay beyond.

He was sprawled on a wide band of compacted ebony-black sand that defined a hexagon enclosing blinding white grit of about the same size. From each vertex radiated more rays of black that formed the boundaries of additional hexagons abutting the one at which he was positioned. Beyond them, yet more radiated outward and tiled a vast featureless plane, vanishing into an indistinct horizon that blurred the separation of ground and air. Just as in the realm of the fey, there was no sun, only a diffuse light that came from all directions.

At his back, he felt the rough bark of a tree that must have sunk its roots through the pathway. Five more stood around the periphery of the hexagon at each of the other vertices, each one identical to the next. A small pool of water was adjacent to each tree.

"An oasis," he muttered. "We are at an oasis in a vast desert."

Kestrel cursed himself for being so impetuous. But then, what else could he have done? When Prydwin called his sentrymen down to Finvarwin's rock, there had been no option but to bolt from cover to offer what aid he could. Phoebe had been in danger, and he could not just idly stand by.

There had been too many of them. Like a bag of trash, he had been hurled through the circle of djinns into the realm of Prydwin's creation.

Dazed from the jarring impact, he had watched helplessly as the others followed. Before any of them could stir, the portal back to the realm of the fey clouded and then closed.

Phoebe wallowed to alertness in front of the tree at the vertex opposite his own, trying to get her bearings. On the one to his left, Nimbia slumped in a disarray of tunic, leggings, and cape. Astron was unconscious, directly across from the queen of the fey.

Kestrel started to rise in order to see farther from the oasis, but felt a great weight that resisted his motion pressing downward on his back and legs. He increased his effort and managed to stand, although his body twitched from side to side from the buffet of small unseen forces.

"Stop," Phoebe cried from across the hexagon. "Stop whatever you are doing. Somehow, you are pulling me upward. I cannot move freely on my own."

Kestrel frowned at Phoebe. She was more or less erect but hunched forward and grasping toward the ground with empty hands like an old hag looking for a dropped coin. He felt his own fingers start to wiggle. Then, when Phoebe flung her arm backward to clutch at the tree behind her, his own body followed in an almost perfect imitation. Kestrel's frown deepened as he released the tension in his legs. He collapsed to the ground. Phoebe did the same.

"Somehow, we are bound together," he said in amazement. "There is great resistance when our motions do not imitate one another. What kind of strangeness is this?" He glanced to his side. "Astron, wake up! Explain what is going on."

The demon stirred slightly. Nimbia began to move as well.

"It is the realm of order," Nimbia said in an exhausted voice. "Prydwin considers it one of his two masterpieces, despite the strife and pain." She drew in a deep breath. "The effort to create is most exhausting. Give me a moment to regain my strength, and I will explain more."

Astron coughed and raised his head. His nose wrinkled in puzzlement and then his dark eyes darted about the black and white landscape. "Symmetries," he muttered, "like the hexagon of identical trees and each of us at different vertices."

"Yes," Nimbia said. "This realm abounds in things that look the same under reflections and rotations. That is the way it was constructed. Actions that build symmetry are reinforced. Those that break them are impeded."

"Most interesting," Astron replied. "I even have difficulty holding my mouth shut when I listen to you speak."

"You saw the battle before Prydwin shifted the view to this isolated hex." Nimbia's voice, rather than increasing in strength, grew still fainter. "This realm is one of violence. We must be away."

"But the reason for our quest," Astron said. "It has not yet been completed."

Kestrel again scanned the unfamiliar desolation and felt a sense of strangeness and dread far more intense than what he had first experienced in the realm of the fey. "Let us heed Nimbia's words and be gone before we encounter something we cannot handle."

"I have no answer to the riddle," Astron persisted.

Struggling against Nimbia's resistance, he pulled himself to a sitting position. "As far as I can tell, the words of the high king about reality and bubbles have little to do with a flame in the realm of demons. How can they save my prince from Gaspar's attacks?"

"Then tell it to the other, the one you call Palodad," Kestrel said. He pointed at the rucksack at his side. Phoebe's arm jerked in response. "Perhaps the one who reckons can analyze some hidden meaning once you have paid him with the pollen."

"Palodad." Astron shuddered. He stopped speaking as membranes flicked over his eyes. "I had hoped to seek out my prince directly, but your logic is correct. It is to the decrepit one that we must turn for aid and succor. Yes, Palodad first, and then, with what hopefully he will add to the answer, search for the hiding place of my prince."

He eyed Nimbia and then Phoebe across the oasis. "A fire, wizards," he said. "Break down the barrier between the realms and contact the one that we must."

"I do not have the strength." Nimbia rocked back and forth like a rag doll that could not quite stand. "Nor the firmness of will that is needed. Let the human female try. She has been most eager to prove her worth."

Despite the difficulty in moving, Phoebe managed to smile. Fumbling with the pockets in her cape, she retrieved several matches but they tumbled out of her grasp onto the ground. She bent forward to pick them up but clutched only emptiness several hand spans from where they fell.

Phoebe bent over awkwardly, deciding what to do next. "There is much resistance," she growled as she wrenched her head upward. "With what little kindling I have in my cape, it is not such a small task as one might believe."

"It is the force of the symmetries," Nimbia said. "If you were broken free you could act alone."

Astron surveyed the hexagon of trees, and his nose wrinkled in thought.

"Yes, I believe it is the fact that you two humans are at opposite vertices about an axis drawn between Nimbia and me," he said. "A half-circle rotation about axis interchanges you — part of the basic symmetry."

"Kestrel, if you can move to Nimbia's vertex while Phoebe remains where she is," he continued, "then the symmetry between you and her will be broken. All of us should then be free to act independently."

Kestrel rose and turned toward the tree on his left, but Phoebe's gasp of breath stopped him short. Her body wrenched to the side, preparing to pace to the next vertex around the periphery just the same as he.

"No, not so fast," Astron said. "Relax your muscles and let Phoebe get situated first, perhaps with her arms wrapped around the tree."

Kestrel did not quite understand what Astron had in mind, but they had to try something other than the first idea that had arisen. As he let the tension out of his limbs, he felt insistent tugs that turned him back toward the tree. He let the forces wash over him like the cascade from a waterfall and, without resisting, stepped up to the coarse bark. His arms rose from his sides and extended about the trunk. With a tight grip, his hands clasped together on the other side. Across the pond, Phoebe was also hugging her tree in the same relative position as he.

"Now," Astron said. "While Phoebe keeps her hands clasped together, release your grip and step away."

Kestrel grunted and began to uncoil his fingers from one another as if he were untying a shoe. He felt the same strong resistance to his efforts, and Phoebe gasped in exasperation as her fingers fought to pull apart. Kestrel stepped backward, and Phoebe arched in response, her feet moving from the base of the tree while she struggled and held her grip firm.

Kestrel took another step and then, more quickly, another. He felt as if he were walking upstream in a swift current. But each step was easier than the one before and finally, midway between the trees, the force vanished altogether. In complete freedom, he turned and walked to the next vertex of the hexagon and joined Nimbia.

Phoebe slid to the ground. Tentatively, the wizard waved her arm and then shook her entire body. The smile returned to her face for an instant, and then she sobered back into seriousness. She retrieved her scattered matches. Reaching into her cape, she brought forth some small twigs and parchment and built them into a paper cone at her feet.

Pulling her robe about her, Phoebe kneeled by her assemblage of materials and struck a match against one of the scraps of wood. The head skittered against the rough surface but did not light. Phoebe cursed under her breath and tried with a second matchstick, this time bearing down harder and paying strict attention to what she was about.

Halfway through her swing, however, the match broke in two. Frowning, she gathered five of the sticks together in a tight grouping and tried again. Even from where Kestrel stood, he could see the force of her stroke. The grate of the yellow-tipped heads growled far out into the featureless expanse of the desert.

Again, no sparks resulted from the swipe. Phoebe's scowl deepened. She clasped the matches with both hands and ground the cluster a second time against the wooden surface. Nothing happened, and she began stroking repeatedly, each time more intensely than before, hardly pausing between swipes and ignoring the splinters of matchwood that spewed away from where she worked. In a few heartbeats, the cluster was destroyed with not even the tiniest glow to show for her effort.

Phoebe looked over at Kestrel, crestfallen. The surge of purpose she had shown in Alodar's cabin now was completely gone. She kicked at her mound of kindling and sent it flying. "The wizards of my council," she said sourly. "They were right after all. When it came time to do my part, even make the simplest of flames, I choked like a doxy from the sagas." She reached for her cape and flung it to the ground. "Even with the mantle of the master, I must turn to another to get the simplest job done."

"My apologies, but I am still too weak." Nimbia shook her head. She gazed out into the desert, scanning the horizon. "It is your powers that we must use, wizard. Get us away before it is too late."

In the tree under which he stood, Kestrel spied a cluster of pear-shaped fruits. "Perhaps we are proceeding a bit too hastily," he said. "We have just been through a great deal. Let us eat first. Then one of you can try again."

"Now that Kestrel and Nimbia are at the same vertex, the symmetry is broken," Astron agreed. "You first, Phoebe, and then I will follow. Move to join them. We can all be together."

To Kestrel's surprise, Phoebe shook her head violently and then sagged to the ground. She stared at the splinters in her hand and did not try to speak. "I have failed us all," she said after the longest while, "Failed us all and precisely when it was needed most. My words in the chamber of the archimage were no more than bluster. I failed in my cabin

205

with the anvilwood and now a second time here."

"It is not so serious, Phoebe," Kestrel said. "Just the strangeness of this realm. With a bit of food —"

"Do you not understand?" Phoebe's voice strained with a hollow sharpness. She waved at the refuse strewn about her. "I cannot start a fire here, Kestrel. I know it. I can feel it. Perhaps it is within the ability of one worthy of the logo, but I cannot, regardless of the kindling."

"Then later, after we have all had a chance to rest."

"You are not listening," Phoebe exploded. Frustration and anger shot from her eyes. She clasped her fists tightly and beat them against her arms.

"It is not a matter of demon control," she said. "I did not even get that far. It is just as pompous Maspanar and the others chided. Experimentation with tiny imps in the confines of one's own cabin is one thing. The measure of a true wizard is quite another — what is accomplished when the consequences of failure are more than the loss of a fee.

"Not a spark. Not even a single spark. It is not a matter of new surroundings either. It goes far deeper than that. I can feel the inhibition. I am no wizard, not in this place, not anywhere in all of the realms. I am sorry, Kestrel, sorry that I made you come."

Her self-esteem began to melt from her expression as Kestrel watched. It was her only reason for the quest, he thought. She had wanted to prove herself the equal of the others above all else. He glanced at the litter of matchwood and shook his head. She alone would know the limits of her prowess. If she could not start a fire, what she said must be true. And now, despite the unknowns they were yet to face, even if he could protect her physically, what could he do to mend the way she had come to feel about herself?

"There is more than my shame, Kestrel," Phoebe said. She lowered her eyes, sighing deeply. "Without a flame, we cannot get passage to any other realm — to that of men, of the skyskirr, or even back to the fey. Unless Nimbia can be aroused, we are marooned here — marooned forever."

Rules of the Game

KESTREL PRESSED his hand against his stomach. Enough time had passed that he was reasonably sure of no ill effects from the fruit. Climbing the tree and tossing some of what he had picked across the oasis to the others had been easy enough, although Nimbia ate little and seemed to doze in a deep lethargy when she was done.

He peered up into the tree. They had consumed all of the fruit that had hung there. Presumably, there were five more meals hanging in the branches at the other vertices of the hexagon, but after they were eaten, then what? The level of the little pool of water that he had used to slack his thirst was noticeably lower. This realm definitely was not like that of the fey.

The fruit had been sweet and tangy, but helped his mood little, if at all. Despite his most careful words, Phoebe refused to be consoled. In an almost mindless obsession, she had assembled specimens of every different type of material she could find in her proximity, a handful of sand, tree bark and fronds, even the skins of the fruit they had eaten. Using one of the water lenses from Astron's pack to focus the diffuse light, she had succeeded no better than with her first attempt. There was no hint of flame, not even the tiniest wisp of smoke.

And now, rather than lifting Phoebe's spirits, he felt the crushing reality of her words growing with each passing moment. The featureless plane that expanded to the horizon in all directions made the feeling of entrapment all the more intense. Perhaps there were great cities and enchanting delights just out of eyesight, but Kestrel thought it unlikely. The glimpse he had of this realm while still with the fey looked very much the same as what he saw now. Except for the presence of some fighting warriors in azure blue, he recalled seeing only the same black paths radiating from a central point into the vast desert that was lacking in detail. They could not long survive here. Nimbia was right. They must get away, even if it were back to the realm of the fey.

He scowled and decided to venture into the center of the hexagon. The sand there was not compacted like that in the ebony borders. Each step in the deep looseness took some effort, not as much as he had felt when breaking the symmetry with Phoebe, but at least as difficult as marching along a beach after a storm. He reversed direction and tried walking out into the vacant hexagon on the other side, but the result was the same. If anyone wanted to go somewhere in this realm they would have to do so on the dark paths.

As he squatted to ponder the almost oppressive symmetry and order, the sky suddenly turned emerald green. His left foot dragged to the side, and his entire body twisted to follow. Phoebe gasped. She reached to fling her arms around her tree, her legs sailing out nearly horizontal. In a flurry of sand and snapping capes, both Phoebe and Astron were tossed into heaps. Like tumbleweeds, they began to bounce out into the desert along one of the paths leading away from the hex. Then, just as suddenly as it had appeared, the green sky turned back to dull gray.

"I surmise it is another symmetry," Astron shouted backward as he managed to regain his balance, his feet moving rapidly underneath him. "Something acting on everyone and pulling us along."

Kestrel tried to turn and snatch the tree now at his back, but he was too late. The unseen force intensified. He too was directed onto the path as if he were part of a marionette' parade, Nimbia brought up the rear, barely able to remain upright. They reached the end of the segment they were on, and without pause were turned slightly and transitioned to the next boundary line. Faster and faster, they zigged and zagged, flailing over the ground until even the wind whistled with their passage.

Kestrel strained to look over his shoulder. The oasis was already a mere speck in the distance. As he watched, it disappeared into a haze. He turned back to squint in the direction they were traveling and detected a similar blur of detail on the horizon up ahead.

The features sharpened as he approached. He recognized the tall trees of another oasis and that it was already occupied — by warriors in red like the ones he had seen fighting within the ring of djinns. What looked like strangely shaped balloons were pulled taut in the center of the hex. He turned his head from side to side to look down the lines of other paths converging from the different directions. Others were also coming — more fighters.

Far more rapidly than Kestrel could think of what to do, he arrived at the new watering place. As abruptly as the forces had torn him from the other oasis, they died away. He tumbled in a heap and offered only token resistance to the waning push that rolled him into the trunk of the nearest tree.

The inrushing warriors came to an abrupt halt at the same time. With the precision of dismounting horse riders, they steadied themselves and remained erect. Kestrel grabbed his dagger, fearing the worst, but after a brief inspection, the other arrivals paid him and his three companions little attention.

Instead, with shouts and upraised swords, they fell onto the original occupants in the hexagon's center, outnumbering them five to one. The fight was swift and cruel. The defenders were overwhelmed and, to a man, dispatched. As they fell, they faded from view. For an instant, the sky flashed ruby red and then returned to gray.

"Move is over," a commanding voice called out. "Prepare for planning."

In a few heartbeats more, Kestrel was surrounded by several dozen lean men with chalky complexions, only a few shades darker than the sand confined by the hexagons. They wore blue armor of thick leather that restricted their movement with squeaks and groans. The first two began to set up a small table from spars and hinged planks they carried on their backs while a third uncoiled a thick parchment covered with brilliant red and blue inks. With a few bellowed grunts that Kestrel thought he could almost understand, the rest dispersed to each of the six trees that ringed the hexagon.

One of the men spoke and Astron immediately answered. Again, Kestrel could make out most of what was being said.

"Since all of this is Prydwin's creation, it is no wonder that we can converse," Astron explained. "It is a small change from the normal speech in the realm of the fey." The demon shrugged. "It is perhaps a detail on which Prydwin did not spend much effort."

"Your presence contributes to our freedom of movement," the first warrior replied, "and for that, you have value. The map did not mark you as either enforcer or berserker, for order or chaos, for red or blue. And from your appearance, it is clear that you indeed are neither."

"Share in our celebration of victory," the second added.

"The berserkers never suspected the cunning of our symmetry until it was thrust upon them. No less than five of the surrounding oases did we command, and now they have been expulsed from this one as well," said the third. "They did not have a chance for an exchange of bodies. Not a single one."

"From which hex did you come?" the third continued. "It must have been the sixth; the one that we had thought to be unoccupied."

Kestrel opened his mouth to speak but Astron was quicker. "What is on this map?" the demon said. "The hexes that are colored — what do they mean?"

"It is the rendering of the great warring field, all that there is within the confining wall that surrounds everything," answered the first. "Already the map is changing itself to mark the victory." The warrior stopped and jabbed at the parchment. "It is all in accordance with the second protocol — 'all moves are simultaneous'. We had occupied hexes here and here and then those three over on the other side. You were at a sixth.

"Look at the map. See the beautiful pattern of blue that is now fading away: invariant if it is rotated one sixth of a full circle about any of the axes? And at the same time, the one in the very center deepening its color to azure blue?" The warrior's face widened in a satisfied grin. "As the first protocol states — 'the greater the symmetry, the greater the power'. In perfect synchronization, those of us occupying the five hexes surrounding this one converged upon it.

"You were on the sixth and were dragged along," the warrior continued. "No matter. The symmetry was close enough to perfect. We struck before they could deploy any of their weapons. We have eliminated all that were here. If we can calculate a few more moves like this one, we might yet regain the advantage."

Kestrel glanced at Astron in confusion, but then relaxed when he saw that the demon had not wrinkled his nose.

"This map then is a reproduction of all that we see." Astron waved his arm outward toward the desert for confirmation. "Most of the hexes are vacant in the realm, and so are they clear of color on the map. But those occupied by you are blue."

"It is a record of the entire realm," agreed one of the warriors.

"And the hexagons that are marked in red are under the control of the ones you call the berserkers." Astron studied the parchment for a few heartbeats. "You hold your territory most unlike the fashion of the realm of men," he said after a while. "Look at how interspersed you are. How can you possibly say who has the greater advantage?"

"It is not a matter of adjacency, but one of symmetry. Look at the beauty of the hexes that we possess. Of very high order are the subgroups that describe our lands."

"And that symmetry gives us the power to use the innate forces of the realm to aid us rather than fight against it in furthering of our aims. The oases are many day marches apart. If we attacked as the berserkers do, we would arrive at a target tired and with no element of surprise. But when five or six squadrons move as one, we almost fly across the warring field, appearing simultaneously, fresh and ready to battle."

"But why fight at all?" Astron asked. "What motivates you against these you call the berserkers?"

"They do not believe in symmetries," the first warriors spat. "They believe in no order at all. To them, chaos is the better. No patterns, no repetition, no planning. They were placed here at the beginning of time from a different realm that has no laws."

"But as the fourth protocol states — 'victory is total'," said another. "In the end, only one of the two of us will be left. It is the duty of every enforcer to destroy berserkers wherever we can; to strive to eliminate them until none is left to poison the beauty of the true symmetries of occupied oases that we will inhabit when they are gone."

"What of women and the crops that supplement these few fruits?" Kestrel asked. "Who weaves the clothes you wear on your backs and from where do your weapons come?"

"Most of your words make no sense whatsoever," the first warrior shook his head. "Our lives are to fight the berserkers until either we receive mortal wounds or have won. The fruit of the trees and the pools of water at the oases provide us subsistence. They renew after every move, either theirs or ours. Our armor protects us from blows. Of other things we have no need."

"But replacements," Kestrel persisted. "What happens when some of your number are indeed struck down?"

"Replacements?" the warrior laughed. "We fight the berserkers until one of us is victor. If some of my comrades fall during our attack, we recompute the symmetries for the numbers remaining, so that we have freedom of movement about the vertices." He waved his arm about the oasis. "As you see, we have done so here. There are no replacements. There never have been since the start."

The warriors deployed in what appeared to be a random fashion only at first glance, Kestrel realized. Closer examination revealed that the subgroups by each tree were different in many distinct ways from all the rest. Each had a different number of men, and the heights and weights were well distributed as well. The camp tasks they had undertaken were all unique and the identical weapons were stacked only where other differences outnumbered the similarities.

Kestrel glanced at Phoebe's almost vacant stare and Nimbia's listless shell hunched next to her. Out on the featureless desert all he could see was no more than the creation of one of the fey, he realized. It all had come into existence only by the force of thought — just like a scribe transcribing flights of fancy for the sagas, leaving out all nonessential detail. One could not expect any more.

There might be sufficient food and water here after all, he thought, but they still were marooned! The words boomed through his mind. Marooned in a universe in which all life apparently had to offer were the rules of a simple game.

Weapons of Chaos

KESTREL FORCED his face into a smile almost as fake as that of a costumed clown as he looked across the hex at Phoebe. After the battle and being accepted by the enforcers, he had lost track of the number of hexes to which they had marched, but it would do her spirits no good to show how low his own had sunk. Far better it would be if they could share the same vertex, but the enforcers, with their rigorously balanced deployments, insisted that they be kept apart.

"The great monotony must be avoided at all costs," the demon had told him when they were back in the realm of men. "Find something to occupy one's musings, or else self-destruction would be the final result." But here, what could possibly be done here! The life of an enforcer was one of almost complete ritual. In a rigid sequence, they would plan, eat, sleep, and then, when they had decided to move across the realm again, simultaneously with all of their other comrades in the realm, rush over the sands to a new oasis that looked almost exactly the same as the one they had left behind.

There may be a battle when they arrived at their destination or they might arrive at an oasis unoccupied. In either case, the cycle would begin again on their next turn. Plan, eat, sleep, and move. They were merely playing pieces on a complex board, jockeying for position without ceasing. The only variation was that a move might not be a change in location, but instead the stockpiling of food and water for a long march that would occur at some later time. And as far as Kestrel could tell from looking at the map, the enforcers were losing. More than half of the oases were marked in red including the one in the very center, the origin.

On occasion, Nimbia seemed a little more alert, but most of the time she still dozed in her stupor at the base of the tree to the right of Phoebe's. Although Astron was at Kestrel's side, the demon occupied himself with learning about some obscure detail of the realm.

Well, one thing was different here, Kestrel thought as he tried to shake himself out of numbness. Although the hex had been unoccupied by the enemy when they arrived, a crate taller than a man and longer than four lying head to toe lay in the center, apparently abandoned as part of some other move.

"Abel, what are these weapons of the berserkers, you speak about?" he called out to the commander of the squadron who shared the vertex with him. "The ones that give them such advantage unless you can take them by surprise. Are such things in this crate?"

One of the warriors looked up from where he had been conversing with two others over the small portable table covered with the map of the warboard. His complexion was slate-gray like the rest, but streaks of black ran through his hair like the accents sometimes affected by the older ladies of the court in the realm of men. . His eyes shown steady and unblinking in a face not creased by either smile or frown.

"They produce chaos rather than order — a violation of the protocols," Abel said with disgust in his voice, "The weapons of the berserker's own realm. It is best that they are destroyed as soon as possible."

"What kind of weapons?" Kestrel asked. "Something that would give you an advantage if you had them instead? Do they, by chance, involve the use of fire?"

"We would never use the devices of the berserkers." Abel pursed his lips. "When we defeat them in battle, we bury the mechanisms instead."

"You are afraid to show them to me then —"

"An enforcer is seldom afraid," Abel cut him off. He stood with purpose and gestured to one of the other blue warriors. "We will look at some now. Then you might better understand."

The second fighter began to protest, but Abel's stare made his stop. The warrior spat at the ground at his feet, dropped his shovel, and then began swinging a heavy sledge at the structure at the center of the hex.

"Note that it has no wheels," Abel said, as the first blow shattered the panel on the left, revealing the contents inside. "In the first compartment are four lifters that hold the crate off of the ground so that it can be easily moved from hex to hex as part of a march."

"I saw what looked like balloons at the hex where we first met," Kestrel said. "But they were not shaped as one would expect."

"What the magicians in your realm call toroids, Kestrel," Astron said as he came to Abel's side. I suspect that the berserkers worried about what would happen if the tether to one of them slipped off during a

214

march. By looping cords through the center of each torus rather than use knots at the bottom, they could ensure that would not happen."

"The lifters are of no concern," Abel answered as a second panel splintered. "Nor are the cranks and frames. They provide the motive power for inflating them and powering the weapons of war."

Kestrel and Astron leaned in to look beyond the splintered wood. In the compartment were hand and pedal cranks, chair backs, gear chains, and boxes of pulleys and wheels. The sledge crashed again, this time revealing tubing of varying lengths and a splatter of bolts and fasteners.

"This should satisfy your curiosity," Abel said as the last panel gave away. "As is characteristic of the berserkers, the weapon issue is not standardized for all their squadrons. Some crates have only two weapons, other three or four. Here it looks like there are three: an immobilizer, a body switcher, and a hallucionator — although the names are only our approximations. Each time they are used, there is some variation in what happens — what you would expect from a realm of chaos.

"Sometimes they work against the berserkers rather than for them," Abel continued. "Sometimes they do not work at all. Sometimes in a way that has never been seen before. Sometimes they disrupt symmetries at more than one oasis at a time."

"You mean like pulling a skunk out of a hat?" Kestrel asked.

"That I do not understand," Abel frowned. "But no matter. As far as we can surmise, berserkers attack oases at random. Most often as single squadrons, but sometimes, rarely, in a coordinated fashion." He paused. "It is well that they do not coordinate all of the time. If they did, if they consistently used only those devices that were proven effective and reliable, we would have been defeated and the contest ended long ago."

"What does a hallucionator —", Astron began.

"Then why are you losing?" Kestrel asked.

"You have not witnessed how chaotic the berserkers are," Abel shook his head. "Some truly live up to their name: wild men who care nothing for their own defense and lash out at whoever opposes them. Others lie down and die rather than stand from where they have been slumbering. Only a few use the laws of symmetry and participate in the dance of engagement.

"It is all very — very disconcerting, the discord, the chaos," Abel lowered his eyes. "Sometimes we get disheartened and just retreat so that our minds remain sane. It is why we strive to always attack with overwhelming odds rather than one to one combats. The same expected outcome is an element of order, the ways things should be."

One of the warriors from another of the vertices interrupted and called to Abel. The commander turned away without another word and resumed his duties. The abruptness of the enforcer did not bother Kestrel. He had come to realize that there was little need for courtesy in a realm such as this, but the information he had learned had been most interesting. Perhaps there was something in what Abel had said that would help them in their plight. Kestrel glanced at Astron, trying to draw out the significance of what he had heard, but the demon was again occupied by the parchment in his lap.

A flash of color at another of the vertices drew Kestrel's attention away. Something was happening that he had not seen before. A giant sling had been strung between two of the trees. While he watched, a roll of brilliant blue cloth was launched in a high arc into the sky. Like a streaking comet, the material unfolded into an eye-catching arch that could be seen almost at the edge of vision, cryptic symbols painted upon it dangling in the sky. After it had plummeted back to the ground, several of the warriors began rewinding a rope that had been attached to the banner's tail, retrieving the cloth so it could be rolled back up into a coil.

Four of the warriors at one of the vertices scanned the horizon, three more looked out along paths that ran to other hexagons, and two others at angles in between. Almost as soon as the signal bolt was retrieved, there was a flash of motion down the line of sight that was farthest to the left. Another banner of blue adorned with symbols soared up into the sky in answer to the first signal.

Then in a wise direction from the first, just barely above the horizon and far more distant, four more banners replied as well. All eyes turned to the right most path, the last of the six, but the sky remained calm. There was no arch of color sailing into the sky.

A sudden babble of excitement erupted from the enforcers. Even though they had not yet eaten, shield straps were tightened and a dozen or more began practicing stylized jumps and feints with their swords.

"What is happening?" Kestrel asked Astron.

The demon stopped tracing his finger across a copy of the tiled plane and listened to the rush of voices that Kestrel could not quite follow.

"The prospect of battle is high." Astron raised his head from the map. "This hexagon can be thought of as a vertex of a larger one, just like one of the fruit trees around the oasis. The enforcers also occupy the two on the left and two more on the right. The berserkers who were in the central target have moved to the vertex at the bottom.

"The enforcers here arm for a fight against an enemy they have not

216

even seen," Astron shook his head in the manner of men. "The maps may show oasis occupancy but not the strength of the warriors that are there. And this time, additional berserkers would be pulled into the central target as well. The odds will be five to one, but only with all of the squadrons, theirs and ours are of equal strength.

"This upcoming move is a good one for us as well," Astron continued quietly. It is in the right direction."

"What do you mean?" Kestrel whispered back.

"It places us one oasis closer to the origin," the demon answered. "Look at the map — the one hex that is the center of all the others. It has a different marking, The rest are arrayed about it."

Kestrel frowned. He still did not comfortably understand symmetries.

"The origin is least bound by the forces of law here," Astron continued. "It is the one oasis for which there need not be the same activities on another in order for things to happen with great power. At the origin, the unusual is more likely permitted to occur. There, we have some hope — some hope of performing wizardry and building a fire."

The woodcutter's spirits lifted. "Yes," he exclaimed, "Far better than just continuing in mind-numbing lock step. You may well be right!"

He studied Astron's map with far keener interest. "After the battle, will we press on even closer to this origin?" he asked.

"Not necessarily. If the enforcers do not see such moves as part of a plan to surround another berserker hex nearby, they will travel elsewhere, and it will be difficult for us to resist being carried along."

"Then, they will need a little convincing." Kestrel smiled and rubbed his hands together.

His thoughts began to jump as he regarded Abel with calculating eyes. "Help me with the details, Astron. Perhaps fanning the fear of a sacrificial gambit just might be a good thing to try."

217

Berserker's Gambit

AFTER CONFERRING with Aston a while more, Kestrel sprang to his feet and walked to the vertex occupied by Abel. Fortunately, the enforcers had so carefully distributed everyone about the oasis that the resistance to maintaining symmetry was small.

"Commander," he asked, "how cunning have the berserkers proven to be in the past?"

Abel looked up from the map he was studying and pursed his lips. "The berserkers do not act with cunning. If they did, I would grant them a small token of respect. Instead, they employ any methods to enforce advantage — poisoning oases just as they leave or imitating our signal ribbons with messages of deception."

"And you?" Kestrel smiled. "The enforcers do not engage in such tactics when the alternative would be a defeat?"

"Certainly not." Abel glowered. "It is the fundamental difference between the two of us. We wish to rid this realm of the berserkers, it is true, but for the enforcers, symmetry and order are everything. The finish does not justify all paths."

Kestrel scanned the horizon and rubbed his chin. "Suppose I can provide you a method that will result in a substantial advantage," he said, "something that might tip the struggle in your favor, but is entirely consistent with the protocols of order."

"I do not know the customs of your realm," Abel replied. "What you judge to be of no consequence might be out of concert with what we enforcers believe."

"It is more a — a matter of cunning than the poisoning of wells," Kestrel said.

"Speak and I shall judge. If what you say has merit, then I will pledge my token to your command and all of those who can be communicated with by sky ribbon as well."

Kestrel peered into the cold gray eyes and hesitated. Among men, he had seen such an expression only in the most steadfast of wizards. "I do not seek your command," he said. "I propose only to offer advice. If it is accepted, then the results will be compensation enough for those who travel with me."

"I command this squadron or I do not," Abel replied. "If your plan is accepted, then you carry the burden of responsibility for its execution. That has been the way of the enforcers since the beginning of time."

Kestrel glanced around the oasis uncomfortably. Enough of the warriors at other vertices had overheard the conversation that they were looking at him. His goal was to get Phoebe and himself back to the realm of men safely so that the archimage could again be approached, he told himself. He glanced out over the sands and felt a return of the feelings that had pulled at him until just moments before. There was no other choice. He would have to see through to the fruition of Astron's insight and work out the consequences later.

"I think that rather than moving to the hexagon that we now surround with five hexes of our own," Kestrel said, "we should strike instead for the origin of the realm by another route. The present maneuver is too obvious. It is most likely a trap. What do you say to surrendering responsibility if such were my first command?"

"Your scheme is one of correct moves and nothing more?" Abel asked. "No special weapons outside the custom?"

"No, none of that," Kestrel said. "But that is not the point."

"That is the point entirely," Abel contradicted. "A scheme that has order is all that I ask. Sketch for me on the map the moves you propose. If they show greater merit than the plan for the moment, then we are yours to lead."

Kestrel stared back at the cold unblinking eyes that resembled those of a horned owl preparing to hunt. He looked for some hint of reservation in Abel's expression, some indication that the blue warrior was merely agreeing until he revealed more of what he had in mind. But the face was void of veiled tension. Provided that it aided the enforcer's cause, the commander appeared quite willing to hand everything over to the woodcutter. The warrior took his words at face value and trusted him in what he said just as if he were a venerated hero from the sagas.

His sense of discomfort grew. This was totally unlike his dealings in the realm of men. There, he always sought to find the hidden failings, the weakness that he could exploit to consummate the deal. And when he was done, his conscience was not bothered. An honest man would not have been tempted by what he had to offer in the first place. In the end, the prey got what he deserved.

But this time, there was no real reason other than his own to move in the direction of the origin. It was an out-and-out swindle that simple beings created by the imagination did not deserve.

"No, forget it," Kestrel said. "Your plan is perhaps best after all. Proceed to seize the surrounded oasis as you have planned."

"Your words cannot be so easily put aside," Abel shook his head. "The origin has been a matter of some concern since it was seized by the berserkers some three hundred moves ago. Taking it back might compensate for some of our recent losses." The warrior touched the sword pommel at his side. "If you indeed have a scheme of merit, you must tell us your plan so that we can judge."

Kestrel hesitated, but Abel did not waver. With a slow deliberateness, the warrior began to withdraw his sword from its scabbard like a dragon awaking hungry from a long sleep. Kestrel glanced at Astron waiting expectantly and over at Phoebe staring vacantly into space. He pointed at the map.

"It is merely a conjecture," he said, trying to buy time with his words. "See, here is the target hex, here are the five surrounding ones occupied by you and the other squadrons. The sixth here is possessed by the berserkers, and by converging simultaneously you hope to draw them into the target with you — just as you did with me and the others."

"That is apparent to all," Abel growled. "What is your plan that has superior merit?" Several other warriors stopped whatever they were doing and drew closer to hear Kestrel's words.

"Apparent to all — as you state, that is exactly what I wish to emphasize," Kestrel said. "What about the ring of hexes that surround even these six that you control — the ones that lie even farther from the target?"

"Yes, that is the trap," he continued before anyone could answer. "When you perform your maneuver and collapse, all six of the surrounding hexagon will be vacated. While you stockpile for your next move at the site of victory, the berserkers might be able to possess a dozen symmetric hexes further out with a few simple moves. Then, added by symmetry, they can converge on you swiftly. You, yes, you will be the ones outnumbered — outnumbered by two to one even if you have no losses in your initial success. The berserkers might sacrifice one squadron the size of one of yours, and in the end, you eventually will lose five in return."

A murmur of surprise erupted from the warriors who were listening. Abel's sword arm relaxed.

"That is not possible," the commander said after a moment. "Berserkers do not coordinate their moves. As I have told you, they are random and result in, at worst, a contest of one on one."

"Not *probable*, I agree," Kestrel said. "But not *possible*? You yourself have said that from time to time the berserkers acted in coordination. And isn't it a bit odd that they would move out of the target oasis just as you occupy the five surrounding, making it so tempting for you to converge and draw them back in?"

"A sacrifice of one to gain five." Abel looked at the map and back to Kestrel with respect. "I would not have thought of it, nor would any other of our side. It would be just like the berserkers, though, shedding some of their own blood, so long as it produced a greater gain." He puckered his lips. "Your logic has great force. What, then, is the alternative?"

"It is merely conjecture," Kestrel repeated, "a thought experiment about what might be the berserkers' intent. I have no proof that it is so."

"But as you said, the convergence to the center of the hexagon is so obvious. Tell us the rest and then you can lead."

Kestrel pointed out over the horizon. "There," he said. "We should move to an oasis in that direction independent of the other four squadrons and they should move in the same lateral direction as well. Then we all should converge on an unoccupied oasis some distance away, and after that, march as a brigade from oasis to oasis towards the origin — five squadrons strong, able to take on anything that stands in our way."

Abel squinted out over the desert a final time and then nodded. He turned back to Kestrel and unclasped his sword belt. "The plan has merit," he said without any rancor. "We will foil the berserkers' plan to sacrifice one for five. Assume the command. We will do as you say."

Kestrel observed Abel's unwavering eyes. He waited for some tiny twinge or movement but saw none. "Signal the other squadrons," he said in a resigned voice. "Inform them of the plan so that there is no misunderstanding." Reluctantly, he took the offered belt and put it around his waist. It felt far heavier than it should.

The Burden of Command

KESTREL WAITED impatiently by the oasis tree for the last of the fruit to be squeezed into the bowl. It was quite tart to be drunk undiluted, as he knew from his first experimentation, but it was tolerable and could just as easily be carried on the march in canteens or a tank on wheels. He shrugged. They could do nothing, of course, until the time of the next move. Perhaps the reason of the empty rituals was no more than to keep everyone occupied and not thinking about what was to come.

Only one of the other enforcer squadrons had also accepted Kestrel's plan. The other three had remained behind to maneuver into new symmetries and continue fighting in the traditional way. Not constrained by coordinating with enforcers at other oases, the two remaining squadrons had followed a zigzag path over the warboard, avoiding coming close to any oasis occupied by the berserkers. But now, nearer the origin, the enemy occupied too many hexes to make further progress unchallenged. Kestrel did not like it, but a battle must be fought for them to move on, and the odds would not be five to one as Astron and he had hoped but only a factor of two.

Abel carefully decanted oasis water into the bowl on top of the thick juice. The liquid ran down the side without mixing and like oil on water formed a crystal-clear layer on top of the opaque orange sludge on which it rode. Besides the former commander, two other warriors flailed at the wrung-out pap on large flat stones, pressing it into a thin layer of sticky paste. Before the next move, the gentle breezes would have dried the pulp into a fine powder that was packed away against the contingency of arriving at a hex with nothing fresh to eat.

After the last of the water had been added, Abel opened a spout near the bottom of the bowl and let the juice flow out to fill a large spoon. Then, with a practiced deftness, the enforcer stopped the flow, raised the spoon back over the top edge of the bowl, plunged it into the water layer, and stirred it about. The juice sprayed into a shower of the fine droplets that added a hint of orange to the transparent crispness of the water but somehow did not disturb the darker opaqueness that rested beneath.

Kestrel yawned, partially from the tension of waiting, but also because by now he had seen the ritual more than a dozen times. The movement along the paths defining the hexagons had been true marches, trudging for full moves without the benefit of any boosts from symmetry. And after each march, many more moves were spent in one place, stockpiling food and water for the next segment of the journey.

Abel returned the spoon to the spout near the bottom of the bowl, collected some of the lower liquid, and mixed it with the top. Again, he extracted a portion of the result and swirled it with the bottom. With each transfer, the water became more and more cloudy, the juice more and more fluid and transparent, and the horizontal line marking the boundary between the two harder and harder to detect.

Finally, after perhaps a score of transfers, the boundary line began to buckle and writhe. Fingers of liquid started to intertwine and merge. In an indefinable instant, the two liquids coalesced into one with no distinction between them. Abel grunted in satisfaction, and the warriors began lining up with their cups and gourds.

Soon everyone at Kestrel's vertex and those at the other vertices as well had his fill of juice and wind-dried bread. According to the plan, the provisions to carry forward had been augmented. In a rigorous sequence, the warriors began nodding off to sleep, assuming a variety of positions, some leaning against the trees, while others curled up into tight balls near the roots.

The eyes of the last one closed, and then Kestrel smiled across the hex at Phoebe. Now that he was the commander, he should at least be able to move about as he decided, especially since Abel now dozed with the rest. With a grin of anticipation, he started to walk toward her vertex, but then halted. Abel always seemed to sense when the next move was about to begin, he thought. The commander would shout the call to order and begin assembling the warriors into formation with just sufficient time to start marching out when the flash of green filled the sky.

Kestrel slapped the pommel of the heavy sword. It would not do if everyone staggered awake in disarray while he was in mid-dalliance with the wizard. He scowled at the direction his thoughts were taking him. Such concerns were madness. What difference did it make what Abel and the others judged of his actions? They were no more than creatures of imagination. He had no real allegiance to them. They were merely the means to the end of achieving deliverance.

He ran his fingers over the smooth grooves that spiraled up the hilt of the sword. It was heavy, true, but even in the short time he had worn it, despite the undercurrent of the entrapment, there was a degree of excitement as well, something he had not felt since before he first met Evelyn. All the warriors now nodded to him with that subtle hint of respect that only Abel had received before. He was now more than just another body that broke the symmetry of the vertex. He was the commander in whom they trusted the course of the next move.

Kestrel sighed. His emotions began to churn in a tumble. Creatures of imagination or not, they deserved better than one such as he. There was no deceit in Abel's eyes or in any of the others that followed him — only trust in the one who wore the commander's sword.

Kestrel stepped back to the tree and folded his arms across his chest as he had seen Abel do before. Slowly, he began counting in his head, ticking off the featureless time as best he was able. After twenty thousand counts, he decided, he will call out the alert.

Attack

KESTREL BOBBED and weaved in the whistling wind. Strong eddies created by the rucksack on his back rocked him about. Unlike the enforcers, he could not help but stumble as they converged on the target. But the grace of his motion was not the primary concern. Far sooner than he wished, the next oasis, the one occupied by berserkers, was fast approaching.

The tops of the ring of trees sharpened in the distance and then the lower trunks. Kestrel had held his breath, hoping that there would be no berserker weapons to deal with, but that was not to be. Sentinels had spotted their movement. Eight lifters were straining to be aloft. There were two squadrons of berserkers at the oasis, not just one. The enforcers would not have a numerical advantage. The battle could go either way.

"Be on your guard," Abel shouted over to him as they neared. "The dance of engagement might be tricky the first time."

Kestrel started to apologize for what he was leading the enforcers into but then thought better of it. Concentrating on exactly where he would land and whom he immediately would be facing was far better to think about for now. He glanced at Phoebe, sprinting along behind him and slightly to the right. He did not like the possibility of her being separated and sent off to another of the vertices, but there was nothing he could do about it. And somehow, Astron and Nimbia would take have to care of themselves as best they could.

As they drew closer, the rest of the details of the oasis crispened in the hazy sky like those of a microscope specimen brought into focus. From the distance, except for the color, the arming berserkers looked no different from the enforcers: pallid complexions, leather vests, leggings and boots of red, and blades of orange-copper at their waists

Four of the enemy ran to the weapon crates, jumped on seats in frames and begin pedaling with determined energy. From their angle of approach, Kestrel could see around the corner of the first crate into the unshielded innards. Cogwheels the height of a man meshed with teeth the size of interleaved fists. A loosely coiled escapement banged against a long ratchet that filled the full height of its partition. Axles squeaked and gears whirled the mechanism came to life.

Kestrel did not have time to observe more. With a final whoosh, he swerved to the right as he approached. His teeth clanged with the contact with the ground. For a moment, his vision blurred from the shock. He shook his head and reached for his blade, finding a sudden resistance to the motion of his arm. One of Abel's lieutenants was at his side and two of the berserkers faced them an arm's length away. This was it! No time to think more. Just concentrate on staying alive.

He strained again for his blade, but the resistance was greater than before. One of the berserkers laughed, and the other eyed him with a satisfied grin. His brow was low and his nose was pinched as if by a crab.

Kestrel again eyed the lieutenant, then the berserkers. With the skill of a synchronized ballet, the two warriors facing them reached in unison for their swords, and the enforcer copied their motion, flowing with it, rather than trying to resist. Kestrel pushed toward the scabbard a final time, but to no avail. He had not noticed it before, but of all those who fought, he was the only one who was right-handed.

With an awkward thrust, he twisted his left arm down his side, fumbling to draw his sword and pushing away the thought of the hopelessness of what he was doing. To his surprise, it did not fall from his grip as he pulled it free, but soared to a guard position in front of his body, just like the others.

The warriors yelled and swung viciously downward, and Kestrel's arm followed through with the rest. With a grating shriek like that of a file against the side of a bell, the blades scraped past one another and crashed point-first into the ground. Then as one, all four of the combatants lifted the swords and lunged forward, turning bodies to the side to avoid the duplicated thrusts by their opponents.

The motions were not precise copies. Straining as best he could, Kestrel was able to twist his blade horizontal as he drew it back. Trembling from the resistance, he turned a cutting edge slightly to the side and sliced into the leather vest of the berserker as the warrior drew back.

A trickle of blood ran down the enforcer lieutenant's right arm, but his eyes were still clear and determined. In a flash, Kestrel understood how the battle was waged. The forces of symmetry compelled all of the lunges to be nearly the same. The strikes were aimed to be near misses, rather than vital thrusts. And then the extra straining effort or slightly longer reach would do the real damage while avoiding a similar wound in return. Kestrel gripped the pommel tighter, but the strangeness did not go away. If anyone would be at a disadvantage, it would be he.

The four closed again, this time with backhand swipes across the body that stopped just short of the neck. Kestrel strained to push his blade forward while tipping his own head to the side. His arm quivered but proceeded no further, while his opponent shook his own blade back and forth in tiny arcs, trying to break it free to strike a finger-width more.

The woodcutter took a deep breath and gritted his teeth. Tightening the muscles the length of his arm and twisting his torso, he increased the pressure, realizing that, if all four pushed too hard simultaneously, they would all suffer the same. His blade covered half the distance to the bulging artery of the berserker, and then he sucked in his breath as a prickly line of pain caressed his own skin. Almost instinctively, he halted his plunge and reversed direction, but the pressure did not release. The grin on his opponent's face broadened. He was trapped immobile and could not move.

Suddenly, clockworks at the center of the hex sounded in a deep resonant gong. There was a cry of surprise and a flurry of motion at the next vertex in line. The clock struck a second time. In a blur, his sword spun from his hand high into the air. Simultaneously, the pressure released from his neck.

Kestrel craned his head upward. His sword and the three others arced in a complex swirl and then fell back toward the earth like spent missiles from sieging ballistas. Spinning with precision, the pommel of one returned to his grip, in the same manner as the first had left it. With a scrape of skin, the pressure returned to the side of his neck. The four swords had been interchanged! He blinked with surprise. Clockwork? Gongs? Abel had not mentioned any of this. What was happening?

The clock sounded again, and the lieutenant at Kestrels side choked a startled cry. Involuntarily, Kestrel glanced to see if his comrade had fallen, but he had not. Instead, the warrior's face contorted into a grim smile as he shifted his blade to point at Kestrel's chest.

At the same time, the pressure at Kestrel's neck fell away and he wrenched his head back to reface his adversary. The smile was gone, and the eyes bulged in confusion. The remaining berserker disengaged and also turned to strike at the one in front of Kestrel.

Kestrel gaped at what was happening. Somehow, his adversary had been switched! And it was not just the externals. The one who had fought at his side was now across from him, the one at the side, the adversary. It was just as Abel had tried to explain. The striking of the berserker clock mixed up things spatially in strange ways — even the inner beings between the enforcers and berserkers were being transformed from one body into another!

On the third gong of the clock, there were more cries from around the oasis. First, one and then two other enforcers were catapulted into the air. Their bodies wrenched into unnatural trajectories and hurled toward the horizon with breathtaking force. Almost immediately, berserkers sailed into view and landed in the spots vacated by their foes. At several of the vertices, the ratio of fighters shifted to a clear disadvantage for the enforcers.

The clock sounded again. This time, Phoebe's shriek intermingled with the rest.as she rose into the air and then sailed from view. He stared at the sword now being drawn back to strike at his midsection and for an instant hesitated, uncertain on how to counter the blow.

Before Kestrel could decide, the clock struck a note deeper than before. A sudden blur of nausea welled up within him. The scene before his eyes shimmered and then turned to a blurry gray. He felt a wrenching disorientation and then a sudden rush of heat as if he had a great fever. His body seemed suddenly strange and he staggered and almost fell. The resistance to his motion changed.

The blur dissolved. Kestrel blinked at what he saw. No longer was he at a vertex with three other warriors but near the clock itself. Berserkers on either side were drawing their swords, arms back across their bodies, preparing for deep thrusts toward his chest. He held his own sword pointed directly out in front. A net of tiny scales on the back of his hand ran up his forearm into his sleeve. Somehow, he was conscious of a stubble of minute bristly hairs in the web of his fingers and between his toes.

Back across the oasis, what could only be an exact image of himself was still locked in synchrony with the lieutenant trying to ward off the attack coming from the side. It could not be possible! Kestrel tried to deny the thought, but the feeling of all of his senses could not be denied.

"Astron," he called across the sand. "Somehow we have been transposed like the others. Do not fight the lieutenant. Turn clockwise with him and swing totally about."

He need not have bothered. With the final gong of the clock, Kestrel's body vaulted up into the air and then streak away like the ones before. Grimly, in Astron's body, he forced his attention back to how he was going to ward off the two berserkers with the sword in his alien left hand.

Around him, the dance of encounter had dissolved into a mêlée of confusion. The color of the armor no longer was a clue as to who was friend and who was foe. Blue warriors fought blue; red fought red. Kestrel glanced to the periphery. Many of the squadron he commanded had started to fall back in confusion. They must be true enforcers no longer able to cope.

"To me, to me," he shouted above the din. Where the words were coming from, he did not know. His sword arm felt free in the chaos; there was no symmetry, no pattern. He warded off the blow to the right and then savagely lunged at the berserker on the other side.

"To me, to me, the one with the scales. I am Kestrel, the commander of the enforcers. Rally about me and follow my example. Man to man, in complete chaos we shall fight them, one to one."

Spare Parts

ASTRON FELT the sand under the strange fingertips. First, there had been the blurring and transformation so unlike a journey between the realms. And then the flight away from the fighting to this deserted hex. He had to still his stembrain before he could think further.

The demon tried to flip down his membranes and then frowned in annoyance when they would not come. He reached for the panic that should be upwelling and concentrated on making it still, imagining pouring a viscous medicine over stormy thoughts.

Eyes blinked open. He looked about, surprised. There was no panic, no rumble at the base of his skull. He felt an internal discomfort from the flight and jarring landing, and his heart seemed to throb for no apparent reason, but otherwise he was in complete control of his thoughts.

Phoebe staggered to standing at the vertex to the left, but Astron noticed no other occupants of the oasis. Dimly, he remembered a berserker passing him halfway in his flight, going the other direction. He released the sword he still held in his left hand and watched it fall at his side. His nose wrinkled as small curly hairs appeared on the back of his hand and arm, providing a wiry cover to a pale, smooth skin.

Kestrel, he thought. What had the human shouted about the transpositions that the berserkers were effecting? He held both arms up and then touched the smoothness of his forehead. He ran a finger over the more or less even row of teeth in his mouth and, reaching to his back, felt no knobs where the degenerate wing stubs should have been.

Breathing deeply, he marveled at the feeling of the air coursing in and out of his lungs. A growl sounded in his stomach and a pleasant longing teased at his mind. Unbidden images of meat sizzling on a spit and the smell of fresh bread flitted, real and compelling, like the lure of an experienced succubus.

"Oh, Kestrel, thank the random factors that you are here," Phoebe shouted as she ran to his vertex. "The blood and fighting with all that overpowering restraint were far worse than the alchemist's foundry. We are lucky to have survived."

He was not Kestrel, Astron thought. Words of denial started to form in his throat, but his tongue felt strange and he only managed a cough instead.

"What is it?" Phoebe asked as she held wide her arms and stepped forward, beckoning.

Astron motioned for her to stop and took a cautious step backward.

"What is it?" Phoebe repeated. "Tell me everything is all right. I can stand no more chaos and surprise."

The tension etched in Phoebe's face like slashes from a knife. The events had been unsettling, perhaps more so to a human than to one of his own kind. Whatever was decided to be done next, he certainly would need her aid. And he knew from struggles through the flame in eons past how fragile was the will to survive. It was perhaps best to explain all that had happened at a better time. He wrinkled his nose and then began to speak. The tenor of the first words startled him, but he held all the tiny muscles that were alive in his face rigidly taut.

"Do not be concerned." He measured his words carefully. "For the moment, we are safe. Take a few heartbeats to bring your stembrain — your feelings under control and then we can proceed."

"But we are separated from the others. What are we to do?"

"To the origin," Astron answered. His thoughts seemed to rush forward without the benefit of deliberation. "There is no change in our intent. There you will summon a demon to get us home."

Phoebe pulled a folded map from a pocket in her gown and began to open it, but then shrugged. "It is kind that you still show faith in my ability, Kestrel," she said with eyes lowered, "but in truth, the reality of my shortcomings has become clearer with each passing moment. Reaching the origin may be all well and good, but without Nimbia fully recovered, there is little point for such a journey."

She looked out over the sands back in the direction from which they had come. "And how can we proceed the way we want when these forces of symmetry flip us from hex to hex? Without Astron, how do we stand a chance? He seemed to have a knack for figuring out these mathematical things."

"Yes, the devil," Astron echoed. He shook his head to keep his thoughts straight. "Once a djinn is under your command, you can task him to soar over this desert until he finds the others. But if such a demon were here, the first thing he would do is …"

Astron stopped and for the first time examined the oasis. It was very much like all the rest, six trees at the vertices of a hexagon. Strewn all about, however, was the debris left by the berserkers who had occupied it before the battle and the transformations that occurred. At the adjacent vertex on the left stood a pile of branches hacked from the treetops to make soft beds. Denuded limbs and an axe were tossed in a heap nearby.

At the next vertex around the periphery was one of the devices of the berserkers in obvious disrepair. Stacks of gears, springs, and pedal cranks were scattered about a nearly empty framework. Three or four thick leather vests stood in a heap next to a pile of eyelets, buckles, and sewing thongs. Two nicked and rusting swords rested against the tree behind.

"From the looks of things this oasis served as a camp for perhaps a dozen," Phoebe said.

"And yet when the battle began, evidently it was occupied only by two," Astron replied. "Otherwise, now you and I would not be the only ones here." He waved his arm out over the bleached sands. "The rest must have dispersed to yet other oases and then converged back to where the enforcers attacked. Perhaps it had something to do with the working of the devices of the berserkers."

He studied the disarray a second time. "One thing is for sure. There is more than enough here to break up the symmetries between the vertices for the two of us. We can move about with comparative ease."

Astron's voice trailed off. The glimmer of an idea popped into his mind. He paced off two of the longest and straightest three branches and dragged them around the periphery to the remains of the weapon crate. He rummaged through the stacks of debris until he found the two matched petal cranks and gear chains and wheels that fit them.

"What are you doing?" Phoebe called out.

Astron ignored the question. "Rummage through the rest of this," he told her, "and start looking for a pump, something that was used to inflate the lifters. And go across to the armory and cutting the vests into leather strips. We will concern ourselves about your abilities later. For now, let us get this thing built before some part of my mind is able to convince me otherwise."

Demonlust

ASTRON UNBUCKLED the harness from his chest with a deep sigh. His muscles ached. What had been the pleas and longing in his stomach had turned into an insistent discomfort. He looked over his shoulder in the dimming daylight. Phoebe was unfastening the half-dozen belts that held her to the long metal frame. She had not complained during the entire trek, and surely, the strains on her body must have been the same as his.

Astron ducked under the branch on his left and smiled at his handiwork. If stood on end, the buggy would tower three times the height of a mundane djinn. At front and rear, gear chains connected to the pedal cranks turned the berserker lifters. Like giant round pastries with holes in the middle, they spread the weight across the sand and allowed Phoebe and him to pedal the contraption directly from one hex to the next. Sometimes, with a burst of energy, they were able to sprint forward against their harnesses and then raise their feet and coast for a few moments before friction brought them to a halt.

Far more important than the practicalities, however, were the other additions to the craft. Five more gear wheels of odd sizes hung along the sides at haphazard positions like the arrangement of a mad artist. Here and there, small clusters of greenery sprouted at odd angles. The rusted swords all pointed skyward from three of the four top corners and the eating utensils and cans of orange powder swung from the cross struts. Even though it gave them some difficulty in steering, the harnesses that connected them to the frame were offset from one another. Astron was near the center of the very front while Phoebe was halfway to the rear and nearly touching the left side.

At first, Phoebe had protested adding all the extra weight and the number of belts that she had to wrap around her waist. But when the first tug of the symmetries had come and passed over them with barely a ripple she understood the intent. They were not two separate individuals but coupled together as one. Their engine was in all probability unlike anything else in the realm. There was no increase in symmetry in transporting it to a particular hex or switching it with anything else. They could move as they chose without constraints or regard to the actions of others.

"Go and gather some fruits." He waved at the hex that was in the middle distance before them. "Then I will pedal the engine the rest of the way to it. We are making excellent progress."

Yes, if not impeded they could reach the origin, he thought. But the map he had studied denoted that there was no oasis there. What then? It was as bare as most of the other hexes. Without food and water, how would they manage to survive for long even if they all got there?

"There is ripe fruit enough that we can provision for several moves," Phoebe said as she returned to the engine. She untied several of the canisters still swinging from the frame and beckoned Astron to the vertex where she had laid out a cloth.

Astron finished pulling the engine to the water's edge at one of the vertices and then sat down across from the meal that Phoebe had prepared. With a dedicated savagery that surprised himself, he began to gobble down the slices almost as fast as Phoebe could place them, hardly bothering to sprinkle on the flours from the canisters that balanced the meal. Only dimly was he aware of the cool pleasure of the juices that dripped over his hands or the tartness that tingled in his mouth.

When he was finally done, he leaned backward with a feeling of contentment unlike anything he had experienced before. He shook his head in wonder. The sensations were quite pleasurable ones, but such a weakness it must be for humans. Without food and drink, their thoughts would soon be driven to distraction. They would abandon all reason, just as if their minds were seized by the most powerful of stembrains. And unlike his own kind, there would be no hope for remaining in control.

Astron studied Phoebe through half-closed eyes. There was much risk in this quest for his prince, and yet much reward as well, he thought. He had learned things that no other cataloguer could have even suspected. Even Palodad probably had no notion of the concept of hunger or of how it truly tugged at one's will.

Phoebe smiled back at Astron and swept the remains of their meal aside. She closed the distance between them and put her hand up to touch Astron's cheek. "I wonder about the others, Kestrel," she said. "But there is some advantage for the events as they have happened. For the first time in a very long while, we are alone."

Phoebe slid her hand behind Astron's neck and put her lips to his.

Astron choked in confusion. Words would not come. He found his arms reaching around the wizard and pulling her even closer to him. As he did, a strange new feeling coursed through his body. He sucked in his breath at the intensity of it.

He was keenly aware of the softness of her back under the palms of his hands, even though her jerkin was between. The press of her body tightened everywhere it touched. Without thinking, he maneuvered so that the pleasure of it would be greater. His pulse quickened and his breath grow more shallow like that of a dog on a summer day.

Desire swirled through his thoughts until only the tiniest ember of rationality remained. This was not like the duty for the broodmothers. No cataloguer had dreamed of its potency, of that he was quite sure.

"You know that it does not matter," Phoebe whispered. "It does not matter, whatever happens, Kestrel, just so long as we are together."

Kestrel. In Astron's mind, the name jarred like a cart losing a wheel and it did not go away. It was Kestrel that Phoebe was giving herself to, and not a wingless demon who could not weave. It should be the woodcutter's pleasure and not his.

Astron peered at Phoebe's expectant eyes in confusion. It would be Kestrel's body, nonetheless. Her sensations would be the same. In addition, he would catalogue yet another experience of humankind. It was his duty to his prince. Astron licked his lips. The yearning was crisp and sharp, like the most brilliant sodium flame. Perhaps if it was not the first time, if he were more jaded to the senses of men, it would feel different, but there was a rush of emotion now and he must decide what to do.

"It is a compelling pleasure," Astron mumbled. "In the realm of men, pleasure is regarded as a great good."

"The pleasure is because it is you," Phoebe whispered.

How much of what he was feeling was merely the construction of the bodies of men, Astron wondered. How much was some part of Kestrel that still lurked around the edges of his thoughts? What happened exactly when two awarenesses were switched, anyway? Was Kestrel, in the body of a demon, experiencing the same temptations with Nimbia? Did the woodcutter still remember his human emotions and seek to gratify them as best he could?

A sudden wash of reluctance cascaded over his desire. Kestrel and Nimbia — it would not be right. She did not deserve to be deceived in the way that the woodcutter exploited his own kind. And if she did consent, it would be because she thought it was Astron the demon, not a weak-bodied human slave given to hunger, thirst, sleep, and who knew what other tugs and emotions.

"What is the matter?" Phoebe said. "You feel so stiff, so uncertain."

Astron pulled Phoebe tight one final time and sighed.

"It is not right," he shook his head. "Now is not the time." With an ache in his loins, he disengaged and gently pushed her away.

"Then when?"

"After we have reached the origin. After everything has been restored to the way it should be."

Phoebe cocked her head to the side but gradually her smile returned. "All right," she agreed. "Perhaps the burden of our escape rests a little more firmly on your shoulders than I realized. I should be carrying more of the load, rather than be the weepy prize of the sagas. There will be time enough when we are safe."

She turned and groped for her cape. "After our rest, let me take the front position in the sand buggy. You will need your wits if we encounter an oasis that is not vacant."

"Sand buggy?"

Phoebe laughed. "If there were dunes here, perhaps the name should be a little different. But there are not, so sand buggy it is."

Astron heard the sound of a blown kiss and then silence. He let his feelings slowly dissolve away. Getting to the origin was of the utmost urgency, he thought, but no more important than reversing the transformation between Kestrel and himself.

The Bargain

THE NEXT moves passed quickly. Phoebe made no further reference to the events of their first rest. As they made steady progress toward their goal, her spirits soared in proportion like a kite buoyed by a quickening wind. Once more accustomed to the sand buggy, they were able to increase the number of oases traversed in a single move from three to five. As with the first, each one they visited had been unoccupied. The berserkers had all moved elsewhere in their struggle with the enforcers. But as they drew closer to the origin, Astron knew, they finally would encounter a challenge and must have an explanation that would be believed.

Toward the end of the sixth move, as they reached an oasis only a hundred or so away from the origin, Astron saw what he had been dreading throughout the trek. The silhouettes of squabbling warriors reaching for fresh fruit stood out from the outline of the treetops. A lookout sounded an alarm and half-dozen swords were drawn in expectation of their arrival.

Astron's discomfort grew. Despite Kestrel's explanations, the concept of deception was still unsettling. This time, it would involve more than merely fooling a sentryman while wearing a hood. He would have to sound convincing, using facial muscles he could barely control. And with no experience, he could not judge the inherent credibility of the tale. He knew it was false. Why would not the others deduce the same? He felt the sweetness of the air course in and out of his lungs, and a slight taste of apprehension not unlike the stirring of the stembrain began to awaken within him.

"We bring greetings from our realm," Astron shouted, as the buggy grew close. "An example of a most powerful device for you to observe. We will use it to recapture the origin for the — I mean *from* the enforcers." He pointed at his chest. "Yes, I wear armor of blue, the result of an exchange in my last battle. Pay it no mind."

Astron's chest tightened while he waited for a response. His eyes darted from side to side, searching for which way to veer if they charged, even though Kestrel had told him that one must look straightforward and smile.

"I am Boltzman, a squadron leader for the berserkers." One of the warriors stepped forward from the rest. He was rail-thin, with eyes set wide as if they were trying to flee from one another. "We have heard of the increase in the vigor of the enforcer attacks, but no word that the origin has fallen as well."

The squadron leader thrust out his chest. An array of medals was randomly pinned there. None were in a straight row. Other warriors crowded about, some also adorned with pieces of leather taken from enforcer armor or carrying enforcer swords on the opposite hip from their own.

Boltzman puckered his lips. "The signal bolts cannot be wrong, yet it is still hard to believe. First, they captured an oasis, although outnumbered. Then, with an almost obsessive passion they have massed, not scores, but hundreds to take more oases from us still. The rumor is that they follow a new leader, but it is hard to see how that could make much of a difference."

Boltzman looked critically at Astron and Phoebe and then up and down the engine that they had constructed. "How can such a machine as this have any power?" he asked.

Astron let out his breath. It was just as the human had predicted! The basic premise was not rejected out of hand, no matter how outrageous it might be. Now if he could only invent quickly enough to fill in the details. With a final surge, he pedaled the buggy into their midst and called for Phoebe to halt. While his mind raced for an answer, he unbuckled the leather straps of his harness.

"This engine has the power of immunity to the forces of symmetry," he said. "How else could we travel from oasis to oasis even when it is not our move?"

"Immunity?" Boltzman asked. "How can that help? Our other devices warp and modify the force, rather than decrease it. Why, with some we can even force exchanges of body or mind." He waved his hand at the center of the hex. "That is what we amass here in preparation for a battle to blunt the drive of the enforcers."

The equipment of the berserkers was configured in much the same way as the first that Phoebe and Astron had encountered alone. This oasis was occupied with over a score of warriors, and not one, but no less than six weapon crates were sitting in the center of the hex. They were all open. Next to each a large clock had been unpacked and erected, a huge gong hanging atop of its steeple.

Boltzman noticed Astron's eyebrows raise in astonishment. "Yes, six," he said, "Six weapons we will activate at once, if and when enforcers next attack,"

"But, we do not even know what the effect will be of even one," Astron said. "What could possibly happen with six?"

"It is no matter," Boltzman said. "The attacking enforcers will be sufficiently dismayed that they will dissolve in disarray."

The squadron leader rubbed his chin. "I am a squadron leader, already bathed with glory for my prowess in battle. Show me this device's use, and then, if it has merit, surrender it to me. I will use it along with the others."

Astron felt the tug of muscles that were not there, but his nose wrinkled slightly, even with the human equipment. He had not expected this. Another false step would be disastrous.

"This device is more powerful than any that you have yet seen," the demon stalled.

"So you assert," Boltzman replied. "I repeat. Show me its use and surrender."

The wheels in Astron's mind whirled like a clock with a broken gear. 'Desire and fear', Kestrel had told him now so long ago. 'If one does not work, then try the other'. What else could he tell the squadron leader?

"The device must be controlled correctly," Astron answered with sudden inspiration. "All other weapons that are too close will not function at all. Such use would tarnish rather than add additional shine to a squadron leader's reputation."

"Boltzman frowned. "You travel to the origin in order to free it from the enforcers?" he asked. "There will be glory for just the two of you?"

"Yes."

The squadron leader thought for twenty heartbeats, eyeing the buggy all the while. "Then take me with you," he said at last. "What acclaim there that will come of it, we shall share."

This is not what was wanted, Astron thought. A berserker, even just one would be a complication that was not needed. But then if that allowed Phoebe and him to proceed, it probably was the best bargain that they could get.

"Agreed," he said.

239

Boltzman puckered his lips. "Wait! The journey *and* explanation for the use while we go," he said. "And — and two more of the squad to accomplish us as well —"

His eyes darted to the other berserkers, as if in warning, and no one spoke. "Once we have retaken the origin, then, in good faith, we will decide what the allocation of rewards shall be. Yes, yes, I think I can agree to that. Of our good faith you can be assured."

Some of Astron's tension dissolved, but not all. He wished he could be more sure, but it seemed to follow the pattern that Kestrel had explained. It was a standard negotiating technique — nibbling at the end. If he could only get Phoebe's flame started before the berserkers discovered that their duplicity was the lesser of the two. One or three berserkers, he consoled himself at last. Would that really matter?

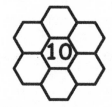

A Hint of Success

"KESTREL, I still do not understand the point of the rush," Phoebe whispered beside Astron as they approached an unoccupied oasis only a dozen away from the origin. "As I have said, without Nimbia or the services of some other wizard, it is futile to press as hard as we have. And even if we get to where you seek, Boltzman and the others will — will expect what you have promised."

"We will face the events one at a time." Astron glanced to the side between breaths. "Do not waste your energy. Concentrate only on our objective."

Astron heard the confidence in his voice as if someone else were speaking. His demon's mind knew the truth of what Phoebe said, but somehow his body would not admit it. Instead, it seemed caught up in pushing onward toward his goal. His mouth was dry. His muscles ached from the strain. Irritating pains shot from his shoulder where the leather armor had begun to chafe the soft, unscaled skin. Even the weight of the rucksack containing the harebell pollen had become a heavy burden. Yet, there was no other choice but to continue. To stop would be to surrender to the despair of the stembrain or whatever humans had in its place.

"The enforcer's next move is about to begin," Boltzman stopped pedaling as they crossed the boundary line around the oasis. He and his two lieutenants freed themselves from the harnesses they had used to help propel the buggy across the desert sands.

"We can stop here until we are refreshed," he continued, "and then on our next turn, we will strike at the origin and you will receive your — share of the reward."

Astron started to reply when the sky flashed red. Almost immediately after a deep vibrant gong like that from a king's audience chamber sounded from the direction from which they had come. He felt a tingling in his feet. The ground started to vibrate at a frequency just below his hearing. His nose wrinkled. A flick of motion at one of the vertices caught his eye. The trees had begun to oscillate. In slow unison, they swayed from side to side like synchronized metronomes. Then the water from the ponds sloshed outward to bathe the roots on one side. A great wave of sand, like a ripple in a blanket, seemed to race toward him with breath-catching speed.

The tremor passed under Astron with a mild shifting of his support. He felt his thoughts turn sluggish and difficult to understand. Then, just as suddenly as it had begun, the tremor in the ground stopped. The distant rumbling died away. Astron's head cleared and he was able to think.

Banners began to soar into the sky from the direction of the resounding gong. Boltzman watched them all intently. "Wait!" he said. "We should not continue on. My comrades there say that they are under attack. If we are to use your device, it will be here and now. The enforcers press too forcefully. We must employ everything that we can."

Astron's nose wrinkled. He tried to capture the subtle flavor of his disorientation, but with each passing heartbeat, it faded further and further away. All that remained stuck in his thoughts was the vision of the swirling juice and water.

"Perhaps it is not so wise," he said. "If your squadron is exercising more than one weapon at once, adding this may produce effects too bizarre even for a berserker. I have experienced full well what happens with two."

"We have a bargain." Boltzman ignored the question. "Your device will aid along with all the rest."

Astron started to say more when the two gongs sounded, one immediately after the other. Again, the treetops started to sway back and forth. The water in the ponds spewed from their banks in a foamy spray. A wave of sand much higher than before pulsed away from its creation.

"Brace yourself!" Astron yelled as he was thrown from his feet.

With a wrenching groan, the long beams of the engine snapped their leather bindings and he tumbled to the ground. As if it were from a stroke of lightning from the realm of men, a painful clap of thunder filled the air and reverberated into a distant rumble that left him dazed. The sky shimmered for a moment, not with green or red, but with thin lines of iridescence arching from horizon to horizon.

Astron breathed the sweet taste of air deeply and shook his head from side to side. As the sky began to return to its former steady gray brightness, Boltzman and his lieutenant started to lash the engine back to the way it had been.

"No, no more use of devices of chaos." Astron's tongue felt heavy in his mouth as he rose. "Stop them all. Wait until we understand better what the consequences truly are."

Boltzman stopped his mending. He puckered his lips and looked at Astron through squinted eyes. "What you say is most strange. On one hand, you speak of the virtues of a device from our realm. On the other, you entreat instead that such engines not be used. That is a behavior inconsistent for one of our own."

Astron felt a sudden stab of panic. "No, there is no inconsistency," he answered. "You see it is merely a matter of, a matter of "hellip;""

He tried to look Boltzman squarely in the eye but when the words would not come, he turned his face aside. Scowling, he wished for Kestrel's quickness of thought.

Boltzman waited a few moments more, then drew his sword. He motioned for his lieutenants to fall in line beside him. "I should have trusted my first instincts," he said. "What is the truth, strange one? Tell me why you and the long hair look so different from the rest we have seen."

As Phoebe regained her footing at Astron's side, he drew Kestrel's heavy sword and pointed it awkwardly at the three who advanced at him with synchronized steps. He felt his chest tighten and the air come in short gulps.

But before Boltzman and his subordinates could engage, they faltered and then fell out of sync. The eyes of the berserkers widened, and they waved their sword arms in exaggerated flourishes off to the side. Boltzman stopped and stared all the harder at Astron.

"Even in disrepair, your device still seems to disrupt the symmetries," he said. "We cannot engage you as one. It feels so very uncertain, the correct steps to take."

Astron seized the opportunity. Continuing to hold the sword in front, he spoke rapidly to Phoebe at his side. "I think we can little afford to wait for another stroke of the chime," he said. You must act now. Perform your craft as never before."

"What do you mean?" Phoebe frowned. "I have told you more than once —"

"Forget what has happened before." Astron shook her shoulder with his free hand. "It is a characteristic of the realm. No one could have started a fire at the spot where we first arrived, not even the archimage himself. But now, we are much closer to the center than we were before, perhaps close enough that the violation of symmetry caused by the flame will be small enough that it can be overcome. The origin itself would be better, but we cannot afford to wait."

He squeezed Phoebe's hand. The thrill of their previous closeness surged anew, but he managed to push it aside. "You are a wizard," he said. "A wizard as much as any other — but only if you practice your art."

"Symmetry has no bearing, Kestrel." Phoebe shook her head. "I can feel the failure even before I begin." She slumped her shoulders and began to sag back to the ground. "There is no point to endure the frustration, no matter whatever else might come. I can imagine the laughs of my council as clearly as if they were here."

A surge of anger and frustration welled up within Astron. He almost choked over the intensity of the emotion. "I do not care about your council," he yelled. "Put them from your mind."

He gulped air and rushed on. "I have heard tales of the encounters with the great wizards, far more than you might guess. I know the characteristics of the ones who were successful, the ones who controlled the mightiest djinns. They did not care about the opinions of others. The practice of their craft was not for fame or good standing with those who would be their peers.

"It was for themselves they struggled, Phoebe," he continued. "The measure of success was against goals that were known by themselves alone. The reward was increased self-esteem — acceptance of their own true worth, not the fickle opinion of the lesser ones around them whom they did not choose to control. Think! Why do you want to be a wizard? So that you can be regarded as an *equal* — or know deep within yourself that you are unique and comparable to none?"

Three gongs sounded; each one much louder than the one before. The sky again began to shimmer, and the iridescent lines stood out in a much bolder relief. Astron thought he could see faint images of gear works at nearby hexes and, with them, shadowy figures of men winding huge springs. Another wave of sand rushed at them from the oasis. This time, he was more prepared, and he pushed Phoebe to the ground before the wrenching jerk ripped away their footing.

As the wave passed, a blur of nausea like that from a tainted meal suddenly bubbled up within him. The trees of the oasis distorted in a blurring rush, as if one were somehow racing by them at a breakneck speed. The broken frame of the buggy creaked and groaned where it had fallen. With lifelike spasms, the twisted frame and snapped leather thongs reached for one another as if they were trying to mend. Some of the spewed orange flour arched upward from where it had struck the sands and cascaded back into canisters just before their lids snapped shut.

Astron felt another wave of disorientation. His thoughts slowed and then started off in a direction that he did not understand. They bounced around his head like fragments from a language not quite his own. He could only sit stunned and wait for the feeling to pass.

Eventually, the firmness of the sands returned, but Boltzman and his lieutenant did not advance, their faces limp with confusion. Astron started to say more to Phoebe, but already she was preparing to start a fire. Clutching a match in her fist, with a sweeping stroke, she ran it along the length the framework at her side.

The matchhead grated with the contact and then glowed red from the friction of passage but did not light.

"Better than before," Astron shouted encouragement. "Better than before. You must try again."

Phoebe grunted. She grabbed three matches together and ground them against the wood. The heads sparked dully and then burst into a feebly smoky flame.

For an instant, Phoebe's eyes widened in disbelief. Then she shook her head. "Some kindling — here in the pouch." She motioned with her free hand. "Make a loose pile of it, Kestrel, before the matches burn out."

Still with his sword on guard, Astron stooped and grabbed at the small pouch with his free hand and pulled out dry needles and bits of string. He smoothed a depression in the sand and clumsily constructed a fragile dome of small struts and spars. Shielding the delicate flicker of fire with her hand, Phoebe bent the matches to the kindling. She caught her breath waiting for the fire to grow.

Tendrils of smoke enveloped the needles and bits of bark. For a brief instant, a small speck began to glow red. But then the weak fire faltered and started to die. Helplessly, she watched as each little tongue of flame grew dimmer and, in a final puff of smoke, wink out.

Phoebe fumbled for more matches. "The last three." She held out her hand. "And I see no way that they can be any better than the rest." She sighed and looked at Astron with tears forming in her eyes.

"No, wait," Astron said. "Keep your composure. It is just a matter of the kindling. We need something that more easily absorbs the heat of the matches, something with a large surface area for a given volume."

He looked about, trying to seize upon an idea. The sound of four gongs filled the air, each more violent than the one before. Perhaps they could not withstand the next. They had only moments left before something must be done.

Ignoring Boltzman and his lieutenant, Astron closed his eyes and wrenched at his memories as a cataloguer. Fires, flames, the barrier between the realms — there must be something that he had learned that could be used. What was the purpose of all of his knowledge if not...

Astron stopped with the sudden thought. Dropping the sword, he lunged at the clutter at Phoebe's feet and pawed through the debris from the engine. "Strike the last three matches," he yelled. "Just as you did before. You are indeed the wizard. Without you we cannot succeed."

Coalesce of Space and Time

PHOEBE HESITATED but then turned back to the twisted frame in front of her. She struck the matches and when they did not light, she tried again. Boltzman and his helper stumbled forward still unsure on how best to attack. Groping in the sand, Astron found a flour tin with weak walls and jabbed a hole in the side near the bottom with the tip of his sword. A sudden slice of pain jolted through his soft hand where he had gripped the blade for control. The wetness was sticky, but he pushed the discomfort out of his mind. He flung off the top of the tin, sending it sailing away like a broken dish.

Phoebe returned with the barely lit matches as she had before. Astron twisted his head to the ground and placed his mouth around the indentation he had made in the tin. He felt the rumble of the ground and had to use both hands to steady the small container in front of his face.

"Here," he shouted, "as soon as you see the spray." Astron filled his lungs and blew into the small hole. At first, the packed flour on the inside resisted the pressure. Most of his breath spilled back out onto his face like a gust of wind. Only a small portion blasted into the tin and bubbled toward the upper rim. A fine mist of flour danced from the surface into the air. "Now," Astron gasped. "Apply the fire when I blow again."

Astron expanded his chest and exhaled even harder, sending a visible orange spray skyward in a tiny geyser. Phoebe pushed the matches forward and thrust them towards the upwelling powder. An orange-red flame with tongues the length of a forearm erupted into life.

"Bring over some of the wreckage of the buggy," Astron gasped between breaths. "Spark, kindling, and fuel — they are all essential for any blaze. Unless we supply the third, the fire will go out as soon as I stop blowing." He resumed exhaling into the tin, each puff sending the flames higher into the air.

Phoebe nodded and twisted one of the jutting branches of the frame over the spot where Astron lay. The bright tendrils from the burning flour bathed the lower contour of the log and then arched around it to flicker higher in the sky. Almost instantly, the peeling bark caught fire and a scant moment later began burning on its own.

Astron ceased blowing and tried to stop the rapid breathing so that he could speak again. The human body had disadvantages that appeared at the most awkward of times. "Be careful, even in your haste," he gasped. "The first mind that you contact might be too pow —"

"Camonel." Phoebe's voice boomed out with a sudden vibrancy. From her cape, she sprinkled into the fire some powder that looked the same as what Alodar had used in his keep. "I demand the presence and service of Camonel, the one who carries." She darted a quick glance at Astron and smiled. "Oh, Kestrel," she said. "You had faith in me when even my own will faltered. Perhaps, I am in some way unique, as each true wizard must be, not the equal of any other but —"

"Careful!" Astron repeated. "You do not know —"

There was a sudden rush of sulphur-tinted air. The great brown djinn that had carried Astron and the others to the realm of the fey stepped from the fire, blocking Boltzman and his lieutenant from view. "The one who reckons instructs that I do not resist," the massive demon said. "Tell me what you wish and I will obey."

"Another of your kind and an inhabitant of the realm of the fey," Phoebe commanded. "Quickly, take us to them wherever they may be."

The djinn bowed. With a powerful swoop of its long arms, he coiled Astron and Phoebe to his chest like a constructor surrounding its prey. A single beat of his wings soared them into the air, but before Astron had time to think, five gongs rang through the air. The sky shimmered into a painful brightness. The network of iridescence intensified and did not fade. Massive clockworks and strangely dressed beings propelled from the glow and raced earthward. Halfway to the ground, the machineries passed startled enforcers hurling skyward in return.

Astron felt another wave of disorientation stronger than before. Although he could not be sure, it seemed that even Camonel faltered, loosening his grip and fluttering to the ground.

"It all runs together in confusion," the djinn muttered as he landed with a slight jolt. "Many oases fused into one. I need not search them out for all who you seek are now here."

Astron felt the wings pull back. With dizzy steps, he staggered from the larger demon's embrace. He was at the edge of a single expansive oasis surrounded by dozens of trees, rather than just six. At most of the vertices, hundreds of warriors flailed away at each other in an immense mêlée, every one of them locked in step.

Astron scanned the nearer vertices and jerked to a halt. Over from the nearest, he recognized his own body backed against a trunk with a bloody sword waving threateningly at a cluster of berserkers who attacked from the interior of the hex. Beside him were Abel and a score of enforcers, each one stabbing and hacking as well. More than a dozen bodies were strewn from the center of the hex to the feet of those who defended against the odds.

"Forget about their squabbles," Phoebe called from the protective cover of Camonel's wings. "Astron, Nimbia. I succeeded after all. After two failures, I have succeeded when it was most needed. Finally, I have been able to summon a djinn and command him to carry us home."

Astron saw his own body jerk in recognition of the voice. The sword dipped in apparent salute but then returned to parry the thrust aimed at his side.

"Not now," Astron heard his own voice say. "It is too soon. They have trusted me without question. More than a dozen oases we have won. Until the last, I cannot let them down."

"But something more has happened," another voice yelled. "Look about you, demon. The chances are too slim."

Astron turned to his right. At an almost deserted vertex, Nimbia held a sword point to the throat of a berserker on the ground and waving with her free hand across the hex to Kestrel. Her tunic was in tatters, one sleeve torn free and the bodice ripped across her chest.

Astron started to call out, but the words choked in his throat. Through Kestrel's eyes, she looked as he had remembered her, but somehow it was not quite the same. Her body possessed a new sensuousness, a compelling beacon of desire that blotted out the urgency of the moment. It was just the same as with Phoebe, he thought in sudden confusion, the same as with the human, except that the exposure and the danger made the feeling much more intense.

Astron glanced at both sides of Nimbia's vertex to see if any berserkers were attempting to attack it. With leaping bounds, he began racing to where Nimbia stood, waving Kestrel's sword above his head.

"Kestrel, what are you doing?" Phoebe shouted behind him. "Help cut a path for Astron. He is the one that needs your help."

Astron shook his head and looked back as he ran to the vertex occupied by Abel and the others. Kestrel, laboring in his slight demon's body, would need aid soon indeed. He returned his attention to Nimbia as he approached, and her eyes widened in confusion. Only at the last instant was he able to force himself to stop. He sucked in his breath and struggled to regain control. Worse than a stembrain, he thought, is this human body with its strange desires.

He stared at Nimbia and let out his breath. The questioning look remained on her face but she did not retreat. No, there was something more than just the impulsive lust. Astron tried to sort through his thoughts. Something was greater than the mere animal passions of the realm of men. What was it that compelled him? In his own body how then would he feel?

The ground shook with an audible rumble. Six clocks ticked in synchrony and prepared to strike. He jerked his attention back to what had been their original plan. "Phoebe, the djinn," he yelled. "Instruct him to contact Palodad as he did before."

"I am already with you." Camonel's deep voice boomed out behind Astron. "I speak with the voice of the one who reckons, the one who is awaiting what has been promised him."

Astron turned. "We did not find the answer to the riddle," he called out. "High king Finvarwin spoke words that do not seem to relate."

"Did you secure the harebell pollen? Have you obtained what I have asked?"

"Yes, more than half-dozen grains." Astron felt the rucksack still on the back of Kestrel's body. "But —"

"Describe them to me."

The clocks' strikers reach back to their maximum extent. "There is no time," Astron said. "Something must —"

"What, did you say, there is no time?" Camonel flung back his head and laughter boomed out over the oasis. "Here there will be time eternal. Do you not see what is happening? Before there were two separate realms. Soon there will be but one. Order and chaos have mixed so that there is nothing to distinguish one universe from another.

"Like two bubbles pressed together, the surface between them has dissolved away. They distort and strain, but inevitably merge into one. The single realm that results will obey the symmetries of time as well of those of space. With the next stroke of the gongs, these beings that call themselves enforcers and berserkers will have their game continue forever, circling about a single oasis in pursuit of one another and playing the same move over and over and over. Yes, a beautiful symmetry that —"

"Tiny barbs and upon them smaller filaments still," Astron

250

interrupted. "The surface of the pollen has a structure finer than that possible from the most skilled weaver. I have had no chance to study them further. But then, how can it matter? Although you might be satisfied, it does not help to answer —"

"Oh, but indeed it does." Camonel clasped his sides to control the laughter. His eyes defocused and took on a faraway look. "Barbs and filaments, you say. Yes, exactly what my calculations predicted. It is but a small reason why I am known as the one who reckons. That is why I sent you. Even without the answer, I had hoped that the pollen would still provide a piece to the puzzle."

"Then Prince Elezar," Astron asked. "How does he fare?"

"Gaspar has found his dark node and driven him from it. The spark of life shines no longer in most of his followers. He is adrift, alone, somewhere in the darkness of the realm, awaiting his end. I must have the pollen and the cataloguer quickly. It is the last hope that Gaspar will not be victorious in the end.

"But enough," Camonel's voice continued. "Now, human, before the strike of the last gong that locks this realm into an eternity of repetition, clasp the pollen and enfold yourself in the arms of my agent. Come, before Gaspar's minions find you. You will be safe here with me."

"There are four of us altogether," Astron said.

"No, just you and the cataloguer," the voice rumbled from Camonel. "Of the others, there is no need."

Camonel stepped forward, stretching his wings out to full span. Nimbia and Kestrel, still slashing with a sword, were three vertices away. "Come." The djinn's voice boomed with authority. "Come, bring the pollen to Palodad's domain, and then we will speak of riddles and the precepts that lie beyond all others. The pollen and the cataloguer — both are essential. For no less will I continue to aid in your cause."

"No!" Phoebe's voice sounded above the demon's own. "You have stated that you have submitted. It is my commands that you must obey."

Camonel hesitated. He turned back to the wizard. "But there was no true struggle," he said. "It was only because Palodad had instructed —"

"I command you to take us away," Phoebe said. "Away from here to safety for the four of us who do not belong."

"Not even a mighty djinn can find his way when the reality about him changes as he flies," Camonel replied. "If we hesitate too long, I cannot be sure of even finding the lair of the one who reckons."

The six clocks struck in synchrony with an ear-shattering peal. The ground began to weave and buckle as if it were water instead of land, making it difficult for Astron to keep his balance. Off in the distance, the sand rose in a huge wave that climbed halfway into the zenith. The sky above blinked in a kaleidoscope of changing colors.

"Away," Phoebe shouted. "To the first flame that you can find. I care not where."

Camonel grunted. "Dominance or submission," he muttered. "There can be no in-between."

The djinn pulled Phoebe to him with one hand and then swooped to retrieve Nimbia with the other. Cradling them in his stout upper arms, he plucked Kestrel's body from the surrounding mêlée and then returned for Astron and the rucksack.

As the wings folded shut about him, there were screams of dismay and pain, and then Abel's strong voice shouted above the rest. "We have broken the protocols and new ones come in their place. Look about you, berserkers, and see what you have done. Unwittingly, you have invoked the strongest, the ultimate protocol of them all — 'coalescence follows from similarity'. We are merged and now are all doomed."

With a crash, the wave of sand hit the oasis. A chant of 'eat, sleep, cycle, eat, sleep, cycle' began to ring in Astron's ears. A wave of nausea far stronger than any that had gone before swelled within him. Everything went blurry, and he felt like he was tumbling head over heel. The sweetness of the air lost its pleasure. His aches and pains dissolved away. In resignation, he succumbed to the protection of what was again his stembrain, only dimly aware of the closeness of Nimbia at his side.

Part Five

The Realm of the Aleators

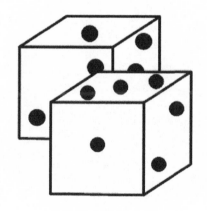

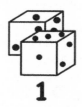

1

Castaways at Sea

KESTREL LOOKED at his outstretched hand. It was his own. The last transformation in the realm of order had restored him and Astron to their proper bodies. He shook his head to clear it of the last of the strange feelings. Like the vanishing dew under a morning's sun, they faded away. For a while, he had felt a robustness that had coursed through his veins with a pounding vigor. His basic needs for air, food, and sleep had been satisfied and had not troubled his thoughts, even on the lowest level. The immortality of a demon's body he could well believe.

But to be facing an existence that stretched out forever with so little control over one's own thoughts! Kestrel frowned at the horror of it. It had been a constant struggle to keep from raising his sword over his head and plunging to certain death against any of a dozen berserker attacks. Eventually, he would have succumbed. It was just too great an effort to remain on guard all the time — on guard against yourself and what your own thoughts might cause to happen.

Kestrel started to sit up and then hesitated as he became more aware of a rocking motion that pushed him from side to side. He was lying at the bottom of a concave wooden hull. Curved spars arched upward from a keel board under his back to gunwales well above his head. The last embers of a fire hissed in a smoky broth of bilgewater and soot. Beyond his feet, he could see Phoebe's crumpled form and, farther behind her, were Nimbia and Astron.

Looking skyward, he groaned. The canopy was pale blue and lit by a small reddish sun, far smaller than what he was familiar with in the realm of men. A few of the morning stars were bright enough to be shining still. Again, they were somewhere else from where they wanted to be! For a while, he lay on the planking, trying to put his thoughts in order. The strain of the last few moves had taken its toll on his mind, as well as on Astron's poorly equipped body. Having to think consciously of every thrust and parry, rather than rely on instincts learned over many years of getting out of scrapes, was as exhausting as heavy labor.

Kestrel sighed. Yes, the effort had been exhausting, but somehow rewarding as well. If not for the gong of the clocks on the final move, the enforcers he led might have captured the origin, despite the odds. They had depended on him, and he had been true to their trust. He had risen to what was his duty and discharged it well. Who knew what could have happened? After Phoebe was safely home, he could have gone back — gone back and rescued those that had put their lives in his hands without questioning that he would respond in return.

"This is worse than the desert," Phoebe rose and came to his side. Her depressing lethargy seemed to have vanished, but her face mirrored a new concern. "Look, Kestrel, there is nothing in sight. In the realm of the enforcers, we arrived at an oasis where we could at least eat and drink." She waved both arms out wide. "Here, it is worse than the wasteland. No oases. Nothing as far as we can see."

Over the gunwale, there was no sight of land on the horizon. Kestrel whirled to look in other directions, but the view was the same. The only feature was a thin line in the distance, separating ocean from sky.

He glanced down the length of the long boat. Except for Nimbia and Astron, the hull was bare. They had no sails, oars, food, or water. Near his feet, the last embers of the dying fire cooled to a soggy gray.

Kestrel put his arm around Phoebe and attempted a brave smile. She drew closer. "At least, this part is better than the last few moves," she said. "You hardly touched me when we were separated from the others."

Kestrel started to explain what had happened, but then thought better of it. There would be time enough for that later after they had reached safety. "How big a fire do you need to summon the djinn again?" he asked, waving at the charred splints at his feet. "Evidently, in this place, a blaze in a small wooden boat is not something bizarre."

"No, do not struggle with a demon now." Astron shook his head from where he was trying to stand like a drunken sailor. "Something is not right about the summoning. There is too much risk."

"What do you mean?" Phoebe asked. "I have brought forth Camonel before, and I can do it again. Do not worry, Astron. I have my full confidence now. Kestrel had faith in me, and that was enough."

"I do not question the power in your craft," Astron answered. "It is the words of the djinn that give me the suspicion. You have taught me, Kestrel, to look beyond them to the meaning behind."

The demon wrinkled his nose. "How do we know that it was actually

Palodad speaking through the mouth of Camonel? The one who reckons is a recluse, more concerned with the flipping of the imps in his own domain than delving into the working of other realms. He wants the harebell pollen grains as part of a bargain, it is true, but the insistence that I must accompany their delivery seems out of place."

"I do not know the workings of your kind." Kestrel shook his head. "So I cannot speak to how well your conjecture hits the mark. But if not this Palodad, then who else would speak through the flame?"

"Gaspar," Astron said. "He is the one who stands to lose if we are successful in our quest. Without the pollen, we cannot expect any more of Palodad's aid. The lightning djinn is the one who is tracking down all those with allegiance to the prince he wishes to destroy, the one who would want my return far more than any other.

"And even though Phoebe controlled Camonel to effect our rescue, the djinn is free to act in matters that she does not explicitly proscribe."

"From what you have told me of Gaspar," Kestrel rose to stand on legs far more seaworthy than those of the demon, "it is unlikely he would have the skill for such complex charades. You even said that his posing of the riddle was a surprise to your prince."

Kestrel tugged at his chin and looked out over the featureless sea. "There is also the matter of the outside influence in the realm of symmetry. Given the confining nature of the rules of the games, why would the berserkers continue when the unpredictable results from using the engines began to interfere with their plans? Who was responsible for the torrent of exchanges at the end? It is as if there were someone else behind all of this, someone far wiser than Gaspar manipulating him as well as other things."

"Prydwin!" Nimbia sat up, suddenly alert. "It all fits together when you think of it. It is his creations that have been coalesced. Although I can think of no reason why he would wish it so, he is the one who knows the details of their creation. No one could cause the merging any better than he. Who else would be concerned about what happens to harebell pollen, if not one of the fey? Suppose that the prince of the lightning djinns did not have a free will of his own, but was under the domination of my kinsman?"

"Yes, Prydwin," Astron replied. "You may very well be right. Most of my kind have little concern for the workings of other realms. Except for cataloguers such as myself, they dwell instead on instant gratifications that forestall the great monotony. Far more plausible is a being from somewhere else manipulating events for his own personal gain."

"Then what is our plan?" Phoebe asked. "We need to come up with one shortly. Without food and water, we cannot stay here long."

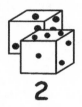

2

A Little Bit of Luck

"DO NOT despair," Astron said to Phoebe as they gently rocked in the boat. "Despite appearances, we have made some progress on our quest. First, we learned that it was the realm of the fey in which we had to look. There we acquired the pollen grains that Palodad desires."

"And in the realms of symmetry," Nimbia cut in, "we heard Palodad say that their physical design somehow was important to the answer of the riddle."

"Only if indeed it was Palodad," Astron countered. "Of that, we cannot be certain." He shook his head. "No, it is the one who reckons whom we must contact directly to be safe. No intermediary agent will do."

"Then tell me of his mental signatures," Phoebe said. "When we relight the fire, he is the one I will seek."

Astron's membranes flicked down over his eyes and his nose wrinkle to the side. "It is not quite that simple," he replied. "I doubt I could accurately describe the character of Palodad's will. He is old, old even by the standards of my kind."

"Mankind would probably call him mad," the demon continued, "and I am not so sure that I disagree." He clenched his fist and suppressed a slight shudder. "No, I must be the agent as we have agreed before. But in light of our suspicions, I must return unaided, return and seek out Palodad directly, rather than rely on the intermediary of any of my kind."

"Would it not be better to take the pollen with you when you go?" Kestrel reached behind his back and patted the pack. "With nothing to offer, what would be the motivation for Palodad to aid us any further?"

"I cannot carry the harebell pollen through the flame, Kestrel," Astron said, "at least not in my — my present state." The thoughts of how he felt with Phoebe while in Kestrel's body flooded back in a wave of passion. "Remember the reason that Elezar directed me to your realm was to secure the aid of mankind to perform the cartage," he managed to continue. "Even the most powerful of djinns has difficulty with objects that do not possess minds of their own."

"Then clasp me somehow to you," Kestrel replied. He smiled at Phoebe. "I have already experienced three realms other than my own in aiding in the adventures of a wizard. One more can hardly make any difference."

"I am not a mighty djinn." Astron shook his head. "Although I require the flame of anvilwood and not simple pine or fir to pass between the realms, skills in weaving or transportation I have none."

"How can you be sure?" Kestrel asked. "With so many fetters of logic about your stembrain, how can you be sure?"

"Fetters? What do you mean?"

"And how can you know the inner thoughts of a demon." Phoebe laughed. "Even the best of wizards can only guess."

Kestrel started to answer but then shrugged. A sad smile came to his face. "It does not matter," he waved his arm. "I doubt we will be able to find the proper wood surrounded by ..."

Kestrel stopped and stared out over his outflung hand. Between the bobs of the waves, he caught sight of a mast and sail just at the horizon. Impulsively, he began to wave his arms like a scarecrow in a windy field. "Look!" he shouted. "Look to port. It is a ship, a large ship, sailing our way. What luck, what incredible luck indeed!"

His feelings flipped with a suddenness that made him giddy. "Enough pondering our future path for the moment." He pulled Phoebe close and gave her a hug. "First, let us attend to our safety in one realm before we take on the challenges of another. "

"Over there on the starboard." Nimbia pointed. "There is one — no, two more, in addition to the first. "

The ship to port gradually drew closer. There seemed little doubt that they had been seen. Kestrel turned his attention to starboard and stared in amazement. Near the stern was another tall mast, and directly abeam was a third. There was such a thing as luck, especially in the sagas, but this was incredible! How could they have landed in the precise center of a circle of ships in a featureless sea?

Phoebe did not seem to care about the coincidence. She was jumping up and down as much as the woodcutter. The boat rocked with each leap, and Nimbia stumbled as she tried to maintain her balance. Astron reached out and grabbed her by the shoulder. The demon's nose suddenly wrinkled with the contact. Eye membranes flicked into place, and he withdrew. Nimbia smiled and reached out in return, grabbing Astron's retreating hand. The demon held his arm out stiffly like a stick figure drawn by a child. Nimbia steadied herself and closed the distance between them.

"The retriever of harebell pollen, the swordsman leader of the enforcers, and even the gentleman-in-waiting for a queen of the fey," she said. "One has difficulty remembering that you are a merely a djinn from beyond the flame."

The crook in Astron's nose sharpened. "I am a demon, you know full well. But the power of my brood brethren is not mine to command. I am but a cataloguer, serving as best I can."

"And to whom is this service rendered?"

"Why, to my prince, of course." Astron lowered his eyes. "And, as well, to the success of the quest of Kestrel and Phoebe to restore their good names, — and also to a queen of the fey."

"And when these quests are over?"

"I have not thought of it," Astron answered. "It is not the nature of demonkind to think of what lies beyond the present. It leads to brooding on the inevitability of the jaded senses and the ultimate despair of the great monotony."

"But as I have observed, you are no common demon," Nimbia said. "And for me, the end of the quest poses the greatest uncertainty of us four. The two humans will no doubt return to their own kind." She waved her arm in Kestrel's direction. "And you, if you so choose, will flitter back to some depressingly plain patch of mud in the void of your realm. But what of Nimbia, a queen of the fey? There is no place to which to return. Ever so much worse than before, there is no one with whom to share. Who will serve me with distinction in a manner of which I could be proud?"

Astron wrenched his hand free of Nimbia's grip. "Your words prick at my stembrain. It is difficult to maintain rational control. "

For a long while, he stood silent. Then his membranes cleared and the muscles in his face relaxed. "Do not be deceived," he said. "I am no weaver of matter. No wings of great lift sprout from my back. I am only a cataloguer whose power derives from the few facts that no other has learned. There is no special destiny for one such as me."

"In the realm of the fey and, I suspect in others as well, one is measured by his deeds, rather than his inherent potentials, whatever they might be. I remember tasting your inner doubts when you rescued me from Prydwin's sentrymen, demon. And I have seen you lead hundreds of enforcers with clumsy hands and little regard for your own safety as well."

Nimbia reached out and touched Astron on the cheek. "There is much more that you can learn, cataloguer," she said, "much more you can learn of yourself."

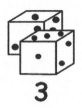

3

Powerful Suction

"AVAST, YOU in the dory," a deep voice boomed across the waves like the roll of distant thunder. "Reduce your efflux so that the others will sail away."

Kestrel turned his attention from Astron and Nimbia and studied the ship approaching from portside. It was nearer than the others, and details of its superstructure could now be discerned. A single short mast stood in the middle of a deck that was both wide and long. A single lateen sail billowed in a stiffening breeze. The broad bow and even broader beam were wider than those of any barge that Kestrel had ever seen. It seemed hard to believe that the small area of cloth presented to the wind could be adequate for a hull the length of two score men.

Even more remarkable, Kestrel thought with a start, was the fact that he understood perfectly the words that had been spoken. Except for a slight accent, they sounded like the speech of an Arcadian from across the great ocean in the realm of men. This, then, was not another creation of Prydwin, but if not, how amazing that the language turned out as it did.

"Reduce your efflux," the voice repeated. "You have impressed me as much as you can. I regard you as wealthy. To spill more luck to the winds will increase my assessment not a quantum more."

Kestrel stared up at the deck, puzzled. On it stood a rotund man wrapped in pinkish silks and a purple sash pulled tight into an overflowing girth. Bushy black hair, as dark as night, tumbled out of a small turban down the sides of his face into a curly beard. The heavy-lidded eyes squinted into the reddish sun. The smile wrinkles were shallow and seldom used.

Three or four others dressed like the first huddled about their leader, each one holding high a small cage of gold that contained some small white-furred rodent munching away on greens. The neck of each man bowed under the weight of at least a score of chains. On every one hung small trinkets: some mere gauze bags tied with ribbon, others intricately veined leaves pressed flat on slabs of slate.

"Why you carry no plenuma," the black-headed one continued as the two vessels drew quite close, "no plenum chambers at all." He reached for a monocle of colored glass hanging from a chain about his neck and cocked it into his eye. "By the rush of entropy, it is a spontaneous discharge from all four of you. Spontaneous discharge, as if you had been building pressure for a lifetime and using none of it until now."

He waved over his shoulder to the center of the ship. "All right, I withdraw my words. I am impressed, more certainly than I have ever been before."

He intertwined his fingers across his expansive girth, rocking back and forth as if enjoying a secret joke. "But understand," he said, "I am not so awed as to forgo absorbing the flux for myself. And if you do not have plenum chambers, let us find out how good are your wards against the sucking chambers of yours truly, Jelilac, the most fortunate."

A man much smaller than Jelilac vaulted over the gunwale of the larger ship and, with hardly a glance to see where he was going, landed in the dory between Phoebe and Nimbia. He carried a bowl of soapy water in one hand and a large pipe in the other. Without spilling a drop or hesitating to catch his balance, he settled into a squatting position and submerged the pipe into the bowl. He had as many chains about his neck as the rest, perhaps even more. All along the arms and legs of his silken tunic were embroidered tiny leaves of clover, and each of his fingers was wrapped in bows of red ribbon.

"Luck begets luck." The newcomer noticed Kestrel's stare. "It is the third tenet." Then, without further comment, he began to blow on his pipe, causing a bubble to form in its bowl. His first few puffs seemed easy, and the glassy surface expanded with rapid jumps. But when the bubble had reached the size of a fist, the veins in the pipeman's neck began to stand out like knotted cords, and his cheeks reddened from the effort to force air down the stem of the pipe. It reminded Kestrel of the sport of the fey, but it was somehow different, and he suspected the effort served a practical utility.

The surface of the bubble began to darken and take on a tough, leathery texture, far less elastic than that of any balloon. By the time the pipeman had finished, he had created a sphere the size of a person's head with a dark opalescent surface that light just barely shone through.

The piper dropped his grip on the pipestem. With a grunt, he removed the bubble from where it still adhered to the bowl. Then he stretched out his arms and touched the orb to the hem of Phoebe's cape. A sudden spark of light jumped from the draping material into the interior of the sphere. A churning maelstrom of dense red smoke billowed within the confines of the globe, and then as the light vanished, the image faded away.

Phoebe stumbled. Kestrel reached out just in time to break her fall on the hard planking of the small boat. "Just exactly what do you think you are doing," he shouted angrily at the piper. "What is that thing, anyway?"

The piper looked at Phoebe's sprawled form on the deck and then hefted the sphere at his side. "I suppose it does seem a bit uncivil," he said. "Certainly, for this exchange, you deserve at least the most basic of talismans in return." He reached into his pocket with his free hand and offered Phoebe a necklace like one of the many he wore about his neck. The preserved foot of a small animal dangled from the lower end.

"Only good for simple accidents, I admit," he continued. "But then Jelilac covets each dram. It is the way of all who wish to live more than the briefest of moments in the realm of the aleators."

Kestrel grimaced. Understanding the language was almost too good to have happened. Without it, perhaps things would have proceeded more slowly and given him time to size up better the situation they were in. He reached out to grab the offered talisman, but the piper easily whisked it out of his reach. With a deft and fluid motion, he flung it over Phoebe's head, where it settled in a perfect position about her neck.

"For the lady," the piper said. "And watch your manners or Milligan might decide that you end up with nothing at all."

Kestrel reached out a second time for the piper's leg, but the little man was too swift. As the woodcutter's hand closed on air, Milligan had touched the globe to Nimbia's tunic, and a brilliant arc jumped to it as before. Nimbia teetered, but Astron was slightly quicker than Kestrel had been. Not hesitating to avoid contact, he steadied the queen so that she did not fall.

"Hmmm," Milligan mused. "Perhaps it would be better to give this one a chance at food and drink. If you concentrated on subsistence alone and depended on the others for protection, you might get enough to share." He reached into his pocket and withdrew another pendant necklace, this one an ebony lump of wood carved in intricate whirls.

Kestrel lunged out at Milligan from behind, but the little man turned and held the sphere chest high to absorb the force of the rush. The spark that jumped from Kestrel's outstretched hand sent a stab of pain up his arm. He felt a sudden tugging sensation all over his body and then a rushing away of some essence that he could not quite identify. A wave of discomfort swept over his senses. In a weakened stupor, he sagged to the bottom of the dory.

With clouded vision, Kestrel watched the sparks dance from Astron's body as it had the others. Dimly, he was aware of a leather thong pierced by a small heavy stone being placed over his slumping head. Offering only the feeblest of protests, he let himself be hoisted by a crane up to the deck of the larger ship. He clutched his hands to a growling stomach, suddenly quite aware that he had not eaten for what seemed like a very long time.

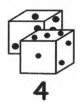

4

Experiment with a Ladder

"YOUR CONTRIBUTIONS have mellowed Jelilac's temper," Milligan said some hours later.

They all had been piled in a tumble about the single mast of the sloop. Kestrel shook his head and willed himself to focus on the little man standing before him. He felt a second talisman being hung about his neck and then a third.

"Ordinarily, with ones as destitute as you, the only choices he would offer would be trials with long odds," Milligan continued. "But the idiocy of such a great concentration and not even the slightest of wards has him most amused. As it is, he needs to refine a rather mundane procedure before landfall at the casino. Surely, at least one of you four will survive."

Kestrel staggered to his feet and looked about. The glassy calm sea was the same, although the other ships were no longer visible. Off the port bow in the distance was a sliver of brown above the horizon that indicated the first signs of land. Except for the helmsman and Milligan, none of the crew were above deck. The dory in which they had arrived was battened to the port gunwale, and a long ladder lay at its side.

"We are travelers from afar," Kestrel said, "and understand little of what you speak." He ran his tongue across the dry roof of his mouth. "But decency anywhere would demand that you offer at least some food and drink."

"Offer subsistence, offer it freely from one to another." Milligan threw back his head and laughed. He waved his arm in a wide, flat circle out to the horizon. "Do your eyes not see the vast expanse of waste — salt water everywhere and only tiny pinpoints of land? There is no food to offer to another. Even one such as I has had occasions of hunger, despite all that I carry about my neck."

Kestrel started to respond, but the doorway leading below deck slammed open, and two seamen appeared, carrying a long table between them. "Ah, spinpins," Milligan said. "Jelilac is feeling mellow indeed. He must think that crown is certain to be his."

The seamen positioned the table crosswise on the deck just in front of the mast where Kestrel stood. On one end stood a simple maze, a box of wooden partitions divided into compartments, each the height of a hand. Doorways were cut in many of the walls connecting the confinements together. Some were empty, but in most were standing geometric arrays of tiny bowling pins. A single doorway pierced the perimeter. Near it lay a carved spintop and a pile of string.

A third seaman appeared from below deck, carrying a small vertical frame on which near the top was hung a blade of shining metal. At the bottom were two sheets of wood paneling between which the sharp edge could drop. The panels were plain and unadorned, except for a hole about the size of a finger that had been drilled through them both. The seaman positioned the apparatus near the spintop and clamped it to the table. He ran a string from a hinged release mechanism for the blade and tied it about one of the pins standing in the maze.

"The principle is quite simple," Milligan said as he moved to the ladder at the side of the dory. Struggling with its long length for a moment, he thrust it into a vertical position and twisted its orientation with a flip, so that the topmost rung fell against the mast.

"Even the simplest child knows that one's luck decreases by walking under a ladder," Milligan continued. "The effect can be reversed only by retracing one's steps the other way."

"We have such a tale from whence we come," Kestrel said. "But it is the nonsense of ancient crones, nothing more."

Milligan frowned. "Minions of the crazed Byron," he muttered while he clutched at the talismans about his neck. "Minions of Byron, and not one, but four."

His eyes narrowed, and he eyed Kestrel keenly. "No, that cannot be. You are attempting some sort of a deception to free yourselves from your plight. No fatalists could have accumulated such auras as yours. You struggle for the crown, just as does Jelilac and the rest."

Kestrel frowned in turn. Very little of what Milligan was saying made any sense. He glanced down at Astron as the demon stirred and struggled to sit. Kestrel wished that he were fully alert. Some of his deductive observations would be quite useful about now.

"Anyway, the reversal raises an interesting question," Milligan continued. "It is one that Jelilac stumbled upon, the kind of insight that makes him a true contender to be archon over us all. The throne has been vacant since Sigmund's luck suddenly turned sour. Soon we will all assemble to judge which aleator now possesses the greatest power."

Milligan stroked three of his talismans hanging on his chest. "Although, under the right circumstances, who is to say what will happen in the casino where the die is cast? Yes, who is to say which is the most deserving, the most faithful to the tenets of our creed?"

Milligan's eyes focused far away as if his mind was burning with secret thoughts that could not be shared. Over the bow, the land was growing on the horizon. Kestrel eyed the two battens that held the dory and scanned the deck for signs of any other useful gear. With so few crew members on deck, the right circumstances were the ones he was interested in as well. He began to think more clearly. Perhaps it was best to keep Milligan engaged in conversation until the others were fully alert. Then they just might manage an escape from whatever Jelilac had in store for them.

Kestrel glanced at the ladder and then back at the table. The construction for both was rather crude and unvarnished, like something built by a peasant child too young to work in the fields. He could see that more than one type of wood was used in each. Maybe the risk of confrontation was not even necessary. A fire on deck could serve just as well. That was a possibility worth exploring before attempting the longer odds of an escape.

"What do you have that is carved of anvilwood?" He smiled innocently. "I am a collector and most interested in any small figurines that you might have to show."

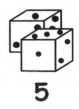

5

A Simple Enough Escape

MILLIGAN BROKE out of his reverie. "Anvilwood?" he laughed. "There is none here on Jelilac's barge, to be sure. You must indeed be from an islet far away. Every aleator who has stopped sucking his thumb is taught to avoid such a luck drainer whenever he chances upon it."

He laughed again. "It would just be the perversity of luck that such as you would be desirous of finding some. Throughout the realm, prisoners convicted of the worst crimes are sent to uproot the trees when they are discovered and forced to hack the branches to bits. For others, the risks in touching are just too great. The only piece that I know of is at the casino for the trials to be archon. And even that Jelilac and the others will strive to destroy if given half the chance."

Kestrel frowned. They would have to get away after all, he thought. And then, from the sound of it, journey to one very special place. He speculated about the ladder. Perhaps it could serve another use. They would need oars, even if they managed to drop the dory over the side. He glanced back at Milligan. The little man seemed to enjoy talking. For the moment, it probably was best to keep him occupied.

Kestrel fingered the three talismans hanging about his neck. "This one looks something like a match stick." He held it out to Milligan. "Where we come from, it is a mark of great honor, since only a few we call wizards have the capability to build a flame. I suppose that here such skill is also a great rarity. No one such as yourself could hope to accomplish such a feat."

Milligan cocked his head to one side. "If it were not for the aura you possessed, I would agree with Jelilac and judge you most insane," he said. "Of course, you can light a fire. Why, so could any child. It is not a question of ease, but one of law. On all corners of the great sea, a flame is prohibited under penalty of death."

Kestrel frowned as Milligan continued. "The second tenet states that the entropy of luck always increases. There is no way it can be avoided. Each transfer from one to another, even those that dilutes it back to the ether. All such transferals reduce its potency. The last thing that anyone would want is a flame that disorders its fine crystalline structure and renders it useless.

"Why even an archon could become a pauper, if he approached too close to a fire, Milligan continued. Without his luck to guard him, all of his great displays of state on the islands would be washed away by the next giant wave that sweeps across our sea. Even if he possessed the strange book of star sightings and maps that Myra is reputed to have found, his ships would start to wander aimlessly, missing all of their ports. In the time of a single sigh, he would find that he had come to possess nothing, neither food for his next meal nor even clothing to ward off the chill. And everyone who but an instant before stooped in the greatest collection of bows would shun his misfortune, casting him aside and letting him wander to his death, unheralded and alone.

"No, the object of us all is to find ways to increase our luck, to concentrate it into tighter and tighter confines that enhance its potency. It is the only way to survive, to move ahead, and to strive for the mantle of the archon. The fatalists cannot be right. Things should not be left to the will of the cosmos. Outcomes are determined by men with luck. He who has the greatest will emerge the winner."

"I would think that skill or wit would somehow be important as well," Kestrel said. Cautiously, he placed one hand on the ladder and studied the rungs. Perhaps, if the sidebeams were ripped apart, they would serve well enough. He smiled inwardly and looked at Astron. It was something the demon probably would have thought of, and yet it came to him first.

"In the dim past, skill and wit did determine the outcome of many events," Milligan answered. "We contested by might of arms and clever strategies of state. But then, as our legends record it, wise archon Williard, with overwhelming favorable odds, was defeated by a force a tenth his size when his horse stepped into the only squirrel hole on the field of battle. An errant arrow hit his second in command in the throat, and, without a leader, the army stumbled into a mire.

"Luck triumphed over all else, and from that day to this, everyone who strives for power concentrates on increasing his own and dissipating that of others. Skill and talent mean little to one who can select a marked token from a bowl of thousands with but a single thrust of his hand."

"Then what need do you have of this experimentation?" Kestrel asked. He placed his hand on each of the ladder's sidebeams and strained outward while smiling in Milligan's direction. "If starting a fire is of no use, then whatever else of value can we be for you?"

"The means for accumulating and dissipating luck are not written in stone monuments for all to see," Milligan said. "It is only by centuries of trial and error that the methods that we use have come to light. Doubtless many more efficient techniques yet remain to be discovered." He waved his hand in a wide circle. "Luck is all about us, albeit at very low pressure. Certain actions seem to compress it into smaller volumes and increase its potency to alter events.

"As I have said, when one walks under a ladder, a portion of whatever one possesses leaks out into the ether. Immediately reversing direction prevents the loss before it can transpire." Milligan ran his tongue over his lips. "But what if one circled back and walked under the ladder again in the second direction, the one that prevented the loss. Perhaps then the vector of transaction would remain fixed in a positive way, each circuit under the ladder increasing one's luck, rather than dissipating it away.

"That then is the test. The first of you, I care not which, will walk once under the ladder and then spin the top through the maze. He will be what we call the control. The second will walk once and then reverse before taking the test. The third, after reversing direction, will continue around the mast and back under the overhang a dozen times more. The last will not reverse directions at all but rotate the dozen times in the same sense as the first."

"What will the spinning top prove?" Kestrel asked while he slid his arms up the ladder to feel another rung.

"It is a test of luck, to be sure," Milligan said. "The spinning top caroms through the compartments in a manner that no one can predict, scattering pins at random. The count of how many are felled is the measure we wish to monitor. If all the pins are toppled before the one attached to the blade, then the game is stopped, and you are lucky indeed."

"And if the blade topples," Kestrel asked. "What does that prove?"

"The finger you place in the hole will be severed, a most unlucky outcome," Milligan replied. He gazed back at the maze on the table for a moment and then smiled at the woodcutter. "The beauty of it is that you all have ten. We will be able to run some forty trials before we are done."

Kestrel decided he had heard enough. It did not matter if the others were alert or not. With or without oars, they must be away. "Astron," he yelled, "unlash the dory. Get it back over the side." With a grunt, he twisted the ladder from its resting place and crashed it downward on the middle of the table, hoping that the force of the blow would break it apart.

The ladder bounced off the horizontal surface, however, the bottom end kicking up painfully into Kestrel's thigh. He staggered a single step and then sagged to one knee, his leg refusing to give him support. As he fell, he pushed at Phoebe, propelling her forward toward the gunwale where the dory was lashed. He rolled over on his back, expecting to see Milligan spring at him with some weapon. Instead, the little man, like a magician trying to stop a ritual gone suddenly awry, feverishly fingered the brightest talisman that hung from his neck.

"Jelilac, Jelilac," Milligan screamed. "They are followers of Byron. Despite the great auras they once possessed, they follow Byron, to be sure."

Kestrel rose to kneeling and grabbed Nimbia about the shoulder. Crawling with one hand on the deck, he urged her in the direction he had pushed Phoebe. Astron fumbled with the mooring knots like an arthritic crone, not making any progress in getting them untied.

Two seamen came forward, their fingers out-flexed like the tentacles of a squid and reaching for the thongs of leather about Nimbia's neck. Kestrel staggered erect and pointed wildly into the sky. "Look," he shouted. "Not one shooting star, but two. Not to witness is a great misfortune."

He held his breath for an instant, but the two sailors were unaccustomed to such a blatant deception. Like conjoined twins, they turned and began searching the clouds. Kestrel limped forward a single step. As his leg again gave way, he staggered against the nearest of the seamen. A ring on the sailor's hand scratched his cheek as he fell. Concentrating as hard as he could, he managed to grab hold of the loops and chains about the sailor's neck and pull the man to the ground.

Kestrel gathered up as many talismans in his hands as he could manage. With a back-wrenching yank, he snapped them from the seaman's neck. The sailor screamed. Like a lion cornered by a pack of dogs, he began clawing at Kestrel's arms to get them back.

Kestrel flung them in the direction of the dory. Although several went over the gunwale, two landed at Astron's feet. Almost at once, the knot on the last fetter unraveled. The demon reached down, cradled the bow in his arms and hoisted it up over the low railing. Phoebe and Nimbia reached the stern and lifted it up as well. In an instant, the small boat splashed down onto the waves.

Kestrel crawled forward to the gunwale, blocking out the seaman who scrambled on the deck with him to retrieve the two talismans that remained. Kestrel reached to scoop them up a second time but grimaced as sharp splinters from the deck dug into his palm.

Astron bent down, grasped the talismans in one hand, and then grabbed Kestrel by the arm with the other. The woodcutter reached out for Phoebe and Nimbia. Without thinking further, they jumped together over the side. The salt water stung Kestrel's cheek when he hit, but he paid it little heed. Lashing out blindly, he felt the side of the dory and grasped for a hold.

Milligan leaned over the rail, cupping his hands to his mouth. 'There is little enough gain in what you have stolen," he yelled. "Basic enhancers and navigator's fetishes are all. They are organic and soon will decay. About enough to see you to the island in the distance and survive a wave or two, but little more. And there, if you stay out of the clutches of doubting Myra and her arcane devices, you will learn well enough the difficulty of finding food and drink with what little auras you now possess."

Milligan looked back over his shoulder and laughed. "Followers of Byron," he said. "With the spintop, at least one of you might have had a chance."

The distance between the dory and the sloop begin to widen. From somewhere, a fresh breeze had begun to blow them apart. He tried to hoist himself a little higher to see the direction they should begin to paddle. Despite the aches and pains, he felt the cold of the sea and the renewed gnawing of his hunger. Basic enhancers and navigator's fetishes, he thought. Even if they were lucky, would so little be enough?

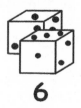

6

The Restless Sea

ASTRON STIRRED with discomfort, his patience growing thin like the last bit of road ice about to melt. Kestrel clutched a tripstring, preparing for the moment that he would jerk away the twig that propped the splintered beam from the sandy beach. The small quail was just partway into the trap. It would be the dozenth try, and Astron doubted it would be any more successful than the rest.

He cast an eye at Phoebe and Nimbia, huddled near the wreckage of the dory. The heavy wave that had dashed them against the beach had destroyed their only means to travel elsewhere with any speed. The small, reddish sun was almost to the crest of the hill spine that hid the interior of the island. A heavy copse of trees covered the entire slope. Only the sandy beach that curved out of sight in both directions was devoid of the thick vegetation. Perhaps in the interior, they would find bigger game or even someone more sympathetic to their plight. But nightfall was coming too soon. For the moment, they had to hope for a single meal and find what cover they could in the wreckage of the boat.

Astron twisted his shoulders, ignoring Kestrel's sharp glance to be still. He wished he could be more sure of the path they were taking, seeking out anvilwood rather than letting Phoebe summon some other demon to their aid. But if she did, she might connect with one of Gaspar's minions searching for them. Which was the lesser risk he could not decide. The uncertainty stirred his stembrain, forcing him to tighten his control.

He peered again at Nimbia, trying to recapture the pounding emotion that had gripped him when it was Kestrel's body he had possessed. It was not the same now, of course, but the experience had touched his rational centers as well. He remembered their closeness when hiding from Prydwin's pursuit: the piercing inner sadness that she had exposed to him more than any other, the strength of duty she felt to her hill dwellers that was stronger than that of any prince. Even in abstraction, sharing more of her thoughts would bring a great pleasure, perhaps as keen as the discovery of new facts from beyond the flame. What would it be like, he wondered, if their relationship went deeper than that of a broodmother and sire?

Astron stopped the direction of his thoughts short and wrinkled his nose. He shook his head in the manner of men. She was a queen and regarded him in quite a different light. At no time had she even bothered to call him by name. She spoke with kindness and praise, but always as she would to a servant, one perhaps to a loyal retainer when the quest was finally done.

If only it *were* finally done! He had been away from Elezar far longer than he had intended. Could there still be any hope that his prince was alive? And with Gaspar triumphant, his own grisly fate could only be a matter of time. Somehow, he must get the harebell pollen back to Palodad and trust that whatever he had learned would provide a sufficient clue to solve the riddle. Without that, nothing else mattered.

Astron pushed away the reverie. He turned his attention back to the immediacy of their problems. The quail took another timid step under the overhang of the beam. Its tiny head twitched from side to side, looking for predators. Then, in two quick thrusts of its bill, it poked at the seeds that Nimbia had gathered along the beach. Kestrel yanked on the string unraveled from Phoebe's cape and wrenched the twig free. The beam seemed to hover for an instant in mid-air and then crashed to the ground, shearing away a few feathers from the quail as it ran clear.

Kestrel pounded his fist into his hand. "So close," he spat. "I should have waited an instant more until the bird was more centered under the beam."

"Such is not our luck," Astron said. "And if the words of that Milligan are true, never will it be. It was only the lifetimes of unspent luck that we brought with us upon entry to the realm that ensured our rescue from the sea and a language that you and Phoebe understand as well as I. But Jelilac and Milligan have drained all of that away. The ordinary trapping skills from the realm of men will do us little good here. We must approach the cause of our problem, rather than deal with its symptoms."

"That is easy enough for you to say," Phoebe growled. "You do not need food and water as do the rest of us."

"I am well aware of the metabolic needs of men," Astron rebutted. He waved his arm toward the tree line in the distance. "Despite the peril, we must leave this beach."

"Or perhaps we should all clutch these talismans and hope that a game fowl walks out of the forest and lies down at our feet," Phoebe said.

"That is the essence of the solution," Astron agreed. "In this realm, we must strive to increase our luck and raise it to the point that the improbable happens as a matter of course. Then whatever we need will follow."

"Yes, Astron is right." Nimbia pulled at the chains about her neck. "We have survived as well as we have because of whatever minimal protection these necklaces provide."

"And how does one go about effecting this increase?" Kestrel asked. "We have no masts or ladders here, and even Milligan was unsure of what would be the result."

"That is only one way," Astron replied. "Surely, the aleators have many other means. We must approach them again, only this time much better prepared."

"I do not care for the likes of Jelilac." Phoebe shook her head. "Perhaps others will be the same. We must instead act on our own. Despite your misgivings, Astron, contacting Camonel is our best chance."

Before Astron could reply, a deep sighing noise like that of a dying swan came from the direction of the water. The foaming crestline of waves began a rapid retreat, exposing the slope of land far beneath the extent of the lowest tide. Although he could not be sure, farther out over the ocean, the line between the water and the sky seemed much higher than he had remembered it before.

"What is it?" Kestrel asked.

"A wall of moving water," Astron said. "Just as Milligan hinted — what some among your realm of men call a tidal wave. There is little time. Run for higher ground and climb into the trees."

He raced over to where Nimbia sat and pulled her to her feet. Spinning her about, he shoved her in the direction of the slope rising from the beach.

Kestrel pounded his fist into his other hand. "What rotten luck," he growled as he lifted Phoebe from the ground. In imitation of Astron and Nimbia, they began running hillward on a slightly different path.

7

Toboggan to Safety

ASTRON AND Nimbia sprinted up over the sandy ground into the darkness of the forest without speaking. Nimbia paused at the base of the first climbable tree she found, but Astron motioned her onward. Stumbling into darkness, they picked their way into the dense canopy like explorers searching for the best way through a bramble. Behind him, Astron could hear a muted roar drawing closer. Kestrel and Phoebe were nowhere to be seen.

Finally, Astron stopped and pointed at a low-hanging branch. Together, he and Nimbia scrambled up from limb to limb into the foliage. Despite his scales, rough branches scraped against his hands and snagged his leggings, but he did not stop to pick at the splinters. His head poked through to sunlight as he pulled himself to a slender, swaying branch that barely held his weight. Seaward, the huge wave crested and toppled over upon itself. With a booming crash, a wall of foaming water pounded onto the beach and began racing uphill.

In an instant, the sandy slope began to disappear. Like popping embers in a fire, the trunks of the closest trees snapped from the impact and then disappeared under the waterline. The dense grove of timber slowed the advance, but still it roared up the hillside. Astron flicked down his membranes, hoping that the fury of the onrush would be spent before it reached them. Row after row of treetops disappeared beneath the churning sea, and huge trunks bobbed up behind, completely stripped of foliage. The cool sea-green muted into muddy browns, and a web of debris formed on the once clear surface of the water.

The wave front surged closer, slowing as it came. Midway up the slope, the breathtaking speed blunted. The wave top crashed, to rise no more, but the water level climbed higher in a relentless swell. The first tendrils snaked about the base of the tree in which he had climbed and then the water level rose even higher. Swiftly, the lower branches were submerged. Astron tested what remained of the trunk above his head, but he already knew he could climb no more.

Nimbia hung awkwardly on the branch across from his own. Before he could warn her, the cold water reached his feet and then surged over his head. With an irresistible pull, he was yanked from his perch and then struck in the side by an uprooted trunk. Astron thrust his hands into the thick and deeply grooved bark and grabbed hold of the log as it passed. He scrambled around the side and thrust his head into the air, just in time to see Nimbia floating past. Releasing part of his grip, he grabbed and pulled her to the trunk. Dimly, he was aware of passing over a crest and then tipping downward to cascade into an interior valley below.

The next few moments were a blur of splashing spray and jarring caroms off the trees on the downslope side. Somehow, Astron and Nimbia managed to hang on to the trunk that bore them and at the same time avoid being caught between it and the other trees into which it crashed.

They reached the bottom of the small valley and then hurled partway up the other side. The water slowed to a halt. With a ponderous motion, it reversed direction and began to move back down toward the valley floor. But its momentum was nearly spent. The trunk moved sluggishly with the flow. With one final bone-jarring jolt, it crashed to the ground, letting the burbling water race ahead like broodmothers finally abandoning their offspring.

Astron held on to his grip a while longer, listening to the hiss and gurgle receding into silence. He dismounted and slid his feet to the ground. Nimbia joined him, her face blanked in a daze. Oblivious to their deliverance, she grimaced at the wet clothing that cloaked her.

"If you had the power of weaving, you could dry these instantly," Nimbia said. She fussed at her tunic, still not mended from the battles in the realm of symmetries. "But since you do not demon, turn your head while I disrobe."

Mixing with the dizziness of their ride, Astron felt a subtle stirring in his stembrain, a tantalizing feeling from before, which he could not quite recognize. They should immediately begin searching for Kestrel and Phoebe, but something else tugged at him.

Astron started to answer and then halted. A flicker of movement up the interior slope above the high-water mark had caught his eye. Almost thankful for the distraction, he touched Nimbia's shoulder and pointed at what he saw. A small tendril of smoke struggled skyward from the foliage.

"Perhaps another aleator," he whispered. "One with luck to burn. Keep on your clothing. This time, we will be more forewarned."

Astron led Nimbia up the hillside. The ground became more rocky and the canopy of trees gave way to scrubbier underbrush and finally to an open clearing. The demon strode forward boldly, mustering as much dignity as he could in his soggy clothing. A single figure sat on a rock beside a small fire, over which was roasting some sort of pig. A horse hobbled nearby. Next to it, a large pack was propped against a small tent of azure blue.

Upon the noise of their approach, the man looked up from his contemplation, but no expression of surprise crossed his face. Cold green eyes stared out under a head of golden blond hair, cut shoulder length and straight, with no curl. The face held the smoothness of youth, unwrinkled and without trouble — almost that of a child just aroused from sleep. Broad shoulders, heavily muscled, flexed under a thin, sleeveless shirt that sparkled with an iridescence in the last rays of sunlight filtering into the clearing. The throat of the shirt was open. Not a single talisman dangled about the sinewy neck.

"Whom do you seek?" A measured voice cut across the distance, each word unhurried and more of a command than a question.

"Did you not hear the crash of the wave?" Astron walked forward, motioning Nimbia to follow. "I would not expect to find anyone on low ground calmly fixing a meal."

"The wave would have reached Byron or it would not," the man shrugged. "There is no need to prepare for what is meant to be."

Astron searched about for one of the spheres that Milligan had used to capture his and the others' luck. There were no signs of one, and he took another step forward. After his experience with the berserkers, it seemed far easier than before. "You are one of exceedingly good fortune," he said. "I have heard that even the smallest fire dissipates what one has accumulated back into the ether."

Byron looked at Astron sharply. "Are you here to tempt me?" he replied. "To test and see if I am worthy?" He stopped and darted his eyes to Nimbia as she approached. His nostrils flared, and his hands coiled into fists. His's eyes ran over her body and torn tunic. The beat of his pulse stood out strongly on his neck.

"You tempt me, indeed." Byron's voice rumbled quietly. "What is it that you would have me do?"

Astron scowled in annoyance. He recognized the reaction and understood it far better than before. Stepping in front of Nimbia, he threw wide his arms, shielding her as much as he was able.

"We might have something of great benefit," he said. "It all depends on what you can offer as a fair payment in exchange."

"If it is luck of which you speak, there is no basis for a barter," Byron shook his head. "I have none to offer, nor do I seek any for what I must do."

Astron stirred uncomfortably. "What exactly is it that, ah, that you must do?" he asked.

"Why travel to the grand casino to contest for the crown with all the others," Byron answered. He slapped the long broadsword at his side. "But not in the same manner. If I succeed, it will be because fate wills it, not because of twists of luck."

Astron's interest heightened. The grand casino! According to what Mulligan had said, exactly where he wanted to go! Only with a firm resolution did he stop himself from looking back at Nimbia with a smile.

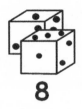

8

The Darling of Destiny

"WE HAVE experienced firsthand what happens without luck," Astron said as he studied the man before him. "Just to survive takes more than a little amount."

"Only because some of the aleators have so distorted it," Byron spat. "They lead the realm to destruction with their tinkering. They work with fluids better left alone.

"Look," he warmed to the subject. "The first tenet says that luck is a gas, a perfect one that flows from high pressure to low. Without interference, it distributes itself evenly throughout the realm, favoring no one over another. The forces of fate are free to operate, to work the destinies that are intended for us all.

"But what happens when it is compressed, scooped up from everywhere into a small number of concentrations under the control of only a few? There is less left in the ambiance. Without participating in the forbidden rituals, everyone else is stripped of what is his due share. To step from a hut becomes a great adventure; to fill one's stomach is a hunt of great exhaustion. Even the elements are perturbed into extremes. For the fortunate, the air is always clear and balmy. In compensation, gentle rains and waves are compressed into great disasters that prey on those who do not have the protection of the proper talismans.

"With the great accumulations come great new strains and forces," Byron went on, "distortions in the very fabric of what must happen to us all. Those who have accumulated luck must dispense some modicums to their followers, constructing all sorts of amulets like those useless husks that drape about your necks. They war not with merit, but depend instead on chance outcomes to go their way."

Byron stopped and set his lips in a grim line. "But I will stop them all," he said defiantly. "It is my calling, and to it, I will be true."

"You say you have no great accumulation of luck of your own," Astron asked. "How do you hope to accomplish your goal?"

"Soon my followers will return and report what they have seen in the bay on the far coast. There, Myra has dropped anchor with both of her ships. We will attack on the morrow, and one of them will become mine. With it, we will cross the great sea. I will stride into the grand casino and win, although luck I have none. 'Luck favors the believer' states the fourth tenet. 'Luck is fickle' and hence runs in streaks, professes the fifth. Great manipulations for enhancement and devices for reversing good to ill are built upon the two of them, but neither shall I use."

"But if you have no advantage and they —"

"I am destiny's darling," Byron thundered. "The great sagas of our past have been incarnated in me. I am untouched by wind or wave. I am the one to weave together the last threads of the tapestry of our fate into one final design."

Byron stopped and looked into the growing darkness. "It is true that how I will triumph is hidden. Even I do not know the means. My journey to the grand casino may be but a testing, a proof that I am worthy of being the instrument of fate. But in the moment of crisis, in the final spin of the wheel, my power will be revealed, and I will be victorious as from the beginning of time it was written that I would."

A sudden shout from up the hill cut off Astron's reply. At the crest were torches in a staggered line.

"I am here," Byron called back. "I am here, and the way is safe. There are no concentrations of luck with which you must contend."

With excited voices and the sound of crunching underbrush, the group on the crest began to pour down the hillside like swarming ants. Although the way was clear and the torches gave sufficient light, two dozen men, women, and children picked their way carefully, holding on to one another for additional security and giving the fallen snags and large bushes a wide berth.

In the very center of the group, supported on both sides, was one far older than the rest. Wisps of long white hair streamed from around a crown splotched with spatters of red and veins of purple. The eyes were nearly closed, and a trickle of spittle ran from the corner of the face that sagged. Bare stick-thin arms flapped idly with the jostle of each step. The feet shuffled after one another as if actuated by the mechanism of a child's toy.

"We call him Centuron." Byron nodded in response to Astron's gaze. "His fame among the aleators is almost as great as — well, almost as great as mine. For over one hundred cycles of the sun, he has survived without the benefit of the magical arts to shape his luck. He is the living proof that my cause is right and that I will succeed."

The procession of gaunt and sallow faces drew closer. Except for the excitement of meeting, they showed animation only slightly greater than Centuron's. With stooped shoulders and panting breath, they converged on Byron's camp, some looking with hungry eyes at the roast pig like dogs returning from a failed hunt. One separated herself from the rest. Dirt streaked her face, and her hair was in tangles. Suitably cleaned, the woman would be a beauty, but the rigors of the trek had made her barely distinguishable from the men.

"We must move on quickly," she said. "The minions of Myra have found two others adrift in the wake of the last wave. We overheard them talk of two more whom they wanted as well. Soon there will be search parties throughout the hills."

"Kestrel and Phoebe," Astron shouted. "Were they injured?"

"They seemed to walk well enough with no assistance from their guards." The woman shrugged. "But, of course, such a condition is only temporary if Myra wants to be amused before she uses them as shields in the games at the grand casino."

"Then we must get to that beach and —" Astron began, but Byron put up his hand to stop.

"What else, Sylvan, what else do you bring?" he asked.

The woman nodded. She pulled a pack from her back and dumped its contents at Byron's feet, a dozen ears of a black-kernelled corn, three large apples, and a scattering of small seeds.

"We saved as much as we could for your great contest, Byron, but the little ones need more than an equal share."

Byron waved at Astron and Nimbia. "It is well that you have procured what you did, Sylvan. There are two more, and I have not yet decided if they should be fed as well."

"Wait," Astron said. "By all means, let the little ones eat. I, for one, have no need."

"No, I have spoken," Byron thundered. "I am the chosen one, and my commands must be obeyed. The sacrifice of all others is of no importance. Their destiny is only to ensure that I succeed."

"We do not question." Sylvan lowered her head and stepped backward. "Even old Centuron has taken less than we might otherwise offer."

"Ah, if you do not know exactly what power you will have," Astron said, "what convinces you that you indeed are this darling of destiny?"

Byron's eyes blazed. "You *were* sent by the fates to tempt me!" he yelled. "You wish to test how firm is my resolve."

He eyed Nimbia again and drew his lips into a grim line. "Very well. I will show to the overseers of our fate the extent of my mettle. You shall accompany me and yet both remain untouched." His stare locked on Nimbia and he ran his tongue over his lips. "Yes, untouched," he continued, "until it is properly time."

Astron's stembrain bubbled with a fiery vexation. "Do not be overly concerned." He turned and spoke to Nimbia in the language of the fey. "Despite my size, I will serve you still. You merely need ..."

Astron stopped as he noticed Nimbia's smile. She let the top of her tunic sag in disarray. "It sounds as if he invites us to join him," she said. "Accept, accept in the name of a queen of the fey."

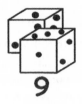

9

Fatal Amusements

KESTREL HELD his breath as the rope-suspended blade oscillated back and forth like a giant pendulum over another captive's outstretched body on the cabin deck. The prisoner was bound hand and foot, spread-eagled between four pegs anchored in the polished planking. Only by pressing himself against the horizontal could he just barely avoid the swipe of the sharp edge across her neck.

The aleator named Myra sat in the corner behind a small table and tracked his darting eyes with a cold stare like that of a panther about to strike. Grabbing her chin between thumb and forefingers, she brought her fingertips together, gathering up the loose flesh. A raspy scrape resulted from the contact like the sound made by a man testing a half-day growth of beard. A loose fitting tunic did little to hide the angular bones underneath, and patches of splotched skin shone through thin white hair pulled straight back and tied in a knot.

Myra's two ships lay at anchor side by side, far closer than the mooring one would expect in the realm of men. But with each wave that shifted them about, the two craft always avoided colliding at the last instant. The massive vessels seemed to be ably manned by very small crews, although the hold of the other ship, Kestrel had noticed when he was hustled aboard, was full of hammocks, men-at-arms, and others fettered with heavy chains.

"Just one more toss of the ball into the hoops," Myra said. "Just one more and I will be satisfied for today."

Another captive squeezed the rubber ball in his hand. The array of small circular openings in the slanted panel across the cabin were beginning to become indistinct in the dimming light, and the gentle rocking motion of the barge did not help. Without any luck to aid him, there was no way to ensure that the sphere fell into one of the hoops that he wished.

The ball arched through the air, hit an opening a little off center and caromed away. A geyser of blood erupted from the bound captive's throat as the slightly lower swinging blade sliced through his neck. It happened so quickly, he could not even cry out.

"Why?" Phoebe exclaimed at Kestrel's side. "Why are you doing this? What can you possibly learn from such an experiment?"

"Experiment?" Myra answered. "That was no experiment. I do not dabble in useless exercises like that pompous little man, Jelilac."

"Then, why?"

Myra smiled. "Because it amuses me," she said. "You, your companion, and the rest of the captives I have assembled have squandered away all of your luck. In a short time, you will die of starvation anyway."

"And I have overstocked," she continued. "I have more than enough to serve as shields at the casino." She stared at Phoebe as a cruel smile curved her lips. "It is best for you to not attract so much attention. I have my fill for today. But tomorrow, tomorrow I will select again. Perhaps I will remember how you spoke out when I make my selection."

Kestrel glanced at Phoebe, trying to smile encouragement, although he felt little inside. They had been apprehended after the passing of the wave almost as easily as they had by Jelilac on their arrival in the realm. This time, however, since they had no real luck to be siphoned away, the glassine spheres did not become charged with the oily, amber smoke. Somehow, he had to convince Myra that Phoebe and he were of value to her, but if not for having luck then what?

Kestrel took a deep breath. He had to make use of what little knowledge he had. "The book with figures," he said, "the one that Milligan says you possess. It sounds to me to be a navigator's almanac. Is that what you use to plot your course in this featureless sea?"

There was a sudden flicker in Myra's cheeks. Her eyes widened almost imperceptibly but then returned to their piercing stare. He waited expectantly. The signs were not much, but perhaps indeed he had chanced upon something he could twist to advantage.

"Who could be so bold?" Myra asked, "So bold just to follow the instructions as they are written, without knowing the consequences?" She waved her arms about the cabin. "None of my minions would dare attempt it."

"To do so would be counter the basic tenets of any aleator," she continued. "We sail where the winds take us, and, if we truly believe, it will be where we desire. Our luck provides. To use a calculation, no

287

matter how reliable it might be, is a statement of distrust."

Myra leaned forward until her face was a hand span from Kestrel's own. "Luck favors the believer," she said, "just as the fourth tenet states. If you sincerely trust in it, you will weather your trials unscathed. If you doubt, then it gives the fifth tenet — 'luck is fickle' — a chance to wreak its havoc.

"The book and the device labeled as a sextant which accompanies it," Myra continued in a hushed voice, "they must come from someone beyond the farthest extent of our realm — from someone whose wish is to do us harm, to make us doubt in our very foundations and in our reasons for existing at all."

Myra drew back and squinted at Kestrel. "No, it would do great ill for me or one of my minions to perform the calculations that would point us where we wish to go. I have often wondered if it were good luck or ill in the first place that led me to find it in the smoking ashes of a lightning-struck fire."

"So luck is expended to take you to the casino?" Kestrel asked. "Luck that might better be of value once you are there."

Myra stroked her chin and then shrugged. "Jelilac does have a great store of luck for use in the games, perhaps the greatest of all. And I do need to husband each dram of mine and not waste any on getting from here to the casino, wherever that might be."

She considered for a few heartbeats, and then reached out and tapped a long slender finger against Kestrel's chest. "But for one who had no luck to put in jeopardy, to him there surely could be no harm, now could it? He would not fear the misfortune that might result from following the ritual or the weight upon his thoughts about what he has done."

Kestrel stared back into Myra's eyes, unblinking. An idea came to him. He weighed the risks and decided that the chance was worth it. It might not take more than simple sightings, and he would be done. With just the right words, it would free Phoebe and give her a chance at Camonel as well.

"Of course, I understand the third tenet — 'luck begets luck'," he said, "But consider. The rituals in the book might not be one of misfortune. Instead, performing the calculations could enhance whatever one possesses. Yes, do release the woman, and we will do as the book instructs. We will calculate the bearing for the casino and inform you of the result.

"But be warned of the consequence, Myra," he continued. *I* believe. I believe deeply that our luck will be restored by our actions — restored to perhaps a level even greater than your own."

"Your speech is glib," Myra frowned and rubbed her chin. "Most glib for one so close to disaster."

Her eyes lost their focus, and she looked past Kestrel out onto the sea. "Jelilac," she muttered. "It is he that I fear the most. Against him, I must marshal every resource. It would be folly not to take advantage of all my luck that I have accumulated." She paused. "But then, another rival is not a prospect that I relish either."

"It sounds as if you want to save your poison and use it too," Kestrel said. "Get the navigation instruction and dispose also of any luck that Phoebe and I might acquire in the process."

She looked back at Kestrel and smiled. "As the second tenet states, 'the entropy of luck always increases'. Even if the reading of a navigation direction does concentrate a large quantity of luck, I doubt that it could withstand the heat of a flame."

Kestrel steeled himself from smiling in return. Finally, things were pointing in the direction he wanted. He forced a look of apprehension onto his face. "Just a moment." He licked his lips. "I said nothing about being subjecting to a fire."

"Ah, I see your composure does seem to waver a bit," Myra's smile broadened.

Kestrel put protest into his voice and waved his arm about the room. "Never mind what I said. You can do with us what you will with any of your devices, but like everyone else, we shun the flame."

Kestrel stopped and lowered his eyes. "Please! We have struggled too long to survive as long as we have. Anything but a fire."

"Thus, it shall be." Myra slapped her side. "Yes, this will be far more rewarding than any of the other amusements that distract me." She looked over her shoulder and yelled out onto the deck. "Bring the kindling and the spark. We shall set them out on a raft where the logs can be the fuel. After he has performed the ritual as the tome instructs, whatever luck they might accrue will be burned away."

"But —" Kestrel began.

"Silence," Myra commanded. She motioned to a sailor in the hatchway, and he came forward, clutching a large leather-bound book like a servant with a tray. Balancing on its upper surface was a sextant of gleaming metal.

Kestrel forced his eyes to open wide and then slumped his shoulders. He squeezed Phoebe's hand as a signal for silence. With just a little more luck …

He stopped the race of his thoughts. As a final piece of convincing, he offered a token resistance to the arms that propelled him out of the cabin. The entire crew came alive with a blur of activity. A small raft was lowered over the side of the ship, tethered to a long rope.

Matches and kindling were assembled, and an archer donned a thick, padded vest and hood. At arm's length, he struck a spark that caught some curly shavings on fire. The archer dipped a tar-soaked arrow tip into the blaze, flinching backward as it burst into a smoky flame.

In silence, the Kestrel and Phoebe were lowered onto the raft and pushed onto its rocking deck. The tether played out, and the small platform drifted a distance away. The archer placed his hands in gloves so thick he could barely grasp his bow. Bulky shields were placed behind his back. Aiming awkwardly, he nocked the shaft and pointed it at the raft.

Kestrel turned to Phoebe and smiled with what he hoped looked like conviction. "This idea is a much better one than tossing the ball into the hoops," he said.

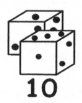

10

Book and Sextant

KESTREL PUT down the book and arched his back. He steadied himself to the roll of the raft. Most of an hour had passed. The archer still strained at attention on Myra's barge. He felt a grim satisfaction at the bowman's discomfort. Of course, it had been too much to expect that he could read as well as understand the language of the realm, especially since Milligan had siphoned away all of their luck. A little more time would be a reasonable enough amount for study, he judged, and then he would go through the motions of sighting.

"When I am done and shout back the heading," he said to Phoebe, "they will undoubtedly give the instruction to fire the shaft. Let it start the raft burning and then use some of the powder you obtained from the archimage to summon Camonel to our aid."

"What about the sextant and book?" Phoebe asked. "If they are from beyond this realm, might not they reveal some clue about Astron's riddle as well?"

"The sextant is of some arcane design, but I think I have figured out how to use it in a convincing fashion." Kestrel shook his head. "Except for a few unusual features, the book appears much as one would expect: page after page of navigation tables. Take the sightings to find out where you are. Then read the bearing for the destination in which you should travel."

He shrugged. "If Astron were here, he might make something more of the instructions, but the significance I cannot tell."

Kestrel thumbed through the bulk of the volume, grunting as the pages fell through his fingers. "It must have been constructed by more than one scribe, and it looks like they did not talk to one another. The style changes with the entries for every few days.

"At the first, there are four columns on each leaf," he continued.

"With what I guess from the accompanying logos to be the position of the sun on the upper half and the brighter stars beneath. Next, it changes to data in rows, if the headings are to be believed, and after that, the solar elevations are separated from the rest. On and on it goes, with fancy scrollwork and then harsh starkness, changing the format every fortnight or so."

He set down the tome and laughed despite himself. "It certainly was designed to be well used. The entries run on and on for what must be hundreds and hundreds of years. I doubt that anyone would care unless it was passed on from one generation to the next. What is here could last Myra and her crew for a long time."

Kestrel hefted the sextant. "But enough of that. Prepare to toss your powders into the fire." He turned in the direction of the setting sun and found the brightest of the evening stars. The slosh of the waves against the raft was greater than against the massive sides of the barge. Only with difficulty was he able to keep what he sighted in the center of view.

He grunted at the heaviness of the sextant, swinging it slowly to the second sighting. The screws felt awkward to his touch and wobbled in their shafts as he tried to adjust a cursor. He ran his hand over the blistered skin of iron that framed a cloudy lens. The artisanship was quite primitive, but he supposed it did not matter. The heading he would shout back to Myra's barges would be the first that popped into his mind. It would depend upon her luck if it were accurate or not.

When he had completed the last sighting, Kestrel thumbed through the book as if he were searching for corresponding entries. Phoebe tensed at his side with her hand in the pocket of her cape, ready to toss out the powder. After a moment, he stood up on the rocking platform and cupped his hands to his mouth.

"A third of a circle away from the direction of the setting sun," he shouted. "The calculations have been made, and there is no doubt about —"

Before he could finish, the archer released his bow. The arrow sliced through the gathering gloom of night like a comet and hit the raft on the side closest to Myra's ships. Kestrel bent over and fanned the flames, no longer caring about what the aleators thought of his actions. Phoebe's face glowed with confidence. With clenched fists, she waved her arms upward, as if adding energy to the flame. The sparkling powder danced from her hand like a collection of fleas and fell into the blaze.

Kestrel's own tension grew. Soon it would be over. Without the rush of combining realms, Camonel could head to wherever they wished. He could find Astron and Nimbia and send the small demon back to his own realm. Then with Palodad ...

He had not thought through the reason they wanted to find the anvilwood and send Astron home alone in the first place. Suppose the demon was right, and Camonel was under the control of some wizard. Perhaps even Prydwin was manipulating things beyond his own realm. Kestrel touched the sextant at his side and frowned. Manipulations in another realm — a navigator's almanac and sextant served the same end.

Panic suddenly welled up within him. Kestrel grasped Phoebe's shoulder, even though he knew he should not. "Wait a moment. Perhaps it would be better if it were some other demon that you —"

His words were cut short. With a hiss of foul tasting air, the massive djinn stepped from the flame and stood as a sinister, dark silhouette against the last rays of the sun.

"I, Camonel, submit to your will because my prince Palodad instructs it," the demon said. "There is no need for a struggle of wills. Speak your command and it will be mine to perform."

"Never mind about princes and allegiances in the realm of demons," Kestrel replied before Phoebe could speak. Her eyes darted to him, but he rushed on, ignoring her puzzlement. "It is your mastery which we wish to know. Yes, not princes but *masters*. Is the wizard here the one who dominates your will so that you must do all that she asks, or is there another who instructs you instead to say the words that prevent any true struggle from taking place?"

Sparkles of blue like emerging stars in the twilight began to dance about Camonel's teeth. In the faint glow, the demon's scowl grew into one of true menace. For a long while, the djinn was silent. Then his rumbling voice again came forth.

"Where is Astron, the one who walks? It is not only the pollen. He is needed as well."

"Your master — who is it?" Phoebe asked, catching the drift of Kestrel's thought. "Now that I think of it, each time was too easy. I was too flushed in victory to examine closely how I felt. You merely said that you were mine to dominate, but never was there a true test."

"Prince Palodad instructs that I serve and —"

"Not him," Phoebe interrupted. "Not another demon — your master. What is his name?"

Kestrel sucked in his breath. He could not pull his eyes away from the glowing yellow eyes of the djinn. A cold numbness crept down his spine. If Camonel were *not* under Phoebe's control, what would happen then?

Again, Camonel was silent. His face distorted in indecision. Finally, he answered in a staccato popping of sparks that shot from his teeth and lips. "I am to do whatever I am asked by you, provided that it does not conflict with what I otherwise have been told."

"Then the need for Astron to accompany the pollen, Palodad's words that the grains held some clue to the answer —"

"The why of that I know nothing." Camonel shook his head. Kestrel grabbed the sextant, just as a large wave sloshed into the raft and tumbled Phoebe into his side

"Is your master the manipulator?" He waved the instrument in front of Camonel's chest. "Is it he that brought about the collapsing of the two realms of symmetry? Did he leave the sextant here so that those like Myra would doubt, so that there would be damage here in addition to the rest?"

"Yes," Camonel said. "To speak of the manipulations themselves I am not bound. But this is only one realm of the many that swim in the void. What is your command? There is much yet to be done."

"And Gaspar," Kestrel continued. "Is your master behind his riddle as well?"

"Gaspar is a demon of little brain," Camonel answered. "Even so, you must make haste, mortal. His minions are close. They have observed this very flame through which we are speaking. They now know the realm in which you hide. In a few ticks of time more, they will —"

"Take us back to the realm of men," Phoebe shouted. "Then return and find Astron and Nimbia as —"

A sudden wave bigger than any before raced under the raft. Kestrel tipped forward, just barely managing to grab Phoebe before she fell. The water lapped over the edge of the logs and spilled into the fire. In a flash of smoke, the flame was doused, and Camonel was gone.

Kestrel tried staggering back to his feet, but the agitation of the sea increased. Stunned by what had happened, he looked out in the growing blackness toward Myra's ship.

"The fire is spent, but it has done its job," the aleator called out over the bulwark. "See the increased agitation of the surf. A great wave is coming, and they no longer have luck to ward it away. Pull them back aboard and we will slip offshore a league or so until the disturbance passes.

"Then on the morrow we will set sail as the glib one has directed," Myra continued. "Keep them in bondage. If I can think of no new amusement, especially for them during our journey, then they can serve as shields on the floor of the casino along with the rest."

Almost in a daze, Kestrel pulled Phoebe to him and held her tight. The last wisps of smoke curled from the doused fire. He cursed his luck, what little there was of it. What had he done? He had learned that Astron's conjecture about Camonel was true, but at what cost. Phoebe and he were just as much prisoner as before. Yes, now they would travel to the casino. But there would be no chance that Myra would be persuaded to light a fire again. And as the djinn had warned, now Gaspar would be close behind.

He kicked the sextant overboard and then gave the almanac a shove — devices of the manipulator, the one behind the merging realms and the riddle as well. There must be something of significance that could be deduced from these facts, but it would take someone like Astron to figure out what it was. Now, until they dropped anchor, he had to focus all his attention on keeping Myra's thoughts away her swinging blade.

11

A Treasure of Talismans

ASTRON PEERED out from the cover of the brush at the line of the crest. Leaves of deep green scattered tiny droplets of dew as he pushed them aside. Behind him, buzzing insects filled the interior slopes of the island with a blur of sound. Was the noise all from bugs or were there an imp or two adding to the drone as well? In this realm, even with his demon senses, he could not be sure.

No one had yet stirred from either of Myra's ships lying at anchor in the bay below. In only a few moments more, Byron's force sneaking down the hillside would inevitably be discovered.

From the look of the anxious faces of those who had followed the tall swordsman, not everyone was as convinced as he was about their role in his destiny. Armed only with blade and shield, they would be no match for aleators with necks ringed by talismans. But at least some would survive long enough, Astron thought. Long enough to bolt and flee back up the slope along the wide path that ran by his hiding place. And just as surely, some of Myra's aleators would follow.

Astron tightened his grip on the rope of twisted vines that ran from his hand down onto the wide path past the bush. There was every chance that it would break or even come untied from the base of the tree across the way, but he could think of nothing better to try. He glanced at Nimbia, kneeling at his side, a sword of steel dangling from her hip.

"The words you had me say to Byron about my prowess in battle felt most uncomfortable," he said. "I am a cataloguer, not a hewer of men."

"I saw how you led the enforcers at more than a single oasis," Nimbia answered. "Do not be concerned about the discomfort, demon, though the modesty is becoming."

Astron wrinkled his nose. He should have felt pleasure in Nimbia's words, but he did not. Somehow, the aid he offered to Byron increased her stature, rather than his own.

"Nevertheless," he growled, "too much time has been wasted in my translation of fluffs of conversation back and forth. It is better spent in observation of the realm, collecting facts that later can be used to advantage."

Nimbia smiled. "I do not consider the exchange of information a waste," she said. "You are serving me well. Without the facility of your tongue, I would know nothing of Byron beyond grunts and stares." She stopped and lowered her eyes. "And just as important, he would know as little of me."

Astron annoyance grew. He did not care for the way that Byron stared at her when she was distracted elsewhere. When in Byron's presence, she behaved like a human female from the sagas. Her interest in the aleator went beyond the needs of their riddle-quest or even wresting some anvilwood from the grand casino. More than once she had laughed when he translated Byron's words and shook her head at the chastisement he suggested as a reply.

"Byron has made clear more than once that his destiny is his primary focus." Astron pulled on the rope. "Everything else is of little concern."

"A secondary position would not be so bad." Nimbia shrugged. "I have not fared nearly so well in the realm of the fey." She flipped golden curls over her shoulder. "He is comely enough so that no one would whisper when we are seen together. Among his own, he commands a station of respect, one that fittingly links with a hillsovereign."

Nimbia stopped and looked Astron in the eye. "Besides, when all is done, and you return to your own realm, what then is to happen to me?"

The wrinkle in Astron's nose deepened, but Nimbia did not seem to notice as she rushed on.

"I can tell that he is interested," she said. "Constantly, he devours me with his eyes. His boldness is far better than the hesitant glances and turned-away faces that were the features of most when I was the one who held sway. Yes, he has great interest, and yet, at the same time, he shows measured restraint. Unlike the others who became victims of their own lust and interpreted each gentle hesitation as a stunning rebuke or a sure indication that there is someone else, he is game for the chase."

"You have special qualities as well." Astron stumbled. "Your creations were as much for your minions as yourself. No prince have I seen display such concern. You would have earned your diadem, even if it were not acquired by default. And a wizard besides — only ones of that ilk can a djinn ever truly respect. You shielded me in the tree when —"

"Enough." Nimbia laughed. She reached out and touched Astron on the cheek. "You need not sing of my virtues, demon. Your place in my retinue is secure. It is rather I that should list the praises so that you are encouraged to even greater glories for your queen."

Astron started to reply but then snapped shut his mouth. He halted the idle flexing of his grip about the rope and froze dead still. Without moving, he looked at Nimbia expectantly.

Nimbia's face clouded in puzzlement. "Demon?" she said. "What is the matter? Did something happen in that stembrain of yours?"

"I am waiting," Astron answered. "Waiting to hear the list."

Nimbia threw back her head and laughed. Her voice tinkled like a shower of golden brandels tossed against a shield. "Very well," she said. "You deserve no less."

Nimbia eyed Astron critically and then touched her index finger to the palm of her other hand. "First, there is the keenness of mind. In no other of your realm have I observed such an ability for deduction."

"Palodad and other princes that rule." Astron blurted, suddenly as uncomfortable as he had been before. But Nimbia put her finger to his lips for silence and then placed another beside the first.

"Secondly, there is the dedication to your quest," she said. "Despite the hindrances and dangers, you pursue the goal with an unrelenting intensity. I have seen it matched in none of the mighty djinns with their easily distracted flitter of thought. And, now that I think of it, none in the realm of the fey would have persisted as long as have you."

A smile appeared on Astron's face, despite the discomfort. Other delicious feelings began to stir underneath. He wanted again to protest the sweep of her hyperbole but thought better of it as Nimbia retracted her hand and began to say even more.

"Last, and perhaps most important, demon," she smiled, "is the comfort that you bring when we are together. I do not have to worry about breaking through an impenetrable shyness or warding off a jealousy that never can be quenched. I do not have to remember that I am a woman and you are a man."

The seductive sweetness bubbling up inside Astron turned sour like milk left in the sun. Somehow, Nimbia's words of praise were no longer a delight. Despite his best efforts to keep a placid composure, he felt his eye membranes quiver and his sternbrain stir from its slumber with discontent.

Astron shook his head in the manner of men. Why did all of her words now affect him so? Was there a residual effect from his transposition into Kestrel's body that he somehow still retained?

Before he could begin to sort out any of the confusion of his thoughts, the first of Byron's men appeared on the crest. The aleator had discarded sword and shield and was running as fast as he could. Astron scowled and pushed his feelings away. They would have to be examined later. First, there was the matter of the darling of destiny and passage to the grand casino.

Three more of Byron's minions crested the hill in full rout and then six after that. Behind the last, tall, well-fed swordsmen with purple surcoats over close-knit mail came racing close after.

As the first of Byron's men staggered past, he checked with Nimbia to see if she were ready. The rest of darling's followers sprinted down the path into the interior of the island with the first of Myra's aleators on their heels like hounds after a fox. A half-dozen talismans danced about the necks of each of those in the foreground. Gritting his teeth, Astron let them pass. A score of swordsmen sped by, shouting and laughing as they ran. Behind them came a dozen stragglers more, not so richly endowed as the rest.

Astron waited until the last three were just beginning to rush past the hidden rope. Then he jerked it tight and held it as firmly as he was able. The first aleator leaped over a small boulder jutting in the way and hurled clear of the trip rope, evidently not even noticing its presence. The other two, however, were caught just above their ankles and pitched forward onto the ground. Both landed gracefully on glove-protected hands; but more importantly, just as Astron had hoped, the talismans about their necks hurled free to land a few body lengths beyond.

"Now," Astron shouted, "now, Nimbia, while we have a chance."

The hillsovereign sprang out onto the trail, her sword pointing the way. The two sprawled warriors rose to their feet and then their eyes widened in terror as she moved between them and their amulets. They returned to their knees with hands spread wide, indicating surrender. One looked longingly at what lay a few feet away and began to sob.

Astron ran out behind Nimbia and scooped up the treasures. He flung them over his head and then turned after the third warrior who had stopped to see what was happening behind. Astron waved his sword with one hand while pointing at his own chest with the other. "Not one standard issue, but two," he said. "You do not have a chance."

The third warrior froze. He unbuckled his sword and let it fall. Sagging on one knee, he bowed to the ground. Astron did not hesitate. He ran forward and, despite the small rocks that seemed to get in his way, pulled the third set of talismans away from their wearer.

"Over there." He pointed his sword back to Nimbia. "Do exactly as she says."

The man-at-arms nodded in submission. Without waiting to ensure that he fully complied, Astron began running down the trail as fast as he could manage not to stumble. So far, everything was proceeding as he had hoped. The aleators were so conditioned to depending on luck in everything they did that, without their amulets, they felt completely helpless. When confronted with an opponent better endowed, they gave up rather than attempt a fight.

Astron caught up with two more warriors who ran behind the rest. He tripped over a bared root in the trail, but like an accomplished dancer, he did not fall. Circling his sword over his head, he froze his face in a berserker's stare, yelling an incoherent challenge. A half-dozen talismans now bounced from his chest as he ran, and the men-at-arms' eyes immediately focused on their dance.

Just as the others before, the two warriors assumed postures of surrender, letting Astron snatch their amulets with a clumsy swipe before they guessed his intent. More aleators looked backward, and a shout of warning coursed through their midst. The pursuit of Byron's followers slowed and then halted.

Those fleeing sensed the slacking of pursuit and halted their own flight. With a cheer, they turned and began to strike at the aleators who were looking over their shoulders at what was attacking their rear.

Astron yelled as fiendishly as he could and slashed left and right. Aleators on both sides stepped backward, tumbling over one another and off the trail into the brush to get out of the way. One of Myra's captains in the vanguard caught sight of Astron's weight of treasure. He stared down at his own chest, barely ducked a swipe at the side of his head, and then with a shudder, bolted into the brush. Two more followed his lead, then a half-dozen more on the other side of the trail. In barely an instant, only five men-at-arms remained, all offering their swords in surrender.

Astron pulled to a halt, hardly believing what had happened. More than a score of well-armed warriors had been routed by a single foolhardy rush. Shaking his head, he grabbed the talismans that remained and added them to the rest. With stooping shoulders, he walked back up the hill to see how Nimbia was faring in her stint at guard duty.

He was elated. He had performed as well as could have been expected of even a mighty djinn. But then, just as quickly, he put the thought aside. He was still a long way from securing any anvilwood.

There was yet the rescue of Kestrel and Phoebe to be managed. The lightning djinns that pursued might discover them at any time. And Byron? If he had survived the rush down the slope, what more could be expected from the one who seemed to covet Nimbia more and more with each passing moment.

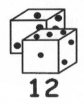

12

Dissipation

ASTRON APPROACHED Nimbia on the far side of the evening campfire erected just down the seaward slope from the crest of the hill. Nimbia watched with interest the preparations of Sylvan and Centuron for destroying the captured talismans. When the demon and the others had returned in triumph up the hill, Byron had insisted. The luck had to be dissipated back into the either. To do less would not be true to his quest.

Wounded by the first man he had met, Byron had been left behind when his ranks broke and retreated up the hill. Now, while hobbling around the campfire, he talked with two of his lieutenants as if the day had been the same as any other. The bloodstained rags that bound his leg looked blotched with black in the dimness of the evening.

"Of course, Myra's aleators that remained all transferred onto a single barge and sailed away," Byron said. "She had reasoned that she was confronting a force much more powerful than her own and did not wish to suffer the same defeat One ship is ours, just as I had predicted."

Astron ran his hand over the nape of his neck. Reluctantly, after the abandoned ship and the prisoners had been secured, he had given up all the talismans he had captured to be destroyed with the rest. His arguments about the men-at-arms who had run into the forest possibly returning were ignored.

He also was interested in what was happening with the talismans. It probably was the last chance to talk to the hillsovereign without Byron being in the vicinity. Tomorrow they would be confined together in the barge for the final journey across the sea. Then, once in the grand casino, from what little Astron had gleaned, there would be little time for anything other than struggling for survival. And if by luck, they did …

Astron shook his head in the manner of men at the thought. And if by luck they did, Gaspar's djinns would probably be upon him.

302

Nimbia peered over Sylvan's shoulder and gestured while the aleator stirred the contents of a small cauldron over a sputtering flame. Nearby a second fire was roaring fiercely as it consumed branches of dry pinewood that Byron's followers had carried with them from the beginning of their trek.

"I think I understand what you ask," Sylvan said, "but a more intense flame makes the film too fragile. The only purpose of the heat here is to thin the liquid to the proper consistency."

"It looks like the sap of what we call the soapbark tree in the realm of fey," Nimbia turned to Astron as he drew near. "Here, the aleators tap the trunk and let it drip into waiting buckets."

"The same is done for syrups in the realm of men," Astron answered as he fell into the mode of automatically translating.

"This is for a greater purpose than delighting the tongue," Sylvan said. "Without its protection, the risk of contamination is far too great."

"I thought that fires destroyed the concentration of luck," Astron replied. "If you must ruin the talismans, why not just toss them under the stewpot while it heats?"

"The heat would crack the shell that resists the great pressure of the gas, it is true," Sylvan explained, "but when it rushes out in a burst, there is no way to tell which way it will surge. It might all lodge in a nearby tree or worse yet, in one of us who attends the fire. No, the luck must be released slowly in a way that we can control."

"Then you coat the talismans in this paste?" Astron asked.

"Watch and you will see." Sylvan ignored the question. She motioned for Centuron to come forward, and the old man lumbered up, holding one of the talismans at arm's length as if it had a foul odor.

Sylvan dipped a circle of wire into a cauldron and then drew it back. It emerged with a thin film of the soapbark sap stretched across its interior. She blew on the film, deforming it from a plane into a bulging hemisphere. Centuron continued forward until the dangling talisman met the shiny surface and then passed through it to the other side. Sylvan exhaled one more strong burst of air and a glassy bubble separated from the ring, enveloping the amulet.

"Now we can apply the heat." Sylvan looked back at Nimbia. She took the leather thong from Centuron's grasp and moved the bubble encompassing the talisman over toward the second fire. The orb bounced slightly, but remained suspended, not touching the amulet at all but somehow remaining hanging from the point where it was pierced by the thong.

Sylvan held the bubble over the fire so that it warmed in the rising heat, but the flames did not touch. Two or three others of Byron's followers gathered around her as she adjusted the height of the little sphere, all silently waiting for what would happen.

For a long while, Astron detected no change. The fire crackled and wisps of smoke rose into the air, enveloping the bubble in a sooty haze as it floated skyward. Then, just as his interest began to sag, he noted a slight change of color on the surface of the brightly painted wood inside the glassy globe. The yellows and reds began to fade. The blues paled into gray; the whites started to blister. In three heartbeats, the polished surface turned to a dull, ashen indistinctness. The amulet seemed to start vibrating, although Astron could not hear a hum. The sharp outlines of the intricate carving blurred. With a sharp crack like the breaking of an egg, a jagged rip appeared down one side from top to bottom.

A sparkling iridescence shot from the fissure and dissipated itself against the interior curve of the bubble. Like the spout of a tiny geyser seeded with reflective glitter, the essence of the talisman rushed out of its confinement. Sylvan waited a while more until the exhaust from the amulet had slowed to a barely discernible trickle. A slight opaqueness filled the bubble, where before it had been transparent and clear.

"Now for the controlled outgassing," Sylvan said, motioning to Centuron, who was already making his way forward with a circle of twine in one hand and a needle in the other.

"Popping the bubble would serve no better than cracking the talisman unprotected," she continued, "But the strength of the soapbark film is high. It allows us to proceed with much more care."

She took the circle of twine from Centuron with her free hand between extended thumb and forefinger, placed the ring against the surface of the bubble, and then withdrew,

The band of twine did not penetrate the surface but instead floated on its glassy slickness, pulled into a tiny, perfect circle.

"I recognize what is happening," Astron said. "It is the surface tension in the liquid. The same force that holds the bubble together in a sphere against the gasses inside deforms the string into a ring."

Sylvan ignored the comment. She turned so that the floating circle was aimed away from the rest of the camp and outward toward the open sea. Reaching from the side, she stabbed the needle into the small ring of film trapped by the twine.

Astron expected the bubble to pop with an explosive spray of what was contained inside, but it did not. Instead, only the small ring of film within the circle vanished, leaving the bulk of the bubble intact. Wisps of the glittering gas oozed through the opening out into the air in a gentle flow.

The bubble contracted. Unlike a fragile sphere of film and rather like a balloon made of a cow's bladder in the realm of men, the orb grew smaller in a controlled manner. As more and more of the glittering gas vented to the outside, the surface tension contracted the sphere into a tinier and tinier volume. Finally, the radius became so small that the film touched the ragged edge of the rip in the talisman. With a tiny pop, the bubble flashed into nonexistence.

"Most interesting," Astron said. "I suspect that such a procedure would work with the soaps in the realms of men and the fey as well."

Back near the main campfire, Byron threw back his head and laughed at something his lieutenant had said. Nimbia looked his way and then flushed when she noticed everyone watching what she had done.

"It is too bad," Centuron rumbled. He waved at the two fires as Sylvan stirred the small cauldron. "Only some luck can be undone." He glanced at Nimbia and shook his head. "Yes, the dabblings of men can be unmade, but that which is bestowed by fate at birth is a burden forever."

"What do you mean?" Nimbia asked after Astron translated. She glanced at Sylvan and hesitated. "Are you the one until now the most in his favor? I am sorry, but if nothing yet has been decided, then surely there is no harm ..."

Nimbia's words trailed off. Sylvan looked down at the cauldron and began stirring more vigorously without answering. The queen eyed the old man carefully. "What is your wish in the matter? Is Sylvan here a personal favorite? If not, the words of one so venerated will carry a great weight if there is to be a decision."

"If somehow, without manipulating the tenets of luck," Centuron answered, "the pompous one manages to survive to the final struggles, then there is where I want to be — at the very center of the realm, when all those who have cast their lot with the vagaries of chance begin to doubt the foundation of their existence.

"So you see, your question does not require an answer, unfortunate maid. With either outcome, your wish will be denied. Either the sands will run with Byron's blood or —"

"Do not mind his prattle," Sylvan cut in. "I suspect that it depresses him that you are so unlucky, and there is nothing that he can do."

"Without luck, yes, I understand that," Nimbia frowned. "It is what happened when we first arrived — but unlucky? What do you mean?"

"Why, your beauty, of course. How unfortunate to be saddled with such a burden."

Nimbia's frown grew deeper. She reached up and straightened a loose strand of hair. "I know that I am fair," she said. "It is what gives me an advantage when it comes to Byron's affections, I do confess, but —"

"Think, woman," Sylvan cut her off. "Byron cannot be the only one. The souls of how many men have been warped by the closeness of your presence so that their inner worths were hidden? Whom do you know that has acted so that you could judge him as he truly is?" She glanced at Byron. "What you do is tempt him from his destiny, and if you succeed, then whom will he blame?"

Sylvan shook her head. "No, I do not rue the fact that you have him smitten. I pity you instead."

13

The Grand Casino

KESTREL STEADIED himself against the gentle roll of the ship in the quickening breeze. He shielded his eyes from the emerging sun on his starboard and squinted at the smudge directly ahead of the bowsprit. The air was hazy with the remains of a clearing fog, but already he could see what must be the tall, thin towers that marked the corners of the casino

They had been beset by calm for most of the first day at sea. At the dawn of the second, a lookout had spied a mast on the sternward horizon. The crew had buzzed with the speculation that they were being followed by the savages who had captured the entire company of men-at-arms. Little that Myra had said changed the growing apprehensiveness of their disposition.

Kestrel had listened closely to the description of the one who had led the charge down to the beach and almost succeeded in boarding before they were safely away. He dared not hope too much. But perhaps there was the slimmest of chances that it was Astron who followed their every move through the swirling fog and occasional gusting winds. He shook his head. No, the description of the leader of the savages did not sound right.

Phoebe came to Kestrel's side and reached up to massage the tense muscles in his neck. He felt tight and drawn out, like an archer's bowstring before its release. For the two full days at sea, he had just barely managed to convince Myra to seek her amusements elsewhere and save him and the wizard for the contest in the casino.

"It is not your burden," Phoebe tried to comfort him. "Myra would have toyed with the others, regardless of what you said. Your words were not responsible. They did no more than shield me from certain harm."

Kestrel shook his head again. For each time that Myra had been dissuaded, cries of pain and pleas for a quick death for some other prisoner had echoed through his mind. A terrible weight bore down on his shoulders.

"But for what?" Kestrel said. "I have done no more than postpone the inevitable. Myra has made it quite clear that our purpose on the casino floor is to be human shields against the weapons directed at her by the other competing aleators."

He grasped Phoebe's hands in his. "I am sorry, sorry that my wit has not been as strong as it needs to be."

Kestrel looked at the cabin in the stern. He released Phoebe, and his fists clenched tight. He remembered Milligan's theft of his luck without even a hint of warning and the small value Jelilac placed on their lives.

This quest had become one of mounting obligations, he thought. First, his pledge to Phoebe, then the debt he owed to the enforcers who trusted him as leader, and now, if somehow he could manage it, Jelilac, Milligan, Myra, and the others like them should be made to pay for all they must have done.

Like a nervous cat, Kestrel examined the shore. The towers of the casino become more crisp and clear. He sucked in a chestfull of air and then spilled it back into the salty spray. Brave words, he shook his head, not what one might expect from a scheming woodcutter — especially not from one who could calculate quite well the chances of surviving without luck in a casino filled with talisman-wearing aleators. He flexed his fingers about the sword pommel that was not there, trying to fan the flame of his conviction so that it masked the growing fear.

Finally, he pushed the bizarre thoughts away. He stood, silently watching and waiting for what would happen next. In a little more than what he judged to be a few hundred heartbeats, Myra's ship would cast anchor in a crowded harbor. Her followers and prisoners would come ashore into a surging mass of aspiring aleators and their own retainers. Everyone in the realm, Myra had said, would be there — if not a possessor of enough wealth to compete, then to watch to see who the next archon would be.

In the confusion of mingling bodies, one might expect someone to break for freedom, but those without talismans knew better than to try. With faces heavy with resignation, they shuffled into position as their masters directed. Kestrel kept Phoebe close, his eyes darting all about, looking for a sign of Astron or a chance to communicate through the flame.

Except for the casino itself, the island was bare of structure, low and sandy with no plants taller than bushy shrubs. The building was shaped like a huge octagon with high walls that Myra had said enclosed a many-tiered stadium. From each vertex, towers soared even farther into the sky. At the apex of each, attendants stood ready near the signal beacons that would flash the results of the competition across the sea to those whose luck prevented them from arriving in time.

The walls were thick, covered by many layers of fading paint that had withstood countless years of high surf and spray. Portions of old murals peeked out from behind the peeling layers of those placed on top. Faded scenes of previous victories; cornucopia brimming with talismans and devices of chance blended into the mute drabness that surrounded them.

Midway in the face of each of the casino walls, high doors thrice the height of a man stood open. Into each snaked the retainers of the aleators, climbing into the stands to cheer their lords onward.

"You two shall be in the vanguard of my contingent." Myra pointed in the direction of Kestrel and Phoebe as other aleators jostled past. "For each contender, a full dozen is allowed on the floor, but it is folly to have every minion's neck heavy with capsules of great fortune. A single reversal could spell the end of serious contention. I think it is better for at least four to be luckless as newborn babes. Let the machines of Jelilac and the others do their worst. It will not be talismans of true power that feel the slings of their wrath."

Myra waited until all the aleators at the nearest door had entered. Then, with a majestic swirl of a cape she had donned for the ceremony, she strode into the casino. Inside the outer shell, the stairways lead up into the stands on either flank. Pressed against the high ceiling, globes of bioluminescent fungi bathed everything in an eerie soft light. Directly ahead, a tunnel ran onto the floor of the casino itself. The ground underfoot was bare earth, almost muddy from the humid air.

Myra motioned her followers, except for the chosen twelve, to take the stairs to the left and ascend to the highest seats, as far removed as possible from the rest of the spectators. When the last had begun to climb, she nodded to Kestrel and Phoebe to begin their entrance.

Kestrel clutched empty air at his side with a feeling of futility. His pulse begin to race. On Jelilac's sloop, he had managed to escape, but here in the casino, there would be too many to fight. He started to speak when a sudden crashing boom exploded outward from the casino floor and echoed down the tunnel walls.

"Minefields," Myra grunted without losing a stride. "Evidently, one of the contestants did not enter sufficiently prepared."

Another explosion ripped down the passageway. Then a third came, this one mingled with cries of pain and a roar from the crowd. Kestrel moved forward as slowly as he could with the tip of a sword planted in the small of his back. He stepped in front of Phoebe just as he reached the tunnel entrance and looked out into the bright light of the contesting field, squinting to see what was happening.

From the other entrances were emerging more contingents, each with a dozen retainers surrounding an elegantly dressed aleator shouting commands. Nearer the center of the casino floor, still other groups surrounded their leaders, but in most cases, their number had been reduced from the original dozen. Only six still protected a corpulent, well-dressed lord in their midst, and one of those limped, with his left arm hanging useless at his side. Myra's goal was the same as the rest of the contenders, to reach one of the shallow pits dug into the ground and surrounded by chalky white boulders and low barriers of tumbled logs.

The group proceeded cautiously and then, with no apparent reason, veered sharply to the left. With a flash of angry yellow, another boom ricocheted through the stadium. The retainer on the far right suddenly hurled up in the air, his body bent like a handful of broken twigs.

"Come," Myra said. "We will show them that my luck is sufficient to find a path to a fortress without fear or hesitation." She prodded one of her talisman-protected men-at-arms forward, and he began walking rapidly out onto the casino floor. "Follow his footsteps, follow them exactly," Myra commanded. "Match him step for step, if you wish to survive for when you are needed later."

Kestrel hesitated. The man-at-arms veered sharply to the left and then just as quickly resumed his course toward the protective barricades. He felt the sharp prodding in his back and sucked in his breath. Stepping out into the warrior's footprints, he reached behind to pull Phoebe's hand. He took two tentative paces and then half a dozen more, matching the zigzag path of his predecessor as best he could. Moving with increasing haste so that he would not lose the trail, he pulled Phoebe after, only dimly aware of Myra and her other followers snaking behind.

A sudden crack sharper than the boom of the mines pierced through the din on Kestrel's right. A sudden rip of pain shot into his hand. There was a streak of blood as if he had been neatly nicked by a blade. He snapped Phoebe forward and tumbled her over the nearest boulder of the barricade just ahead, just as a second pop sounded behind him. As he jumped for cover, what sounded like a shower of pebbles skittered against the thick granite to his rear.

"A grenade," Myra muttered behind him as she was helped over the rock by two of her retainers. She stopped and coughed, trying to blow the

310

dust from her lungs. "Shrapnel will find the unlucky. About that there can be no doubt."

14

Challenges for the Aleators

ELSEWHERE IN the casino, the other contesting groups were also seeking what shelter they could. Those who arrived last began to erect makeshift barriers of shields and protruding lances on open ground, and as far removed from the other contingents as possible. More grenades began to soar through the air, lofted from one group to that immediately closest. The staccato pop of many projectiles replaced the dull boom of the mines.

One of the less protected groups sallied from their cover and raced with swords drawn at the adversaries on their left. Kestrel expected to see a protracted and grim struggle like the carefully choreographed dances of the enforcers, but instead, in a brief mêlée, the encounter was over. Half of the attackers stumbled and fell when they engaged their opponents. The rest were dispatched by the first lucky swings of carelessly aimed swords. Another brief flurry erupted on the opposite side of the casino floor and, far to the right, yet two more.

"The ones whose wishes exceed their stores of wealth," Myra said at Kestrel's side. "They mimic the contest of old when strength of arm and cleverness of siegecraft determined the victor. Soon they will all be gone, and those of potential, those that believe, will struggle as it should be done."

Fulfilling her prophecy almost at once, a strong voice suddenly rang through the din. "A challenge, a challenge of true virtue to masqueraders on our left."

The crowd fell silent, and all the hostilities ceased on the casino floor. Kestrel craned around to see Milligan standing on the top of a small boulder near one of the tunnels with a megaphone to his mouth. Jelilac's had been one of the last contingents to arrive.

"We do the great practice of our art disservice by such crude measures," Milligan continued. "Avoiding mines and the shrapnel of grenades takes a measure of luck, to be sure, but it in no way answers which of us has the greatest power and hence the authority to rule."

Milligan circled to address the stands at his back. "Remember our heritage," he said. "This very edifice is enshrined with the name of the grand casino — not the arena, not the stadium, but the *casino* where all is ruled by chance. The events to be decided here are to be based upon the pristine twisting of gaseous luck, not the slashing of bloodied blades."

The crowd roared in approval, but Milligan motioned them back to silence. "Yes, luck is to be the mechanism of decision — luck, pure and unsullied with irrelevant skill."

He pointed at his side to a large glass bowl filled with tiny white spheres and with two transparent tubes snaking out of the top. "Of all those who have assembled to struggle here Jelilac is the mightiest, the one with the greatest hoard of fortune. He issues a challenge to all. The first to have three chosen numbers discharged will be the victor. The vanquished will cease their struggles and submit all talismans to aid in the greater cause."

Milligan shut his eyes. Extending his arm, he pointed out across the casino floor and spun about three times, pirouetting to a sudden halt. "You!" He laughed as he sighted down the length of his arm toward a small fortification across the floor. "You shall be the first to test that Jelilac's luck is the most potent of all."

A young aleator rose from cover and shook his head. "No, that is not my plan," he protested. "My only hope is to win against others similarly endowed and capture what luck they have remaining after the battle. Only by that means would I have the chance to face the likes of Jelilac in the end."

The crowd roared in disapproval. For a long while, the high walls of the casino echoed with their lust for the confrontation. Kestrel squeezed Phoebe's hand and tried to settle into a comfortable position. At least for the moment, everyone was distracted, and no grenades were hurling their way.

Milligan and two other retainers set up a large wooden frame and then draped it with tapestries embroidered in intricate designs. A long hose was connected to one of the tubes protruding from the glass bowl and run back behind the panels where Kestrel could not see. In an instant, the tiny spheres began to dance in the confines of the bowl, like a boiling liquid just about to erupt. Each ball was inscribed with a few strokes of precise lettering in black ink.

"Your numbers," Milligan shouted over the fading din of the crowd. "Everyone here demands it. Remember the fourth tenet — 'luck favors the believer'. If you have doubts and hesitate, then you will fail."

The aleator across the casino floor looked wildly out into the stands and then slumped. He grasped at the handful of talismans about his neck and tightly clenched shut his eyes "Seven, nineteen, and thirty-seven," he said weakly. "And by the third tenet, may these amulets beget all the fortune that I will need."

Milligan laughed and marked the selected numbers on a huge slate handed to him from within the canvas framework. "Nine, forty-two, and forty-three," he called out and added them in a line below the first. "Now we shall contest in the manner that has always been intended."

Milligan removed a cover from the second tube emerging from the bowl, and the crowd again fell silent. No one moved while the white spheres churned and frothed. After a short while, one of the balls bounced into the conical orifice that fed the tube's exit and popped out into Milligan's waiting hand. "Forty-two." He laughed as he held up the orb and waved it over his head. "Forty-two on the very first ball, even though over two hundred spin about."

Before Milligan had finished speaking, a second sphere followed the first. Another of Jelilac's retainers dashed out from the cover of the framing and caught it as it arched into the air. "And forty-three." Milligan laughed again. "I can see the marking clearly from here."

He looked across the casino floor and shook his head. "You may as well make ready. It appears that the wealth you wager against Jelilac is meager indeed."

Milligan turned his attention back to the glass bowl just in time to receive the third ball emerging from the tube. "The third is nine," he said. "Yes, after the first two so suddenly, there could be no doubt."

Most of the crowd broke into enthusiastic cheering, although one small grouping high in the stands sat silently with faces pulled to their chests. Milligan waved both arms over his head to keep up the volume of sound as he tripped across the casino floor to the aleator who had been defeated. With a theatrical flourish, he accepted an armload of talismans and carried them back to Jelilac's framework.

"Who is next?" he shouted. "Who is next to challenge? Jelilac is ready to battle with all."

Kestrel glanced at Myra out of the corner of his eye. The old woman shook her head. "Not yet," she muttered. "Each contest dissipates a little of Jelilac's wealth back into the ether. And there is always the chance that he will not be able to beat them all. I will wait until the last, when my own opportunity is the best."

The banner from another of the fortifications began to wave. A new cheer went up from the crowd. "Five, thirty-nine, and fifty-two," a voice heavy with resignation sounded in the distance. "I may as well be next. It seems that at the last moment, my luck turned fickle. This fortification is made of anvilwood, not simple fir or pine like the rest."

The cheer reverberating in the stands suddenly stopped. Milligan doubled over with his laughter. "Barrier logs made of anvilwood," he said. "The custodians of the casino have prepared for this contest better than most." He waved back at the glass bowl and the churning balls. "One, two, and three. Let us proceed so we can get on to the next."

Anvilwood, Kestrel thought, the very reason for coming to the casino in the first place! He touched the rucksack still hanging on his back. Again, he scanned the rising stadium seats and the array of contestants on the casino floor. "Astron, where are you?" he muttered.

He glanced down at Phoebe and shook his head. With a sigh, he settled beside her and watched the dance of tiny, white balls. With all the contingents on the casino floor, it would take some while to get to Myra. Maybe by then the demon would appear.

15

The Relationships of Numbers

THE ROAR of the crowd was deafening, like that from a waterfall one hundred man-heights wide. Of all the contingents that had swarmed onto the casino floor so many hours before, only Myra and Jelilac remained. The tension grew in Myra's retainers. With each new challenger, they had hoped that Jelilac's luck would turn, but it held steady and true like a compass always pointing north. Some of the opponents had taken more effort to defeat than others. For one, over seventy spheres of no consequence popped free of the miniature maelstrom before Jelilac's third selection emerged. Another, for a moment, trailed only two to one. But in the end, Milligan's master emerged triumphant over all, collecting the largesse of talismans and adding them to his store.

"And now Myra!" Milligan pointed at the one fortification still occupied in the center of the floor. "What are your guesses, old crone? The hour grows late. We have been at this for the better part of a day."

Myra grasped the talismans about her neck and hesitated. She squinted at the bouncing spheres while the bowl was being reloaded and then around the vast interior of the casino as if looking for a sign. "We both have warriors and shields still unspent," she called out in a hoarse voice that betrayed her true age. "It has made no sense to bring the fated twelve if they are not to be used."

"You talk as if you had a great store of wealth, Myra," Milligan shot back. "As great as Jelilac's own. But having the dozen slash at one another is only a distraction. Eventually, it will come down to the spheres."

"If you wish to increase the stakes, then it will be done," he continued. "All talismans forfeited by the loser as before — but in addition, the retainers are to be given to the victor to do with what he will."

Kestrel felt Phoebe tighten against him, but he did not know what to do. Myra or Jelilac — which one emerged the winner did not matter; in either case, their fate was equally grim.

Myra tried to force her face into a grin. She counted the talismans about her neck and then looked around the now nearly deserted casino floor. "Luck favors the believer," she muttered, and then with greater conviction, "Luck favors the believer."

Grabbing the largest stone hanging on her chest, she stared back at Milligan. "Done," she said. "Only instead of three balls, let's make it two."

Two of her retainers bolted to their feet like frogs dropped on a griddle, but Myra motioned them to be still. "Why not?" she muttered. "You have seen what has happened to all the rest. They did not believe as fervently as do I."

"But only two numbers increases the variability of the outcome even more," Milligan protested. "A truly lucky stroke could win, despite where lies the preponderance of wealth."

"Precisely." Myra cackled. "Luck favors the believer, and I will take what is my best chance." She reached into the paraphernalia her retainers had lugged out onto the floor. Kestrel watched with surprise as she extracted the navigator's almanac and opened it to a random page. He had thought it was at the bottom of the sea, but apparently, it had not quite gone overboard from the raft.

"Eight and twelve," Myra called out after she had stabbed her finger down onto the parchment. "I do not need fickle luck. Calculations shall help me instead."

She held up the volume with both hands over her head and turned slowly around so that everyone could see. The shouts of the crowd suddenly fell silent, as if their tongues had been sliced by a blade. No one stirred. Then a troubled murmur arose from the far end of the casino and flowed around the tiers.

"Calculations," Milligan said. "It is not our way — worse even than the slash of sword and clang of shield."

"Eight and twelve," Myra insisted. "Perhaps now even Jelilac is beginning to have some doubts?"

Kestrel studied Myra's face. The signs were subtle, but he had been in too many games of cards not to see them there. It was a bluff. She had not wavered in the strength of her beliefs about luck. Her strategy was to make Jelilac begin to doubt his.

Jelilac was silent for a dozen heartbeats, and then he spoke "Never!"

he said from the protection of the canvas framing, although his voice was not as forceful as that of Milligan, his spokesperson. "I choose thirty four and, and one hundred forty two." His voice trailed off. "Let the mixing begin."

Milligan hesitated. His shoulders twitched like those of a nervous horse before he motioned for the air to begin pumping into the bowl. Almost instantly, a ball popped out the second tubing, and everyone waited in hushed anticipation to see what it would be.

"Thirty four!" Milligan called out in triumph. "I admit that you will not be as easy as any of the rest, Myra, but even with calculations, Jelilac will prevail."

Myra stared back with unblinking eyes. Kestrel could see the stringy muscles in her arms draw into tense bands. The confidence slid from her face. Her strategy was not working as she had hoped. Everything now resided on one element of chance.

He should do something to push the outcome in the way that was best for Phoebe and himself. But which way? Milligan was as much a predator as Myra, but at least he gave out basic talismans so that his victims did not immediately perish. On the other hand, Myra was more of a known quantity. He had interacted with her far more. As the old saying went: 'better to cast the charm you know than the one you don't'.

Another ball exited the pool. "Thirty two," Milligan called out and set it aside.

He had to try something, Kestrel thought. Anything was better than just waiting to see which would be the victor. "Follow my lead," he whispered to Myra, "Just follow my lead."

"Yes, thirty two," he shouted. The prattle of numbers he had used many times before when posing as a magician came easily to his mind. "Eight and twelve are Myra's numbers. But eight and twelve are twenty, and thirty-two minus twenty is twelve again. It is not an irrelevant draw. Myra has won!"

Milligan frowned but said nothing. He reached for the next ball.

"Ninety six —" he began, but Kestrel cut him off.

"Yes, in the nineties," he said. "Eight times twelve is ninety-six. Another agreement with Myra's choice. The numbers emerge according to plan."

"All of those numbers cannot be yours," Jelilac protested.

"But they are," Myra caught on to what Kestrel was attempting to do. "Each of my numbers is the parent of — of dozens more. When the next is chosen, my retainer will explain how it is tied to my choices of eight and twelve. Three in a row, rather than two should be enough to prove that I have won."

Another ball bounced up to the exit orifice, but before it could start its journey, it suddenly fell backward into the rest. The whirl of random motion died away. In a heartbeat, all the spheres were lying quietly in the bottom of the bowl.

Jelilac emerged from the confines of his shelter. With a waddling gait, he walked out to stand at Milligan's side. "I have stopped the blower," he said as he glanced at Myra's tally on the board. "If you truly believe in the power of your calculation, I have another proposition to offer instead."

Myra tossed back her head and laughed, the tension suddenly gone. She glanced once at Kestrel and smiled

"I am willing to up the stakes still further," Jelilac offered, "and give you better odds."

"You heard what my minion said," Myra answered. "The flow of luck is in my direction. There is no incentive for me to change."

"If we employ the giant spinner instead, I will give you nine portions out of ten of the field," Jelilac said. "And in addition to the twelve, I propose that we become part of the prize pools ourselves."

"No, not the spinner," Milligan pleaded. "It is not proper. We have agreed not to deviate from the plan. Let us continue with the dancing spheres. Surely you will prevail."

Myra squinted. Her confidence rebounded. "Nine out of ten," she said, "Ten to one odds, and your body to probe with my pinchers when you lose as I see fit." She slapped the almanac at her side. "Why not?" she cackled. "Your luck is potent, but it cannot be that much greater than mine."

Jelilac grimaced and motioned back to his retainers. "I will be archon," he answered the question forming on their lips. "If we do not duel with the same tools, then how can we be sure?"

Milligan opened his mouth to protest, but Jelilac's stare turned him aside. He stood silent while two of the aleator's retainers emerged from behind the tapestries carrying a large wooden frame into which a hundred pegs had outlined a great circle. With his head shaking, Milligan propped the panel upright. He offered no more aid as the helpers affixed a stout shaft onto an axle that protruded through the center of the frame. A flap of stiff leather was affixed to one end of the shaft and protruded just far enough to touch the circle of pegs.

"You may start the spinner into motion, Myra," Jelilac said, tension in his voice. "Then before it has completed its third spin, I will call out the ten numbers that I select as my own."

Myra stepped from the fortifications. With a flourish of her cape like one who fought stadium bulls, she walked across the casino floor, avoiding the mines that remained. When she reached the frame, she bowed slightly toward each of the eight sides of the casino. Then, with an elaborate gesture, she grasped the opposite end of the spinner from the one that held the leather flap. The few remaining murmurs of the crowd vanished in anticipation.

"A moment." Jelilac held out his hand. "Please do not begin until I am ready." Moving as quickly as he could, he joggled back into the cover of his canvas-draped box. For a few heartbeats, there was silence. Myra scowled, but waited, a smile of anticipation growing on her face.

Kestrel twisted uncomfortably. He had changed the contest slightly, but not enough to make any real difference. After one spin of the wheel, what hope did he and Phoebe have? If only there were some way to get a flame going before …

"I smell smoke." Phoebe sat up out of her slump at Kestrel's side. "There behind the tapestries, I am sure of it. Jelilac is starting a fire."

16

Calculation and Skill

THERE WAS a sudden whoosh of heat that billowed from behind the tapestries, straining them against the hooks that held them to the frame. Kestrel smelled the odor of rotten carrion, a small like that he had detected before.

"Camonel!" he exclaimed. "Phoebe, can it be? It smells just like Camonel." He shook his head, confused. "But Milligan had said that the aleators avoided fire at all costs because of the second tenet."

Phoebe's answer was cut off by Jelilac's command. "Now," he shouted. "Perform your best calculation, Myra, because no matter what the method, I am the one who will win."

Myra ignored Kestrel's words and gave the bar a mighty wrench to send it whirling about. Just as she did, a burst of yellow flame shot upward above the tapestries for everyone to see. In a sudden panic. Jelilac's retainers exploded out of the box, rushing onto the casino floor. Two stepped onto mines, and startled cries mingled with a spray of hurling limbs and blood. The spectators in the stands astride the tunnel behind Jelilac's framework screamed with fear. Those in the rows nearest began climbing into the tiers above, trampling on those not fast enough to get out of their way.

"Mark." Camonel's deep voice rumbled above the din. The djinn pushed aside the canvas and stepped next to the rotating spinner. "It passed vertical, Master, just as I spoke."

"Jelilac, what is this?" Myra backed away from the demon that towered over her. "I saw this monster on the raft. You deal with the forbidden far more than have I."

"You stoop to using calculation. Then do not be surprised if it is employed by others as well," Jelilac followed the djinn into the open. A dark curl of smoke indicated that the fire that summoned Camonel still smoldered inside. "I will be archon, woman. Soon it all will be decided."

"Mark," Camonel shouted again. "I have timed the duration of one complete rotation, Master. You have said that that would be enough."

Kestrel grabbed Phoebe by the arm, lifting her up to standing. They had another chance to bind Camonel to her will, and this time, there would be no water to douse the flame. He started to leap over the barrier and run to the demon but then hesitated. He glanced at the craters and twisted bodies between his fortification and Jelilac's canvas box. Scowling, he pulled her back down to safety.

'There is too much risk of the mines," he said. "Phoebe, you must try to control him from here."

"It is too far." Phoebe shook her head. "I have already attempted the binding of his will, but the control of his master is too strong."

"Eighty-three through ninety-two," Camonel boomed for all to hear. "One tenth of the numbers, but that is the region in which the spinner will finally reside. My master has calculated it, and there can be no doubt."

"Calculation," someone shouted in the stands. "Not calculation! No!"

"Calculation," another echoed with a groan. "In the final battle, luck is pitted against calculation and skill."

A wave of agitation radiated out from those nearest Jelilac's box. The aleators in the stands were mere spectators no longer. Even those scrambling to safety slowed and turned back to watch. On the side of the casino farthest away from the action, a low murmur tinged with despair began to build and grow.

"But if luck loses to some other method, then what is the purpose, what is the meaning?" Myra shrieked above all the rest.

The moaning of the crowd increased. An entire section clasped hands and begin swaying back and forth to the cadence of a chant: "Calculation, calculation and skill."

Kestrel felt a twinge in his stomach. The ground under his feet suddenly was less firm like a street of tar heating on a warm day. He glanced up at one of the large windows in the far wall. The fog had begun to move back onshore. A subtle vibration began tickling the soles of his feet and migrating up his legs into his spine. Obviously, the use of something other than luck in the confrontation of Jelilac and Myra was deeply disturbing to all those who watched. And somehow, the mood was contagious, affecting everything about them as well.

"Something is happening." Kestrel drew Phoebe close.

Something, something — the thought hit him something like two realms of symmetry starting to merge.

322

"Yes," Phoebe said. "I feel it, too. Only this time, there is no other realm of which the aleators speak." She glanced at the dimming rays of the sun, filtering through the colored glass, and pressed herself into Kestrel's side. "If not merging, what transformation could it possibly be?"

Kestrel stared at the distance to the fire behind the tapestries and the mighty djinn standing arms akimbo in front, watching the spinner slowing to rest. The heel of his boot began to sink into an oozy soup. Except for the burning tapestries, the high corners of the casino seemed to start fading away. Things were converging too fast. He would have to chance getting Phoebe closer to the demon, no matter what the risk.

Kestrel took in a deep breath and prepared to vault over the barrier. Perhaps if he ran ahead, she would see where it was safe to follow. But before he could move, a new voice sounded from a tunnel behind him.

"Stop," it said. "The contest has not yet run its course. There is the entry of one more who destiny decrees will win. Yes, it is I, Byron, who has come as it has been preordained."

17

The Will to Believe

ASTRON SCANNED the nearly deserted casino floor. Only two contingents remained of what initially must have been many. The djinn, Camonel, stood next to a spinner that was slowing to a stop. Behind him, Jelilac was waving his hands in the air like a crane supervisor in a quarry, motioning the sluggish beam onward so that it would come to rest just to the left of the vertical.

Smoke curled above the canvas tapestries from the fire that had brought forth the demon and, not far away, anvilwood in another of the low barricades. Near the center of the floor, the second group of aleators stood transfixed, all watching the final sweep of the spinner. Astron's membranes flicked down over his eyes. In their midst, there could be no mistake. There was Kestrel with the pollen-filled knapsack still on his back.

Astron eyed the scatter of small craters and mangled bodies and hesitated. Kestrel would use some clever tactic, he thought, rather than rushing pell-mell into certain danger. His stembrain strained to be free, but, despite the urgency, he had to think and plan.

Byron started out onto the casino floor. Astron tugged at his arm. "Why challenge two groups when, if you wait a moment, you will have to contend only with the victor?" the demon said. "Fate will determine which of them it is to be."

Byron grunted. He relaxed the tension in his sword arm. The blade arched earthward and buried its tip into the soft ground. The aleators in the stands saw that the tall warrior had stopped his challenge and turned their attention back to the slowing spinner.

"Ninety-one," Camonel called out as it barely slid past one peg and then stopped as it touched another. "Ninety-one, within the band of ten, just as it has been predicted."

The murmur of the crowd grew in intensity. Only a few shouted accolades pierced the indistinct rumble that coursed from tier to tier.

"Your talismans, Myra." Jelilac beamed in triumph. The aleator paid no attention to the waves of sound mounting behind him. "You were the most likely to offer serious competition. With your defeat, no other can seriously offer a challenge now. "

"But you used calculation." Milligan suddenly shook off his restraint. "It is not right. Not by such a means should you become the archon."

"The most trusted advisor is a position coveted by many." Jelilac frowned in Milligan's direction. "Do not protest too much, or I will have to select another." He motioned to the retainers that remained, directing them to fan out and receive the spoils of their victory.

Myra slumped into a heap, her spirit seeming to ooze out of every pore. She squinted at the spinner, resting clearly in the region that Camonel had predicted, and shook her head. "Nine chances out of ten," she muttered. "It was worth the chance." She glanced at Jelilac's smile and then turned away.

"I will offer no resistance to the removal of my amulets," she said, suddenly sounding far more ancient than she looked. "Remember, I am but an old woman." She waved her arm back to the central barricade. "Come, my followers, come. Do not resist. It would be ungracious to prolong my harm."

Kestrel and Phoebe joined the procession winding its way across the casino floor to Jelilac's canvas frame. Astron studied Byron, but the warrior had not yet lifted up his sword. Moving the pollen closer to the fire could only help, but it was not yet time to act.

"No! I cannot let it happen." Milligan sprang away from the rest. He drew a short dagger from his belt and waved it over his head. "It is luck that shall triumph in the end. It must be the stronger. It must. It must."

Jelilac's frown deepened. He motioned to two of his retainers, and they drew their swords. Cautiously, they began to close in on Milligan from both sides. A great roar of approval ripped through the stands as Milligan deftly dodged the attack. He drew his own blade and slashed at one as he passed, streaking the tunic sleeve with red. Ducking his head, he just barely missed a tumbling grenade that exploded harmlessly behind.

Short strokes of the dagger somehow darted through hastily erected guards, and two more of Jelilac's followers sagged to the ground. Jelilac's eyes widened. He stepped backward and looked at the massive djinn standing by the motionless spinner.

"Help me!" he cried as he clutched at his chest. "My talismans are many, but now that I have experienced the power of your master's predictions and been close to the flame, I no longer feel so confident that they ..."

Jelilac's voice trailed off. He stared down in disbelief at his stomach and then clutched his hands over a gaping wound. His face turned ashen white. With eyes staring into nothingness, he slid to the ground.

Milligan stood silent, staring at what he had done. Then, as the realization dawned, like the doll of a thaumaturge, he jerked back into life. "I am the victor, the archon." He danced back with his bloody blade. "As our creators must have intended — 'luck favors the believer'."

The roar of the crowd intensified. Some started leaping up and down, shaking the tiers in violent oscillations. Milligan smiled and waved his dagger over his head with one hand while fondling the talismans about his neck with the other.

"No!" Camonel's impassive expression distorted into one of malice. His voice was heard even above the chanting spectators. "Luck is not to be the victor. My master does not wish it so." With a speed surprising for his size, the djinn batted at Jelilac's framework, tumbling it aside. He reached backward and extracted a burning branch of pinewood from the still smoldering fire.

"I am a weaver of matter," he growled as he waved it menacingly in front of Milligan's face. "Here, in a realm other than my own, it is easy." Deep furrows etched into the djinn's forehead. He studied the dance of flame, and then the log seemed to burst asunder. Five globes of white-hot magma arched from his hand and landed in a pentagon around where Milligan stood.

"My master has calculated, and five will be enough," the djinn boomed out so that everyone could hear. "The heat is intense, and eventually, each and every amulet he carries about his neck will crack. The one you call Milligan will succumb to calculation, just as have all the rest."

Camonel tossed back his head and laughed. "Let the fogs of nothingness come forward," he yelled. "Let them come forward and dissolve all that there is. Then there will be one less. Where once there was a realm, there will be only the nothingness of the void." He stepped back suddenly into the flame. The fire roared with a burst of yellow brightness. Then he was gone.

The yells of aleators in the stands stopped just as suddenly as they had begun. The low murmur of unrest and disbelief from before returned.

Like a pendulum somehow gathering energy with each swing, their emotions rocked back and forth, each time more violently than before.

Milligan tried to dance between two of the glowing globes of fire on the ground, but backed up and hesitated when the outermost of his talismans began to blister. Beads of sweat popped out on his forehead above eyes starting to fill with helpless panic. He bent forward and blew on the fiercely glowing spheres of light, then shook his head when he saw that they were not perturbed at all. He raised his hands expectantly as if calling for the intervention of unseen gods. For a moment, he did not move. Then, in an almost perfect imitation of Myra, he slumped into the center of the pentagon that surrounded him. One by one he began removing his talismans and tossing them at the flames.

"Then the newcomer," Someone in the stands nearby shouted. "The one on the sidelines yet to be heard. He is the chance, the final chance that luck will triumph after all."

Somehow, the spectators all understood. Again, they stopped their keening. As one, they held their breaths.

"Luck has nothing to do with my presence here," Byron called back. "It is the decree of preordained fate. I carry no talismans, and I do not need their aid in my fight."

Shrieks of despair exploded from the crowd. Their emotions swung back to despair far deeper than before. Whole blocks of spectators rose from where they sat. With eyes brimming with tears, they began to embrace those next to them with heart-wracking sobs. The caress of a chilling wind touched Astron's cheek, and the ground trembled as it had done in the realm of order. It was as if a dam had finally broken. There was no hope left that would stem the outrushing tide.

18

Centuron's Delight

"IT IS just as I was foretold such a long time ago," Centuron called out behind Astron in flushed excitement. "And by the fates, Byron is not even needed. The self-doubt has started even before he appeared. I have survived long enough, long enough to see it happen. Even if he does not triumph, the end will be the same."

The keening of the crowd rose to an ear-pounding crescendo. Moans of anguish became more frequent, and loud sobbing mingled with the rest. Astron wrinkled his nose. The ground under his feet definitely felt less firm than when he had first entered. The pillars and arches that held aloft the roof of the casino were somehow less distinct than before. Only a deep black painted the high window where the sun had been.

A growing uneasiness coursed up Astron's legs and into his chest. The phenomena were interesting, but he could not allow himself to consider dispassionately what was taking place. His stembrain writhed within the confines of his control with far greater power, straining to be free. About the casino floor, all of the aleators there had fallen to their knees. With eyes focusing on nothing, they rocked back and forth and keened with the rest. Only Kestrel and Phoebe were still alert, looking all about. Astron had waited long enough. Now was the time.

He eyed the beckoning anvilwood and then turned back to Centuron. "The mines of which you spoke as we entered," he asked. "What is their danger? Quickly, I must know."

Centuron squinted at Astron and then threw back his head. The laughter tumbled from his lips in gasping wheezes. For several heartbeats, he shook in spasms, unable to regain control. Astron clenched his fist in frustration, eyeing again the distance to the anvilwood, Camonel's smoldering fire, and Kestrel and the pollen, unable to decide which was to be the first objective.

"Byron and the others." Centuron ignored the question when he finally could speak. "They are all one and the same, driving down the one path to mutual destruction like crazed rats to the sea. Each in his own way has surrendered his free will to the ether and has given up any stake in determining events by his own volition. And with each such submission, on a level far below their conscious thought, the self-doubt has increased, and the reason for existence has become less firm. We indeed are the mere puppets of some other creator, a bubble of life breathed into being by gods that have walked away."

"Demon," Nimbia cried out. "I do not like what I see. The fey can create realms out of their thoughts, but that is not what sustains them, once they are born. Only so long as the occupants believe in their own reality does what they inhabit continue to resist the pressures that push against them from the outside. All the aleators here — look at them. They slump and —"

Centuron interrupted Nimbia with another peal of laughter. "We are all gathered here, almost all of the occupants of our realm. We now face what we have hidden in our hearts and refused to believe. There is no purpose to existence. The triumph of predestination over luck proves it. It is the end of the universe and everyone that it contains."

"There are thousands here." Astron shook his head. "One spin of the wheel and a few words cannot affect everyone so."

"Despite your great misfortune, you are not one of us," Centuron said. "You cannot know the importance of what has transpired."

"I wish to continue living," Nimbia cried fiercely as she placed her hands around Byron's arm. "Surely others do as well."

Centuron waved at the casino walls a final time. "Observe the dissolution of the fabric of the realm," he said. "You and your companion are too few to keep alive an entire universe when it no longer has the will to live."

Byron looked down at Nimbia and then glanced at the fuzzy haze seeming to blur the spectators on the wall farthest away. He licked his lips and patted Nimbia's hand on his arm.

"Perhaps Centuron is right," he said in a husky voice. "Perhaps afterward there will not be enough time."

Byron released the grip on his blade. He wiped the back of his hand against his lips and looked with glowing eyes at Nimbia. "There is nothing more I can do about the others."

He waved back toward the center of the casino floor. "But now, at least I can succumb to the joys of my temptation." He spread his hands wide and, with a slow, deliberate motion, reached to draw Nimbia to him.

"Wait, wait a moment, Byron." Nimbia hesitated and then smiled. "I know you do not fully understand my words, but this is not what I had in mind."

She waved her arm around the casino like a guide for a peasant's day at a lord's castle. "First, we must do something about the will of the people. If you truly are a leader, then rally their beliefs to save us all." Her smile brightened. "Do your duty. Then you will deserve the reward."

Astron's stembrain boiled. He gritted his teeth, pulling it back under control. He took in Nimbia's smile and then stared back at Byron, baring fangs that were no longer there.

"No!" Astron exclaimed. "The hillsovereign is not yours to do with what you will. As she states, her favor is to be for the most deserving — and not because of what emotions she excites, but the qualities she has inside. She is not yours, Byron; she is — she is mine!"

Not realizing what he was doing, Astron fumbled for the sword at his side. He glanced around the casino. The closing fog was now obscuring the farthest stands. The sound of the keening faded into softness and then vanished altogether. The ground underneath his feet now was like a thin sheet of linen loosely stretched over a tub of water. The wetness of the swirling fog began to glisten on his cheeks as if he were exposed to a gentle rain.

"Do not be alarmed, demon," Nimbia said. "I am sure that Byron has sufficient nobility to be different from the —"

She stopped when she saw the gleam in Byron's eye intensify. Nimbia took a step backward and then halted as her foot touched the edge of the stadium wall. She looked back helplessly, her eyes growing wide with fear.

"It is your fate to be so unlucky," Byron said. "Such beauty was meant to be consumed."

"Underneath it all, I am a person like anyone else," Pain and disappointment putting a bitter edge to her voice. "Judge me for that and nothing else. That is all I ask."

"The allure is too great." Byron shook his head. "There is no one who can resist, no one who can look past the exterior with dispassion to see if there is any other value inside."

"Somewhere there must be at least one." Nimbia put out her hands to ward off his approach. She looked about frantically and then focused on Astron rushing to her.

"Dem — Astron!" she shouted. "Astron, help me. He is like all the rest. Only you are different. Please, do something. There is so little time."

"The mines! Where are they?" Astron yelled at Centuron as he stepped in Byron's way. "Tell me so that I may act."

"We do not know where any are buried." Centuron waved his arm. "But it does not matter. They will dissolve with the rest. Far better that —"

"Buried," Astron interrupted. "Did you say buried?"

"Why, yes —"

"That explains the blotchy appearance of the casino floor," Astron said. "With my membranes down I see far into the red, even into what is called heat in the realm of men. And turned earth is colder than that which has been in contact with the air."

He broke off and reached behind to grab Nimbia's outstretched hand. Ducking to the right, he avoided the swat of Byron's arm and started running out onto the casino floor, pulling her behind. He jogged to the right of a different-textured plot of ground and then veered back to the left. Behind him, Nimbia stumbled after, Byron's heavy tread in pursuit.

Astron cut to the side, and his heel ripped into the softening earth. Like a folded blanket, the ground wrinkled under the thrust. His foot dug deep, and then, with a sudden lack of resistance, seemed to poke through into a chilling nothingness underneath. He tumbled down to sitting and jerked his leg free. An inky blackness curl upward out of the hole.

Byron retrieved his sword and waved it over his head.

"I am too swift for you," the demon called out suddenly as a glimmer of an idea darted into his mind. "And until you catch and overcome me, you will not have the hillsovereign."

Byron ran up to where Astron sat. He moved one step in Nimbia's direction and then hesitated. "Guard your backside," Astron said, waving his own blade as convincingly as he could.

Byron turned and looked down at Astron. The look of lust on his face distorted into one of battle rage. He gripped his sword with both hands and raised it high in the air. With an ear-piercing yell, he brought it down in a vertical swipe over Astron's head. The demon waited until the last possible moment and then jerked aside, just missing the slash.

Byron's sword dug into the softening ground, this time burying itself almost to the hilt. The warrior tightened his grip on the pommel and strained to extract his weapon.

As Astron had hoped, the blade trembled but did not bulge. He scrambled to his feet, and again took Nimbia's hand. "To Kestrel and Phoebe. It will be a while before Byron is a menace again."

Together they zigzagged their way to the remains of Jelilac's contingent. The swirling fog had penetrated almost to the first few rows of seats. Astron could no longer be sure that any of the aleators in the stands were still there.

"The pollen," he shouted, pointing at Kestrel's rucksack as he dashed up upon them.

"The anvilwood," Kestrel answered as he motioned to the abandoned fortification to the right of where Camonel had stood.

"And the flame." Phoebe pointed at the remains of Camonel's fire. She smiled at the crumpled tapestries lying nearby. "There is wizard's work to be done."

19

Power of the Clutch Brother

"WAIT A moment," Kestrel said to Astron as the demon dropped Nimbia's hand and started to head for the anvilwood. "I have learned some things that might be important in the quest. Whoever merged the realms of symmetry also planted the seeds of calculation in this universe as well. Look, there is the evidence of the navigator's almanac."

Astron skidded to a halt. "A book, did you say? That is most interesting and might indeed provide a clue."

"Not now," Phoebe shouted.

"I have tried to analyze the facts just as you would and extract the most important," Kestrel yelled at Astron's back when the demon resumed running to the other fortification. "Of all of the features of the almanac, it seems to be most strange that it lasts for centuries, and yet, every few days, the format is different."

Astron started to wrinkle his nose, but he realized he did not have the time. Reaching the anvilwood barrier, he began hewing with the sword as if it were an axe, sending splinters flying. He managed to dislodge two large logs. Abandoning his blade, he lifted them in the circle of his arms. Staggering with the load, he weaved his way back to the fire that Phoebe had fanned into a respectable blaze, despite the growing wetness of the air.

The tiers of the casino had become completely hidden in the dense black fog, and only hints of the massive support pillars were outlined where the high ceiling should be. The illuminating spheres of fungi had been reduced to dull glows. Only the fire pushed back the darkness of the encroaching gloom. It looked as if they were on an island in a fogbound sea.

Astron tossed the logs onto the fire and prepared to step into it himself, but then hesitated. "There is insufficient time." He shook his head. "You all will be gone before I can return."

"Then transport us to another realm," Phoebe said. "Like a mighty djinn, you must somehow carry us through."

"There is no time for that, even if I were able," Astron replied. "Piercing through one barrier to the realm of demons is hard enough, let alone two."

"You must think of something, Astron." Nimbia touched his arm. "Look! At the very edge of the mists, I see Byron wrenching free his blade."

Astron considered the inviting lick of the flame. The color and smell beckoned him with an almost irresistible allure. He could step into the warm, enfolding embrace and vanish from the peril. He watched the shrinking horizon of visibility as his stembrain screamed in panic. He reached out and felt the softness of Nimbia's hand still on his arm. Memories of the passion he had felt in Kestrel's body returned with a surprising sharpness. He stared into her eyes and saw the confidence in his abilities that she seemed to radiate back to him.

"I will try as would my clutch brethren," he said as he walked into the flame. "The arc will be small, so you will have to squeeze as much as you can."

"Where will you take us?" Nimbia asked.

"If I am successful, just into the realm of demons," Astron answered. "To the darkness of my own den. Perhaps none will be waiting for us there."

He studied the expression on her face. "It will be quite strange, but perhaps, after what you all have experienced, not so bizarre that you cannot act. We must get the pollen to Palodad. Remember, without that, eventually, we will still fail."

Astron turned away his face and pulled his thoughts within himself, trying to shut out the collapse rushing inward. Groping, he felt the fabric of resistance between the two realms and probed it for the flaw, the subtle discontinuity created by the burning of the anvilwood that would create the opening back to his home.

For how long he searched, Astron could not tell, but finally, he found it, a slight thinning in the essence of resistance that could be pierced by the strength of will. He concentrated on the familiar comforts of his own den, the ruggedness of the rock-like walls, and the shelves that protruded from them, displaying the artifacts he had collected from the other realms. He envisioned with satisfaction the three volumes standing in a row between the shell and rock crystal that he used as bookends in the manner of men.

Astron strained against the resistance, pushing it inward, thinning it further, making it more transparent so that he could see and smell what he desired. There was a small pop and then a sudden ripping. He felt himself being drawn away, shrinking into the flame and tumbling into the comforts of his own lair.

For a moment, Astron let the feeling build within him, seeking to slip away and vanish from the dangers all about. His toes slid through the flame and dangled into the ceiling of his lair. Then his ankles followed.

Astron stopped his slide with a start. This time, it had to be different. He could not luxuriate in the narcotic sweetness of coming home. He stilled himself and stopped his transition. Instead, he concentrated on building an arc in the flame such as he had seen the mighty djinns form in the realm of the fey.

The ripping of the barrier halted, barely big enough for him alone to slip through and little else. He arched his back and placed his hands down into the fire, knotting his muscles and straining against the increased resistance. The fire of the anvilwood climbed up on his legs and arms and eventually met in the small of his back. Sharp tendrils of pain accompanied their journey, somehow racing along the fibers of his being, reaching even into his fingers and toes and screaming with hurt.

Astron's jaws tightened and his vision blurred. "Quickly," he croaked. "I do not know how long I can maintain an opening this large."

"But I cannot see anything." Kestrel peered into the arch beneath Astron's body. "It is a wall of flames and in its very center a dark disk hardly big enough for a child."

"It will have to do," Astron persisted. "First Nimbia and Phoebe, and then you can follow."

Phoebe gathered her cape about her and ducked her head between outstretched arms like a diver preparing to leap from a high cliff. She aimed her fingertips at the dark disk and began to work herself through the opening.

Astron gasped as her head slipped through and he felt the widening bulge of her body. The pain intensified into an agonizing torrent. Only dimly was he aware of her passage and that of Nimbia, who followed. He tried to focus on how close the swirling fogs had converged on them, but in the blur of his vision, he could not tell.

Kestrel came last, and Astron could no longer remain silent. He howled, as the searing pain seemed to rip him asunder. Flashes of reds and yellow washed over him. Wave after pulsing wave dug deeply into

335

his torso, seeking out every atom of his existence and wrenching it about.

"I cannot get through," Kestrel called out. "It is the rucksack. The opening is too small to let it pass."

"Then take it off and try the grains one by one," Astron answered. He ground his teeth and gasped to make his tongue do as it was commanded. He felt his last reserves of strength begin to wane. The nearest corner of his stembrain was dangerously close to breaking free.

"Kestrel," he choked. "If, by some chance, I am unable to follow, you must act with my kind just as you have done with the imps in your own realm. Convince whatever demon passes by my lair to transport you to Palodad." He sucked in his breath in a spasm. "But do not let Phoebe wrestle with the old prince. Just get the pollen to him so that, in the end, Nimbia can be safe."

"One grain will just have to be enou —"

Kestrel's answer was drowned by an increased roaring in Astron's ears. Dimly, he was aware of the prickly barbs of a pollen grain being passed through the barrier to waiting hands on the other side and then Kestrel's all too massive bulk straining to follow.

Astron muscles began to tremble, and his consciousness faltered. He could resist no more. The barrier closed with a sudden pop and he collapsed onto the flame, the last remnants of his tunic and leggings vanishing in smoke.

"Where have you hidden her?" Byron stood above him with the sword aimed at his eyes. "Tell me. There is so little time."

Astron's thoughts bounced about his head. He could not control their direction. He tried to push his chest from the smoldering ashes, but his arms shook, and he collapsed back to the earth. Pools of wetness lapped at the flame. In front, three or four of the giant pollen grains began to shake and bob as rivulets of water wound their way through the dense thicket of radiating spines. Beyond Byron's boots, all he could see were the dim glows of Camonel's fire globes and the shadow of Milligan still slumped in his confinement.

"Talk!" Byron persisted. "Tell me in which direction she has run."

Astron viewed Byron through glazed eyes but did not speak. The chaos continued to build in his mind. Lead balloons, pollen grains, ultimate precepts, bubbles of reality, symmetries, talismans, almanacs, lightning djinns, the archimage, Nimbia — they all boiled and churned, linking together in strange patterns that the ordinary discipline of his mind would not allow.

Byron scowled and pushed the tip of the sword to Astron's nose, but the demon did not move. The warrior pressed against the guard, bringing forth a drop of ichor and then abruptly pulled the blade away.

"An aleator until the end, I see," he growled. For a moment, he studied the sputtering remains of the anvilwood fire and spun on his feet. "Let us see how loose your tongue becomes when you are faced with your bane."

20

The Riddle's Solution

BYRON MOVED out into the dimness and thrusted savagely with the sword. He returned in an instant with one of the fireglobes affixed to the tip of his blade. Despite the drenching wetness that seemed to drip from the heavy air, it still managed to sputter and glow. Byron studied the dance of flame and then thrust it at the nearest of pollen grains at his feet, plunging the two globes together into the soggy ground.

As Camonel's fireglobe submerged into the water, the fire sputtered out. But just as it did, the pollen grain touching it burst into a white-hot blaze of its own, glowing with a piercing intensity far more fierce even than what had ignited it.

The burning harebell pollen floated in the pool of water and burned at the same time, sending up a bubbling cloud of steam to add to the inky fog. Astron stared at another of the grains in front of his face and almost admired the beauty of the branching net of spines that bristled almost into nothingness.

"Of course." His mouth suddenly seemed to move of its own volition. "It is the same principle as the flour in the realm of order. The tips of the barbs are so sharp and fine that they are perfect for the beginning of a flame. The pollen burned in the realm of the fey. Even here in water, it can sustain a blaze."

Astron tried to shake his head free of the ricocheting thoughts, but the undisciplined stembrain would not be re-confined. Byron freed his sword from the fireglobe and stabbed instead at the burning pollen grain. With cruel menace in his face, the warrior brought it forward toward Astron's unprotected eyes.

"And the more difficult the environment, the more intense the fire," Astron babbled on. "The grain smoked and smoldered in the realm of the fey. Here, even water cannot stop the rage of its blaze. In a realm in which it is truly diff …"

Astron stopped. Despite his fatigue, he bolted up to sitting. With a wrench, he forced back his stembrain trying to regain control of his mind.

"It does no good to back away." Byron pressed forward with the burning orb. "A few more steps and you will dissolve into nothingness, as have most of the rest."

"I have solved the riddle!" Astron yelled, ignoring Byron's threat. "It is as Palodad suspected all along, but probably did not dare voice for fear that he might be wrong. The evidence we have here is proof enough. How do you start a fire in the realm of demons?

"Why, with harebell pollen, of course." he continued. "It is the kindling where nothing else will do. Harebell pollen, harebell pollen! It was with us all along. The quest truly is over. The ultimate precept — I have discovered the answer at last."

Byron watched Astron's apparent disregard for the burning globe and hesitated. "The ultimate precept," he said, puzzled. "Old Centuron used to speak of such a thing. Destruction is preordained, he would say. Destruction is preordained — either the sphere of existence is pierced from the outside or the will to believe decays from within."

"No, all of that speculation does not matter." Astron pushed aside Byron's blade. "The wise men of the realms guessed, but they did not know. 'Reality is a bubble,' Finvarwin said. 'Like the pipers blowing into the bowl of quickening gel, it is created by thought.' 'Coalescence follows from similarity,' Abel shouted when his realm was merged with another. Just as the juice and water were mixed for his warriors, two bubbles can be melted into one. And indeed, if the will to believe decays from within, the bubble will col —"

"Luck will be archon." A voice sounded behind Byron. The warrior spun just in time to see Milligan stagger forward out of the gloom with his dagger still in his hand. "With one vertex of the pentagon removed," the aleator said, "I was no longer confined. Luck will be archon, even if I am the only one left who believes."

Milligan lunged at Byron but the ground under his feet gave way, and he sank up to his waist. "The cold! My legs!" he shouted. "It feels as if they are no longer there."

An expression of deep shock began to spread over his face as he sagged. With a desperate stab, he reached out with his dagger and swiped at Byron's calf. The warrior staggered to one knee and swung his sword, forcing the burning pollen grain toward Milligan's head.

"If I shall not succeed, then neither will any other," he cried as he smashed the blazing globe against Milligan's cheek. He grunted as the little aleator's blade struck home again, this time in his chest.

"It is my destiny." Byron coughed up a spatter of blood. "My destiny just as Centuron said."

Byron's final swipe caught Milligan squarely on the jaw. With a cry of pain cut short, flesh and hair were suddenly consumed in a sickening belch of smoke. For an instant, blood spurted like a fountain from the top of Milligan's neck. Then the small aleator slumped forward to bleed over Byron's more massive form.

Astron hesitated as the black mists sweep even closer. The remaining fireglobes could no longer be seen. In addition to the whirl of thoughts he could barely control, he felt the pounding panic of his stembrain increase. His limbs stiffened, and he could not move. He must get the anvilwood burning again — but he could not.

Despite himself, Astron wrinkled his nose. Besides the solution to the riddle, something else was bothering him. How could knowing about harebell pollen be such a powerful secret? Like mismatched elements of a magician's ritual, not everything fit into a harmonious whole.

Astron gritted his teeth and tried to calm the rush in his mind. Wisps of fog coursed about him. There was a prickling on his skin as if he was covered with strong acids to dissolve him away. In front of him, the bodies of Byron and Milligan, beginning to fade into the blackness.

He must remain in control, he thought as he struggled with the forces inside himself. He had to marshal discipline as never before. To succumb now certainly would ensure defeat. He had his duty to his prince; he must …

No, the passion thundered in his head. If only for his prince, then indeed he need not struggle more. With a stembrain running amok, to dissolve here in the realm of the aleators was as good a fate as any. But it was no longer only for his prince. The quest was for Nimbia as well.

She had called him by name, he recalled with sudden clarity — not 'demon' but 'Astron, Astron, help me,' she had said. It was a recognition that he served her not as subject but as equal. Yes, she was the one for whom he would continue the struggle. It was for Nimbia, Nimbia, Queen of the Fey.

Astron took a deep breath in the manner of men. The thought of pleasure not yet tasted flowed through his mind, bringing a small measure of calm. Yes, for Nimbia. For Nimbia and — and for himself being with her as well.

Straining against the stiffness in his limbs, Astron reached down and picked up Byron's sword. With jerky spasms, he touched the pollen grain to the remains of the anvilwood. Despite being half buried in the ooze, the logs again sputtered to life. Just as the last rush of blackness reached him, Astron struggled to merge with the flames.

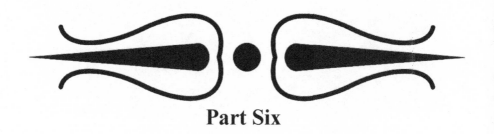

Part Six

The Ultimate Precept

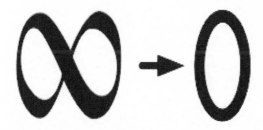

∞→0
1

War of the Realms

"I DO not like it." Kestrel frowned, as Phoebe pulled away from the embrace. "What little strength we have grows weaker the more separated we become."

"The devil is hardly bigger than Astron." Phoebe waved at the demon struggling to grasp Nimbia around the waist. "It is clear that, at most, he can carry only two." She put a finger to the woodcutter's lips. "We lose time by churning again through what has already been decided. Nimbia and I are to take the harebell pollen to the one called Palodad. If any problem develops, it makes more sense to have available the skills of two wizards, rather than one. You are to stay until Astron appears, and then he will somehow figure out a way for you to follow."

Kestrel scowled at the demon standing in the wash of light that flooded outward from the open doorway. The devil beat his leathery wings, pulling at Nimbia a hand span away from the brief landing that ringed the hollow stone. Sprays of hair from the ears and nose formed long stiletto shadows that fell across a pockmarked face. The lower jaw merged into loose, hanging flesh that hung from the neck like a bulging sack.

Kestrel had found the devil cowering under the lowest shelf in what must be Astron's lair shortly after he recovered his senses from the transition. Only with difficulty was he able to interrupt a frightened babble of abject submission to explain the task that must be performed.

Now, in troubled resignation, Phoebe surrendered to the folds of the demon's free arm. In a heartbeat, both she and Nimbia were gone into the deep blackness that seemed to permeate most of the realm.

Kestrel turned his attention back to the curving walls of Astron's lair. He touched the rough surface and felt the stone warp and flex. Thinner than paper, he thought. It was remarkable that it was able to hold a shape with his weight pressing on a membrane of similar material that divided

345

the hollow sphere horizontally in half.

Only the single circular opening to the outside broke the blank expanse of the walls. All available space was covered with shelves or pierced with hooks from which hung lamps, flower petals, spoons, key rings, thimbles, scissors, squares of printed cloth, and a lock of hair.

A single cushion sat on the rough flooring next to a pipe, a pile of small bones, a pen, and bottle of ink. The low-hanging lamp nearby illuminated a scrap of parchment on which a line of script had been abruptly halted in mid-stroke like a thought that would never be completed.

Kestrel stepped around the cushion and headed for the dim outline of a spiral staircase disappearing into a circular opening near the far wall. He should have explored thoroughly before Phoebe's departure, he thought, but the presence of the devil was too great of an opportunity to waste. The bottom half of the lair was probably like the top and, once Astron appeared, it would not really matter what ...

A sudden wheeze of pain filled the confines of the chamber and stopped Kestrel in midstride. He scanned the collection of artifacts and grabbed a long, two-pronged fork. It would be of little use in the realm of demons, but he could find nothing more potent.

A second wheeze followed the first, and then a rustle of movement from down below. Kestrel retreated a step, gripping the fork warily. A deep glow of emerald eyes emerged, and then a figure loomed into the light.

A ragged robe with one sleeve torn away hung over a slender body that limped with each step. A wide and angry scar ran from brow to chin on an otherwise delicate face like a river of lava creeping down a mountainside. The remains of an upturned nose sat atop once slender lips, now swollen and red.

"I am Elezar, the one who dazzles." A voice rasped with difficulty between each dragging step, "I knew that my cataloguer would return as was his duty to his prince. But I fear it is far too late."

Kestrel raised the fork and held it in front of his chest. His eyes darted about the confines of the lair, trying to locate where the demon had materialized and hence, where Astron was also likely to appear.

"You speak in the tongue of men," Kestrel said. "I understand, even though I am not the one you seek."

"I heard your petty debate and the final resolution." Elezar sagged to the cushion. "Since the outcome was the proper one, I did not interfere. Getting the harebell pollen to the one who reckons is all that is important now, despite the risk that Gaspar's minions might see the transit. It is the last hope. If it fails, then I am resigned to what will follow."

Elezar waved at the fork. The edge of a smile tugged at his lips. "Put away the weapon. I do not have the strength to harm you, mortal. If you strive for the same goals as my cataloguer, then it is not my intent to do you harm."

Kestrel eyed the prince, but could read nothing in the damaged face. "We had heard that Gaspar even drove you from your hidden node and pursued you into the very blackness of your realm."

"Gaspar does not have the wit to know where to look," Elezar spat. "To find me in the well-lighted lair of the vanished cataloguer after he once had determined it abandoned is beyond his ability to reason."

Kestrel could not bring himself to relax. Astron should have appeared by now. Without the demon's aid, who knew what Phoebe and Nimbia were getting themselves into? And a prince of demons, even if sorely wounded, would be more than a match for a man with no skills at all with wizardry.

'Then what now?" he asked. "What is the will of the prince?"

"We shall wait," Elezar answered. "Wait and see if Palodad has sufficient time to unlock the secret to the riddle."

Kestrel did not reply. He lowered himself to the stone floor but kept the fork at his side. Imitating the impassive resignation of the prince, he steeled himself into inaction.

TIME DRAGGED by. For what seemed like eons, Elezar did not move. Occasionally, a soft wheeze escaped from his lips. With each one, the glow in his eyes dimmed even a little bit more. Finally, Kestrel could be still no longer. He stirred from where he had slumped against the wall. The inward sloping curve pressed against the base of his head and gave no support to his back. He glanced at Elezar, sitting in regal quiet on the cushion, and scowled.

With each passing moment, his agitation had grown, but he did not know what to do about it. Hours must have passed since the prince lapsed into silence, and even though Astron had said that the flow of time was not quite the same between different realms, surely he would have appeared by now. He glanced again at Elezar's crumpled form. Even if wounded, could a prince be persuaded to carry a single man to the lair of ...

"Gaspar, Gaspar, the prince of lightning djinns has observed my passage!" A sudden shriek cut into Kestrel's thoughts. The devil that had transported Phoebe and Nimbia was twitching with spasms on the landing just outside the entrance to the lair.

"Grab control of your stembrain, or I will do it for you." Elezar sprang to life. "Speak with coherence. I, your Prince, demand it."

"He observed my passage to Palodad's lair, and upon my return, forced upon me where you were. I, I am —"

"Silence," Elezar tried to thunder, but only a labored whisper came forth. "The risk was worth taking. If you have failed, there is no point now in lamenting what might have been. Into the sky with you, assemble all that remain from their hiding places, and draw them here." The prince looked at Astron's artifacts and smiled. "Yes, here at the den of a mere cataloguer. For a final battle, it is most fitting."

"If Gaspar has defeated you before, what hope do you have now?" Kestrel sprang to his feet. He felt his apprehension tighten like an alchemist's vice. Everything was crashing down, just as Astron had feared from the first. Even Elezar seemed resigned to his fate, and Kestrel and his friends were in the middle of it, with little hope of escape.

"Do not give up," Kestrel said. "Get help from the other princes."

"More than half have thrown their lot in with Gaspar," Elezar replied. "The rest await the outcome before they declare. No, none in the realm of demons dare light their domains to aid the one who dazzles."

Elezar stopped speaking and looked past Kestrel into the wall behind. "At least, it will not be surrender to the great monotony. The few weavings of energy I have saved for the last will give Gaspar as much pain as he plans to inflict upon me."

"If not your own kind, then from the other realms," Kestrel said. His thoughts spun. He would have to come up with a plan as he had never before. "From the archimage, the fey, the skyskirr, and maybe even the enforcers as well."

Elezar's eyes narrowed. He eyed Kestrel speculatively. "The denizens of other realms regard my kind either with fear or loathing. What would make them want to enter into a struggle not their own?"

"Let me handle that," Kestrel answered. "First the archimage, and then we can appeal to the others. Contact any wizard in the realm of men and state that you have news of the woodcutter and female wizard. I heard Alodar asked to be informed, just as we vanished into the universe of the fey."

"Your words disturb my stembrain," Elezar said. "I was prepared to meet Gaspar even on his own terms if there proved to be insufficient time to unravel the riddle. Now you give me one more tendril of matter to grasp. Even for a prince, there comes a time when he must put aside the last of foolish hopes."

Kestrel waited without daring to speak again. Heartbeats of time throbbed away. Finally, a cloud lifted from Elezar's face. The fading spark in his eyes glowed with a new life, and he nodded.

"Tell each that you contact that they must first attempt to bridge through the flame," the prince commanded the devil just as he was about to leave. "Get the message of the woodcutter to the archimage so that he, in turn, will try to contact me here."

The devil shuddered a final time. Then, with a trembling beat of his wings, he fluttered away. Pinpoints of light in the distance behind Kestrel assembled into a precise row, and Elezar followed his gaze.

"Each one is a lightning djinn," the prince said. "They are forming a barrier between me and Palodad's lair. Soon they will move forward to attack us here. Your tongue must not only be glib but quick as well."

∞ → 0

2

Acceptance

"THE RISK is a great one." Kestrel heard Alodar's words come from Elezar's mouth. The contact had been established quicker than the woodcutter had hoped, but, as he glanced out the entrance of the lair, he wondered if even what the archimage proposed would make any great difference. The pinpoints of light had intensified to eye-stabbing glows. Their number had increased until a continuous arc streaked across the black sky like a far-flung galaxy of stars. With each passing moment, it grew thicker and longer, arcing outward to surround Astron's lair so that there would be no escape.

"But if the risk is not taken," Kestrel shot back, "then the loss is certain." Somehow the archimage was able to hear what he said because of his contact with Elezar's mind. It was as if the two were together in the confines of the hollow stone, rather than an indescribable distance apart.

"When you agreed to help send Phoebe and me through the flames before," Kestrel continued, "it was because of what would happen to the realm of men if Elezar should fall. Nothing has changed to alter the validity of your decision."

"I still am not sure of the truth of your words," Alodar said. "And if I and the wizards of other realms come forward and fail, there will be no defenses left."

"Would you rather wait and take on Gaspar's might one by one?" Kestrel asked. "Which strategy offers you the better chance to turn aside the threat?"

Elezar sat on the cushion, unblinking, with his hands folded in the lap of his tattered robe. "Your arguments are persuasive," the demon mouthed Alodar's words at last. "They ring true despite whatever other doubts I might have."

Kestrel felt a slight prickle of amazement mingle with the urgency that bubbled within him. He was using no deception at all. He did not have sufficient composure to think through all the twists and turns that would be necessary for one such as the archimage. And yet, it was working. He was speaking the truth, and Alodar was taking him at his word.

"But perhaps most telling is the fact that you are there," Alodar said. "There and willing to take the risks along with the rest. It is the mark of a hero, rather than one looking out only for himself."

Kestrel's thoughts jerked to the side. "No, not a hero," he replied. "Not me. I am not concerned about helping to save the baseness of other men. It is only for myself, only for —"

Kestrel slammed shut his mouth. Only for Phoebe, he thought — and for the enforcers, for Nimbia's underhill, and even for any of the unlucky aleators who still survived — any who had to endure the tortures of their fellows who did not care.

The injustices that had befallen him were not unique. They extended through seven realms as well. And they would continue to do so until someone came forward and took the cause of many as his own, until someone like the archimage felt the duty to look beyond himself and to strive against the Prydwins, Jelilacs, and Gaspars to save the worthy and unworthy alike.

The feeling of amazement grew. Was what he had been striving for on this quest actually anything less? He could not turn aside now, regardless of what escape he was offered. If that was what constituted being a hero, then perhaps being one was not such a foolish role after all.

"Yes, I think that we will need someone to coordinate all of the contingents," Kestrel said. "Someone with experience in all the realms on which we will call for aid. I am ready to serve. Even though it might be hopeless, I will carry out what is my duty and that of no one else."

"Then it is decided. Send what demons through the flame that you can, Elezar. I will have the wizards ready to be ferried back for your aid."

"Next the fey," Kestrel said to Elezar as Alodar's presence faded. "And then the enforcers and perhaps the skyskirr as well."

A hint of annoyance at being ordered about washed across Elezar's twisted face, but Kestrel hardly noticed. Despite the growing terror outside, he felt far better about himself than he had in a long, long time.

$$\infty \rightarrow 0$$
3

The Consequences of Flame

"NIMBIA, NIMBIA are you safe?" Astron shouted as he squeezed through the vanishing opening between the realms. He felt the chill of nothingness on his legs and barely managed to pull them through just in time with a loud pop. What had been the realm of aleators had completely vanished, collapsed into nonexistence by the pressure of the void.

Astron sagged to the familiar stone flooring of his lair in a heap. The struggle against Byron had been draining, and his body cried out to rest. But his stembrain still bubbled in agitation. He knew he could not stop, not until he was sure Nimbia was safe and his alone. Immediately, he must carry the harebell pollen to ...

Astron stopped. His lair was empty. They had gone on ahead without him. He rose to his feet, looking about for some clue, and spotted the pen and ink next to the pile of fish bones where he had left them in what seemed like long ago. He scooped the scrap of parchment from the ground and read the script that had been added to his own.

Almost in disbelief, Astron stared out of the open portal to his lair. The glowing sky confirmed that the words were true. Phoebe and Nimbia had been transported safely to Palodad, but Gaspar now assembled all of his might to strike a final blow. Elezar had gone to direct his resistance, while Kestrel, carried by a broad-winged devil, led the wizards assembled from many realms. As Astron let the scrap fall back to the floor, a swarm of imps buzzed up from the stairwell, but he paid them no heed. The sky was almost as bright as day in the realm of men; so many djinns had Gaspar rallied to his side. With what meager forces Elezar had left, it was doubtful he would have any more need for his tiny entertainers.

Only if Palodad were swift enough to test the pollen and show it blazing in triumph would any who followed Gaspar realize that the

Elezar had won. Otherwise, the one who dazzles was lost, and, in the end, all who strove for him as well.

Astron regarded the sphere of bright lights converging on the darker knot of men and beings from other realms, now standing off in the distance and awaiting the strike. He reached out once with his empty hand, then pounded his sides in frustration. Astron, wingless Astron, the one who walked! In the end, he was reduced to being a mere spectator while others decided the fate of the realm.

Astron pushed against the tug of his stembrain. It continued to stir and boil. There was something that still bothered him, some additional conclusion that could be drawn from all that he had learned. He settled on the cushion, not bothering to bat away the imps as they swarmed about his head.

"Reality is a bubble," he muttered. "I have seen realms created, merged, and destroyed. Aleators like Centuron believe that such destruction is preordained. Either the will to believe decays the pressure within or the bubble is pierced from —"

Astron stopped again. The already high state of agitation of his stembrain grew with a deep terror he had never felt before. Why the knowledge of fire in the realm of demons held such power became clear. He knew why it was the ultimate precept, the greatest of them all.

Astron bolted to his feet and ran back to the open portal. "There is a reason why there is no fire in our realm," he shouted in panic to no one, "a reason most profound. Fire breaks down the barrier that keeps our bubble whole. It creates an opening in the surface that protects it from the void."

He glanced at the still brightening sky. He knew that the distances were still far too great for his voice to carry, but he had to continue. The battle between Elezar and Gaspar suddenly was of insignificant consequence compared to what actually was at stake.

"For all the other realms, the opening is to our very own," he yelled. "The pressure on both sides of the breach is the same. Except for creating a portal of transport, nothing else happens as a result.

"But a flame in the realm of demons!" he shouted although no one would hear.

When it pierces the skin of the bubble, where then will it lead? he thought. Not to another of the realms, other flames already provide those connections. No, it can only be to the void. Like the spheres of the aleators that surrounded the talismans, a small rupture lets out the essence inside. The realm of demons would collapse into nothingness just as surely as if all demons had ceased to believe.

"It is not only our own universe that would wither away," Astron continued aloud. "All the other realms are connected to ours by the other's flames. Like the merged realms of symmetry, they would all vanish as well, first oozing into ours and then following us into the chilling void. It would mean the end of everything, all existence, *all that there is.*"

Astron shook his head and tried to regain a measure of control. The battle of warring princes for supremacy in a single realm was only a shadow of what confronted him. The death of a single realm or two was nothing compared to the end of them all!

"But who would wish such a fate on all existence?" Astron wondered aloud. "Who could be so tired of living that he would succumb to the great monotony in such a fashion? Who would have the power to manipulate ..."

He stopped and tried to look beyond the glare of the djinn light. "Oh, what have I done?" he shrieked. The greatest insight of all descended on him like a weight of the densest matter.

"Nimbia, Nimbia," he moaned. "I have sent you to the worst possible place.

"It is Palodad." He whirled and explained to the buzzing imps. "Palodad, the one who reckons, is behind it all! I now understand it so clearly. He is the old one like Centuron whose only desire is to see the final end. He is the one who controlled events that combined two realms. He is the one that cut away the beliefs of all the aleators so that they vanished as well. Yes, who else but a demon would design an almanac with entries beyond the lifespan of a man? Who else but a demon would think it important to change the format of the entries so that the user would not get bored over such a span and succumb to a great monotony? Who else provided Jelilac with the calculation of where his spinner would come to rest.

"It is all part of his plan, the same one that he constructed to get harebell pollen to him for the final step. It is Palodad who has computed everything along the way. Gaspar's challenge, sending me on the quest, instructing Camonel merely to appear dominated by Phoebe while retaining allegiance to his prince — there was no other wizard involved at all. It is Palodad who must be stopped. Gaspar is merely a cog in his machine like the rest."

Astron watched the converging djinns. Somehow Gaspar's rush must not only be halted but pierced as well. He had to get to Palodad's lair and stop the pollen grain from being ignited. Once it was ablaze, it would be the beginning of the end. He was the only one who knew the true peril. Not only Nimbia, but also all existence was forfeit if he should fail. He regarded the imps still swarming about him and grabbed at the thought that sprang into his head.

"Servants of Elezar," he commanded. "Each of you, grab hold of my flesh where you can. Together you will transport me across the realm."

∞ → 0
4

The Final Computation

GASPAR'S DEMONS zoomed in for their first attack, and Kestrel held his breath. His pulse raced. What he had chosen to do was right, but he could not keep the chilling reality of likely outcome from his thoughts. Even with a score of wizards from each of the realms of men, fey, and skyskirr, Elezar's forces were spread far too thin. The lesser devils in the hastily constructed inner sphere that faced the lightning djinns were outnumbered at least three to one.

Kestrel pressed his foot down on the unseen blackness beneath him, still not quite believing it was there. He and the legion of enforcers stood in relative darkness on what Elezar had called an unoccupied node. Scattered throughout the realm were many such points, the prince has said, loci that remained fixed in the sky and did not fall toward whatever tugged on everything from below. On them, the djinns and lesser devils accumulated and weaved their meager treasures of matter, transforming the blank nothingness into elegant distractions that forestalled the great monotony. Kestrel pushed aside the wonder of it all. For now, although surrounded by Gaspar's forces like the rest, Abel and the others were ready to act in synchrony, and that was all that mattered.

Near the center of the spheres of converging attackers, not far from Astron's lair, Elezar blazed with a brilliant light, no longer hiding but daring Gaspar to come forward. In the direction of Palodad's domain, Kestrel had posted the fewest of the defenders in the hopes that, when the lightning djinns did swoop for the kill, their path would be through the middle of the two lines of waiting warriors.

The already bright sky blossomed into splashes of intense color. Simultaneously, Gaspar's lieutenants unleashed bolts of searing energy at those who rose to fight them. Two devils and a smaller demon enveloped in crackling tendrils of plasma, their shrieks of pain blotted by the rumble of the blow. He clenched his fists. Soon, one way or another, he would experience the fate of the hero.

More demons streaked outward, ducking past the spray of ichor and bone and launching strikes of their own. Behind them, broodmothers beat the air with heavy wings, carrying wizards in their outstretched talons. Gaspar's lesser devils swooped in behind their lieutenants, eyes wide with the choice of targets and sticky drool streaming from their chins as they contemplated the lust of battle.

Bursts of light flashed into incandescence. Kestrel had to shield his eyes with up flung arms. Three more defenders exploded in balls of boiling flesh, then a half dozen more. The deep booming laugh of Gaspar's lieutenants resonated with the rolling echoes of the explosions.

Still, Elezar's defenders rose to meet the attack. The broodmothers climbed upward, and the wizards they carried projected their wills. The arm of one of Gaspar's lieutenants jerked in a spasm. A half-formed streak of energy sputtered and flew wide of its mark. The djinn scowled and turned his head to launch another bolt at the one who had interfered with his thoughts.

Before he could, a brown-skinned devil soared past his outflung arm, blasting out with three sharp stabs of crackling pain. Elezar's smaller devils closed in on the mightier djinns. Even tiny imps harried them in vicious swirls, biting earlobes and cheeks when flailing hands could not keep them away. A random blast ricocheted from a defensive shield and struck a wizard from the realm of the skyskirr in the chest. One of Gaspar's minions shook his head at the sudden release from sluggishness. With a wild yell, he waved to the others, indicating whom they should attack.

All around the enveloping sphere, the word passed as fast as the bolts of plasma. Elezar's demons were ignored. The strikes were aimed instead at the broodmothers and the loads that they carried. The defending demons swooped to intercept the new focus of attack, but the first were blasted out of the way. One wizard fell, then two more. The others tried to maintain their concentration, but each misdirected bolt now did not stray as far from its intended target. The uprush of defenders halted. Gradually, they began to give ground.

The warriors on the dark node stirred, but Kestrel indicated for them to be still. He glanced at Elezar and then back to the crumbling defense. Just as it looked as if the thin surface of protection would be pierced in a half dozen places, the prince gave the sign. The broodmothers and other demons along the weakened corridor turned in midflight and began to dive. With wings folded, they plunged toward Elezar, shooting between Kestrel and the two lines of enforcers.

Gaspar's minions hesitated. Then, with a shout of triumph, they came plunging after. The lieutenants saw the collapse. As Kestrel had hoped, they abandoned their own battles to join in the destruction of Elezar the Prince. In an undisciplined riot, the mighty djinns circled to where the resistance had become nonexistent and poured down the corridor, striving to be the first to strike a blow at the one who waited below.

Elezar released two tremendous blasts of power of his own just as the first of Gaspar's devils sailed into Kestrel's midst, forcing them to stop and throw up their wings to shield off the power of the blow.

"Now," Kestrel shouted. "Demon of many heads, close your ranks just as we have planned."

The enforcers on the ends of the two rows nearest the djinns heeled and rotated their lines inward. Like the lid of a box, in synchronized step they closed off the path to Elezar, presenting a perfect repetition of the lines that flanked the demons on either side.

More of Gaspar's lieutenants raced up in a flurry of wings. Crashing into one another, they puzzled at the silent lines of men linked together and marching in perfect step.

"And the bottom," Kestrel shouted when the last of a dozen had come. "Seal the one remaining means of escape and then they are ours. What can be the hope of a single djinn, no matter how mighty, against a foe with eight score heads and twice as many arms with which to unleash his awesome power?"

Kestrel bit his lip as he peered over Abel's shoulder. The lines of enforcers swung shut just as had the ones in front. For a precious moment, none of the djinns within the box moved or released any of their energy.

"Yes, eight score bodies all connected into one," Kestrel prattled on. "It must be so. Look at the unity in movement. That would be impossible if each were somehow disjoined. One hundred and sixty torsos and hence one hundred and sixty times the strength. You have met your superior, minions of Gaspar. Surrender now so you can observe the extent of this power."

Kestrel reviewed his logic. The demon mind freezes with the unusual, and it does not immediately consider the possibility of falsehood. With just a moment's more hesitation, a major part of Gaspar's strength would be neutralized.

"Inward with swords drawn," Kestrel commanded. "They will not resist one mightier, one who cannot be brought down, no matter what happens to a single limb."

For a few heartbeats more, the lieutenants remained silent and unmoving, almost mesmerized by the cadence of the enforcers' march. Then one shook his head. A jagged bolt of blue lightning arched from his fingertips toward the warrior who was closest.

The enforcer exploded backward from the line with blood boiling from his chest, but he did not cry out. The line immediately closed and, in perfect cadence, resumed the march inward toward the puzzled djinns. Another blast erupted and a third. Two more enforcers were hurled away, but their positions were again immediately filled, pulling the perimeter even tighter.

A fourth lieutenant raised his arm with sparks crackling between his fingertips but then hesitated. His eyes danced as he tried to decide where to aim his bolt. Finally, he slumped against the djinn next to him and let the plasma die away. What Kestrel hoped was the beginning of despair start to form in the devil's eyes.

"Who plays with the minds of my lieutenants?" A gruff voice behind Kestrel shot a sudden chill up his spine. He turned to see Gaspar hovering behind him, not quite touching down to land on the darkness of the node. The prince had not rushed forward with the rest.

Kestrel gaped at the huge form of the djinn and shuddered. All the terror that man had for demonkind spilled over him in a crashing wave. Meeting Astron, Elezar, and even Camonel was one thing, but the presence of Gaspar was overwhelming. The crackles of energy arching between the fingertips, the twitch of massive slabs of muscle barely under control, the swarm of mites about the bristly chin, and worst of all, the smoldering eyes that were focused on him alone.

"Who twists their minds?" Gaspar repeated. "Who has closed off even the suggestion that all they need do is fly upward and then they would be free?"

"It is the many-headed demon from the far reaches of the realm," Kestrel forced himself to say. "Palodad found him and instructed him in Elezar's defense. You may as well surrender as well."

"Palodad? Palodad helping Elezar, you say?" Gaspar tossed back his head and laughed. "Your words do not match the facts, mortal, and I have been warned there might be such as you." The demon looked about at the last of Elezar's defenders fighting his lesser devils.

"Even without my lieutenants, the outcome is still determined — although it might take a little longer than had originally been calculated. And since you are the apparent cause of the delay, it is only fitting that you also provide my diversion until it is done."

∞→0
5

Spark of the Splendorous Djinn

ASTRON IGNORED the barbs of pain that stabbed his back and legs. It was better that the grips of the imps were sure, rather than comfortable. He did not like the heavy and labored sound of their buzzing wings, but what would happen if they faltered? That he did not want to dwell upon.

The sphere of Gaspar's minions converged on his lair. He had half expected to be blasted out of the sky by one of them as he struggled away, but they all had rushed past in their haste to attack the prince. One small demon in a cloud of imps was something that could be taken care of later.

The escape gave him little comfort. A few moments more of existence was all that he had gained, unless he could stop Palodad from lighting the harebell pollen. His stembrain bounced around the confines of his mind, unable to find peace with what it knew. He could no longer force it back into a quiet slumber. Only by straining with all his thoughts could he keep some degree of control on the impulses that threatened to fling his body into twitching spasms.

Astron did not note his passage through the darkness of the realm or the descent down Palodad's long entrance tunnel. Only by forcing his arm to move in clumsy jerks was he able to fling aside the barrier that opened into the interior that was blazing with light.

As the imps lowered him to the ledge that circumnavigated the huge globe, Astron froze, transfixed as he had been before by the enormous display of matter, the bizarre arrays of bound devils, the tugging fetters, and the booming cadence of whirling machines. Somewhere in the midst of it all was Nimbia, Nimbia and the pollen that had to be destroyed.

Astron ran to the first pulley basket and climbed inside. He unwound the rope from its stay and began lowering himself hand over hand into the interior of Palodad's domain. His memories of the first visit were hard to keep in focus, but at each junction, he was able to recall the direction he should take.

While he navigated the vast interior, Palodad's giant machine clanked onward, oblivious of his presence. The small, free-flying sprites darted from array to array, shuttling messages to the demons that were bound. The intricate lines of djinns that flipped from upright to standing on their heads paid him no heed when he passed.

Astron spied the central platform that contained the plane of shimmering glowsprites. Huddled in front of the screen, clasping the pollen in his hands, was the ancient prince. Only hints of his raspy voice could be heard over the background, but Palodad was evidently waving his treasure about the two captives imprisoned in cages to his left.

Nimbia and Phoebe! Astron stopped his rush. They looked unharmed, but now that he was here, what was he to do? Palodad could summon any of a hundred djinns to snare him like the others. How could a cataloguer and one barely in control at that, stop a prince of demons who had plotted for eras before Astron was even hatched? What good was it to have guessed the answer to the riddle, if the result was the same in the end?

Astron's panic grew. His limbs stiffened. He knew that this time he would be unable to make them move. He strained to open his mouth and yell, knowing not what, but even his jaws grew rigid. Like a statue of inert matter, he watched Palodad cackle and preen with his prize.

The old prince seemed to babble for a while longer. Then a motion on the screen caught his eye. He glanced upward and watched for a few heartbeats in silence. Then he threw back his head and laughed raucously, his frail voice loud even over the clatter.

"It is time," Palodad burbled. "It is time for the final ingredient to come." He whirled and looked at Astron. "Do not bother that your mobility is gone, cataloguer. Sprites are on their way to bring you to my immediate presence." He waved his arm at the expanse of his domain. "You have come in duty to your prince, just as my calculations said that you would."

Astron should have felt shock at Palodad's awareness of his presence, but he did not. Only dimly was he aware of being lifted and brought to stand in front of the one who reckons.

"It is about time," Palodad continued, a thick drool beginning to form down the side of his chin. "The ultimate precept is about time and nothing else. Time, time, time — of all the forces, it is the greatest, relentlessly pressing onward, unable to be turned aside by any of the other princes.

"But my power is far more potent still — more so than Gaspar with his bolts of lightning or even Elezar and his keenness of mind. I will not merely harass time in its passage, but stop it altogether. The pollen at your feet, cataloguer, is the kindling, the great store of matter I have accumulated over the eons is the fuel. I will destroy this realm and all the others that connect to it. When I am done, there will be nothing left to measure the tick of time's passage. It will be gone. I will have been the one to see it finally destroyed."

Astron glanced down at the pollen grain at Palodad's feet, a small shred of puzzlement tugging at the muscles in his face.

"You wonder why I have not already set it ablaze, do you not?" Palodad asked. "Think, cataloguer! Besides the fuel and the kindling, what is the third ingredient for a flame?" Palodad's rheumy eyes widened. He pressed the metal ball in his hand against Astron's chest.

"It is the spark, the spark that ignites the kindling and sets the events on their way, in our realm, a special spark that only a most unique demon can provide. That is the final ingredient, cataloguer. That is why I had to bind you to the quest, to manipulate things so carefully that in the end you would be here."

Astron tried to shake his head in protest, but Palodad ignored him and rambled on. "Yes, the spark cannot come from any demon. My calculations have shown me that, within our realm, just any shape and intensity of the energy will not do. It must originate from one for whose entire existence the stembrain has remained under control, a clutch brother of mighty djinns, but one who has repressed even the slightest hint of undisciplined thought."

Palodad pressed his face against Astron's own. "Now, cataloguer, to make the final calculation complete. Surrender, surrender at last to what has churned within you for so long."

Astron attempted to shake his head. He was merely a cataloguer, a stunted djinn without wings, one who could not weave. How could he provide the essence of what the mad demon sought? It could not be true, and yet, as the feelings churned within him, he could not deny what the prince had said.

Palodad was correct, the certainty swelled. He had been correct from the first. All the events had been calculated, and there was no other outcome possible. The mad one's great machine, his incredible store of matter, and the pollen that would surely ignite — there was no logical way to resist. Not only would everything that existed vanish, but he, Astron, the one who walked, was to be the instrument of that destruction.

Astron tried to cry out, but he could not. A ripping pain coursed through him as if his very being were being torn apart. Thoughts exploded in all directions and bounced about his head. Through eyes wet with tears, he saw Nimbia's face contort with concern. He felt a strange tingling and then sharp nips of pain. His stembrain danced as it had never done before. Crackles of energy popped from his fingers and up his arms. They were tiny and feeble as they always had been before, but this time, purple and brilliant red streamers surged from his arms to his back and then onto his thighs. Palodad kicked the pollen grain between his feet, and the angry pulses of energy spurted and jumped to meet it.

Astron felt himself slipping away into a maelstrom of confusion. The lust for destruction within him grew like the pressure from a volcano about to erupt. With the last shred of consciousness, he struggled to pull back the crackling power that radiated from him and keep it away from the prickly sphere waiting for its touch. But he could not hold back the flood. Past his knees, the sheets of plasma danced down onto his shins. White-hot sparks exploded out into the air. In a brilliant flash, globs of pulsing energy rained onto the floor.

$$\infty \rightarrow 0$$
6

Dominance or Submission

"I HAVE let you agonize long enough in anticipation." Gaspar stepped forward into the darkness of the node. "Now you shall experience a hint of what is to come." He extended his arm and pointed at Kestrel's chest. A tiny arc of energy shot from the demon's fingertip and struck the woodcutter just below the throat.

Kestrel staggered to one knee as the stab of pain exploded across his torso and ran down his arms. He gasped, then gritted his teeth, determined not to cry out. For the longest while, Gaspar had stood silently taunting him while the battles behind the two of them still raged. Now only a few cries and bursts of light illuminated the darkness of the demon realm. Elezar's last defenders swarmed about their prince, but not even the most hopeful could now dispute the final result.

"What, no pleas for mercy?" Gaspar asked. "No appeal to some better part of my nature to make the ending swift?" The djinn stepped forward and grabbed Kestrel beneath the arms and lifted him to eye level. "You will grovel before I am done, mortal, grovel like all the rest when they feel the wrath of the prince whose power is the greatest. Grovel and beg that I rip you limb from limb so that you find final peace from the pain."

Gaspar's hands started to glow with pulses of energy. Kestrel felt the fabric of his tunic shrivel and part. Waves of heat radiated into his chest. His skin began to blister and flake away. He shook his head from side to side, trying to find the words that would turn Gaspar's attention somewhere else, some clever stratagem that would misdirect even a prince of demons from his fiendish pleasure. He stared into Gaspar's eyes and saw only the twisted desire that would not be denied. In despair, he realized that there was nothing that he could say that would save him now.

Gaspar understood the expression on Kestrel's face and threw back his head with a booming laugh. Short stabs of plasma arched from the demon's shoulders and elbows and smashed into Kestrel's arms, adding rips of pain to the boiling heat that was already almost too much to withstand.

As the agony intensified, visions began to swim in Kestrel's mind. He thought of Phoebe and what would be her fate after he was gone, of Abel and the warriors behind him still confining the lieutenants as he had commanded them, and of Astron, a demon most unlike all the rest ...

Kestrel reached out and grabbed at the thought as it flitted by. He closed his eyes and concentrated on where it was leading him. Astron would not challenge Gaspar with wily words. He would use whatever solid facts he could and from them determine what must be done.

Kestrel shifted his focus as quickly as he could through the numbing haze of pain. Gaspar — what was all that had been said about the prince in the times that Astron had spoken of him during the quest? He was a most powerful djinn with his weavings of matter, indeed perhaps the most powerful of all. But in Elezar's rotunda, he had been chided for his lack of wit and unwillingness to challenge any wizard who sought.

Gaspar was a powerful weaver; it was true. Kestrel churned the thought in his mind. But what was Gaspar's strength of will? How well could he fare against the archimage, or Phoebe, or even ...

"Surrender," Kestrel yelled at the top of his lungs as he seized at the last chance. "Surrender to him who will be your master. It is dominance or submission. There can be no in between."

"You are no wizard —"

"Nor need I be. It is only a matter of will," Kestrel gasped. The pain in his sides had become excruciating. He thought he could smell the burning of his own flesh. But he lashed out with his mind, seeking the essence of the demon that held him, ready to twist and turn with his last dying gasp. There was nothing else to try.

Kestrel's sight dimmed into hot glowing yellows. Blindly, his thoughts exploded, not knowing what it was that he sought. He felt his awareness expand in all directions, pushing everything before it. All of his essence of being, his pleasures, his hopes, his fears, and everything of consequence boiled and churned, blasting all else aside.

Then Kestrel felt resistance, something that slowed the outswell of thought that swirled midst the pain. Impulsively, he crashed against the barrier, at first skittering against the surface, but then striking it again and again like a battering ram in a siege. Visualizing mental arms and legs, he tore at the covering, trying to rip it asunder so that he could plunge inside.

The images whirled in his mind, but somehow even in the delirium of his pain, he stalked like a hunter, testing the seams of Gaspar's essence one by one. He jabbed a finger into a dark crevasse. When he felt something softer than the rest, he thrust in his hand. Whatever was inside attempted to wither away, but Kestrel was quicker and grabbed and twisted as savagely as he could.

"Your minions might have victory," Kestrel shouted, "but you will not share in it, Gaspar. I have come too far and changed too much to let it be so. I cannot weave, but it does not matter. My will is the greater because I fight for what I believe, not for some idle amusement to forestall an eventual fall of night."

Kestrel felt his fist rip and tear. A shudder coursed throughout all his body. He reached with his other hand and pulled at Gaspar's being, spreading it open so that it was exposed. He felt a sudden wave of pleading protest, and then a smell of self-loathing that shook him to the core. Fear and submission flooded over him, drenching him in doubt and ultimate despair.

"Desist, Master, desist," Gaspar said. "Stop your smiting. I am yours to command."

Kestrel opened his eyes and blinked. He was lying astride Gaspar's chest as the demon sprawled on the inky blackness of the node. The woodcutter examined his bloody hands where he had been ripping at the djinn's face; the flesh of one jowl was hanging there, limp and oozing green ichor.

Tears sprang into Kestrel's eyes. Mingling with the lingering pain, he felt a deep catharsis wash over him. After all these years, the burden was finally lifted. His first deceptions and everyone that followed he could finally put aside.

He started to speak, but the node beneath him suddenly rumbled. There was a flash of light that lit the sky from the direction of Palodad's lair.

"Ah, even in my defeat," Gaspar slurred through the wreckage of his face. "Even in my defeat, it sounds as if my master has still achieved his own triumph — whatever it was that caused him to direct me so."

∞→0
7

Sacrifice

ASTRON'S EYE membranes snapped into place, but they did not help. The harebell pollen glowed with a white-hot intensity that was greater than any normal flame. Through a series of mirrors, the blinding glare ricocheted out of Palodad's lair and across the darkness of the realm in the direction of Astron's den, a signal that the deed was done. Like a boiling sun, the sphere roared in incandescence, churning the air that surrounded it into waves of convective force. The metal platform on which it rested began to pool into a slaggy liquid. Nearby spars blistered and twisted. The wings of close-flying imps burst into fire.

Worst of all was the roaring hiss. Scraps of parchment and small loose objects tumbled toward the flame, accelerating as they grew near. Then in a final rush, they vanished into the whiteness. The surface of the realm of demons had been ruptured. Now its very essence was leaking away to the void of nothingness on the outside.

Palodad knelt down on his haunches and watched the sucking pressure increase its power. Oblivious to everything else and cackling at the top of his lungs, he snatched imps out of the air and cast them into the flame.

"The rupture is but a beginning," Palodad cried. He waved at the expanse of his lair. "As more fuel is consumed, the opening will grow. Stronger will become the force pushing every object into its ultimate dissolution. No matter where they hide, no one will be able to resist It. Eventually, all must tumble past Palodad, the one who reckons."

The wind pushed against Astron's back and rushed into the orb of destruction. His entire body was alive with dancing sparks, but he no longer cared. Despite his last futile efforts, he had been unable to stop the mindless rush of his stembrain and to restrain the power that gave rise to the all-important spark. Now all he felt was the compulsive desire to flee, somehow to shake off the rigidity that gripped him, and to hide from the growing suction as long as he was able.

He looked wistfully at Nimbia, a small part of his mind dimly aware of how in the end he had not saved her from Palodad's fate. Phoebe stood next to her, dumbfounded, her mouth open and watching the all-consuming energy of the fire.

Phoebe, Phoebe and Kestrel, Astron thought. If only the woodcutter had been along for the final confrontation. He would not have let his stembrain get out of control. Somehow, he would have used its power instead, exploiting its irrationality rather than becoming its slave. But for himself, a demon, a cataloguer, Palodad's logic had been inescapable. There was no way that …

Astron gasped. Indeed, Kestrel would not fight the vagaries of the stembrain. He would not try to keep it under restraint. He would let it roam wherever it led him, seeking out solutions rooted in emotion that mere logic could never find. Astron regarded Nimbia a second time. With a shudder, he surrendered the last vestige of control. Unconstrained, he let his stembrain take over his body and do with it what it would.

The sparks that raced over Astron intensified. Like Gaspar, tendrils of blue and green flame filled the spans between his fingers. Glowing plasma danced over his lips and across his cheeks. The rigidity that held him melted away. Surrendering completely, he was able to sag to the ground with his legs trembling in mighty spasms and his head jerking from side to side. His tongue poked out between his teeth. A meaningless cry escaped from his lips.

And inside Astron's mind, the images swirled. The safety of his den, Elezar's beautiful spires, the mysteries of the realm of men, the constructions of the fey, the lust for the human body, the merging of two realms into one, the collapse of the universe of the aleators — they all danced and swayed like pieces of meat in a boiling stew. Colors fused and melted, the touch of smooth surfaces transformed into pungent odors and smells. He sensed his feelings for Nimbia grow into a passion that cataloguer did not resist. Instead, he added his own momentum to Palodad's thrust. Together they tumbled off balance. Holding the surprised prince tightly, Astron plunged headfirst into the center of the pollen grain just as if he were vanishing into a common fire.

The scene around Astron twisted and shimmered. He felt an immediate numbing cold and a total blackness, deeper than any he had ever seen before. Instinctively, he clamped shut his mouth to preserve what little breath remained in his lungs.

Astron felt Palodad twist free, but he did not care. The feeling of numbing coldness began to grow. His chest started to expand painfully, and there was a sudden bubbling in his ears. His eyes bulged, and he could not quite bring them into focus.

Astron whirled about. The feeble glow of the pollen grain stuck through from the realm of demons into the void. The outrush of air batted against him, forcing him backward. He was in the void, outside the realm and beginning to drift away.

With a frantic swipe, the demon reached out and grasped at the burning pollen, feeling a numbing pain that roared up his arms and into his chest. He was not sure that what he was going to try would work, but there was no other choice.

Palodad saw what Astron was attempting and banged the ball in his claw-like hand down on the cataloguer's elbow, trying to force him to release his grip. But Astron's senses were overloaded. The burning flesh in his hands, the numbing cold of the void, and the pressures within trying to dissipate him into the nothingness left no room for anything else. He wrenched at the pollen grain and felt it tremble slightly, like a giant root that would not quite pull free.

Tightening his grip and ignoring Palodad's rain of blows, Astron pulled himself to the surface that confined the realm — filmy like the mist on a foggy day in the realm of men. He planted his feet on its strange, spongy surface and arched his back. With a grunt that emptied his chest of any remaining air, he ripped the burning grain free and pulled it out into the void.

For a heartbeat, nothing happened. The light from Palodad's domain outwelled into the blackness. Astron could see the hem of Nimbia's tunic and behind her the rest of the prince's machine. He began to get dizzy from all of the churning impulses in his brain. His thoughts began to slow. His grip on the pollen grain loosened as Palodad scrambled to rip it free.

But as consciousness finally faded, Astron noted that the size of the hole into the realm of demons had begun to shrink. It closed to the diameter of Palodad's metal ball, then to a coin in the realm of men. With a final rush, the rip vanished altogether, and the realm was whole.

Astron turned his attention to Palodad, frantically clawing away at what he possessed. For a moment, the two demons wrestled with the sphere that no longer burned. Then with a final burst of energy, Astron steadied himself against the outer surface of the realm and heaved the pollen as hard as he could deeper into the fathomless depths of the void.

Unable to surrender his most precious treasure, Palodad held his grip on the orb as it sailed away. He opened his mouth to scream a protest and no sounds came forth. In a spew of blood and foam, the prince arched into the nothingness and out of sight.

Astron watched him go. Then he collapsed into a ball as he also began to drift away. He was ready to surrender to his fate. His job finally was completed.

He had done it! Nimbia, the realm of demons, all of existence, everything had been saved!

8

Wisdom of the Stembrain

HOW MUCH time passed in the void, Astron did not know. Why he still had a glimmer of consciousness, he did not understand. Dimly was he aware of the transformation taking place around him, the formation of solid rock, shelves, a small pile of bones, pen and ink, a lock of hair, and three books and other artifacts from the realm of men.

The stembrain, he mused in misty incoherence — it had been right, even to the last conjecture, the slender chance that convinced him to take the risk. And she must have had deep feelings for him after all! For a mere subject, she would not have paid so much attention to the detail.

∞→0
9

Restoration of Order

"AND SO Astron gambled that Nimbia would be able to construct a new realm for him in time to save his life," Kestrel explained to the wizards who had assembled in the library of the archimage. Over a dozen score were there, sitting in precise lines and following each of his words with frowning concentration. The archimage sat in the first row, with his consort Aeriel robed in the ruby red of the ministry of Procolon at his side. Crowded about the periphery behind them, scribes squeaked their quills across thick parchments, mingling with emissaries from Arcadia across the great ocean and other masters of the five arts. The setting sun cast long shadows through the high windows, and serious faced pages began to light the sconces that would continue the meeting far into the night.

Kestrel glanced at the demon next to him on the dais that was shyly clasping the hillsovereign's hand, and smiled. Behind the four of them, the fire that had brought them back to the realm of men flickered silently. "If her feelings had not been sufficiently strong, she might not have succeeded," Kestrel said. "But, as you can see, Nimbia was able to create a safe haven out of the void just in the nick of time."

"Astron's mind was never besotted by my — my external attributes." Nimbia's hand squeezed the one she held. "He alone judged me for my inner worth. Once I realized that, I knew that the quest that I had pursued almost unknowingly for so long was finally over."

"Then with Palodad out of the way, it was a simple matter for the hillsovereign and me to bring the demons in his lair under our control," Phoebe said. "We dispatched scores to all corners of the realm to announce the answer to the riddle and to explain that it was Elezar who had won the contest. All the other princes stopped their struggle against him and, with the prince of lightning djinns himself defeated, brought Gaspar's minions under control. Now they all defer to Elezar's leadership in fear if nothing else, so close was there almost disaster for all."

372

"So the dazzling one is back in command, and I am still his master." Alodar rose from his chair. "The realm of men is safe once again." Holding a scarlet ribbon that pierced a large circle of gold, he stepped onto the dais. He cleared his throat and placed the medallion around Phoebe's neck. "The councils are unanimous in their vote," the archimage said. "Wear the logo of flame proudly, wizard. You have been accepted by all, the equal of any man."

"Far more important, I have accepted myself." Phoebe shook her head. "Man, woman, demon, hillsovereign of the fey — none of the opinions of the others matter. Once a person is at peace with herself, then everything else will follow."

Alodar turned to Kestrel and held out his hand. "To one who is not a true student of the five magics, the councils cannot convey any largesse. But somehow I suspect that the fame of the master of lightning djinns will keep your pockets filled, nevertheless."

Kestrel shook Alodar's hand, and his smile broadened. "I have gained what no amount of gold could ever buy," he said. He put his arm about Phoebe and pulled her tight. "Trust in one's fellow men — a sense of belonging — is worth far more than even a treasure from beyond the flame."

Kestrel contemplated his friend. "Of course, I must admit, demon, to having learned a few other things as well. Before our journey together, lead balloons and pinhole glasses, I never would have suspected. Your use of them illustrated a powerful discipline. It was because of examining the facts of the situation that I found the way to defeat Gaspar when my glib words were sure to fail."

"Logic and calculations are indeed powerful." Astron pulled his eyes away from Nimbia. "When the quest began, it was for such knowledge of things that I hungered. Yet now that I ponder, it was knowledge of self that I gained the most.

"No logical demon would have rushed toward the burning pollen grain when every impulse was to flee," he continued. "Not even the mightiest djinn willingly would travel through the fire into nothingness and then pluck away the one apparent means to return. None would think that they could pull matter through into the void if it were difficult for them to transport it between universes that are known. Without a demonstration, who could know for sure that a creature of the fey would have feelings intense enough to form a new realm in time?

"It was not logic but the freedom of the stembrain that gave me the plan, as irrational as it was. Palodad never suspected until it was all too late. We have both learned, Kestrel from each other, you of things in the realms about you, me of the emotions that slumbered within."

Astron stood up and tugged on Nimbia's hand. "But enough of analysis after the fact. We should return to the lair that you constructed for me. We must give the tiny realm more thought and soon so that it will grow. Together we can mold it into whatever we desire."

"After a moment, Astron." Nimbia did not rise. She pulled on the demon's hand to have him resume his seat. "I first wish to hear more of the legends that humankind have about the realm of the fey."

"But we have pledged to one another." Astron wrinkled his nose. "According to the sagas, the wishes of one are to be the other's command and — and I desire to go."

"You do not quite have it right." Nimbia smiled. "It is my desire that is the wish; your part is the command to be obeyed."

"But ..." The wrinkle in Astron's nose deepened.

"Astron, there are still many more riddles in your future." Kestrel laughed. "And I think that you will find that Gaspar's was just one of the easy ones."

Astron glanced quickly at Kestrel, saw Phoebe smiling with the rest, and then turned back to Nimbia. His stembrain told him that the words of the woodcutter were all too true.

Author's Afterward

SECRET OF THE SIXTH MAGIC was published in the mass-market paperback format in 1984, four years after *Master of the Five Magics*. Just as before, I did not start writing another book immediately after submitting *Secret*. A few years went by. One morning, out of the blue, a thought flashed in my mind, 'What about the demons? What was their realm really like?' The urge to write had returned.

The Seven Realms

This time, I knew better than try to come up with a title like *Quest for the Fair Lady* or *Metamagic* that dDel Rey would not approve of. It had to be something like Blank *of the Seven* Blanks. And if the book was going to be about the goings on in the realm of demons, then *Riddle of the Seven Realms* was an obvious choice.

OK, something more than just about the realm of the demons. I needed six more. Well, there was the realm of men in which the first book took place, and the realm of the skyskirr in the second. I needed just four more, not six.

A realm of fairies was an easy choice for the fourth, but the last three took some thought. Finally, I came up with the ideas of a realm being no more than a battle game and another in which all of the laws were based on luck. The seventh turned out to be elusive. And besides, if I followed the format of trudging through one realm after another, writing a seven part book was daunting.

So, the skyskirr became bit players in the realm of men, and I added a second realm to the one with the game. There were to be two realms involved in the game, one governed by symmetries of space and the other by symmetries in time.

As I reread the original publication more than thirty years after I had done so before, I found that the realm of time symmetry — inhabited by the mysterious chronoids — no longer worked for me. Rotators, reflectives, and chronoids to boot — it was all too complicated.

So, I reduced and renamed things. There were still two interacting realms to deal with, but their inhabitants were the only adversaries. Then I looked again at the rules of the game. Those needed more clarity as well.

Cleaning up the rules was the hardest part of the rewrite. I kept coming up with loopholes and exceptions. I took care of some, but I am sure that the astute reader can find more. Creating a game is both not trivial and that at the same time actually can be played for enjoyment is a hard thing to do!

Some memories

I incorporated several of my personal favorite concepts in the original *Riddle*, but without any reference from which one could learn more. This second edition has the references, and here are some memories about three of them.

The Growing Power of Computers

The first computer that I worked on was a Librascope LGP30. It had all of eight kilobytes of memory. That's *kilo*, not mega or giga. It was the size of a washer-dryer combination with a teletype, a fancy typewriter on a pedestal, placed nearby. For the LGP30, only sixteen of the teletype keys were functional. This meant that inputting alphabetical information was quite laborious. One had to strike two keys in succession for ten letters of the alphabet.

Writing efficiently was as much an exercise in correct placement of instructions in the drum memory as it was of logic. One did not put one instruction immediately after another. After the first was read into the processor logic, the computer would have to wait for a full rotation of the drum to fetch the next one. Instead, you would look up how long it took the first instruction to execute, figure out how far the drum had rotated in that time, and place the second instruction at just the right location to be read right away. As programs grew, finding locations for new instructions and perhaps moving those already there became quite challenging.

Needless to say, productivity was not great. But at the time, except for something like the LGP30, the only other computers around were the expensive monsters built by IBM, CDC, Burroughs, and others that were attended to by a high priesthood of gatekeepers.

In the eighties, the time that *Riddle* was written, minicomputers were the rage. They still were big, filling racks of equipment, but compared to the 'mainframes', they were relatively inexpensive.

Teletype entry was gone. Instead, you were connected by a CRT terminal. But even these were a shadow of the capabilities we take for granted today. Most of us to some degree are fumble-fingered typists. We make a lot of mistakes. In the eighties, if you mistyped, you first had to hit the backslash key for as many letters as you wanted to backup. These strokes showed as well as the original mistake. Then you typed in the correction. What one typically saw on the screen was something like this:

Now is the tyme\\\\time for all god\\ood men to come to the aid of their country.

I remember the day when an upgrade to the software from Digital Equipment Corporation for our PDP-45 arrived. Going forward, no more backslashes were needed. When one hit the backspace key, the offending letter actually vanished from the screen! It was heaven.

In *Riddle*, I wanted to capture a little of these early years of computers. Demons had difficulty importing matter into their realms. It was a precious commodity. They had to make do with what they had. The basic computer logic elements were not electronic but instead, imps constrained in a lattice who stuck out their tongues or not depending on whether or not they were representing a one or a zero.

The Paradox of Beautiful Women

In the sixties, I read a paper by a famous psychologist — Havelock Ellis, I believe — but I am not sure about the name. The paper, titled *The Paradox of Beautiful Women*, asserted that the popular belief — the more beautiful the woman, the happier was her life — was false. Unlike the fairy tales, she did not live happily ever after.

Yes, there were the men who fawned over her, the attention that she got in a public place, and the help she received when she smiled. However, romantic relationships were the pits. Most men, when contemplating the prospect of approaching a woman of great beauty, would shy away instead. They felt that they had no chance with someone so beautiful and attractive to many. Only men so egotistical, so filled with themselves, would even try.

These men were completely self-centered, A beautiful woman was no more than a trophy, a conquest, another proof of how truly cool they were. The relationship was not one of equals sharing a life together, but that of master and slave.

Furthermore, these men were insanely jealous of any one who interacted with their trophies. A smile, a kind word, a helping hand, every innocent gesture was looked upon as betrayal. Someone was stalking his possession, and worse, the possession was conspiring with the stalker.

As a result, the romantic relationships of beautiful women were not pleasant ones, but tormented from the start. The women went from one to another seeking what they could never have.

This is how I remember the paper after some two decades of having first read it. I do not know how true it is, or what evidence substantiated the claim. When editing this second edition, I tried to track it down with no success. Google let me down. Perhaps an astute reader will be more successful and point me to what I am referring to.

Anyway, true or not, the idea formed the basis for the character of Nimbia, a queen of the fey.

Cellular automata

John Conway, the famous British mathematician, invented one called 'The Game of Life'. The glossary gives a link to more information. When it came out, CRT displays had improved yet again. One could download the software that followed Conway's rules and showed on the screen what happened in each succeeding generation. It became great fun to start with an initial creation of your own and watch it evolve. The basic trick was to get one that did not eventually die out completely.

Conway and others invented and named special initial formations like the 'glider'. With each generation, it moved a few cells down to the right. Then there was the 'glider gun'. It created a series of new gliders and recreated itself in place so that it could continue firing.

Stephan Wolfram, in his book, *A New Kind of Science*, speculated that perhaps some physical phenomena can best be modeled by automata rather than by differential equations as we use mostly today.

Wikipedia:

Battle Board Games

In the sixties, I played several World War Two board games produced by the game company, Avalon Hill. One I particularly enjoyed was titled 'Stalingrad'. This game simulated the German invasion of Russia, and begins in June of 1941. The two sides place their pieces — infantry, cavalry, armor and such on the hexagonal game board of Eastern Europe. A move is made each month. Battles are fought when one side's piece or pieces tries to occupy a hex held by the other.

For the Germans side to win, the player must occupy the three key cities of Leningrad, Moscow, and Stalingrad for two consecutive moves before May of 1943.

Play of the game seemed to me to be quite realistic. The German side would siege Leningrad, and when it fell, send the troops to help the siege of Moscow. They reach the outskirts of the city as winter comes and the advance halts. The Russian side holds out and wins. I was never able to play the German side and be victorious.

A typewritten 'Instructional Supplement' was included in my edition of the game. It contains the statement "Because we have re-created the real situation in STALINGRAD, games involving players of equal ability will result in Russian victory most of the time." Wow, I thought. If the German army had been able to play the game before the start of the war, what would have happened then?

The original instructions also stated that, when placing the German pieces before the start of the game, they could not have any units in Finland — presumably because of historical accuracy. The supplement allowed this to happen. As an experiment, my game-playing buddies and I tried a game in which this rule change was taken advantage of; German troops started the game with units in Finland in June of 1941.

When we played, these troops swooped around Lake Lagoda, cut off Russian units coming to aid, and Leningrad fell quickly. With the attackers able to move further into the heartland sooner, Moscow fell before the winter of 1942 and then finally Stalingrad before May of 1943, winning the game. Wow again! If the German army had the game in 1939, what indeed would have happened?

Yesterday and Today

Of course, today, such things as sassy imps, lead balloons, Conway's game of life, board games, and predicting the outcome of roulette spins are, if one is charitable, regarded as quaint. Things such as Minecraft and Destiny are their replacements.

What's next?

WHAT'S NEXT? I am not sure. The three books *Master of the Five Magics*, *Secret of the Sixth Magic*, and *Riddle of the Seven Realms* are a loose trilogy. The first book established the basic premise of fantasy governed by some rigorous rules. It was modestly successful, but I resisted the temptation to start a long series with a sixth magic, then a seventh and so on.

The second book instead focused on a deeper layer of fantastic reality. Just as in our own universe where our basic laws of mechanics and electromagnetism are just the surface manifestations of the rules of quantum mechanics and relativity, the laws of magic were just a shadow of a deeper complexity governed by metalaws — the laws about the laws.

I could have attempted yet another layer beneath the metalaws, but I felt if I did, the explanations would be even more complex and unintuitive, just like those describing our understanding of quarks and gluons, the particles that have replaced protons and neutrons as being truly elemental.

Instead, I expanded sideways and wrote about a multiverse of realms, each with its own first level laws and, as best as I could make them consistent within themselves. I could see nowhere else to go. The trilogy was complete.

However, three decades is a long time for the subconscious to be pondering. Who knows? Maybe there is another novel in me that might make sense if I now put some effort into it. I will just have to see if there is enough gas left in the tank.

Thanks to all of you who have shared the long journey.

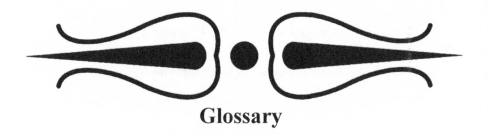

Glossary

Abel

The six rotation operations on a hexagon that leave it invariant can be represented as members of what is called a commutative or Abelian group — one for which the result of two operations does not depend on the order in which they are applied.

Abelian groups are named for the Norwegian mathematician Niels Abel.

By an amazing coincidence, the squadron leader that Astron and the others encounter is also named Abel.

Wikipedia: https://en.wikipedia.org/wiki/Abelian_group

930,000 Google results

alchemy

On earth, the root of the word comes from the Greek for transmutation. In the Middle Ages, alchemy focused on changing baser metals into gold, finding an elixir of life and a universal solvent. Some alchemical practices ultimately became the basis for modern chemistry.

In Master of the Five Magics and its sequels, alchemical procedures were described by formulas of arcane symbols kept in grimoires. Formula success was governed by probability; the more potent the result the less likely it was to succeed.

On earth, the most similar craft is that of a chemist.

Wikipedia: http://en.wikipedia.org/wiki/Alchemy

3,790,000 Google results

archimage

A master of all five of the crafts of thaumaturgy, alchemy, magic, sorcery, and wizardry.

archon

The ruler of the aleators.

Wikipedia: https://en.wikipedia.org/wiki/Archon

7,200,000 Google results

attack symmetry

The warboard in the realm of order has hexagonal symmetry. It looks the same when either rotated by a multiple of sixty degrees or reflected around axes going through opposite vertexes or midway between them.

The laws of the realm support actions that are symmetric and retards those that are not.

Movement between hexagons is assisted from hexes that are symmetrically placed on the warboard. The enforcers use this to cover distances quickly rather than by slow independent marches.

In the illustration below, five of six oases that are symmetrically placed around a target contain attackers. The sixth is occupied by Astron and the other adventurers. If the squadron at each of five hexes starts moving in a manner that preserves the symmetry, their steps take less energy and happen more quickly.

The symmetry is not perfect, but it is sufficiently close so that Astron and the others are swept along as well.

For the purpose of illustration, the figure is not to proper scale. On the warboard, there are many intervening hexagons between the attackers and the target, not just a few.

ballista

A siegecraft that used the principle of a bow and arrow to hurl large projectiles.

Wikipedia: http://en.wikipedia.org/wiki/Ballista

1,200,000 Google results

berserkers

One of two types of inhabitants in the realm of order. The other is the enforcers. Berserkers are transplants from the realm of chaos.

Berserkers are clad in red leather armor and generally disregard

387

symmetry when making their moves across the warboard. In addition to the sword worn by a single warrior, they also carry with them crates of weapons that can have unexpected effects when used. Their one goal in life is to rid the board of berserkers.

Boltzman

Ludwig Boltzmann was a physicist who, among other things, developed the kinetic theory of gases — an explanation of the statistical properties of what otherwise would be considered completely chaotic motion.

By an amazing coincidence, the berserker squadron leader encountered by Astron and Phoebe had the same name — except for missing one letter at the end.

Wikipedia: https://en.wikipedia.org/wiki/Ludwig_Boltzmann

5,280,000 Google results

cantrip

On earth, cantrip is a word that means a spell of any kind. In Master of the Five Magics and its sequels, it means the sorcerer's charm for prophecy.

Wikipedia: http://en.wikipedia.org/wiki/Cantrip

100,000 Google results

charm

On earth, a synonym for spell in general. In Master of The Five Magics and its sequels, a sorcerer's spell in particular.

Wikipedia: http://en.wikipedia.org/wiki/Charm

demon

Resident of another realm different from that of the universe containing the earth and the world of Master of the Five Magics. With the exception of djinns, of limited physical power in our realm. Synonymous with devil.

Wikipedia: http://en.wikipedia.org/wiki/Demon

Wikipedia: http://en.wikipedia.org/wiki/Devil

Wikipedia: http://en.wikipedia.org/wiki/List_of_fictional_demons

14,200,000 Google results

devil

A synonym for demon in Master of the Five Magics and its sequels.

Wikipedia: http://en.wikipedia.org/wiki/Devil

Wikipedia: http://en.wikipedia.org/wiki/Demon

Wikipedia: http://en.wikipedia.org/wiki/List_of_fictional_demons

20,300,000 Google results

djinn

The largest and most powerful demons physically, and a considerable challenge for any wizard to dominate.

Wikipedia: http://en.wikipedia.org/wiki/Jinn

1,580,000 Google results

dodecahedron

One of the five so-called Platonic solids. It has twelve pentagonal faces, twenty vertices and thirty edges.

Wikipedia: http://en.wikipedia.org/wiki/Dodecahedron

85,000 Google references

enchantment

On earth, to cast a spell over someone. In Master of the Five Magics, a sorcerer charm in which the sorcerer takes complete control of the enchanted.

Wikipedia: http://en.wikipedia.org/wiki/Enchantment

3,980,000 results

enforcers

One of two types of inhabitants in the realm of order. The other is the berserkers, transplants from the realm of chaos.

Enforcers are clad in blue leather armor and use the laws of symmetry to make their moves across the warboard more efficient. They plan their moves carefully and often involve coordiated moves of several sqadrons. Their one goal in life is to rid the board of berserkers.

ensorcellment

On earth, bewitchment. In Master of the Five Magics, the sorcerer charm of moving the consciousness from one animate object to another.

Wikipedia: http://en.wiktionary.org/wiki/Ensorcellment

5,640 Google results

entropy

In Riddle of the Seven Realms, entropy refers to the fact that all luck transactions are not 100 percent efficient. Each time a little is lost to the ether of the realm. Similar to the entropy of our universe.

Wikipedia: http://en.wikipedia.org/wiki/Introduction_to_entropy

17,500,000 Google results

flour fires

Many substances not regarded as inflammable can quite easily burn if the ratio of surface area to volume is large. Fine dusts in an enclosed area can lead to violent explosions, such as those that occur in structures in which flour is stored.

Wikipedia: http://en.wikipedia.org/wiki/Flour_bomb

http://en.wikipedia.org/wiki/Dust_explosion

galena

A major ore of lead.

Wikipedia: http://en.wikipedia.org/wiki/Galena

269,000 Google references

glamour

Many meanings on earth: a magazine title, appearance of attractiveness, a shape-shifter, and others. In Master of the Five Magics, the sorcerer's charm of illusion.

Wikipedia: http://en.wikipedia.org/wiki/Glamour

hexagon

The warboard in the realm of order is inspired by the battle games created by Avalon Hill in the 1950s and 60s. One of their key innovations was the use of a hexagonal grid rather than a rectangular one for the surface on which the game was played.

Wikipedia: https://en.wikipedia.org/wiki/Avalon_Hill

557,000 Google results

The hexagonal grid is also used for path completion games such as:

Hex
Wikipedia: https://en.wikipedia.org/wiki/Hex_%28board_game%29

Kaliko
https://boardgamegeek.com/boardgame/4178/kaliko

imp

The smallest of demons and mostly just pranksters.

Wikipedia: http://en.wikipedia.org/wiki/Imp

5,130,000 Google results

keep

A fortified tower within a castle that is the defense of last resort.

Wikipedia: http://en.wikipedia.org/wiki/Keep

57,700,000 Google results

lead balloon

Riddle of the Seven Realms originally was published in 1988, 20 years before the possibility of one actually flying being proved on the television show Myth Busters.

Myth Busters Lead Balloon

Some poetic license is still called for, however. The Myth Buster balloon flew within the confines of a hanger, shielded from any winds that would blow against the structure in an open atmosphere. To combat these forces the thickness of the lead sheeting would have to be much greater, and an internal structure like that used for a rigid airship such as the Hindenburg employed.

Both of these increase the weight. This in turn means that the volume of the balloon has to be larger to displace more air in order to carry the increased load. Theoretically, there is still a radius that would work because of the square-cube relationship of the surface area of the sphere to its volume.

Radius	Area	Volume
1	1	1
2	4	8
3	9	27
...	...	...

But it is unclear just how gigantic this sphere would be. It is probably better to just relax and enjoy the story.

magic

The use of means outside of normal availability to affect change. On earth, the terms magic, sorcery, thaumaturgy, and wizardry are roughly synonymous.

In Master of the Five Magics and its sequels, each, along with alchemy, have distinct meanings. Magic is performed by the exercise of rituals, the steps of which are derived from extensions of rituals deduced previously.

The goal of these exercises is the production of magical objects, things that are perfect in what they do, such as mirrors, daggers, swords, and shields. Once created, with few exceptions, they last forever.

The power of magic is limited by the time and expense involved in performing magic rituals. Some take several generations and the involvement of many participants. Because of the time and effort involved, magical objects are quite expensive.

On earth, the most similar craft is that of a mathematician.

Wikipedia: http://en.wikipedia.org/wiki/Magic

63,900,000 Google results

manipulant

A magic worker in the realm of the Skyskirr who follows the instructions of a metamagician. Metamagicians can perform no magic themselves. Instead, they can change magical laws.

mêlée

Disorganized close combat.

Wikipedia: http://en.wikipedia.org/wiki/Melee

1.070,000 Google results

multiverse theories

A theory that our observable universe is but a part of a larger universe, sometimes called a multiverse. One such theory, black hole cosmology, is that our universe is inside of a black hole.

Wikipedia: https://en.wikipedia.org/wiki/Black-hole_cosmology

Other possibilities are at: http://www.space.com/18811-multiple-universes-5-theories.html

1,700,000 Google references

nibbling

a standard negotiating tactic which, after the deal has been agreed to but before the final signing, one of the parties asks for something extra.
Give and Take by Chester L. Karrass

Amazon:
http://www.amazon.com/Give-Take-Revised-Negotiating-Strategies/dp/0887307434

pinhole glasses

They actually work! Those of you who are near-sighted might want to experiment. Take an old pair of glasses and remove the lenses. Replace the glass with two pieces of cardboard — a single small hole in the center for each eye. Go into bright light and look around. Compare with what you see with having no glasses on at all.

Or, if cardboard is not currently in fashion, you can buy inexpensive pairs on the internet.

Wikipedia: https://en.wikipedia.org/wiki/Pinhole_glasses

478,000 Google results

plenum chamber

A container of a gas that has a pressure greater than that of its surroundings. Talismans in the realm of the aleators are plenum chambers for luck.

• Wikipedia: https://en.wikipedia.org/wiki/Plenum_chamber

359,000 Google results

realm of life

The realm created by Nimbia is an example of a cellular automation like that invented by the mathematician John Conway.

Wikipedia:
http://www.conwaylife.com/wiki/Conway's_Game_of_Life

366,000 Google results

realm of order

The realm of order is a wargame.

The protocols that govern the realm are:

Protocol 1 — the greater the symmetry, the greater the power

Protocol 2 — all moves are simultaneous

Protocol 3 — [not determined before the collapse with the realm of chaos]

Protocol 4 — victory is total

Protocol 5 — coalescence follows from similarity

realm of the aleators

Aleator is a synonym for a gambler.

The realm of the aleators is governed by luck. Things happen to advantage to those who have it, disaster to those who do not.

Five tenets govern the realm:

Tenet 1 — luck is a gas

Luck can be captured into talismans and thereby enhance the luck of one wearing one. Otherwise, it dissipates throughout the ether that permeates the realm.

Tenet 2 — the entropy of luck always increases

For each transfer of luck from one to another, or its use to enhance one's odds, some of it returns to back to the ether.

Tenet 3 — luck begets luck

The more luck that one has, the more that is attracted to it.

Tenet 4 — luck favors the believer

If one does not believe in luck, they will not have it.

Tenet 5 — luck is fickle

Even if one has a lot of luck, it runs in streaks. There is no guarantee of outcome in every instance.

realm of the fey

The realm of the fey is distinct from those of men, Skyskirr, and demons. On earth, it is viewed as the legendary home of fairies. All of the fey have the power of wizards and can summons demons to do their will. More importantly, they have to power to create new realms out of nothingness, and compete among themselves for who has the most artistic and interesting constructions.

Five dictums govern the realm:

Dictum 1 - reality follows from passion

Dictum 2 - strength comes from the lattice

Dictum 3 - weakness comes from contradiction

Dictum 4 - two is greater than one

Dictum 5 - reap what you sow

Perhaps even the realm of men is a construction of the fey in an age long ago.

Wikipedia: https://en.wikipedia.org/wiki/Fairy

917,000 Google results

realm of the skyskirr

The word skyskirr is a loose translation of what the natives of the realm call themselves — the ones who fly through the air.

The entire realm of the skyskirr is confined to the interior of a giant icosahedron, one of the five so-called Platonic solids. This solid has twenty triangular faces and thirty edges with five of the edges meeting at each of its twelve vertices.

Wikipedia: http://en.wikipedia.org/wiki/Icosahedron

675,000 Google results

Faces on opposite sides of the icosahedron are composed of a single mineral, ten minerals in all for the twenty faces.

The skyskirr uses these forces to propel their homes called lithons throughout the 'hedron in order to harvest and trade. A particular type of mineral only feels these forces when one of two associated magic laws is in effect. One of the two laws causes lodestones to attract one another. The other for them to repel. By carefully turning on an off which laws are operating at any given time, the skyskirr are able to perform necessary maneuvers.

Of course, the Postulate of Invariance dictates that when one law is turned off, another must turn on in its place. Although not mentioned in the text, it must be that the skyskirr have other weaker laws that can be turned on when one that moves lithons is turned off, and hence the status of the other lithon moving laws are not disturbed.

The Right Hand Rule

Just as moving charges in our realm are subject to magnetic forces as well as electrical ones, so are moving minerals in the realm of the skyskirr. One of the twenty triangular faces of the hedron is the 'top'. Its opposite is the 'bottom'. The lateral force on a lodestone in motion is perpendicular to both the direction of that movement and that of the line running from 'top' to 'bottom'.

Was this complication necessary? Well, of course not. But I thought that a closer analogy to electromagnetism in our realm was a neat concept, even if things are not exactly the same. It explains the existence of the great right hand.

robe

Practitioners of each of the five magics are distinguished by the capes and robes they wear.

Thaumaturges wear brown covered with what is on earth the mathematical symbol of similarity.

Alchemists wear white covered with triangles with a single vertex bottom-most symbolizing the delicate balance between success and failure when performing a formula.

Magicians wear blue with the palest for a neophyte and the darkest for the master and covered by circular rings symbolizing the perfect mathematical object.

Sorcerers wear gray covered with the logo of the staring eye symbolizing the ability to see far in time and place and into another's inner being.

Wizards wear black covered with wisps of flame symbolizing the portal by which the realm of demons and the realm of men are connected.

skeeball

An arcade game invented around the turn of the twentieth century.

Wikipedia: https://en.wikipedia.org/wiki/Skee_ball

478,000 Google results

skittles

Skittles is an outdoor game played with bowling pins in the United Kingdom. An indoor variation called carom skittles is readily available for purchase.

A spinning top is introduced into the confines of a partitioned box that contains pins standing on scoring positions. In one rule variation, each player starts with a complete pin set up. How many pins are knocked over determines a player's score — perfect for the realm of the aleators where everything that happens is determined primarily by luck.

https://boardgamegeek.com/boardgame/3276/skittles

soap bubble holes

You can actually create holes in bubbles and see them empty their content rather than popping. (Unlike what happens in the realm of the aleators, here on earth, because the surface tension is so strong, the outflow is robust rather than gentle.)

The first thing to do is create a soap solution that has an added ingredient — glycerin.

Glycerin bubbles are far less fragile than bubbles made only from soap. Some experimenters have made ones that last for more than a year.

There are many recipes available on the internet. I have not tried any of them. Just google on "Glycerin soap bubble" in order to see what is out there.

Once you have become proficient in making robust glycerin bubbles, you can try to duplicate the method in the text to free the content of luck-containing talismans.

http://www.scientificamerican.com/article/experiments-with-soap-bubbles-and-f/

sorcery

The use of means outside of normal availability to affect change. On earth, the terms magic, sorcery, thaumaturgy, and wizardry are roughly synonymous.

In Master of the Five Magics and its sequels, each, along with alchemy, have distinct meanings. Sorcery is performed by the recitation of charms, the steps of which are revealed from self-enchantment.

The power of a sorcerer is limited by the fact that each casting takes some of his life force, and eventually he succumbs when he has no more to give.

On earth, the most similar craft is that of a psychologist.

Wikipedia: http://en.wikipedia.org/wiki/Sorcery

5,070,000 Google results

spell

401

On earth the terms cantrip, charm, enchantment, glamour, incantation, and spell are synonymous — the performance of an act of magic.

In Master of the Five Magics and its sequels, except for the word spell itself, each of the others have particular meanings, and the word spell is a generic umbrella for any of them.

Thaumaturgy — incantation
Alchemist — formula performance
Magician — ritual exercise
Sorcerer — charm recitation
Wizard — invocation

spinner prediction

Narrowing the range of possible outcomes for a spinning wheel is not a fantasy. In fact, the more difficult problem of roulette was tackled by students at the University of California at Santa Cruz as chronicled in the book The Eudemonic Pie by Thomas A. Bass.

Amazon:
http://www.amazon.com/The-Eudaemonic-Pie-Thomas-Bass/dp/0595142362

sprite

A demon that is larger than an imp but smaller and less powerful than a djinn.

Wikipedia: http://en.wikipedia.org/wiki/Sprite

3,590,000 Google results

subordinate

The first four crafts have named subordinates in Master of the Five Magics and its sequels.

Thaumaturgy — Journeyman, Apprentice

Alchemist — Novice

Magician — Neophyte, Initiate, Acolyte

Sorcerer — Tyro

succubus

A seductive female demon.

Wikipedia: https://en.wikipedia.org/wiki/Succubus

1,840,000 Google results

talisman

An object that provides good luck.

Wikipedia: https://en.wikipedia.org/wiki/Talisman

24,400,000 Google results

thaumaturgy

The use of means outside of normal availability to affect change. On earth, the terms magic, sorcery, thaumaturgy, and wizardry are roughly synonymous.

In Master of the Five Magics and its sequels, each, along with alchemy, have distinct meanings. Thaumaturgy is performed by the reciting incantations that bind together objects at a distance that once had physically been together and with a source of energy that can perform work.

The power of thaumaturgy is limited by the fact that all incantations must conserve energy or, as sometimes stated, the first law of thermodynamics.

On earth, the term derives from the Greek for miracle and the most similar craft is that of a physicist.

Wikipedia: http://en.wikipedia.org/wiki/Thaumaturgy

118,000 Google results

toroid

A three-dimensional object shaped like a donut.

Wikipedia: https://en.wikipedia.org/wiki/Torus

Wikipedia: https://en.wikipedia.org/wiki/Toroid

vertex symmetry

The warboard in the realm of order has hexagonal symmetry. It looks the same when either rotated by a multiple of sixty degrees or reflected around axes going through opposite vertexes or midway between them.

The laws of the realm support actions that are symmetric and retards those that are not.

Initially, Kestrel and Phoebe are at two vertices that are symmetric about the reflection axis going through the vertices occupied by Astron and Nimbia, and hence are influenced to carry out the same actions.

When Kestrel moves from his initial vertex to Nimbia's, the symmetry is broken, and everyone can move freely — so long as they do not create new symmetries by moving to other vertices.

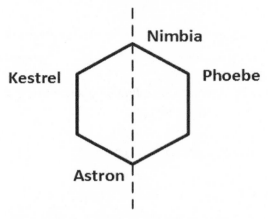

Axis of reflective symmetry

Nimbia

Kestrel   Phoebe

Astron

Positions before Kestrel moves

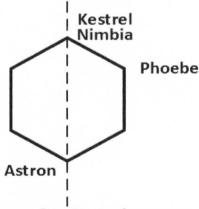

Axis of reflective symmetry

Kestrel
Nimbia

Phoebe

Astron

Positions after Kestrel moves

wizardry

The use of means outside of normal availability to affect change. On earth, the terms magic, sorcery, thaumaturgy, and wizardry are roughly synonymous.

In Master of the Five Magics and its sequels, each, along with alchemy, have distinct meanings. Wizardry is performed by the invocation of demons from another realm from that of the earth.

The potency of a wizard is limited by the power of the demons that he can dominate.

On earth, there is no such craft as such, although one could argue that the practices of witches and warlocks is similar.

Wikipedia: http://en.wikipedia.org/wiki/Witchcraft

3,050,000 Google results

Made in the USA
Coppell, TX
15 December 2021

68742146R20246